The Osterling Weekend

A MUSICAL MISADVENTURE

Steven Duff

The Osterling Weekend by Steven Duff
Copyright © 2006 Steven Duff

This novel is a work of fiction. With the exception of the distinguished composer/arranger Eric Osterling, names, characters, places and incidents are the product of the author's imagination or are used fictitiously and any resemblance to actual persons living or dead, events or locales is entirely coincidental.

Library and Archives Canada Cataloguing in Publication

Duff, Steven
The Osterling weekend : a musical misadventure / Steven Duff.

ISBN 1-897242-17-4

I. Title.

PS8557.U285O88 2006   C813'.54   C2006-904154-7

Aydy Press
www.aydy.ca

To Anne and Hugh Horler
Friends, confidants, lovers of the arts, and shipmates,
in loving memory.

OVERTURE

The Osterling Weekend had its genesis over a four-year span from 1990 to 1993, while the writer was an administrator at the Scarborough Board of Education's Music Camp. The magic of that time, it is hoped, will emerge in the telling of this story; at the same time, the reader must be assured that our operation went far more smoothly than the Osterling Weekend. However, there was much speculation about what could have gone wrong, and, whether we like it or not, it is things gone wrong that make a story all the more fun to tell.

There were many wonderful people at the Scarborough Music Camp: our instructors and conductors, both from Scarborough or visiting from other places; our Junior Administration, made up of Scarborough music graduates; our Mentors and Mentors-in-Training; and, of course, our students.

To mention everyone connected with this story would take many pages. However, particular recognition is due those who put our Music Camp together: Christopher D. Howells, Inge Herrmann, L. Garth Allen, David R. Graham, Lee Willingham, Mark Ruhnke, Donna Dale Smith, Ken Ferdinands, our secretarial staff, and, finally, my particular and special friend Donald Coakley.

The Overture is finished. Now you may turn the page and begin The Osterling Weekend.

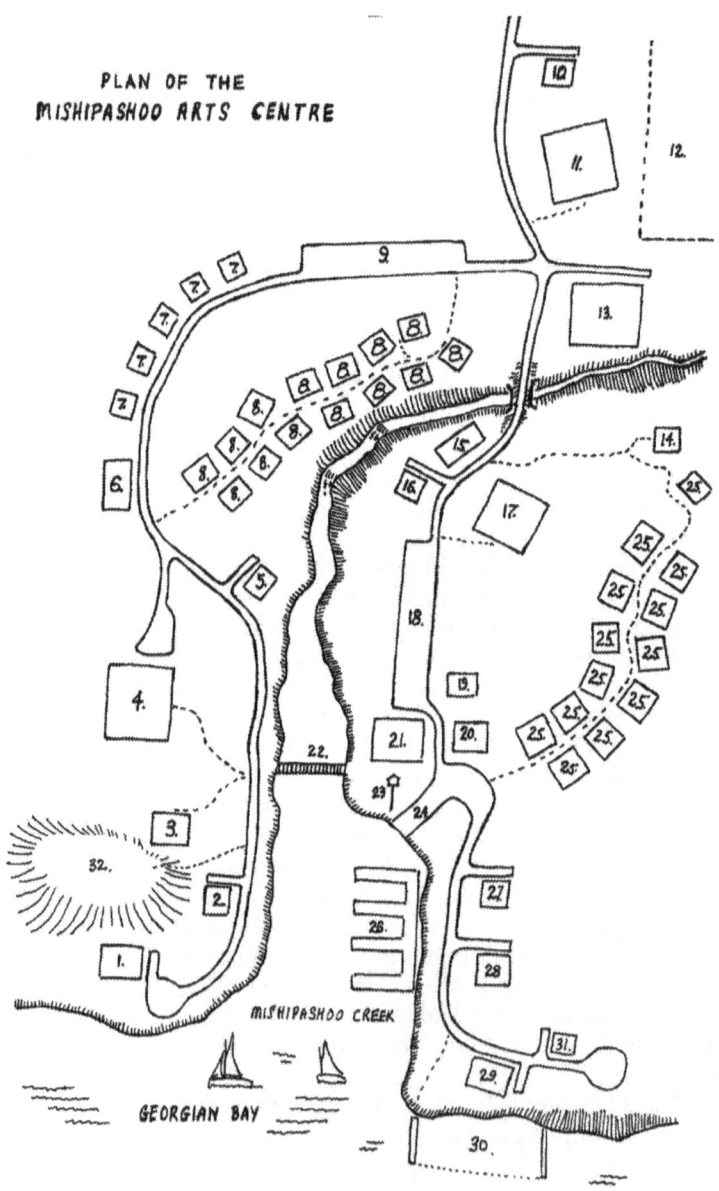

PLAN OF THE
MISHIPASHOO ARTS CENTRE

MISHIPASHOO CREEK

GEORGIAN BAY

KEY TO THE PLAN OF
THE MISHIPASHOO ARTS CENTRE
As it was at the time of the Osterling Weekend

1. Brideshead Cottage: K.Y. Jackson, Fr. John Oakley, Eric Osterling.
2. Wenlock Edge: Charlie, Michelle, and Jenny Cowell.
3. Wuthering Heights: Dunstan Corrigan, Israel Bond.
4. The Old Lodge: Concert Orchestra
5. Valhalla Cottage: Antonio d'Averso
6. Art Studio: Symphonic Band
7. Staff Cabins: Junior Administration
8. Boys' Camp
9. Parking
10. Constable and Mrs. "Beaver" Lumber residence.
11. Concert Tent: Symphony Orchestra
12. Cow pasture
13. Dining Hall: Choir
14. Piano Studio
15. Theatre Workshop: Concert Band
16. Pete and Rosie's house
17. Theatre: Wind Symphony
18. Parking
19. Utility Shed and camp equipment storage
20. Tuck Shop
21 Camp Office
22. Footbridge
23. Purple martin house
24. Launch ramp
25. Girls' Camp
26. Docks for camp canoes, dinghies, and Hugo's boat collection.
27. Infirmary: Mrs. Vomet
28. Egdon Heath: Neville and Violet Park
29. Tintagel Cottage: Hugo and Anna Harland
30. Swim Area
31. Linden Lea: Angela Rumley and Gianetta d'Averso
32. Arthur Ransome Memorial Outpost

MISHIPASHOO ARTS CENTRE
SATURDAY, JUNE 7, 1991, EARLY AFTERNOON

"And so it begins," said the Rev. John Oakley, S.J., as the first of our campers came down the road laden, not with tents and camping supplies, but with trumpets, clarinets, violins and the like. "Hi, dear, how are you doing?"

"Fine, Father, thanks. Where does the Symphonic Band go?"

"Just back right up, dear, and you're there. That sort of barn thing right over there."

"Thanks, Father."

"Okay, dear, hang in there. Enjoy yourself. And you know where you're going…okay…have fun…no, the Concert Orchestra is over the footbridge in the big lodge on your right at the top of the path…"

"Thank you, Father."

"A pleasure…have fun…are you okay? …good…they're cute, aren't they?"

"Yes, they are, kind of," I said without conviction.

"You said that without conviction."

"Nailed again. Now, there's one that's really cute…my God…"

"Kenneth, contain yourself…Symphonic Band? The brown barn, right behind you. You with the cello…don't know? How old are you? Okay, Concert Orchestra, across the bridge, in the big cottage to your right…okay there? Good…enjoy…Symphony Orchestra? Up the road and you'll find a sort of circus tent…oh, you're most welcome, dear…(very aesthetic, isn't she, Ken?)…okay? Good…have fun…now, you don't look at all happy, young fellow. What's the trouble?"

Two eyes glistening with sorrow looked up from a height of barely five feet. Nothing was said. Father Oakley tried again.

9

"What's the trouble, now? We can't have you being sad at Music Camp."

"My mum gave me a twenty dollar bill for tuck and treats and I lost it."

"What did it look like?"

"It was, er, green."

"And whose picture was on it?"

"Uh, it was the Queen, Father."

"Well, now," said Father Oakley, rummaging in his pocket, extracting half a dozen phone messages, a bent stick of Beeman's gum, two lock washers, and, praise Jesus, a twenty dollar bill. He held it out to the little boy. "Did it look like this?"

"Yes, Father."

"Well, I found it on the path by the dining hall. It must be yours. Be careful with it, now."

The little face lit up like a neon sign. "Oh, thanks, Father. Thanks a lot! That made my day. Uh, where's the Concert Orchestra?"

"Across the bridge there and on your right. Hustle, now."

"Yeah. Thanks again, Father."

"Father Oakley," I said as the small figure vanished along the road, "Did you really find that money somewhere?"

"I have to go. Got to make a phone call. Hang in here for me would you, kid, and make sure the stragglers know where they're going."

THE SERVIETTE UNION
PARRY SOUND, ONTARIO
SUNDAY, JUNE 15, EVENING

"And so it ends," said Father Oakley. "The Last Supper is nigh. We owe ourselves a good one."

Indeed we did. A week had passed that we would never forget, a fulminating admixture of struggle and triumph, of horror and exaltation, and now that the week was over, the experience of an entire lifetime packed into just seven days. The campers and junior administration had left and all that remained of the venture was myself, Father Oakley, and the co-owners of the Mishipashoo Arts Centre, Hugo and Anna Harland; our indispensable equipment manager, Charlie Cowell, who could have organized the D-Day landings; the gentle Sister Ingrid, peerless in the interpretation of choral music; Mrs. Schwarzkopf, who until just that day had been my nemesis; and the crown jewel of the operation, our resident composer, Eric Osterling.

"Good heavens!" exclaimed Hugo.

"What?"

"Well, here's the way to start our celebrations." He showed Father Oakley the menu.

"Oh, my goodness," said the Father. "It must be some drink to call it an Orgasm. Oh, pardon me, Sister."

"Don't worry, Father, I've heard a lot worse. Right at camp. From you."

"I never said stuff like that to you!"

"Of course not. But you do speak to others and I do have ears."

"Father, you look so sweet when you blush. It does things to me," said Charlie in a hoarse whisper.

"Charlie, don't start that on me now. I can't deal with it."

"I will deal with it," said Hugo grandly. "I will see who would like to join me in an orgasm. Darling?"

"Oh, yes," said Anna demurely. "I'll try one."

"You're being most demure, darling. Sister?"

"Hugo!"

"You're Anna, at least you were this morning. Sister, an org—"

"No, thank you, Hugo. I don't...I mean, I don't...well..."

"Hugo, stop it. You're being awful," scolded Anna. I could sense an exquisitely terrible punishment in store for Hugo at evening's end.

"Sorry, darling. I was just trying to be a good host. Father Oakley?"

"Jesuits don't usually do this, but there has to be a first time for everything."

"Aha, up to three. Eric?"

"I'll have to pass. I want to get to Toronto unimpaired. A cola would be fine for me. Not a decaf."

"Still at three. Mrs. Schwarzkopf?"

Mrs. Schwarzkopf laughed breathily. "Nein, sanx, Mr. Harland. Yinyer ale iss fine mit me."

"Still stuck on three. Charlie?"

"Ginger ale as per usual. I too have a long drive ahead, back to dear old Birkenstock, and do not wish to be distracted by the demon drink. That's my story and I'm sticking to it."

"Ken. Want to make a *ménage a quatre*?" offered Hugo.

"Count me in," said I. "Je suis curious."

"Oh, man," sighed Charlie, a self-described "regular guy" who despised anything artsy, even that which was rendered in fun, even that rendered by himself.

"Have you decided on something from the bar?" asked the young waitress, hardly older than some of our recent charges.

"We have," said Hugo commandingly. "Two ginger ales, one cola with caffeine, what for you, Sister? V-8? A V-8 for the Sister, and for the rest of us reprobates, four, count 'em, four—"

"Hugo, not so loud!"

"Was I loud, darling? Where was I? Oh, yes. Four orgasms! What is that, a multiple orgasm? Or a group orgasm? This is a cunning exercise for linguists..."

"Hugo!"

"No problem at all, sir," assured the waitress. "I'll be right back with your org...your drinks."

"Oh, don't rush. I prefer to linger."

"Hugo, I'm warning you..."

"Of course, darling. Excuse me."

"This is shocking," said Charlie. "These pillars of the church and of musical society having orgasms in public. Some of us have elected to remain pure. You can respect us in the morning. The rest of you can go right ahead and sully yourselves. When we do get our, um, our drinks, what shall we drink to?"

"Survival," said Father Oakley tonelessly.

"Come on, Father," I provoked. "Any ding-dong can survive. I thought our mandate was to excel."

"It was. But there are no guarantees in this life and we ended up doing what we had to in order to survive. Wasn't there a certain triumph to Dunkirk? Aren't we all still here? Will we not arise to fight another day?"

"If they give us the chance," I remarked.

"The cost and the constant notoriety…"

"Not to mention what's happened to my name," inserted Eric. "I'd love a few minutes with the reporter who dubbed the whole thing the Osterling Weekend, as if I wrote it or something. I was just there."

"And, bless you, you were one of the few things that went right," said Father Oakley. "But don't blame the reporter. We called it the Osterling Weekend the moment we knew you were coming."

"A V-8 for the Sister…an orgasm over here…a cola for the gentleman…no, it isn't decaf…ginger ale for you, sir…another here…an orgasm, Father…"

"Thanks, dear, you're one of the great ones."

"Another orgasm…there you go, sir…and one for you." The waitress's voice had become progressively more silken and she was practically purring when she got to me.

"Did you hear how she purred at Ken?"

"He's going crazy," said Father Oakley.

"Come on, you guys." My voice was almost a whine.

"A toast," pronounced Hugo, coming to my rescue. "To paraphrase our Jewish friends, next year in Parry Sound."

"You want to do this again?"

"I'll just put away my toys first. I wouldn't have missed it for anything. The Osterling Weekend…it was too wonderfully preposterous…I want to write about it."

"So do I," said I in the light-headed bravado induced by my orgasm. "God, Hugo, what the hell's in this, anyway?"

"Drunken sot," murmured Charlie.

"It's on the menu," said Hugo. "Let me see…oh, she took it away…"

"We need some of this at the manse," said Father Oakley. "Sherry and port get dull after a bit. Say, Hugo, I guess you could say this gathering is loaded with *mise-en-scène.*"

Charlie rolled his eyes.

"But this is the end of the story, John. *Mise-en-scène* sets the mood, sets the scene. It's too late. It's the end."

Father Oakley rose to his feet. "Oh, no, it's not. We're going to do this again, just as you said, next year in Parry Sound, and we're going to get it right."

Out of a sense of imperial grandeur, I began to sing Rule Britannia and was promptly suppressed by Father Oakley, who generally wished nothing to do with the monarchy and whom I sometimes derided as a drab republican.

We did not tarry long once the Last Supper was finished and the lights, reflecting long and liquid, came on about the harbour. Anna and Hugo had to return by water to their home, the Mishipashoo Arts Centre, the site of the Osterling Weekend and never to be the same again. Eric Osterling faced a long journey home to Connecticut and wished to get at least as far as Toronto this night. And the rest of us were headed to our various homes in the county of Birkenstock, just an hour or so short of Toronto.

Father Oakley and I had to take a walk to clear our heads. And Charlie and Sister Ingrid had some brief business to attend to before starting their own journey; Charlie's new pride and joy, a fearsome black vehicle called the Hog, had been mixed up in a cattle stampede earlier in the day and was in desperate need of a trip to a car-wash.

The spectacle of the gentle Sister Ingrid riding in the Hog was, by a considerable margin, the oddest contrast I can ever recall. Sister Ingrid was a Sister of the Ursuline Order. The Hog was a High-Mobility Multi-Purpose Wheeled Vehicle, more widely known as a HumVee following service in the Gulf War, and Charlie's was the first civilian model to be brought into Canada.

"I have my standards, man," said Charlie. "Can't have the Hog going to town looking like a pig."

MISHIPASHOO ARTS CENTRE
THURSDAY, JUNE 5, EARLY AFTERNOON

"Good afternoon, Birkenstock County Roman Catholic School Board."

"Music Department, please." I felt as if someone had stuck a golf ball down my throat; only a few hours had gone by on the grounds of the Mishipashoo Arts Centre and already we'd been overwhelmed with disaster.

"Music Department. Mrs. Quail speaking." Mrs. Quail was my step-mother-in-law. She was two years younger than I. I liked to call her Mummy from time to time, but this was not one of those times.

"Hi, Suzi, it's me."

"Sweetheart! Oh, God, I miss you! I don't know how long I can stand this."

"Suzi, I need to speak to Neville. Now."

"Darling, what's wrong?"

"A lot. I need to speak to Neville."

"He isn't here. It's Thursday, which means he's you-know-where with you-know-who."

"How about Father Oakley?"

"Yes, he's here. Sweetheart, I'm just going right out of my—"

"So am I. Suzi, would you put him on before I have a heart attack?" I could sense the pout at the other end of the line.

"John Oakley speaking," rasped the phone.

"Father, it's K.Y."

"Hey, kid, how are you?"

"Not well at all."

"What's the matter?"

"The moving van took a swim." Silence. "Father?"

"Took a swim?"

"It's lying half under water by the sailing dock. Or I should say, it smashed up half the sailing dock and took out the bow of Hugo's 1925 Ackroyd dinghy along with it. Hugo is about to have a cow. He's yelling about suing somebody, but he doesn't know who and it's frustrating him."

"Kenneth Yardley Jackson," said Father Oakley with steel in his voice, "this had better not be some sort of joke. You have my job as of September. There is no need to get it by inducing an aneurism."

"Father, I'm not trying to be funny. The moving van got here, oh, half an hour ago and the drivers parked it near the dock and went off to see where to back it in to unload the instruments and stuff. Charlie and Sister Ingrid and I were hanging about waiting for the truck crew to get back and the damn truck started off by itself towards the lake. We didn't realize what was happening, there was no engine noise or anything, we didn't know, didn't realize until it was well on its way—"

"Calm down, K.Y., you're starting to babble."

"Sorry, Father. Charlie took off after it and got in the cab, but he couldn't stop the bloody thing. We think the air for the brakes had all leaked out, that had to be the problem."

"How is Charlie? Is he all right?"

"He rode the thing right into the bay."

"Jesus, Mary, and Joseph! Is he all right?"

"He's very wet and very angry. He's also being very Charlie. The cab went completely underwater and he was blown out the window in a great bubble of air. He was, well, sort of emotional…"

"I'll bet he was. I'm about to be as well."

"…and he got Sister Ingrid and the truck crew and the Junior Admin to bring ashore what they could. I've phoned to Parry Sound for a heavy-duty tow truck, but I'm told it'll be a while until he gets here."

Father Oakley cleared his throat. He was behaving magnificently. So, in retrospect, was I. "So," he said, "the most important thing is that Charlie is okay." Father Oakley was sensitive about his priorities; a story still endured about how one of his student musicians had fallen downstairs just before a concert and Father Oakley's first question had been, "Is his clarinet all right?"

"Charlie is just fine." I paused to give the Father his opening, now that the niceties, such as they were, had been observed.

16

"Well, then, how about the, er, equipment? Did the entire truck go under, or what?"

"The cab part or tractor or whatever is right under. There is a fair slope to the bottom and just the forward quarter or so of the trailer part is in the water."

"Well, thank the Lord for at least that. But you still have no idea of the damage. Where were the cellos and basses stowed?"

"I think toward the back. They should be all right."

"What was up front?"

"Tubas, percussion, music stands. We can speculate until the end of time, but I've told you all I can for the moment. I'd better go out and help. I can hear Charlie. I can hear Hugo. I bet the whole of Georgian Bay hears Charlie and Hugo. I'll phone you again as soon as I have more to tell."

"I'll just camp here in the office and wait to hear from you."

"At the moment, Father, camp is a dirty four-letter word."

"We might have to postpone, although for how long…well, kid, I'll just wait to hear from you."

"I wonder what Neville will say."

Father Oakley snorted. "That idiot! He'll be too sozzled and spent in the loins to give a rat's ass. What a miserable turd." Father Oakley never missed a chance to editorialize on the subject of the Director of Music for the Birkenstock County Roman Catholic School Board. And his editorials were not generally couched in language associated with men of the cloth, but then Father Oakley was not your ordinary man of the cloth. "It's up to us, pal. Keep in touch. Good luck."

"Okay, Father. Look, I'm sorry—"

"Not your fault. I'm going to call Panama Van Lines right now. I'm going to sue the bastards. And tell Hugo to sue them too if he wants someone to sue. He should. Those boats are like pets to him. Hey…talk to you later, kid. Hang in there."

I hung up the phone and started at a trot in the wake of the ill-fated truck's voyage into Georgian Bay. The spectacle was so hideous that it would have been better if the truck had simply disappeared under water and we wouldn't have to look at it. But there it sat like a relic of Pearl Harbour, an iridescent slick of diesel fuel radiating forth upon the waters of Georgian Bay. This was certainly not on the program for the first annual Birkenstock Music Camp. Our student musicians were expected in just forty-six hours. I was in charge here until Neville Park, our esteemed director, would be here the next day. I was in command. I was responsible.

17

Hugo was still by the wreckage of his dock, staring at the poor, bowless dinghy, and looking only slightly less apoplectic than when I had gone to make my fateful phone call. The truck had in its wanton journey demolished a purple martin house, throwing its inhabitants into a state of twittering disarray. Hugo was yelling at the purple martins to shut up. Truth to tell, my concern for Hugo was even greater at the moment than for our equipment. The camp sailing fleet was a collection of antique wooden dinghies, lovingly refurbished by Hugo over the last dozen years, in many cases with my help. They were his babies and one had nearly been taken from him, her lacerated bow stranded beneath the truck. Hugo spoke of burning her timbers and scattering the ashes on the bay.

Charlie, in the meantime, was hard at work, framed by the open doors of the half-sunken van, a dark, wet demon hurling pieces of musical equipment to anyone within catching distance: truck drivers, the nine university students who formed our junior administration, and Sister Ingrid, at the moment wading ashore holding a cello over her head. A police car pulled up nearby and a constable got out to take a statement from Hugo, interrupting a threat to dispatch his pet crow Herbert von Carrion against the purple martins.

It may be inferred that Hugo tends to be emotional. It is part of what people call the "artistic temperament", an expression which I personally dislike because of certain pejorative overtones. But Hugo is an artist of the first order and therefore entitled to all the emotions of his heart's desire. The Hugo in question is Hugo Harland, a writer of considerable renown and known in particular for his trilogy of Asian thrillers: *A Bungalow in Bangalore*, *The Eyesore of Mysore*, and *Chaos in Laos*. What made the current situation all the more piteous was that a photographer was to come the next day and record pictures of Hugo's fleet for his work-in-progress, *Roman Catholicism and the Art of Wooden Boat Restoration*.

It was my long friendship with Hugo and his wife Anna (the same Anna Harland whose syndicated television show "Yoga and You" is watched by adoring men all over North American) who'd brought this together, truck and all. The two of them had bought a derelict camp a few miles northwest of the vacation community of Parry Sound; this was twelve years before and the initial cost was only what was owing on taxes to the township of Carling. The camp in its original form had been a combined farm and fishing lodge; subsequently, it had become a summer camp for teenagers, but after some time, it had been done in by cheap vacations abroad and a growing tendency for young people to take summer jobs. What arose in its place, however, was a summertime colony for writers and artists, a place to work in peace and take professional training and advice. Now, thanks to ourselves, Camp Mishipashoo—re-named the Mishipashoo Arts Centre—had diversified into the field of music. And thanks to ourselves, Hugo was, as in the poem, lying down to bleed before rising to fight again. The process would not be long. I knew how much Hugo hated to bleed.

"Here's the fun part, kids," pronounced Charlie from the truck. "The music took a bath. I don't know if it got screwed, but I want each box carried by two people in case they fall apart."

Fourteen sodden cartons were brought ashore, fourteen cartons containing music for two orchestras, three bands, and a choir, plus assorted chamber music and supplementary teaching materials. If any of this had to be replaced, someone would have to raid the music libraries of several Catholic schools in Birkenstock County in the next twenty-four hours. But it was not as bad as we had feared; our status was codified in the next communication with Father Oakley.

"Mixed reviews," I reported. "We've unloaded all of the cargo. The other truck, the one with the pianos, has been here all afternoon, but we haven't got to it yet. We're doing it after dinner. Now, the computers and electronic keyboards are all totalled."

"Predictable. We'll just have to can the computers-in-music elective."

"And so are the bass and guitar amplifiers."

"Also predictable. How about the percussion?"

"Full of water but otherwise all right. The bassoons took a drink and are pretty iffy. The low strings all made it, except for a cello that had its scroll snapped off. Some of the music got soaked, but Ingrid and the girls spread it all out in the dining hall to dry. God, I have no idea how many hundreds of pages there are there. The folders are warped all to hell but are useable. We'll make it, Father. The organization won't be immaculate, you know, band and orchestra chairs tagged and that sort of thing, but we will open on time. It'll be like Dunkirk. The Birkenstock County Roman Catholic School Board is made of stern stuff."

"That we are, kid. We're a team, which is why I hate what I have to tell you."

"What is it?"

"There's been a complaint."

"How can there be? We haven't even started."

"It was Mrs. Schwarzkopf." Mrs. Schwarzkopf's daughter, Liesl, was one of our unit heads. Mrs. Schwarzkopf, by reputation, was also no stranger to the Birkenstock County Roman Catholic School Board.

"What was her problem?"

"The video you showed the unit heads last night."

"Jesus Christ!"

"K.Y., don't say that, at least not that way. We're Catholics."

"I know, people of substance with taste and standards." These were favourite words of our superior Neville Park, although he seldom lived up to them. I sighed. "I swore those kids to secrecy."

"Liesl is incapable of secrecy. Remember that sexual harassment thing two years ago?"

Even in my agitated state, I could laugh. Liesl was a cellist and one day had been playing her instrument side-saddle because of the constrictions of a skirt reportedly so tight it looked as if it had been sprayed on her. Rather than negotiate with her, the orchestra teacher had simply grabbed her by the knees, forced them apart to the accepted width, and in the process had split Liesl's skirt to the waist. The teacher, Israel Bond, was known more for his actions than his words, earning himself both adulation and opprobrium in equally generous portions. Israel was to be on our camp faculty, although to his disgust, was to conduct a band rather than an orchestra.

I sighed. "I'll call Mrs. Blackhead."

"Call who?"

"That's how you translate Schwarzkopf."

"Well, don't go calling her that, K.Y. She demanded that you phone… 'I vant zet young man to call me tonight, Vater Oakley," clucked Father Oakley. "He better haf eggsplanation, und good vun. Good Catholic child like Liesl, being eggsposed to such sings…"

"Some child!" I screamed. Liesl had left a trail of broken hearts through her traversal of Golgotha High School and was now doing the same in her second year of university.

"I know, I know, kid. Here's the number: 464-2860."

"Thanks so much, Father. Cheerio."

"Hang in there, kid."

My downfall had been a simple function of being in a hurry. I'd stopped in at a video store in the Parry Sound Mall on my way to camp the previous afternoon to arrange some entertainment for our nine Junior Administration people, all recent graduates of the Birkenstock County Roman Catholic School Board, and had grabbed the first thing I saw on the shelf, a potboiler called "Skin Deep". What had paralysed us with laughter but had allegedly offended Liesl was a scene in a darkened room in which two men were wearing luminescent condoms. It was like watching a couple of fireflies gone crazy and we'd thought it was so funny that we had to rewind three times to see it again.

I'd been far more embarrassed than Liesl, but despite my explanation of being in a hurry, Mrs. Schwarzkopf elected to be difficult. "I kennot ackzept your eggscooses, Mr. Checkson. I eggspect better chudgement from zose who shape ze minds of our young pipple. I vill write complaint for inclusion in your personnel file, und if I hear of any more escapades soch as zis, I vill call for your resignation."

This was not something I needed, even on a good day, and this had not been a good day. I reported the conversation with Mrs. Schwarzkopf to Charlie, hoping for a modicum of sympathy, but his only response was, "Outstanding."

"What else can go wrong today?" I said plaintively.

"Nothing," soothed Sister Ingrid.

"A lot," reassured Charlie.

"Charlie, Charlie, Charlie. Where would we be without you?"

"Nowhere, man. You need me. I'm a realist."

After dinner, when we should have been relaxing or sailing one of Hugo's dinghies out on the bay, we were moving pianos to their required locations. As observed earlier, they were in a second truck, one which had no maritime aspirations, and for a spell the job went without mishap. We came to the last piano, destined for a little hut up a steep trail into the woods, too narrow for the truck.

"Maybe we can carry it," suggested the driver.

"Nah," said Charlie. "No way."

"What about the Hog?" I tried.

"K.Y.," said Charlie with a patience so heavy that it had actual mass, "the Hog is my newborn. I literally drove it out of the dealer's to get here. The Hog I shall protect as a mother bear does her cubs."

"So no Hog."

"No Hog. But I think I saw a tractor and a wagon back of that barn thing. Maybe Hugo'll let us use it. Otherwise, the piano either goes back to Birkenstock or takes up residence in the great outdoors."

We had to negotiate with Pete the caretaker for the use of the tractor, whose primary function was in maintenance of the camp and to move various units of Hugo's fleet as required. In line with Hugo's passion for ancient things, it was a villainous old 1951 Cockshutt, and, as Pete explained in the sparse delivery of Northern Ontario, "She's got no batt'ry, eh, you gotta crank her, just like in the old days." Pete had to run an errand into Parry

21

Sound and couldn't show us what to do, but Charlie, out of his own love for machinery, undertook the task.

"Start, you pig...don't fuck with me...Sorry, Sister...Unnnh! When was this bitch last overhauled? Unnnh! All right, it's just you and me, babe...now, start, or you take the big dive...all right! She's all yours, K.Y."

"Hey, shit, I'm not driving that thing. Beg your pardon, Sister. You're the mechanical wizard. You drive it."

Charlie folded his arms. "No, babe, I want to see you drive it. You need to diversify."

What Charlie thought I should diversify from was never made clear, but I took the challenge and mounted to my lofty perch. I put the tractor in gear and it stalled.

"Oh, man!" cried Charlie in exasperation.

"You wanted me to drive," I reminded him.

"I wanted you to drive the bloody thing, not kill it. This sucks the bag, man. What's this thing called again? A Cocksucker?"

"Cockshutt," I corrected.

"That's almost as vulgar. Well, here we go again...Unnh!...It runs, boys and girls. Now, K.Y., try not to humiliate yourself and make me mad all over again."

I persuaded the tractor to my bidding, we coupled a trailer on behind, loaded the piano, and started up the trail, Charlie walking ahead, "scouting for unfriendly natives."

This was fun, I thought, my initial reservations overcome. The old Cockshutt throbbed and purred, I was its master, oh, we were rolling right along, a steep bit here, whoops, more gas, oh, here we go! Charlie was doing a funny sort of dance, perhaps from the sheer joy of triumphing over impossible odds. I could hear music too; it was wonderful, because music was my life.

"Ken, stop!" Charlie screamed. I hit the brake, forgetting the clutch and stalling the tractor with a strangled gurgle. The music continued, great cascades of tone clusters that receded curiously down the hill. Behind me reposed the trailer about thirty feet away, its corroded hitch rearing impotently skyward. The truck crew and junior administration were scattered randomly about the landscape, the piano cartwheeling cacophonously down the slope, shedding bits of itself on each revolution. Its shattered carcass lurched to a stop in front of an astonished Anna, who was out for an evening jog with Herbert the crow flying air cover.

"Ooh, Jesus!" she screeched in apparent oblivion of Sister Ingrid and the rest of us who did subscribe, though in varying degrees, to Roman Catholicism. Then she laughed hysterically as a confounded Herbert von Carrion assaulted the instrument, pecking out a furious jumble of notes. "What is it?"

"It was a piano," I sighed. "Time to call Father Oakley. Again."

"John Oakley," rasped the phone. That was the Father's response even when in his residence at the manse.

"Hi, Father, it's K.Y."

"Hey, kid, how are things? Talk to Mrs. S.?"

"I talked to Mrs. S. and she's sending a letter of complaint to be included in my personnel file."

"Don't take it so hard, K.Y. I'll have the letter directed to me and I'll shred it or wrap fish in it or something. So cheer up and enjoy. I know it's been a tough day for you. But cheer up. I'll be there about ten tomorrow morning. Just got the car tuned up and the tires checked, went through a car wash, one of those Tidy-Car places, you know, they vacuum and clean the windows and everything. Smells just like a new car. You'll have to smell it."

"I can't cheer up. We had another disaster."

"You're trying to give me a stroke again. Or is it a heart attack just for the sheer variety?"

I related the whole sorry tale of the piano, but with the reassurance that nobody was hurt beyond a skinned knee and Anna's close brush with cardiac arrest.

"Well," said Father Oakley, "as long as it wasn't the new Yamaha."

I gulped. I fought for breath.

"It was the new Yamaha, wasn't it, K.Y.?"

"Yes, it was, Father."

"Why did the trailer unhitch itself, K.Y.? You guys coupled it up, didn't you?"

"We did, but what we didn't know was that the threaded part of the ball was rusted all to rat-shit and just snapped off."

"Tell Hugo he owes us a piano. I'll be calling him in the morning. Meanwhile, I'll rent another one and have it sent up. I'll talk to Hugo in the morning. This is not a profit-making organization. Hang in there, K.Y."

"I hope."

MISHIPASHOO ARTS CENTRE
FRIDAY, JUNE 6, MID-MORNING

Father Oakley was one of the most inconspicuous people I have ever met. He had the somewhat bland look of an accountant, was of less than medium height, and had a surface austerity that betrayed nothing of an enormous intellect that embraced music, education, art, politics, and religion in far from moderate helpings. He was also hilarious company. On first meeting, he could be downright formidable, but once trust and respect had been gained, it was quite a different story. I, happily, was in that pantheon of the blessed, but those who were not had to be prepared for suffering beyond their worst imaginings.

When Father Oakley said ten in the morning, he meant it. "Hey, didn't I say ten o'clock? Hey, dear, how are you doing?" to Sister Ingrid. "You're one of the great ones. But you look hung over. Your eyes are all red."

"We were up most of the night drying music and getting it back into the folders. It was a long night, but the Lord was with us." Whenever Sister Ingrid spoke of the Lord, her face lit up in a smile that made me regret profoundly that she was married to Him and was therefore unavailable to Me.

The Hog rolled up in a cloud of gritty dust, Charlie at the helm. Father Oakley had not yet seen Charlie's new vehicle. "My goodness," he remarked. "Isn't that something! Look at those tires…and all those lights…air conditioning and stereo…the crucifix looks a bit, well, incongruous, but I'm glad you have one."

"For protection, man. Hey, Ingrid, are the Symphonic Band folders done? I'll take them to the brown barn."

"Liesl has them."

Charlie tore off to the dining hall, serving as it was as a temporary depot for our music. "Get that stuff out here, Weasel!"

we could hear him yelling. "We don't have all day! Come on, come on! Get with the program!"

Hugo came strolling up, his cat Kitty Sark tagging along. "Hugo, how are you doing, kid?" said Father Oakley disarmingly. "Hey, there, Kitty. I gotta talk to you. About pianos. We're going for a walk." He put his arm about Hugo's shoulder and they started up the road.

"Poor Hugo," said Ingrid.

"I don't think so," I said. "If there is a battle, it will be a battle of the giants."

Musically, organization was proceeding once again, if behind schedule. Because of our location on Georgian Bay, however, there were other considerations to be dealt with, particularly to do with water safety. Part of our contract with Anna and Hugo required all of us to have basic training in cardiopulmonary resuscitation and in the Heimlich maneuver and since Anna was certified from here to there in the necessary procedures, she would be giving us group instruction.

Likely because of our prior acquaintance, I was selected as Anna's demonstration partner, to the disappointment of our male staff, prey as they were to the universal admiration of Anna. The tensions of the day before, in concert with an involuntary state of bachelorhood, in further concert with a regard for Anna beyond the bounds of ordinary friendship, worked their worst upon my overtaxed synapses. I could not help being visibly agitated through the whole procedure.

Charlie and Father Oakley recalled the event during a coffee break the following winter. They always enjoyed discussing anything connected with me between themselves but in my presence, as if I were not there. I think it was a sickness.

"K.Y. doing the Heimlich maneuver on Anna Harland was too much!" recalled Charlie. " 'Higher, K.Y., higher, right under the rib-cage.' "

Father Oakley took a mouthful of coffee, gave it a ritual swish in his mouth, and swallowed it. "She was, er, in the way."

"I'll say she was. I bet she's a real tempest in a C-cup when she gets mad."

"I thought K.Y. was going to shit his pants. A body like that is truly the Lord's work." Another swished mouthful of coffee. Charlie guffawed and several stern clerical heads turned in disapproval at adjacent tables.

"And then there was the mouth-to-mouth," continued the Father. "Anna must have been a closet woodwind player, the things she was doing to Ken with her tongue. My goodness!"

"Father, your secularity will be your eventual doom," said I. I was ignored.

"He didn't just blush," said Charlie. "He was actually sweating."

"Ingrid thought it was funny too," said Father Oakley. "There is definite hope for the good Sister."

"She needs another man in her life besides the Lord," said Charlie.

"Charlie!" cautioned Father Oakley.

"Sorry, Father." Charlie pulled out a cigarette. "Hail Mary full of Grace, blessed art thou among women...gotta step out for a butt."

I tried to divert the conversation away from my own embarrassment. "Whatever perils I had to endure, you have to admit it paid off." I was referring to my own rescue of a saxophone player who'd almost drowned in the creek; without Anna's training, I would certainly have lost her. But there was still no escape from Charlie.

"Too many sax players, man. All you did was tamper with the balance of nature."

MISHIPASHOO ARTS CENTRE
SATURDAY, JUNE 7 - LATE MORNING

The remainder of Friday and all of Saturday morning at Music Camp was a Canadian Dunkirk. The Hog plied the roads of the camp in comets of yellow dust, the unit heads worked furiously setting up the chairs and music stands for the various ensembles, Hugo rented some extra chairs to cover an unexpected shortfall, the chairs were tagged with the names of the students. But for the loss of the electronic equipment, the camp was prepared just the way we had intended.

Our office was set up in what had once been a store by the creek, a holdover from the camp's origins as a fishing lodge. Now that all was in order, I had a bit of time to absorb the atmosphere of the place and admire the mounted fish on the wall, newspaper clippings about sundry local dramas on a bulletin board dating back to the 1940s, a truly formidable crank-operated cash register that out of some bygone economic optimism would display dollar figures in seven digits, a 1956 Canadian Pacific calendar, even some Reckitt's laundry blueing on one of the shelves. I had not seen Reckitt's laundry blueing for many a year, nor had Hugo, which was why he had left it there. We had, however, introduced some modernism into the place with a computer, a photocopier, and a couple of file cabinets with the camp records, all of which had travelled with the pianos and had therefore survived the Big Dive.

The faculty were to begin arriving shortly and on that account I was afflicted with something of the sick yearning of the average seventeen-year-old, just at a time when I should have been in a state of well-being at our comprehensive level of preparation. I felt all shy and nervous, an absurd situation for one in his thirties who'd already been in and out of a marriage and therefore had

27

Experience. But the nature of the Experience had not encouraged self-confidence and now that I had a definite goal in the person of one of our faculty, and camp presented a unique opportunity to achieve it, I felt hopelessly shy and inadequate and almost crippled with the terror of possible disappointment. Awful as the last three days had been, at least they had been a diversion from my apprehension.

Our office manager was a frighteningly efficient young lady named Alice Nestleton, who in the few days previous had earned herself the label of Miss Moneypenny. The phone rang, she answered it. "Birkenstock Music Camp...no, he isn't...no, Father isn't either, but you could speak to Mr. Jackson. Sir, it's for you. It's Mr. Foley."

If it were Rob Foley, it meant trouble.

It was indeed Rob Foley and it was indeed trouble.

Rob was the instrumental music teacher at Mount of Olives Elementary School, not his heart's desire, but he had some years before, as the British like to say, blotted his copybook. Rob's specialty was jazz, in which he was regarded as one of the half-dozen best teachers in Ontario, but therein lay the problem: he had so little interest in any other kind of music that during his tenure at Crown of Thorns High School he had not only neglected what had been a first-rate concert band program but had started refusing such routine musical assignments as graduation and Remembrance Day. Lengthy absences had followed, so lengthy that we thought Rob was dying; prayers were said for him at musical functions all over Birkenstock County, and not only in the Catholic school system. Candles were lit in churches. He was remembered at Sunday Mass.

And then there was the day Father Oakley went on a routine errand to a percussion store in Toronto called "With Mallets Aforethought" and found Rob behind the counter, drawing salaries both from the store and from the Birkenstock County Roman Catholic School Board. Such was the Father's rage that he'd woven a tapestry of obscenities calculated by another of the store's staff as lasting fully twenty-eight seconds. Twenty-eight seconds of unbroken and comprehensive profanity does not sound like much until you try it. Normally a great impression would have been created, but in this instance it was heightened by one of Father Oakley's rare appearances in clerical garb. "You're fired!" he'd screamed, stamping out of the store, his errand forgotten.

To his frustration, Father Oakley did not have the authority to fire Rob himself, though the Personnel Department undertook the task. But they too were frustrated, nay thwarted, by the power of the Teachers' Union of Ontario, whose teams of lawyers had negotiated a settlement ("paid for out of our dues, the sons of whores") and had Rob assigned to Mount of Olives, as they put it, "for a fresh start". There was no jazz at Mount of Olives. However, there was to be a jazz program at camp and over some protests from Father Oakley, Rob had been selected to teach it. There was no question that he did have enormous ability when fully functional.

All these thoughts raced through my mind in the dozen steps to the phone. And what had happened to Rob eclipsed my unhealthiest imaginings. "Hi, Rob. What's up?" I thought perhaps he might have been delayed by car trouble at Waubaushene or Mactier.

"I'm at Windsor," said Rob with the suggestion of a whine in his voice. Windsor was virtually in the opposite direction to where he should have been.

"Windsor? You're supposed to be here." Moneypenny craned forward with a look of perverse anticipation.

"I was in Chicago, man. My mum died there."

"Oh, God, Rob, I'm so sorry. Don't worry—"

"I was bringing back the ashes and the customs people, can you believe this, looked in the, uh, container…"

"They what?"

"They looked in the container the um, cremains… and found half a mil worth of heroin. They had no right to do that. I called my lawyer and I'd have called you, but I was allowed only the one call and I had to wait until my lawyer got here before I could call you and—"

"Slow down, Rob. Okay." Like hell it was okay! "Now, this heroin…" Moneypenny's mouth fell open. "…this heroin…"

"Can't tell you. Can't talk to anybody. But I've been charged and I, uh, can't come to camp."

I wasn't sure quite what to think or feel. Horror at another crisis was tempered by sympathy over Rob's mother, so I told him not to worry and that I was sorry and I hoped things would work out for him.

"Shall I call Mr. Park on the P.A.?" asked Moneypenny, a smirk teasing the corners of her mouth.

"I don't think he's here yet. Call Father Oakley, would you? Oh, hello, Neville."

"Hi, Mr. Park," chimed in Moneypenny. It was a miracle she knew what he looked like, so seldom was he seen at the office: there were endless meetings, interminable luncheons, recurrent conferences, those Thursday afternoon trysts he thought were so discreetly handled. He was always busy with things that seemed to

29

have no direct bearing on the daily functions of our music program.

Neville Park envisioned himself as a Captain of Education and on the Cutting Edge of Music, but looked anything but the part. He brought to mind Erik Satie's Three Pieces in the Form of a Pear; he had been quite skinny until a few years back, but unwholesome eating habits, coupled with borderline alcoholism, had given him an obscene bulge about his middle, and, to complete the picture, he had an oversized bald head with skin so translucent that Charlie called him the Walking X-Ray.

"Good drive up?" asked Moneypenny cheerily.

"Oh, yes, it was just…awfully wonderful," beamed Neville glassily. "Everything ready, Ken?"

"Yes, sir. Everything's all set, accident or no accident."

"Accident?"

What was this? Surely he knew of the accident. "With the moving van."

"What moving van?"

For God's sake, hadn't Father Oakley told him? He had, as it was to turn out, but innocent of the fact. I recounted the whole sorry tale while Neville gazed blankly about, grey tufts of cigarette ash rolling down his gourd-shaped front. "My," he said flatly, "that must have been quite a business."

Moneypenny was becoming as irritated as I, but conducted herself as the Complete Innkeeper. "Mr. Park, you're in Egdon Heath, just along the road on your left." With a marionette-like wobble, Neville bumbled off back to his car, and before Moneypenny could summon Father Oakley, there he was as the Hog slithered to a halt, trailing a great banner of dust. The Father, ordinarily fearless, was terrified of driving with Charlie and had himself thoroughly braced against the dashboard, knuckles gleaming dead white.

"Glad to hell I said confession this morning. Charlie does not revere life. Did I just see Neville creeping about?"

"You did. John, he knows nothing about the truck. You did tell him, didn't you?"

"Of course I told him!" exploded Father Oakley. "What a useless turd. Oh, my, I shouldn't say things like that. I just get mad at people who don't do their jobs. He isn't even entitled to the cubic volume he occupies. I wonder what sort of mess he left at the office. Oh, my goodness, another big confession…I must be strong…"

Charlie put a hand on Father Oakley's knee. "Father, I love it when you talk dirty," he purred. "It just makes me feel all crazy inside." As Charlie's driving was the only earthly thing that scared the Father, it was also Charlie alone who held the key to defusing his periodic outbursts. A blushing Father spilled out of the Hog.

"Father, come back to me!" bleated Charlie.

"Cut the shit, Charlie, you know how I hate that."

"Only in front of others," simpered Charlie. And then in his normal voice, "Are you going to help me fix those choir risers, Father, or do I get to do it by myself?"

"I'll help, but keep your hands to yourself."

"But, Father, you have the cutest kneecaps…"

"Before you go off, Father," I said tightly, "there is something to be dealt with. Rob Foley called. He's been detained at the border. They found heroin in his mother's ashes."

Father Oakley doubled up with laughter, steadying himself against the Hog, his fingers etching wavering lines on the dusty paint. Moneypenny watched in horror from the front porch of the office, thinking he'd gone mad. For my own part, I had no idea what to think. Dumfounded, we watched for a fateful minute in which the camp's composer-in-residence, Eric Osterling, happened to make his entrance.

I tried to ignore Father Oakley. "Mr. Osterling," I said formally, shaking hands, "welcome to the Birkenstock Music Camp. It's an honour to have you aboard."

"It looks like a happy place. I'm glad to be here. I'm really looking forward to meeting the students and getting to work…sorry, I can't keep a straight face…have I missed something?"

"Oh, goodness," sighed Father Oakley. "Eric, this is a zoo! You're going to love it. This is K.Y., I mean to say Ken Jackson. He's my assistant, confidant, and general schlepper. K.Y., where's Eric staying?"

"With us, Father."

"Poor soul."

"We're over the footbridge, follow the creek to your left, and we're in the white cottage by the water. Better yet, double back in your car and take your first left turning and just follow the road. Save you a walk."

"Thanks. See you for lunch."

Father Oakley started to laugh again.

"Father, what the hell is so funny? We have a jazz elective and nobody to teach it."

"Don't look at me, man," said Charlie.

"Ohh, my," sighed Father Oakley. "My last phone call before I left yesterday was to Mrs. Foley."

"At seven a.m.? She was alive?"

"Quarter to. Best time to get people. She's chairing the Music-in-Education committee next year, so I hope she isn't dead. She certainly wasn't then. So what are you trying to tell me?"

I reported the conversation with Rob; Father Oakley tensed with anger as he listened. "That idiot never learns. I'm calling his mother."

I missed the ensuing conversation as more faculty members arrived and I carried out my designated duties of greeting them and directing them to their cabins.

Israel Bond was next, one of the very few non-Catholics working with us: "Iss all right, Kennet, ve are all God's children in same business." During the winter months, Israel divided his time between teaching strings at Golgotha High School and conducting the Ouentaron Symphony Orchestra, an ensemble with a recent and volcanic record of birth. Israel, it may be recalled, was the unfortunate who'd split Liesl Schwarzkopf's skirt; this was one of the reasons Israel was to conduct the Wind Ensemble at camp.

Israel did not like bands; to him they were a bastardized performing medium and a poor second best to the symphony orchestra. "Goddamn bands," he'd lamented to me on the phone when appointed to a band at camp. "Zo much chunk for ze children to play. Vell, Fadder Oakley und Mr. Park vant me to do band, but no chunk." Father Oakley hated symphonic transcriptions for band, but he had yielded to Israel on this point.

"Nossink but ze best," continued Israel's harangue. "Bands iss bastard, see, but, okay, I do vat I got to do. But ve gif children only ze best moosic...Schumann, Bach, Beethoven...moosic mit spiritual substance. Fadder vant a march, he get ze vun from *Fidelio*..."

Israel taken care of, my next client was Pat MacKenzie, the choir director at Mount of Olives Elementary School and therefore a stable-mate of the self-destructive Rob Foley. Her camp duties were to accompany the choir and faculty soloists at evening concerts and any vocal coaching as necessary. Among us she was known as Fat Pat and because of her notoriously unclean habits she'd been assigned a cabin on her own. She travelled in a perpetual miasma so terrible that she'd been referred to health officers and hygiene counsellors, but to no avail. On one memorable occasion, one of her own choir members, downwind of Pat during the Birkenstock Music Festival, had succumbed spectacularly to nausea right on stage in front of nearly a thousand people. At the end of camp, Hugo would have to order the burning of her mattress.

32

A brief lull. I stuck my head into the office to see how Father Oakley's phoning was progressing. He was apoplectic and Miss Moneypenny was grinning openly. "Look, kid, you and Charlie will have to cover the jazz elective."

"Meee? Jazz?"

"Yes, yooou. Jazz. I know you're not all that comfortable with jazz, but there's no other way."

Another car crunched to a halt. My heart leapt. Maybe it was...no, it wasn't. It was the camp choir director, Angela Rumley, Father Oakley's choral counterpart at the office and Neville Park's Thursday afternoon inamorata. She was a revolting peroxide blonde and was never seen without streaks of lipstick on her teeth. Father Oakley called her and Fat Pat the Two Gorgons and when called to task for lack of charity, as I regularly felt compelled to do, would natter a Hail Mary with a smirk on his face. Since we, his intimates, had learned how he had become a priest, we knew not to be shocked.

"Ken, how are you?" drawled Angie. "It's so wonderful to be here, you just can't imagine."

"Oh, I think I can. I've been here four days," I said rudely.

"Oh, you have? Isn't that wonderful."

Clueless bitch, I thought. I was thinking like Father Oakley and I didn't like it. "You're in Linden Lea with Gianetta d'Averso. It's just around this bend, near the big log house."

"Isn't that wonderful! Gianetta is so nice." I swallowed hard. I thought so too, to a degree that Ms. Rumley would not comprehend.

The moment Charlie anticipated and dreaded all at once was now at hand—the arrival of his wife Michelle, the strings teacher at Blood of the Lamb High School. Charlie called her the Human Pipe Cleaner with considerable justification, for, though quite pretty, she was the better part of six feet tall and skinny almost to the point of anorexia. Despite her physical shortcomings and a trying aura of perpetual (and I suspect synthetic) enthusiasm, however, she had a hold over Charlie, catering extravagantly to his passion for what he called "ceremonial underwear", which may seem a flimsy basis for a partnership, but, for whatever reason, it worked. With her she had their small daughter Jennie, a sometime playmate of my own two little girls.

"Hi, K.Y., how are youuuu?" she squealed.

"Fine, uh, Michelle, just fine. Good trip?"

"Oh, yeahhh!" My nerves flinched.

"We've got you and Charlie and Jennie in Wedlock, I mean, Wenlock Edge. You can see it across the creek, among those pines."

"Oh, yeahhh! It looks terrific!"

"Well, enjoy it."

"Oh, yeahhh!"

Enter now Dunstan Corrigan, band director at Our Lady of the Seaways Elementary School and director of our youngest ensemble at camp, the Concert Band. Dunstan was a chubby, good-natured fellow, mustachioed like an adolescent walrus, and radiated an infectious though exhausting enthusiasm.

"K.Y., good to see you!" he bellowed. "Nice to be here, is Osterling here yet? He is? This is really excellent, I've really looked forward to it, you know, I was over in Buffalo a week ago, got some new band recordings, you know, some of those ones Fennell has been doing in Japan...what ensembles they have there!...We'll have to get together some evening and give them a spin, I brought a portable C.D. player with me, one of those Hyper Bass things, and it's really excellent—"

"Dunny—"

"As I said, I've really looked forward to this, really looking forward to meeting Osterling—"

"Dunny, your cabin—"

"I brought one of his newer publications to try out with the little guys, try and stretch them a bit—"

"Dunny—"

"It's really well-written. The man's a wizard—"

"Dunny—"

"As I said, I've really looked—"

"—forward to meeting him."

"This is really exciting. Is Father Oakley around?"

"He's on the phone. Has been for over half-an-hour. Uh, Dunny, your cabin is Wuthering Heights, just up that path across the bridge. I think you would like—"

"—to move on. Thanks, K.Y. See you later. As I said, this is great..."

11:14 in the morning was The Moment. She arrived. She was the only woman on the face of the globe who could be mentioned in the same paragraph as Anna Harland. I had pursued and failed. And then the Lord, in His infinite mercy, had not only granted me another chance but one involving a valiant deed. I'd earned her gratitude; had I earned her love? Would there be the same warmth as but a short time ago, a time of compliments and cautious endearments?

"Hello, Ken." A cool handshake. Well, of course, she had to be discreet.

"Hi, Gianetta, how are things?"

"Oh, settled," she said vaguely, staring off over my shoulder. "I'm going to Germany for the summer."

What? Oh, no! I had glorious plans for the summer ahead, plans of walking hand in hand along illimitable beaches, of moments of growing passion, not too fast, please understand, for there was something of a frightened doe about her, insofar as affairs of the heart were concerned. Besides, the evolution of Gianetta was something to be lingered over and savoured, like a glass of Chablis. But it appeared that the evolution would be stillborn.

"Oh…er, that's…wonderful." I tried not to bleat. "When did you decide on Germany?"

"A friend asked me if I wanted to go. I booked my air ticket Monday."

I dared not ask the gender of the friend. "When do you go?" I ventured. Perhaps there would be a few precious days after the end of term to get something developed.

"The day after we end term."

Dear God! Well, maybe there would be time later in the summer.

"That's really exciting!" I exclaimed with a synthetic cheer that was dashed with Gianetta's next utterance.

"I get back on Labour Day. And then it's back to the rat race."

I was stunned. I was numb. But before I could say anything further, Gianetta said tightly, "Where do I go? Here he comes. I have to get out of here…"

"Linden Lea," I said mechanically. "Along the road here and around the bend by the big log house."

With a shower of stones and no parting words, the exquisite but unattainable Gianetta gunned her car up the road. Into the cloud of dust she left, a Jaguar, a British Racing Green Jaguar, pulled up with a flourish. "The Ego has landed," said Charlie at my elbow. "I think we're expected to be impressed."

The driver poured himself elegantly out of the Jaguar. "My," said Charlie, "I think we should go and change. We just won't do!" Charlie wore jeans, I wore some silly shorts with tropical fish printed thereon, Father Oakley favoured an emerald-green track-suit and a conical sun-hat that made him look like a Chinese coolie. After all, it was Camp.

But we were common folk. This was the Maestro, dressed in a white suit, its glare in the afternoon sun relieved only somewhat by an electric-blue ascot. His eyes were hidden behind the latest designer sunglasses. The Maestro leaned on the front fender of the Jaguar, waiting. I stood where I was, waiting also.

"You're expected to go to him, dummy," whispered Charlie. "You handle this and I'll look after the jazz elective. You're too square for that stuff anyway."

"Fuck him," I said abruptly.

"You're sounding more like Father Oakley with every passing day. I love it when you talk dirty. It makes me feel all cr—"

"Can it, Charlie."

I waited. The Maestro waited.

I waited some more. The Maestro waited some more.

"This is like *High Noon*," said Charlie. "Hear those hot little insects."

"Hi, guys, what's happening?" said Father Oakley cheerily, coming back from dealing with choral risers. "Hey, Antonio, how are you doing, kid?"

"He and K.Y. are having a stand-off," explained Charlie. "K.Y. is the Good, Antonio is the Bad, and I'm the Ugly."

"Antonio, you're in Valhalla, that white cabin across the creek," helped Father Oakley. "If you double back and hook a left, you can drive right up to it." And to me, "Don't be a horse's ass, Ken. Just treat the son-of-a-bitch like God."

"But..."

"For me, kid, okay?"

"K.Y. can treat Antonio like God and I'll do the jazz elective," said Charlie. "This is for you, dear Father."

"Charlie..."

"K.Y. would fail at jazz anyway, so it's all for the best. Hey, here come the buses...oh, look, eight of them...boys, camp is ready to begin."

ANNA AND HUGO

A nna Harland was more than just a friend. She was more than just a woman. She was a state of mind, against which all other women had to be measured, were weighed in the balance, and inevitably found wanting. There were only two exceptions: Aileen, my wife, about whom I was to be pathetically wrong, and the elusive Gianetta d'Averso, who was everything that Anna was, except for being firmly moored to the earth.

From the untidy love life that ensued after the collapse of my marriage with Aileen, Anna stood apart, aloof from the carnage, acting as the Queen does for the Commonwealth, guiding me as would a wise older sister. It was Anna who'd sheltered me on the first agonizingly lonely Christmas on my own. It was Anna who'd bought me groceries when I was too poor to afford milk and sugar for my morning tea and had to make do with the innards of a dismembered Oreo cookie.

The potential for a relationship could have been, as our young people say, awesome. I had known and secretly loved Anna for many years. Likewise, I had known her husband Hugo for many years and it was Hugo's existence that demolished the awesome potential for a relationship, although it did nothing to prevent much fantasy and speculation on my part. Insulated from the hazards of marriage, the Anna of my imaginings was unstained and unblemished, like Wordsworth's

"A perfect woman, nobly plann'd,
to warm, to comfort and command;
and yet a spirit still, and bright
with something of angelic light."

Anna and Hugo's reputations in the fields of television and literature are a matter of public record. So how did I, Kenneth

Yardley Jackson, a musician of modest reputation and teller of
tales of outright disrepute ever reach the ken of such a glittering
couple? In a sense, it happened thrice. Hugo and I had first made
acquaintance through a mutual love of wooden boats, a few tales
of which will follow as a relief from musical matters and the
various stupidities of human devising. We continued to cross paths
when my late (not dead, just late) and unlamented wife Aileen
developed a taste for yoga. Yoga was the second movement in the
cosmic symphony that drew me to Anna,

"…a phantom of delight
when first she gleam'd upon my sight;
a lovely apparition, sent
to be a moment's ornament."

More than a moment's ornament was Anna, even well into
middle age. She bore the patina of life flawlessly and stayed
reassuringly the same year after year. Aileen used to fuss and fume
that Anna did not "develop"; had Anna developed any more in the
physical sense, nobody would have believed the spectacle, and as
for personality, no change could have been for the better. Anna
knew who she was and was comfortable with it, unlike poor
Aileen, wherever she now is, in a constant search for self.

We are now at the third incarnation of the K.Y./Anna/Hugo
coalition, or perhaps we should say the third movement of our
symphony. "A real scherzo, this one," was to be Father Oakley's
editorial.

This third movement was principally a matter of business.
Hugo, as we know, was a writer, but far from being a self-centred
one. He had an active interest in what others were up to,
particularly younger writers, and to that end, he and Anna became
patrons of the arts in a highly individual way. They had rescued
Camp Mishipashoo from dereliction and over the years had
developed it as a haven for writers, actors, and artists to work in
peace, to take instruction, to have seminars and discussions and the
like. Old cabins were refurbished, new ones sprouted up, the barn
was remodelled into a little theatre, actors-in-training came for
repertory experience.

Handily, a little creek bisected the grounds of the camp as it
debouched into Georgian Bay, making the perfect harbour for
Hugo's collection of boats, and in the winter, the dining hall
became a workshop for his various refitting and restoration
projects.

Before much time had passed, Hugo and Anna developed a reputation, not only as patrons of the arts, but as gracious, genial, and witty hosts, and the whole operation was a huge success. As Hugo always enjoyed pointing out, "nothing exceeds like excess"; and it was during one of Hugo's many periods of excess that our friendship went in a new direction, diverging from but at the same time complimenting Hugo's appointed destiny as the guardian of the exquisite Anna.

What Charlie Cowell refers to as my "day job" is as Supervisor of Instrumental Music for the Birkenstock County Roman Catholic School Board. A supervisor is this: when you can't do it, you teach it; and when you can't teach it any more, you become a supervisor, which is how I ended up at the end of this saga. There is a certain mad symmetry to the station in life for which the Almighty has ordained me.

Prior to what I think of as the Ascension, I was director of music at Misericordia High School, an institution sometimes nicknamed, out of spiteful envy, the Miserable Accordion. It came to pass in those days that I got the phone call that made this entire epic possible. A firm friendship had already been established with Father Oakley, at the time Supervisor of Instrumental Music for the Birkenstock County Roman Catholic School Board, so I was not exasperated to hear from him at four o'clock of a 1990 Friday autumn afternoon when I had paid my dues with rehearsals on Tuesday after dinner, again first thing Wednesday morning, yet again first thing Thursday morning, and after school Thursday until 5:30.

"Hey, K.Y., how are you doing, kid? It's John Oakley."

"Hello, Father. Well, I could be better, truth to tell…"

"Hey, that's great. Reason I'm calling is this. You know how it is with me, wheels always turning. Good thing I don't have a wife. She'd go nuts. Listen, here's why I'm calling. You'll read about this in the paper, but do you remember old Carleton Lansdowne?"

"Well, yes, he died a couple of weeks ago, didn't he?" Carleton Lansdowne will be recalled as the founding president of a nationwide chain of lamp stores called the Tri-light Zone. He was from Birkenstock and had been a generous supporter of both the arts and the Church. So what Father Oakley had to tell me both made sense and was gratifying in the extreme.

"He did indeed and the terms of his will were made public today. We, kid, are in the money. Big time."

"What? What do you mean?"

"Old Carleton left four-point-three million good, folding Canadian dollars to the Birkenstock Roman Catholic School Board for an endowment of the arts."

"Holy shit!"

"Well might you say. And this is at a time when other boards are too squeezed to even think of any sort of expansion in anything, let alone the arts."

"Holy shit," I repeated.

"You already said that. We've talked about having a music camp for years and this is our big chance. We have to take a proposal to the Board as soon as we can, but what we do not have is a place…"

"What about the Mishipashoo Arts Centre?"

"Bull's eye, pal. Who's your friend there, the writer…"

"Hugo Harland."

"See if you could set up an appointment with him, say, for a week Saturday. Tell him what we have in mind, no commitment or guarantee at this time, because we have to see it first. Maybe in the meantime he could work up a rental cost for us to cover a week."

Father Oakley must not be judged a heartless individual for not inquiring why I had not been better. He was, after all, a fully-ordained priest in the Society of Jesus. But when he was focused on some great venture, as it was every other week, he was impervious to any distractions or diversions. It was really at this point that I became in effect Father Oakley's assistant and soon became acclimatized to what the music department's secretary Marie Cadbury called "the Father's cycle." Marie had it figured that the first and third weeks of each month were the Father's "solar flare" weeks—weeks of intense activity and outpourings of ideas. The second and fourth weeks were times of contemplation and reflection, for Father Oakley and the office staff alike. These times would lead to phone calls like this:

"Hey, K.Y., how are you doing, kid? It's John Oakley."

"Oh, hi, Father," weakly delivered, for it was just short of eleven at night.

"Been thinking. You know when I called you about the camp idea."

"Uh-huh."

"You sounded pretty down and I was so caught up in the camp thing that I didn't think to ask why. It was very thoughtless of me and I'm sorry."

"Well, it was nice of you to call. Now, I mean. I understand. Don't worry about it."

But as in everything else with Father Oakley, the matter had to be pursued until settled to his own satisfaction. "It was a sin to seem so unconcerned about you, K.Y. What was the problem?"

"Let me talk to you tomorrow." I could feel myself being drawn into a vortex of disapproval from the other side of the bed.

"Family?"

"You've got it."

"I somehow sensed it. You haven't been yourself the last while. Maybe I can help. And now that I have my facts straight for confession…"

"Confession? You?"

"No-one is immune from sin, kid. I have feet of clay, just like anyone else. Talk to you tomorrow."

"Meddling busybody," grumbled my dear wife Aileen. "What a time to call. No peace around here…" She pressed her fingers to her temples, a gesture learned in a dramatic arts class at the Mishipashoo Arts Centre a couple of summers before.

The evolution of our camp was what enabled me to survive the winter. When not carrying out my routine schedule of classes and rehearsals at the Miserable Accordion, I was at the Board of Education office, functioning as Father Oakley's ghostwriter and assembling a formidable stack of paperwork for our proposal. In the process, I developed an immediate friendship with Marie Cadbury, a sort of senior edition of Anna and to everyone's sadness due to retire at the end of the academic year. Whereas Anna was a sort of honorary big sister with overtones of imaginary incest, Marie was more like an honorary mother.

I called her Sweet Marie and on the days when I went to the office after school (a handy refuge from home), I took her a Sweet Marie candy bar to demonstrate my appreciation for all that she was doing. To type as accurately as she did from my hand-written notes was no mean feat; they were never a model of legibility at the best of times and these were not the best of times.

"Sweet Mr. Jackson," Marie would beam on accepting my latest offering. "Are you trying to fatten me up?"

"Yes, I confess it."

"Why would you do that to a woman who counts every calorie?"

"And leaves it at that," said Father Oakley sarcastically.

"Just so," I said, "there will be more of you to love."

"Lust is one of the seven deadly sins," said Father Oakley.

"Not to mention lusting for your neighbour's wife, but that is not what I am doing. I am not doing anything. I can only regard Sweet Marie, married as she is, from a discreet distance. Now, tell me, what is the harm in that?"

"I know you, K.Y. You're lusting. Those initials of yours are no accident."

41

"Don't listen to him, Sweet Boy," admonished Marie. "What have you for me today?"

"The candy bar."

"Besides the candy bar. Professionally. Musically. Educationally."

"I have some preliminary figures from Hugo that I think will fly with the Board. As to going for an inspection, there was a storm up there and the road is all washed out and trees are down and it's a real mess. However, Father, if you've no objection, you and I can leave the car at Parry Sound and Hugo and Anna can take us out by boat."

"By boat? Isn't that dangerous?"

"Hell, no. People do it all the time."

"In late October?"

"Their boat is big, I mean, a really serious ship."

"Oh…well…sure. I'll just have to make sure I'm equipped…"

"Now, then, dear Mr. Jackson," said Marie brusquely, "why can't you write neatly? Surely they still taught penmanship when you were in school, oh, you must have been the sweetest thing!"

Father Oakley made a rude gesture with his finger stuck in his mouth. I ignored him. "I write as I do because neatness demonstrates a lack of genius."

Father Oakley laughed. Sweet Marie called him an old horror, and then said to me, "So us common folk get to pick up the pieces, right? Okay, Sweet Boy, give it to me. Oh, I almost forgot. There's a message for you."

"There is? Here? Who's it from?"

"Your wife. Demanding that you phone. Forthwith."

"Oh, sh…ahem." The nausea of apprehension boiled hotly in my vitals. I dialled the number of my house and a child's voice answered.

DOMESTIC BLISS

"Hi, Katie, honey."

"Daddy!"

"Can I talk to Mum?"

"Talk to me first."

"Dear, I can't right now. I'm at the office. I have a report to do." Katie was fascinated at me being at an office rather than a school. That meant Daddy was all grown up now.

"Come on, Dad, talk to me!"

"Dear, I can't."

"Aww!"

"Honey, I'm in a hurry. Please put Mum on." I would far rather have talked to Katie.

"Kenneth," said my wife brusquely, "had you forgotten Evie's doctor appointment at 4:30?" It was just gone 3:30.

"Appointment? Yeah. What about it?"

"You'll have to take her."

"What? Me? I'm at work. This is an office day. You take her."

"I can't. I have an appointment with Mildred Willis in Toronto for 4:30 and I have to catch the 3:45 bus." This was all news to me.

"Well, maybe you'd better re-book with Mildred Willis for 4:30 tomorrow."

My voice was rising. Father Oakley rolled his eyes, Marie tried to look busy.

"Damn it, Kenneth, my work has to count for something too," yammered the phone. "It may not make money yet, maybe it never will, but there's the matter of Self-Expression. Besides, we are equal partners as parents, which means responsibility has to be shared…" I was holding the phone away from my ear by this time. Aileen's shrewish outpouring nattered through the office.

"Doesn't it, though," I retorted.

43

"What is that supposed to mean?"

"That maybe you at least consult me to avoid exactly this kind of situation…oh, hell, never mind, I'll do it." I chucked the phone onto its holder. Another sell-out, albeit a modest one this time, but there had been so many before that Father Oakley occasionally chided me for what he called my Neville Chamberlain syndrome.

I took a deep breath. "Father, this won't get me any brownie points, but I'm going to have to take my daughter to the doctor. I'll have to come back tomorrow to work on this."

"That's all right, kid," soothed the Father with a friendly pat on the shoulder. "I won't razz you with the Neville Chamberlain thing. Family has to come first."

I dealt with Evie's appointment without even the doubtful luxury of reading superannuated issues of *Time* or *Field and Stream* in the doctor's waiting room, as the child needed to be played with and told stories; normally I enjoyed doing that kind of thing to the hilt, but not today, not when I should have been working on the proposal for the camp. Here Father Oakley had the confidence in me to make a major contribution and I was not there to make it.

I remarked on this at dinner (cooked, rather indifferently, by me), an ill-chosen moment, but then these days any moment was ill-chosen.

"Well, that tells us how important your family is!" snapped Aileen.

"So what were you doing at the time of Evie's appointment?"

"I was, as you full know, signing a publishing contract."

"Congratulations. You made both appointments when you knew full well that on Thursdays I go to the office to work on the music camp. I have been professionally embarrassed—"

"Camp, shmamp! That's kid stuff. This is the real world."

"The real world!" I screamed. "That's wonderful! Writing verse that eclipses anyone's understanding of the English language, verse that you have to pay to have published, with money earned by me, and then it comes out bound in plastic like a low-budget cookbook, and you call it reality?" I was boiling over like a runaway kettle, even in the horror of what I was saying and how I was saying it. It felt as if someone else's words were pouring out of my mouth.

"You bastard!" It was Aileen's turn to scream now, fingertips reaching for temples. "You're the big dreamer here. But let anyone else have dreams, well, look out!"

"Dreams," I said tonelessly, ploughing resolutely through my dinner. "If you comprehend any of our recent family history, you may realize that you sort of destroyed most of mine."

"Nothing keeps you from your food, eh, K.Y.?"

"I'm entitled to eat. I earned the god-damned money so I could." Again I could not believe what I was saying. This was horrible. Aileen's fingers whitened under pressure and I wondered stupidly what would give way first, her fingers or her temples.

I had thought I was being more than fair. The fact of us both being in the arts, but not in competition with each other, had initially boded well, but after eight years of marriage, the almost perpetual dissonance in the Jackson household demonstrated otherwise. Aileen's big thesis of late had been what she called my price-tag mentality, that I was dull and lacked the imagination to unfetter my soul and take flight to the stars, soaring off above the common ignorant masses. My price-tag mentality, though, was what put bread on the table and generally, as I was fond of putting it, rented our space in the world.

Aside from fundamental attitudes, one particularly intrusive problem had been one of time. My own work in music education had fairly well-defined time-boundaries on paper, but with rehearsals, concerts, students requiring after-school help (or having it inflicted on them) and the sundry urgencies that were the lot of any music teacher, scheduling my own affairs according to the convenience of others was a virtual impossibility. In my mind, all this was offset by the sorts of Christmas and summer holidays that are the envy of many, but then during those same holidays, I was adjudged to be around too much. I didn't necessarily want to win, I just wanted reason. It just didn't work that way.

The same situation prevailed to an even greater degree with Aileen's writing, though not out of any Neville Chamberlain-inspired instincts. Not only was verse her medium, but it was verse designed to explore the Deepest Meanings of Life and bring mankind Face to Face With the Essence of Existence. You could not say that Aileen was not innovative; she laid out her material on the printed page in a way that, to the reader, would symbolize the Motion of the Cosmos. I would have liked to show some of it here, but it will come as no surprise that I was denied the rights. Intellectually, it was quite beyond me and, I fear, quite beyond others as well, but there was no avoidance of Aileen's feeling that it was something she was meant to do, that she was a tool of Predestination.

Once the children had come, even though it was by mutual consent, their requirements had been completely at odds with Aileen's writing, the ideas for which obviously could not be turned on and off at will. Morning television for the little ones was a blessing, especially on Saturdays with Anna doing Yoga Bear; and my first priority on getting home from work was to take the girls for a walk so their mother could have some time on her own.

While I did what I could, the fact of the matter was that my work, Aileen's writing, and our family was an impossible combination. The whole structure was like three strips of metal of different coefficients of expansion, bonded together and going into all manner of contortions with every change of temperature. In the interests of keeping things together, I had already sacrificed a vital part of my personal life; now my musical life was under fire, but to sacrifice any aspect of it would have been professional suicide. Try as I might to be accommodating, Aileen complained more and more of being trapped, and in her distress had fallen into the habit of pressing fingertips to temples, a warning as reliable as any barometer.

"She's a real pistol," Father Oakley would say. "If it's so horrible now, how did you two even get together in the first place?"

To this day, I cannot really answer the question. There certainly was an attraction, a Fatal Attraction, to borrow the title of a movie of some years back, and the way I have come to phrase my response is that I was attracted to Aileen as a moth is to a candle, and she to me as a piranha to a drowned sheep.

The phone rang. "Oh, Jesus," said Aileen in bland disregard of the fine Catholic upbringing we were trying to give our children, both of whom were weeping at the spectacle of Mum and Dad fighting yet again. "Another part of your little empire calling," she added sneeringly.

I took the call out of earshot in my basement study. "Hey, kid, been thinking about you. Is everything all right?"

"Oh, hi, Father. Well, Evie is okay, just routine maintenance. But I put it to Aileen that she placed me in a very difficult position, I mean I have a role in the camp thing…"

"…a big one…"

"…and she just refuses to take it seriously. Called it kid stuff, said, well, I was pretty awful, to be honest…"

"You were driven into a corner, K.Y. As a clergyman, I shouldn't say this, but as your friend, let me say that I think your wife is an unmitigated horror for what she is doing to you. She has the instincts of a saboteur. Has she something against us, or what?"

"I have tried so hard to be reasonable, I really have…"

"I know. Just don't sell yourself short, kid. You're doing a great job. It just, er…"

"Has to get done".

"Well, yes, to put it bluntly. Can you come in tomorrow after school?"

"Well, uh…"

"Or sometime Saturday?"

"That one's really hard…"

"On Sunday? It's the Lord's Day, but then what we're doing is the Lord's work."

"Sunday's a real baddie."

"K.Y., come on! I don't want to have to turn this over to someone else. With your connection to Hugo and Anna, there is no-one else. We have to have this for the Board meeting on November, let's see, the twenty-first."

"Let me make a phone call and get back to you in a few minutes. You'll be home?"

"Home, work, or church, pal. Any one of those places. None of this debauchery at the Brew-Ha-Ha or whatever that place is that Charlie likes. Yeah, I'll be home. Talk to you in a bit."

The call was to Anna and Hugo. In point of fact, it was to Anna, complete with the quaking heart that even after all these years, even with both of us married, would not go away. But, the world being as it is, it was Hugo who answered; Anna had boated to Parry Sound to see someone off on the train.

I outlined my dilemma of trying to work on the camp project, look after the girls, keep Aileen happy, and myself from having a complete psychic meltdown.

"Keeping that woman happy is like trying to ride a bicycle in sand," observed Hugo.

"What a great line!"

"Thank you, my friend. I wrote it this morning. That's why everyone thinks I'm such a *bon vivant*. I think up clever little bagatelles like that one at work and then work them into conversation. Just don't tell anybody that was *all* I wrote this morning. Now, what were we saying? The strain of writing that one clever little line has put me in a state of mental gridlock…"

"Oh, that's a hot one!"

"Isn't it, though. Let me write it down…now…sorry, K.Y. Where the hell were we? Oh, yes, poor old Aileen. The hounds of hell all rolled up in one being. What else can I say? Can I do anything?"

"In fact, you can. Is there any chance I could bring the girls up there next weekend and they can just do their stuff and Father Oakley and I can get on with the camp proposal for the Board in peace? I feel kind of brazen asking such a thing, but I'm in such a box I don't know what else to do."

"I'll say a cautious yes. I'm quite far into a new manuscript and wouldn't be much company, but I think Anna's free. Just a second, she just came in."

Pause. Then the slightly breathy voice, known to the thousands of participants in Yoga and You and to thousands more adoring observers. "Of course you can bring the girls. You know about our storm; the road is still washed out and blocked with fallen trees, four big ones, but we can meet you in the boat at the Town Dock, say, at about ten Saturday morning."

"That's perfect. It'll give me some time to synchronize things with Father Oakley..."

"I just love Father Oakley! Hugo's gone all sort of turgid the way he does with a new book and the Father'll lighten him up."

I phoned back to Father Oakley to tell him of the arrangements. There was a silence.

"Father?"

"Er, yes. I was just sort of meditating on Anna for a moment. A golden example of the Lord's work. Oakley, watch your mouth. It's like cheating on the Virgin Mother to say such things. Say, what should I do about Mass on Sunday?"

"St. Peter's Church in Parry Sound has a five o'clocker. We can go there before we head back home. I checked."

"Then it's a done deal. Good work, kid. This'll get us back on track."

Convinced that I had done the Right Thing, had given Aileen an entire weekend to explore the Deepest Meanings of Human Existence and accommodate my professional requirements, mundane though they may have been, at the same time, I was therefore nonplussed at her reaction: "What! Leaving me all alone for the entire weekend?"

"To give you the time for yourself you've always wanted, dear one."

"Oh, great, I finally get a publishing contract, I realize my dream after unspeakable travail and suffering, and what does he do, he takes the kids off and abandons me!"

"You could come with us, Mummy!" chorused Katie and Evie. Oh, bite your tongues, my children! Anna could still be pleasant to Aileen, but Hugo wanted nothing to do with her. He hated being treated like a human doormat because his writing did not attempt explorations into the magnum mysterium; and, heaven forbid, he Made Money. As for Father Oakley, he and Aileen were potentially the most unlikely coalition since Churchill and Stalin.

"Oh, no, dear, I think not," said Aileen. "All they'll talk about is music and this camp thing and, oh, God, boats, I've had it with boats."

"I know," I said sourly.

"Now, what is that supposed to mean?" The finger-tips were at the ready.

"You know bloody well. If you would remember—"

The phone rang again. It was Father Oakley, wanting to know exactly what clothing to take on what he perceived to be a dangerous ocean crossing to a remote and hostile land. Anything outside the arts, education, politics, or the Church was a domain whose mysteries could be dealt with only through the most meticulous and rigorous preparation.

"God-damn phone's ringing off the hook," I heard Aileen snap. "Should just leave it off."

"But, Mum, it can't ring if it's off the hook," pointed out Katie.

"That's the idea, honey. Oh, God, what a zoo." The finger-tips reached for the temples.

Father Oakley had never read any of the sailing books by Arthur Ransome that were the cornerstone of my early teen-years reading, but it was as though the genial spirit of Mr. Ransome were presiding over that Friday. Bear in mind, now, that I had gone to school on a cheerless, wet October morning, with the usual spiritual hangover from fighting with Aileen, faced with a full day of teaching. The diversions started at 8:11 a.m. "Hey, kid, how are you? Won't keep you a minute. Should I go and buy a life-jacket, or what? Does Hugo have extras? If I need one, should it be a Mae West? Always thought they were kind of neat…"

10:02 a.m.—"Hello, Sweet Mr. Jackson. How is my perfect boy? Father asked me to phone you between classes. I think he's out getting K-rations or something. He wanted to know what to take to keep dry. He just has that great bag-like raincoat and a Molson umbrella."

"Both Hugo's boats have cabins, so he'll be okay."

"I think he's concerned with his image."

"A priest with a Molson umbrella concerned with image?"

"It doesn't add up, does it, Sweet Boy? All I can think is that he wants to look at home in those surroundings."

12:05 p.m.—"Hey, kid! How are things? You know, I'm really getting excited about this trip. I went to a marine place at Netherlands Landing and priced some of this stuff and I nearly croaked. You boat people must be loaded."

"I'm not a real boat person any more."

"Sorry, that was dumb of me."

49

"That's okay. You can't be expected to keep track of all my life's disasters. What did you look at?"

"Oh, let's see, a Peter Storm outfit and these groovy yellow boots and a Mae West and one of those emergency radio beacons… flares…let's see what else…"

"Father, you don't need any of it. It's just a six-mile gig across the Sound."

"Well, you know me. I like to do things the right way".

1:43 p.m.—"Hi, K.Y., it's Charlie. What the fuck is going on? Are you and Father going to Samoa or something? He's phoned me three or four times…"

3:22 p.m.—"Hi, kid. Hey, our Charlie is aces, isn't he? He lent me a, what the hell was it called, a Mustang floater suit and a pair of those yellow boots, and everything. I'll fit right in. I'll have credibility."

Father Oakley did better that to simply fit in. Even with boats being one of the few fields outside his sphere of knowledge, he not only fit in but actually managed to dominate. We were to meet Anna and Hugo at 10:00 on Saturday morning; the Father, convinced that we would be late otherwise, had us pick him up at 5:00, and as a result, we were three hours early at Parry Sound. We spent some time in a donut shop (Kiwi was fascinated by Father Oakley's odd habit of swishing his coffee in his mouth), and then a chilly hour pacing the wharf, watching for whatever vessel would pick us up. In addition to his dinghies, Hugo had two cruisers (both wood), a 1928 Gidley, *Helen Louise,* and *Screamer,* the 1963 Trojan whose purchase I had witnessed on making his and Anna's acquaintance. It was *Screamer* doing the honours this day.

"Hi, guys," called the Father cheerily as *Screamer* maneuvered alongside. "My goodness, this is quite a boat. *Screamer,* eh? How'd you come up with a name like that?"

"Hugo," said Anna warningly. Hugo paid no heed.

"She's a Trojan and, being wood, has ribs. So, since, in essence…"

"Hugo!"

"…in essence, since she is a ribbed Trojan, *Screamer* seemed just the ticket…"

"Hugo, you are disgusting!" raged Anna. "And in front of Father Oakley!"

"Darling, he asked."

"Aha-ha-ha!" bellowed the Father appreciatively.

Father Oakley cut a figure that morning that has never been duplicated since. The girls and I were dressed in jeans and sweaters, as were Hugo and Anna. The Father, however, was in full regalia with the orange floater suit and yellow boots. He was a walking sauna, refusing to divest himself of all his gear until we were safely ashore at the camp. It was as if we were to traverse the Northwest Passage.

We got under way. And then the questions began. "Hugo, this is some boat. Like a miniature liner. What do you do to all that varnish every year? How do you keep it so nice? How much gas does she use? Is that paint you use for the bottom toxic? Look at that big ship coming in...tanker?...isn't that kind of dangerous? My goodness, this is the Sound, eh? Must get awful rough in a wind. How do you predict what it's going to do? Now, that deviation card. Has that to do with the compass?..."

For me, what Sweet Marie called 'Father Oakley's Great Adventure' had the bittersweet air of a homecoming with something missing. There was the Sound and all its landmarks I knew and loved; Three-Mile Point, Gull Rock, the Hole-in-the-Wall, Huckleberry and Horse Islands, Grave and Goat Islands, and then the little creek at the Mishipashoo Arts Centre, harbouring Hugo's fleet. My own ship used to moor here, my proud beauty, by far the greatest casualty of the alliance with Aileen.

My melancholy, though, was temporarily forgotten in the excitement of our mission. Anna installed the girls in their own little cabin and took them exploring in company with the family cat Kitty Sark, the crow Herbert von Carrion, and a Highland Terrier named Angus of God. While Hugo spent some time on his manuscript, Father Oakley and I walked the grounds, taking pictures of the facilities for the Birkenstock County Roman Catholic School Board. I should say that I did the taking of pictures; while learned in so many different respects, Father Oakley was a card-carrying Luddite when it came to anything mechanical or electrical, and I took over the photography when I observed him trying to take a picture with the lens cap on.

We measured the buildings for floor space and counted the beds in the sleeping cabins, now barren and melancholy in their winter hibernation. We examined and photographed the kitchen facilities, our observations reinforced by data supplied by Anna. We looked at the plumbing, though more as a formality, since I knew little about plumbing and the Father nothing at all.

We looked at the dining hall, a wonderfully primitive building with large screened openings rather than windows. "There'll be some chilly mornings here," remarked Father Oakley, fumbling with the padlock. "Congealed porridge, just like at the seminary. Oh, fuck this lock; why can't I do this stuff?"

"Your mind is on loftier thoughts and is on a perpetual flight to the stars."

"Horseshit. Open the bloody door, would you? Thanks, pal. Oh, my goodness, would you look at this!"

"This" was Hugo's prized collection of wooden boats; the dining hall was their winter drydock. Lovingly cleaned off and covered with plastic sheeting were two Ackroyd dinghies, one of the original Grew dinghies, a two-masted sailing canoe built in 1899, a Peterborough skiff, a Lakefield runabout, two rowboats (one double-ended), and six cedar-strip canoes.

"My goodness," repeated the Father. "Look at this, it looks like a grand piano. Does Hugo do all this by himself?"

"Most of it, except for the heavy structural stuff. Has a guy in Parry Sound do that. Anna helps too. Hugo has her do the varnishing. She lays it down like nothing you ever saw." A mutual sigh.

"You really miss this, don't you, kid?"

"The degree of loss is so great as to be comprehended only by Hugo and Anna and, of course, you. It was a way of life. Thank God I still have my music."

"Never mind, kid, you'll have a boat again some day. Just be patient. Maybe your Aileen will have a tragic, oh, no, forget it. I never said it."

"Said what?"

"What I was about to say."

"What was that?"

"Never mind. Let's just say it's awful enough for confession."

"What a guy you are, Father. I love your mind. You're the most secular priest I ever met."

"Yeah, well, that's a story I'll tell when the time is right. But right now, we have to deal with this."

In the curious limbo of uplift and gloom that equates to hopelessness, I helped Father Oakley to look at the recreational facilities; there was a slightly sloped playing field, once a farmer's field, and an equally eccentric tennis court, so we could offer at least a couple of land sports.

For sports, it was the waterfront that would be our crown jewel. Hugo offered to engage his usual waterfront staff a week earlier and put them at our disposal, factoring them into our overall cost.

"That takes care of swimming, but we should still be in control of it, okay? The kids will want some canoes to paddle, so we'll look into rental costs…"

"What the hell for?" said Hugo. "We have some beauties right here."

"They're eye-poppers, all right, but you wouldn't want…"

"They're here to be used, Father. They aren't just pretty museum pieces. Just tell the tiddlers not to have races or play pirates. Or try that naval battle scene from Ben Hur."

"That was really something," said Father Oakley reverently; he loved a good film. "We can do the leasing cost with or without boats," said Hugo, "but I would prefer it with. Some of those kids may want to come back as adults and I want it to look as good as possible. Now, please understand as far as the boats go, it's all or nothing. No outside rentals. Know why?"

"Why?" said Father Oakley. I already knew the answer.

"No fibreglass boats allowed here. I hate them. They are an abomination, like zebra mussels or pork to the Jews. You show me a fibreglass tree, then I'll listen about fibreglass boats."

"I like you, Hugo. I like guys with opinions. Okay. Let's get into the figures."

We did; and because Hugo did his writing on a computer, we were able to have the machine produce a document that was a true work of art. "Guys," said Father Oakley, scanning it for the twentieth time, "this is a f…pardon me, Anna, a real work of art. If the Board doesn't go for it, it's sackcloth and ashes for me for the rest of the year. Or maybe my life."

The Board voted on it two weeks later. Neville Chamberlain, in a vision, recommended that I should stay home with Aileen rather than attend the Board meeting, which was on a Monday night. Naturally, there was an eruption when Father Oakley phoned at eleven o'clock to say "Well, kid, we did it! God bless capitalism and the Canadian way of life! Wish you could have been there…"

"So do I."

"I know, kid, I know. Won't keep you a moment. Wish you could have been there. Only one dissenter, old biddy Radcliff, what a shit-awful piece of work she is. Wish you could have been there. This is great. I could stay up all night. Fact, I think I will. Hey, listen, we've got to celebrate. Can you pry yourself loose from hearth and home next Saturday night? I want to combine celebrating with spying. Something is going down and it has a funny smell."

"What is it?"

"Too complex for over the phone. Hey, I'll get out of your life now. Call me tomorrow."

ANTONIO

Prying myself loose was like having a bill passed through Parliament, but after being subjected to Aileen's shrewish squallings that I were abandoning her with the girls, I suggested that Katie should go too. Consent was grudgingly given, although nearly withdrawn at least twice during the ensuing week on such various pretexts that I was trying to win Katie away from her, whatever that was supposed to mean, or that I was trying to influence Katie and fill her head up with all manner of symphonic pretentiousness. Ultimately, we did go, and our heads did become filled, if involuntarily, with symphonic pretentiousness of a most extraordinary kind. On paper, it looked like this:

BIRKENSTOCK PHILHARMONIC SOCIETY
Saturday evening, October 28, 1990
8:00 in the Auditorium, Stigmata High School
Conductor: ANTONIO d'AVERSO

Programme
Overture, *La Forza del Destino* Giuseppe Verdi
Symphonic Poem *Les Preludes* Franz Liszt
Ride of the Valkyries, Richard Wagner
from the opera *Die Walkure*
Intermission
Symphonie Fantastique, Op. 14 Hector Berlioz
1. Dreams and Reveries
2. Scene at the Ball
3. Scene in the Fields
4. March to the Scaffold
5. Dream of a Witches' Sabbath

"Hi, Kiwi, how are you doing, dear?" greeted Father Oakley as we settled into our seats. He always enjoyed his role as the only priest who didn't terrify the children, possibly helped by his somewhat rustic image, for the Father hated suits and would not be persuaded to wear one unless conducting the All-County Wind Ensemble. Tonight he looked fairly typically John, appearing in a yellow windbreaker, rumpled corduroy trousers, and running shoes in arresting combination with his clerical collar.

"Just look at this programme! This is even glossier than the Toronto Symphony...wonder how much this set them back...what the hell, excuse me, Katie, is this guy trying to do? This is a community orchestra...and he goes choosing all gut-blasters...brass players'll have no faces left..."

I read the programme aloud to Katie, who had to have all details, including those of the conductor. She thought conductors were Awesome. "The Birkenstock Philharmonic Society is pleased to welcome Maestro Antonio d'Averso as its new music director. Maestro d'Averso brings to our podium over twenty years' experience as a conductor, cellist, and educator, following a path that has led from his native Italy through appearances in France, the Netherlands, Germany, Denmark, and Great Britain, to our orchestra tonight. The Maestro has also conducted extensively in the United States and made his Lincoln Centre debut in New York last spring.

"Maestro d'Averso holds a doctoral degree from the University of Bari and the Diploma di Direzzione from the Bologna Collegium Musicum. He is Director of Music at our 'headquarters', Stigmata High School."

I was agog. "Good God," I said. "I had no idea..."

"Don't be impressed just yet. You know these trips he takes with his band."

"Yes."

"Where did he take them in the spring?"

"New York."

"And the spring before that?"

"Somewhere overseas...Copenhagen, wasn't it?"

"Yes. And the year before that?"

"Oh, hell, I don't know. Germany?"

"Exactly. Get the picture"

"Oh, I see. But Lincoln Centre?"

"His band played on the plaza in front. I'm tempted to check this other stuff out, like this doctoral degree. Fasten your safety belts, here we go."

The house lights dimmed. A spotlight decreed our attention at the side of the stage; and in came Antonio d'Averso in an electric-blue set of tails, a shirt that vomited frills from his waist-coat, a shock of reddish hair carefully coiffed into a sensuously flowing mane, Roman nose held at exactly the right angle. A sigh swept the audience. Katie's eyes were like buttons and Father Oakley looked ill.

The orchestra sprang to attention as if a switch had been thrown. The Maestro gave a sweeping gesture for them to sit and turned to the audience, clasping his hands like an opera singer in full cry. A great smile with the magnitude of a lighthouse was unleashed on the assemblage, giving rise to renewed applause. Father Oakley's look of impending illness was now one of abject pain.

"*Grazie, grazie,*" cooed the Maestro. "So many of'a you came" (chuckle, chuckle) "so'a many who love'a da great'a music. I am'a so honoured, so'a pleased'a to be asked'a to direct such a splendid'a orchestra. I have'a taught in Birkenstock for eight'a years, right'a here in this'a verra school, and'a inna my time'a here have thought'a what great'a things could'a be done'a with'a such a fine ensemble."

"We'll see," whispered Father Oakley.

"Now I am up on'a stage with them," emoted the Maestro, hands fluttering about his head like a couple of friendly moths. "And although I have'a conducted all over Europe and America, as'a da programme'a so kindly tells you, I feel'a dis to be a special'a kind of an evening. I have'a chosen da overture to'a *Forza del Destino* to begin's da evening, since I think it must'a have been'a da force of destiny that brought'a me to you'a tonight." Scattered sights punctuated the audience, sounding like a distant gospel service.

"Gag me with a wooden spoon," I murmured to the Father.

"And when you're done, clean it off and give it to me."

Katie was seated between us and said in her best Aileen imitation, fingers pressed to temples, "Stop it, both of you! This is disgusting!" It was the one time I have ever seen Father Oakley startled into silence.

We really had no idea what to expect. In its nine years of existence, the Birkenstock Philharmonic had functioned as a competent community orchestra of fifty-five or so, presided over by our friend and colleague, Israel Bond, who taught orchestra at Golgotha High School. Israel sensibly chose music either composed with amateurs in mind or works that were clearly within their reach; Haydn and early Schubert figured prominently in his programmes, as well as such titles as Peter Warlock's *Capriol*

Suite. The idea was to have fun with good music and attain a reasonable standard of performance in the process. Dvorak's Symphony in G Major was generally acknowledged as the orchestra's outer limit in the wake of a somewhat untidy rendition the previous winter.

And now here was the Birkenstock Philharmonic not only facing a programme comprised entirely of works thought outside of its scope, but with its size increased by nearly half of the original membership. As the three great brass chords of *Forza del Destino* rang out (and ring they did), it was plain that a whole new game was in town.

Antonio d'Averso was considered a pompous ass and a charlatan of the first order among the musical community. Those of us responsible for the music programmes in our high schools were expected to attend monthly meetings to discuss current issues, sort out mutual problems, plan joint projects, or simply stay in touch, and for a couple of hours dispel the sense of isolation that is the lot of a music teacher. Although it was a job requirement and actually written into our contracts, Maestro d'Averso usually declined to join us common folk for our meetings; he was always too busy with this or that mysterious errand, lacing his telephoned regrets with references to Cleveland, Los Angeles, and Amsterdam. The times he did show up were invariably following some remarkable feat for which he would have to be congratulated; a case in point was the Stigmata band's winning first prize in a band competition in Germany and being hysterically hailed as "the best band in the world" by the local newspaper. Antonio's noble profile took up half the front page and later enjoyed a great survival rate through being clipped out and taped to the bedroom ceilings of countless adoring women.

When not busy being congratulated at meetings, the Maestro would mock whatever anyone else had to say with a laugh accompanied by a furrowed brow, as if he didn't know whether to laugh or cry, a real "what fools these mortals be" look. The only barrier to our outpouring of feeling was our Director of Music, Neville Park, who was fond of reminding us that as Roman Catholics and musicians, we were curators of the utmost in taste and standards. So we could not tell Antonio d'Averso to fuck off; ergo, our collective dislike for him was blocked of all adequate avenues of expression.

All we could hope for was to see the Maestro fall flat on his face with the Birkenstock Philharmonic. It didn't happen that way. *La Forza* was stupendous, even allowing for the Maestro's gratuitous acrobatics on the podium. There was a cloudburst of applause, in which Father Oakley and I reluctantly joined.

"Clap, Daddy, clap!" squealed Katie, bouncing up and down in her seat.

"Now he's sucking in the little ones," sighed Father Oakley.

The Maestro retired to the wings, dabbing at his brow with an embroidered handkerchief. The orchestra gulped and gasped on stage. A young maiden behind us was whimpering.

Moments later, the Maestro was back. "Franz Liszt was'a one of da greatest'a musicians da world has'a ever known," he gushed. "It has'a been said that he was'a da greatest pianist who ever lived, writing for himself'a da music too difficult for others. Well'a, many pianists play Liszt now and'a play'a him well, so we've all'a come a long way.

"Liszt was'a just as brilliant a composer for'a da orchestra. We play'a now *Les Preludes,* which he wrote after a reading of Alphonse'a Lamartine's poem of'a da same'a name. It'a portrays life as a series of'a preludes to a great and'a glorious afterlife. For'a myself, I hope it to be a prelude'a to many, many years with'a da Birkenstock Philharmonic."

"In your dreams, asshole," grumbled Father Oakley. "Oh, sorry, Katie. You didn't hear that."

"Oh, yes, I did."

"Well, don't tell your mother."

"Don't worry, Father."

Les Preludes was another coup; the Birkenstock Philharmonic played as though all their chairs were wired, the Maestro slashed, stabbed, speared, and harpooned the air, Father rolled his eyes, and Katie actually fell off her seat during the coda. The applause was volcanic.

After the obligatory mopping of brow and a brief exit backstage, a freshly-coiffed Maestro had this to say: "It is'a no accident that we'a combined'a Liszt and'a Wagner on'a da same'a programme. Aside'a from their'a being great'a composers, Wagner was'a Liszt's son-in-law, so it's'a kinda like'a in'a da family, as'a you might'a say. Wagner's 'a specialty was'a da opera, and'a being Italian, what'a can I say? Opera's in'a ma blood, so we give'a you now one of'a da most exciting scenes inna da opera repertoire, da Ride of'a da Valkyries."

The Maestro spun around and gave the downbeat in one smooth motion, a bit of bravado that would fall flat with an orchestra that didn't know its stuff. Three months ago this had been but the torso of an orchestra; now it was not only enormous but playing Ride of the Valkyries. And playing it stupendously to boot. Had it been an admired colleague on the podium, and Father Oakley was as admired as any ("Oh, sure, kid, you're just saying that to kiss ass"), I would have been thrilled. But with someone as nauseating as Antonio d'Averso in charge and pulling it off was singularly dispiriting.

Wine and cheese were served at intermission in the foyer, which had been carpeted in red for the evening. The wine and cheese was a total surprise to the principal, Harley Davidson, not the least of whose concerns was the provision of a liquor licence. Sharing his concern was his fellow principal Philip Horatio Quail, who happened not only to be my own principal but my father-in-law as well.

Phil's life model had been Lord Mountbatten. He'd been in the navy and ran his school accordingly; the White Ensign was no stranger to the school's flag pole and the football team were known as the Boat People.

Phil's wife Suzi carried abundant charms of her own. She was actually Aileen's stepmother and by an odd circumstance of chronology was younger than I and only a couple of years older than Aileen, who was (and still is, wherever she is) five years younger than myself. Amused by our circumstances, Suzi and I from the moment of meeting had carried on an innocuous flirtation and found each other to be great company. Unlike many of my confreres, I always looked forward to outings to or with the in-laws and it was always a matter of regret that Aileen loathed her. Suzi was a secretary for the Birkenstock County Roman Catholic School Board, a totally demeaning occupation as far as Alien was concerned, and the peculiar web of family connections had recently been strengthened by Suzi's assignment to the Music Department. She would succeed Sweet Marie on the latter's retirement.

On the evening of Maestro d'Averso's Great Debut, Phil was, as I have remarked, nonplussed along with his friend Harley by the appearance of the red carpet, the wine and cheese, and to serve the wine and cheese a brigade of minions from the Hotel Birkenstock. "I don't like surprises," fretted Harley. "I hope these guys have a liquor licence. And how the hell are they going to pay for it all? Can't be covered in the ticket price..."

"Mr. Davidson, you worry too much," soothed Katie.

"You're right, Katie. Don't worry, be happy, just like in the song."

The orchestra filed back on stage for the second half of the concert. About half the original membership had resigned with the unwilling departure of Israel Bond, and yet the assemblage we saw was the better part of double the size of the original ensemble, a goodly number even allowing for the eccentric requirements of the Symphonie Fantastique.

We scanned the personnel list on the back of the programme; some of our colleagues, including Charlie, were in the orchestra, most of them being from our itinerant staff, each of whom taught at several schools too small to support a full-time music program. They led a sort of double life, teaching by day and performing in the evenings; Charlie, for example, was in the house band at a pub called the "Brew-ha-ha". And since performing accounted for some of the itinerant teachers' income, surely they would not be doing this out of sheer goodwill. Other names were familiar, but then there were nearly forty names that Father Oakley identified as being "up from the city", meaning Toronto, and all professional. "The bastard must have hustled a hell of a lot of sponsorship to put this one together. No wonder he skips all the meetings."

The house lights dimmed, the stage lights came up, the concert master took his bow and fine-tuned the orchestra. Silence. And then a spotlight blazed upon the right-hand side of the stage. Applause. And to our revulsion, some sighs and outright squeals from the women in the audience.

Then began the Symphonie Fantastique, Berlioz' gaudily-coloured drug-induced nightmare of unrequited love, jealousy, murder, the guillotine, and the terrifyingly vertiginous trip down to hell. The colours of the stage lights became more and more lurid during the course of the performance. The final abrupt cadence was drowned out by cheers and roars of approval. Suburban matrons pressed their hands to their faces, screaming. Embarrassed husbands tried to soothe them. "Oh, God, I want to bear his children!" sobbed a teen-aged nymphet behind me. One elderly lady swooned away entirely and had to be removed by an ambulance crew.

I looked at Father Oakley. He looked at me and shrugged. "Well, kid, we'd better just hang up our sticks. There is no way to follow an act like that."

"Maybe he can't."

"Dream on. He's conducting the *Poem of Ecstasy* in February with Charlie doing the trumpet solo and a light show and the whole works."

"Dear God."

The sundered portion of the Birkenstock Philharmonic had recruited some new members and reconstituted itself as the Ouentaron Symphony, named for the lake that formed the eastern boundary of Birkenstock County. They had a concert scheduled the following night in the auditorium of Isidore's school, Golgotha High up in Annville, and doing a programme of the *Magic Flute Overture, In the Steppes of Central Asia,* Beethoven's First Piano Concerto, and Haydn's "Drum Roll" Symphony. Among the players, heading up the oboe section, was Gianetta d'Averso, the recently-estranged wife of the great Antonio.

The Ouentaron Symphony was, as the Birkenstock Philharmonic had been, a strictly volunteer organization, the players performing for the fun of it. But it was not a happy debut, for the hall was less than half full. Katie went with me once again and on the way home said plaintively, "That wasn't as much fun as last night."

"How is that, dear?"

"There were no crashes or bangs or coloured lights. And not enough of those big trumpets you pump."

"I think you mean trombones."

"I like the way they..uh..." She giggled. "I don't know any other way to say this. Please don't get mad at me, Daddy..."

"How could I get mad at a cute thing like you?"

"Well, these...trombones...yes?...they sort of fart. I think it's a neat sound."

"So do I. It was just very different music tonight." And Gianetta's presence added a quiet Haydnesque lustre quite beyond the capabilities of a gargantuan orchestra in full cry.

Something of the nature of Antonio's gargantuan orchestra was revealed to me a couple of days later as the result of a relatively routine errand. At the annual Birkenstock Music Festival the previous spring, the Misericordia High School Wind Ensemble had premiered a new work written for us by Father Oakley, who had christened the piece *Karegnondi*, the ancient Huron name for Georgian Bay. Because of an almost crippling loss I had suffered, John had chosen the title and subject matter, as he put it, "in some small compensation." The piece had been such a success that we were doing it again this year and, in preparation for publication, Father Oakley had made some revisions.

In that connection, there was a disagreement between the score and the individual part for the first alto saxophone; both versions made musical sense, but to verify what Father Oakley wanted, I took a trip to the Education Centre after school of a misty early November afternoon. I went up to the Curriculum Department on the third floor, a warren of frosted-glass partitions that reached only two thirds of the way to the ceiling; what you could not see, you certainly could hear. As I came into the music area, the place was hushed but for a frantic yammering coming out of the Father's office. Sweet Marie and Suzi were listening admiringly.

"Listen to me and listen well! This department is not Daddy Warbucks for your great self-serving enterprises! You want to hire musicians, you find another trough."

61

A voice mumbled in protest.

"No, I won't pay these guys just this once! *You* come up with the money. It's your problem. You had no authority to do this. You're trying to manipulate my people, and if you ever try again, your back end'll get reamed so bad you'll need industrial strength Preparation H for the rest of your miserable life!"

The other voice could be heard more assertively now. "Father Oakley, I'm'a not'a accustomed to being a'spoken to lik'a that…"

"Tough shit!" roared Father Oakley. "I am not accustomed to being jerked around and misrepresented to like this!"

"As a priest, the way you express'a yourself is'a most unbecoming."

"And the way you conduct yourself as a human being is one of the few things that leave me speechless. This goes on your personnel record. Don't ever come fooling with me again. Now get out!"

The office staff suddenly got busy, heads down in earnest as Antonio d'Averso stalked out, a black cape flung about his shoulders. "Jesus, Mary, and Joseph," said Sweet Marie cheerfully. "How is sweet Mr. Jackson today?"

"A lot better than Antonio, likely. Here's my tribute." I passed her the obligatory candy bar.

"Not one for your loving mother-in-law?" pouted Suzi, who had just started at the office in preparation for taking over at Sweet Marie's retirement.

"Starting next time. What kind do you like?"

"Oh, just surprise me. Something you think is me." Her lips pursed in a kiss. Before I could get into further difficulty, Father Oakley boomed from his office, "Hey, K.Y.! Come on in! I need an honest face in front of me."

"What were the fireworks about?"

"Oh, my goodness. That man is absolutely unbelievable, totally amoral. I think he honestly doesn't think he has done anything wrong. But hear this. The itinerant teachers were in on Friday to do their pay sheets and they all put in for eight extra hours…"

"What?"

"Eight extra hours for rehearsal time and the gig with the Birkenstock Philharmonic!"

"What?" I repeated in a screech.

"The Birkenstock Philharmonic Society, Antonio d'Averso, Music Director. Yes. I called up Charlie…hey, Charlie, how are you, kid?"

"Not…good," said Charlie, standing in the office doorway. Charlie was one of the group commandeered by Antonio.

"Come on in, take a pew, ha, ha...just throw that stuff on the floor...tell K.Y. what happened."

Charlie taught band at two of my "feeder" schools, Via Dolorosa and Father Joachim Sweigert, as well as working at the office on a per diem basis, thus his itinerant status. "D'Averso phones me up to do this gig, see," he explained. "Now, I don't do windows, I don't drive automatic, I don't do any legit stuff, except baroque. I said no, until I found out about all this heavy metal and about being paid. He said to me phone up the other itinerants and tell them the deal. Of course, they all jumped at it. The prick said Father had authorized it, so I phoned them up and we sure had a bunch of happy campers. Now they're all pissed at me. And bloody Antonio has me back on the hook to do *Poem of Ecstasy*."

"They should be pissed at me," said Father Oakley. "D'Averso sure is! At $33.80 per hour, times eight, times twenty-four people leaves him holding the bag for $6489.60. We're not paying it. But you guys are going to get paid. I have no idea what he is going to do now, but, man, I thought he was going to shit his pants!" The crucifix on the wall behind Father Oakley's desk gazed down sorrowfully. Father Oakley noticed my glance in its direction.

"K.Y., He's heard it all. I gave d'Averso thirty days to pay up or I'd be on his tail, maybe garnish his wages or something. And I think that wine and cheese business was done without a liquor licence, but that's not my department."

"Gotta go," said Charlie.

"See you," said Father Oakley. "Now, K.Y., there is a problem with our mutual child?"

"Just a small one, but I don't know which you want here in the sax part." Our attention turned for the moment to *Karegnondi*; the score, as it happened, was correct and it was nothing more than a copying mistake, for which Father Oakley refused to forgive himself. It was a matter, he said, for confession.

He stepped out to get some correction fluid from Sweet Marie. A moment later, the phone rang and I moved to his desk chair to answer it. I took a message and in the process I found myself looking at a framed photograph of a young John Oakley with a little girl and a stunningly attractive woman. Woodenly I hung up the phone and was still staring at the picture when the Father came back in.

"You found the picture."

"Um, sorry, Father, I wasn't snooping, there was a message..."

"That's okay, kid, I don't like secrets between friends anyway. I still can't talk about it much...come for a walk."

FATHER OAKLEY

"I'm gone for the day," said Father Oakley. "Got stuff to do with Ken here."

"Bye, Father. Bye, Sweet One."

We went out into the thickening mist, crossed the road to the Church of Saint Columba, and went into the candle-flickering hush. "Sit down, Ken," said Father Oakley, directing me into a pew. "It's time to tell you about the picture. This is the only place where I can do it and not go to pieces."

"It's okay, you don't…"

Father Oakley cleared his throat and blinked. "You confide in me, pal, and I know I can in you. The picture is of my wife and daughter. They were killed in a car crash when we were twenty-eight. She was pregnant, too. It was a drunk driver, going northbound on the southbound lane of Highway 300. I wanted to kill the son-of-a-bitch, then I felt sorry for him, then I wanted to kill him again. I couldn't handle it, so I turned to the Church. Betty and I had had it all, so there was no question about getting married again. I just couldn't even think of it. Still can't.

"If it weren't for the Church, I'd either have killed this guy or killed myself. I ended up going back to school, to a seminary, to take orders as a priest. I already had a career going as a music teacher, but I wanted to put something back into the Church, so I joined the Jesuits so that I could do both. It made me a better person, anyway. I had been a bit wild, did some drinking, and that tongue of mine, well, that's a matter of only too public a record, like that time I found Rob Foley working at With Mallets Aforethought. My goodness, that one sure got around.

"It was one of those situations that either you master or it overwhelms you. I was never accustomed to being overwhelmed…but it was absolutely shattering. Only the Church, only the Lord could help me deal with the enormity of it all."

"And what about now? This happened, what, twenty years ago?"

"Twenty-four years ago. The drunk has been out of jail for fourteen of those years. I still sometimes want to hunt him down and kill him, I still sometimes feel bitter..."

"Who wouldn't?"

"I shouldn't. That's not what the Lord or any of the saints would do, but I'm neither the Lord nor a saint. I'm just a regular guy, as Charlie would put it, who needs, as *you* would put it, a heavy-duty spiritual life-jacket."

Father Oakley held my hand for a moment. I thought of what Charlie might say.

"Yeah, yeah," said Father Oakley. "Charlie'd say something, oh, maybe not. He picks his time well. Hey, pal, do me a favour."

"What, Father?"

"I hate being vulnerable, it's a man thing, I guess, but don't tell anyone about this conversation..."

"Of course not."

"You're the first person I have trusted with this for over a dozen years. Charlie and Ingrid aren't far behind, and I think it's something they need to know if we're working so closely together. I'll just take care of it myself when the time is right. One other thing."

"Mm-hmm?"

"I know you're not as heavily into church stuff as I am, and I still respect how you feel and think, but, before you leave the church, could you light a candle, make it three candles, for the family I could have had?"

THE CAMP TAKES SHAPE

Now that we had clearance from the Board of Education for our music camp, thanks to the largesse of Carleton Lansdowne, it was my lot to attend a lengthy series of meetings, professionally necessary but to the further detriment of my home life. A cost analysis was made to establish an appropriate fee for a week at the camp. A contract was signed with Hugo and Anna and a security deposit was paid. Father Oakley and I took a day to travel down to Scarborough, a suburb of Toronto, that had a long-established and first-rate annual music camp, to do some picking of brains. The Mishipashoo Arts Centre, we found, enabled us to offer a similar, though not quite so large, program of activities, but that was fine with us; we had no wish to start out with anything that would be unwieldy for us.

Potential instruction staff for the camp was the next matter to be dealt with. Although we would have preferred to hire at least some people from outside our board to gain some different perspectives, it was found to be most cost-effective to use our own teaching staff on regular salary and hire substitute teachers for them in their schools for the week they were away at camp.

By virtue of being director of the music program for all Catholic schools in Birkenstock County, Neville Park was to be director of the camp. Aside from Neville's bizarre appearance, the use of a toothbrush appeared to be an unconquerable mystery to him and so fouled were his teeth that looking at his smile was like looking into a bowl of potato salad. It was therefore a puzzlement to us how he was able to conduct what he thought was a discreet extra-marital affair with Angela Rumley, our supervisor of choral music. Charlie called it his weekly Angiogram and knew for a fact that a room was reserved in perpetuity for each Thursday afternoon at the Shut-Eye Motel in the western environs of town. What mystified us was the perceived necessity for an Angiogram in the first place; not only was Mrs. Park a very attractive woman, but financially had made all manner of things possible for Neville, including a Mercedes and a summer cottage on Georgian Bay.

Now that the skeleton of the camp was instituted, the next step, quite literally, had to do with the flesh. A teaching staff would have to be selected from within our system, selected on the basis of proven teaching ability, initiative, originality of thought, and general musical and ethical reputation. Our program was to be built around a number of performing ensembles; a reconciliation between the facilities available at Mishipashoo and our musical requirements validated the establishment of two orchestras, three bands, and one large choir, in which younger males would sing in the treble range.

Neville, I think, had a vision of himself as an Enlightener of Men, and in meetings was in the habit of either stroking his chin in a learned manner or placing his fingertips together in a steeple as he discoursed. Neville loved meetings. "First and foremost," he intoned, "I am designating Antonio d'Averso as director of the Symphony Orchestra."

Father Oakley had an almost pathological dislike of Neville as well as Antonio. He went off with a sort of fizzing sound, like a bottled soft drink about to boil over, and spluttered, "The man is a crook! Look at what he tried to put over on us with that orchestra of his! Besides, who are you to go designating who does what? What are we, anyway, chopped liver?"

"Whatever you may think of him personally, Father Oakley, he is an outstanding musician with a high profile in the community. He is just...awfully wonderful..."

"Jimmy Hoffa had a high profile too..."

"Father Oakley..."

"So did the Son of Sam..."

"Father Oakley! Come, come, now. Among our fellow colleagues, what other choice would you suggest?"

"Israel Bond, without question. He can conduct rings around Pretty Boy and he's honest as well."

"But as to the matter of faith..."

"Better a good man than a bad Catholic. Besides, Israel's as devout as they come, and, as I just reminded you, he's honest. If Leonard Bernstein, for example, could conduct the sort of Messiah that he did, I won't worry about what church the guy goes to."

"Mr. Bond would be well suited to the Wind Ensemble."

"I think not! Israel hates bands!"

I struggled not to laugh. On the subject of bands, Israel had said to me not long before, "In 1974, Richard M. Nixon said 'I am not a crook.' In 1991, Israel Bond says 'I am not a snob.' Draw your own concloosions, Kennet.''

"A true professional will adapt to any musical situation. Now, on the matter of the choir, I think Mrs. Rumley would be the logical choice…"

Angela simpered and bridled. Charlie rolled his eyes and Sister Ingrid's face tightened with displeasure. "I beg your pardon, Neville," said the Sister. "If you are simply designating staff members, why are we even bothering to have this meeting? Why were Ken and I pulled out of our schools for this? My understanding was that all of us here would be forming the camp administration and choosing other teachers to do the actual instruction."

Sister Ingrid Harrington had, like myself, been seconded to the music office for the purpose of helping to organize the camp. As so many women go to great lengths to beautify themselves, Ingrid went to equal effort to render herself austere. Seldom had so much effort been expended to so little avail. Charlie was particularly fond of Ingrid and remarked often enough that I knew he meant it, "If I weren't to a respectable degree happily married and Ingrid weren't a Sister, the course of history would not be as we know it."

Sister Ingrid sat across the table from me at the meeting, draped in her nun's habit, face barren of makeup, a wedding ring incongruously adorning the fourth finger of her left hand. But it was not in lingering memory of a deceased husband; it proclaimed her wedding to the Lord. It was earnestly hoped that He would appreciate Ingrid as we did, for only a Muslim chador could have concealed one of the half-dozen greatest smiles on God's green earth.

Neville stroked his wattled chin. "There is no question that Mrs. Rumley is a highly-experienced choral director and has created a great reputation with the All-County Choir…"

"Exactly," cut in Father Oakley. "I conduct the All-County Wind Ensemble, but I'm conducting nothing at camp. Obviously. Someone else has to have a kick at the can."

A vehement argument followed which Angela exited in a huff. One did not have to be a rocket scientist to divine that Neville had promised the position to Angela within the precincts of the Shut-Eye Motel and what emerged from the whole messy deliberation was the appointment of Pat Mackenzie, the choir director at Mount of Olives Elementary School to work "in close support" with Angela as choir accompanist and coach, as well as accompanying any necessary faculty recitals. The mere thought of having to work in the presence of Fat Pat's monstrous size and powerful odour was enough to make the innards clench, but she was unquestionably a fine musician with an important position to fill, Angela would be happy, and Neville's anomalously outsized backside would be saved.

Our hopes of getting on with it were dashed when the subject of Antonio resurfaced. It emerged that Neville, being "proactive", as he was fond of putting it, had signed an agreement in principle with Antonio in respect to the Symphony Orchestra, and when called to task, explained that Antonio had been invited to conduct "somewhere in the States" during the week of camp and whoever came forth with a formal agreement first would get him. This had happened before the present meeting and there had, he said, not been time for consultation.

Father Oakley was still not mollified. "I still don't like how Antonio tried to take us to the cleaners, hiring extra players, and damned good ones at that. They made the performance, not him. He owes us $6480.60, I gave him thirty days to pay it, and as long as it's outstanding…"

"It has been dealt with."

"What? How?"

"A cheque has been received from him in that amount and deposited to our account. The matter is considered closed."

"You will be making the wrong man very unhappy…"

"Father Oakley, you are verging on being out of order…"

"This music camp is not your personal sandbox…"

"The matter is closed, Father Oakley. Yes, perhaps it was a lapse in Antonio's judgement, but you can't blame him for wanting the best that he could get."

So poor Israel was to do a band, but it was a safe bet that it would be a good one.

"That's settled, now," said Neville importantly, the great impresario and power-broker at work. "Now we must deal with the Symphonic Band. Any recommendations?"

On an idiot impulse, I made one. "How about Gianetta d'Averso? She does first-rate work…"

"Haaaaa!" roared Father Oakley.

"I beg your pardon?" said Neville.

"She and Antonio have split up, none too cordially at that. We'd be asking for trouble, though I must say I'd far rather have her than him. But the two of them at once in that small community, oh, no, thank you."

"I think it would be exciting beyond compare," said Charlie. "Let's do it."

"Charlie!" scolded Sister Ingrid.

"Musically, I think Ken's suggestion has a great deal of merit." Neville's fingers went into their Gothic steeple position.

"Sociologically, it's a disaster," said Father Oakley. "K.Y., what ever put such an idea in your head?"

"Oh, er, well, I'd forgotten about her, ah, schism with Antonio."

"You're blushing, man, really blushing," helped Charlie. "I think our K.Y. has a thing for Gianetta. Let's just put this together and see what happens."

"Mr. Cowell, keep your remarks constructive, if you please. Can any of you think of anyone as well-suited as Mrs. d'Averso?"

"Dunstan Corrigan," said Father Oakley. Dunstan taught band at Our Lady of the Seaways school in Shenaniga, over on Georgian Bay.

"True, but he is accustomed to younger students. He would be ideal for the Concert Band." Neville stroked his poultry-like chin wisely. "The only viable alternative to Mrs. d'Averso would be Ken here and it's really too late to move him out of administration. Besides, Mr. and Mrs. d'Averso are both members of the musical community and will just have to get along like big boys and girls."

"Easy for you to say," grumbled Father Oakley.

"Father Oakley, I am tired of your editorials and asides. May I remind you that I have made a major concession to you, a *major concession* in respect to the array of on-somms to be offered. Although it was in total violation, *total violation,* of my sensibilities, I was persuaded that there should be a dance-band..."

"Jazz ensemble."

"Whatever."

"Jazz ensembles are a reality, Neville, and kids enjoy playing in them. I'm not that fussy about them either..."

"I am!" blurted Charlie, who made a considerable amount of money outside of school hours playing at the Brew-Ha-Ha. Neville ignored him. Father Oakley continued, "Our mandate is to serve the students. What we..."

"We should be moulding their tastes, not catering to them. They are so low..."

"Give them some credit for natural intelligence and let them be kids, for God's sake. Yes, you did concede, I am so grateful. So we have a jazz ensemble?"

"As an elective. I thought that would be a wise compromise."

"Well, hallelujah. Now, who to direct it, unless it has been decreed."

I feared the worst. Father Oakley feared the worst. Charlie would have been the best choice in all of southern Ontario, were he not to be at the camp in an administrative situation. But since Charlie was in no position to direct the jazz ensemble, there was only one other possibility, one that we knew would be instant trouble.

"Mr. Foley," pronounced Neville, "will direct the Jazz On-Somm. Ah! Ah!" he snapped, holding up his hand. Father Oakley looked ready to do bodily harm.

In his time, Rob Foley had dealt even more wild cards than Antonio d'Averso. His personnel file was bloated with a saga of questionable deeds, a sorry direction in what could have been a brilliant career. Rob was the one, it may be remembered, who was destined not to appear at camp because of the presence of heroin among his mother's "ashes", the culmination of a five- or six-year period of professional disintegration. He had been shunted from school to school, leaving a trail of disarray, until ending up in a state of uneasy armistice at Mount of Olives Elementary School.

The only (but potent) force standing between him and oblivion was the Teachers' Union of Ontario, an alarming and exasperating parallel with the demise of the Greatness of Britain. Security and organization were not in Rob's vocabulary; students' years would be made or broken on the strength of one test marked on a scale of one to ten and something like seven thousand dollars' worth of equipment disappeared to equip hundreds of basement rock bands the length and breadth of Birkenstock County. But, reprehensible as it all was, it was not grounds for dismissal. For that, it appeared, one had to violate a nun on the front steps of the school at 8:30 in the morning in front of what Neville called "the children", hence no ejection from the teaching profession, but relocation to Mount of Olives Elementary.

The Concert Orchestra was the last of the "om-somms" to be dealt with; Charlie's wife, "my beloved pipe-cleaner", was to be invited as its director. The remaining staff was to be composed of instrumental and vocal instructors, as part of the camp day was envisioned to include sectional rehearsals and master classes.

The meeting did not finish until dinner time and of course I got screamed at by Aileen for Neglect of Family and Unwillingness to Relate and all the other tiresome allegations. Unwillingness to Relate was a truth by this time, as there was so little left to relate with. Certainly in the Jackson household not all was well, in fact nothing at all was well. As horrible as it all was, though, the thought of being alone was even worse; I felt, and still do, that life after a family, unless nature is permitted to take its course, is only half a life. If only things had been different; but then Katie and Evie as I knew them would not have existed. If only Anna were single, but then that would mean losing Hugo, to whom I had

71

become attached as one would to a wise and kindly older brother. If Sister Ingrid sundered her ties with the Lord, oh, no, out of the question. She and God, said Charlie, were just too tight, man.

Gianetta! Had I this day managed to forge my own destiny? She would be there at camp, I would have to shield her from contact with Antonio, maybe if she learned that I had recommended her for camp, her gratitude and affection would be boundless. This was worth Deep Thought.

GIANETTA

I had loved Gianetta from a distance for a good part of the eight years the d'Aversos had been a greatly-admired couple and a major musical force in Birkenstock County. The premiere sighting was at the Birkenstock Music Festival in 1984; my own "on-somm" had already played, and brilliantly at that, and I was sitting propped up in a state of post-performance euphoria, momentarily oblivious to what was happening on the stage. The band from Golgotha High School, where Israel Bond was music director, was next on the program, to be conducted by Israel's then-assistant, Gianetta d'Averso. I had not met Gianetta as yet, since she was not at the time a department head and therefore not required to attend monthly meetings.

"Sir, wake up," urged one of my students. I opened one eye. I opened both eyes. I opened both eyes as wide as they would go. My irises strained to absorb what I was seeing. My eyeballs hurt. My heart screamed. Very simply, Gianetta d'Averso was the most beautiful woman I had ever seen. Raven hair, black Mediterranean eyes…I found myself speculating whether a parting from the odious Antonio could only be a matter of time. I sat in a state of helpless yearning, watching her back (and backside, to be truthful) as she steered her young players through Eric Osterling's *Totem Pole March* and an absolutely stunning "Montagues and Capulets" from Prokofiev's *Romeo and Juliet.*

My home life in 1984 was hovering on the cusp between its zenith and its long approaching nadir. When first courting and then subsequently being married to Aileen, I had thought she was the most wonderful woman in the world, though with the qualification that she was the only one that could come close to Anna Harland. But this sighting, and that was all it was, of Gianetta d'Averso was a shock to my system, for I had not felt such a powerful attraction for so long. But I was married, she was married, and extra-marital

73

affairs have never been in my life's vocabulary. Nonetheless, such an impression had been made by Mrs. d'Averso that many days and nights would pass before I recovered.

In the course of things, it was a full year before I saw the fair Gianetta again, and it was at the following year's edition of the Birkenstock Music Festival. The aforementioned cusp had passed by, my home life had started its journey to ruination, and so the sense of yearning was even stronger.

Antonio was on hand with his band as well. The dynamics of a household with two music teachers in such a competitive position was a matter of intriguing speculation. Officially, the Birkenstock Festival was non-competitive, but anyone who has ever been in this sort of situation will appreciate the latent competition that, like it or not, lurks in all musicians.

I kept a close eye on both of them, Gianetta more so than Antonio, since she was the prettier of the two. We had still never met and for all I knew, she had no idea who I was, and so my spying had foolish overtones of being back in Grade 11, trying by whatever means of engineering a meeting, of plotting one's movements from class to class in hopes of a chance encounter, of establishing a panel of advisers to guide me in my quest, oh, no, this was lunatic, it was not Grade 11, she was in a different school, she was married and so was I, though by this time more on paper than in fact.

Other festivals, other years flowed by, and although Gianetta was promoted to department head at St. Bernard High School, she attended music directors' meetings only when Antonio didn't, but discreet inquiries revealed nothing. Her status only started to become clear at the 1990 Festival, the year our music camp venture would have its beginnings.

Antonio's band went on stage to do the *Toccata Marziale* of Vaughan Williams and some tricky thing of Vincent Persichetti. Lunatic, I thought, sitting back to wait for a catastrophe. But, as had already happened with the Birkenstock Philharmonic, it was infuriatingly good. "Good God, sir, how are we going to beat that?" whispered Hughie, my principal tuba player.

"This is not a competition, Hughie," I reminded.

"I know, Mr. Jackson, but how are we going to beat that?"

"Very carefully."

Throughout Antonio's performance, I watched Gianetta. She sat stony-faced and at the end of the Vaughan Williams she applauded with six widely-spaced claps. Maybe it was the stress; the two of them would certainly have debated the merits of their respective bands well into the night after previous festivals.

Perhaps the strain was too much for their marriage, oh, a plan was taking shape! As Antonio's ensemble (or "on-somm", as Neville would have it) left the stage, I hastened over to him to offer congratulations.

"Thank'a you, thank'a you verra much. Could'a have been better, though, but okay it was. Need'a more work before'a we go to'a Toronto for'a da Kiwanis…"

Next was the St. Bernard High School Band: director, the unspeakably and impossibly lovely Gianetta d'Averso. The fairest of Hollywood could not compare. I fought for breath as she went on stage and took her bow. Most festival performances have come and gone in my recollection, but this was another that has remained with me. Morley Calvert's *Romantic Variations* (sigh!) and another Vaughan Williams, the *Prelude on Three Welsh Hymn Tunes*, were her two offerings. Be good, please be good.

"Sir, what was that?" It was young Hughie again.

"Did I say something?"

"It sounded like 'please be good'."

"Funny, I must have been thinking out loud. Well, we're one band after these folks, so, yes, please be good."

"Of course, sir. Count on it."

The St. Bernard Band was indeed good, so good that in all good conscience I could go and congratulate Gianetta. "Hi, Gianetta, we haven't actually met, er, spoken before—"

"No, we haven't."

"Uh, I'm Ken Jackson—"

"I know."

"From Misericordia High School—"

"I know."

I gulped. This was not going well at all. "I just wanted to, um, congratulate you on, er, a really fine performance." My voice had degenerated into a dry croak. I felt a sheen of perspiration break out on my forehead.

She looked at, or rather through me, with the darkest eyes I had ever seen. They were, I noted, a bit small and set close together, which does not sound too appealing, but be assured that she was every bit as stunning close up as in the distance.

But instead of a friendly and appreciative response, what I got was "Well, isn't that what we're here for?"

"Oh, er, yes, of course." Now my voice was turning into an electronic squeal. "Anyway, just…uh…wanted to let you know…uh…really enjoyed your band…"

"Thank you. I think they want you in the warm-up room now."

"Uh, nice talking to you. Bye." Gritting my teeth, I trotted down to the warm-up room to get my troops all in order. Maybe Gianetta wasn't as indifferent as she seemed, maybe she could communicate only through music, well, think about the music now, fool, and get focused...Lord above, she had no wedding ring! This bore investigation, but now was the time to concentrate on one thing only: the first public performance of *Karegnondi*, Father Oakley's elegy to my past life on Georgian Bay.

"Okay, dear children, tuning time. Denise, here's a B-flat...you're a little sharp...okay, got it"...why wasn't Gianetta more friendly?...didn't even thank me..."Flutes, now, one by one, checking with Denise." Denise was our oboist and one of the very few I have ever met who could play in tune. "Sharp, Joanna...okay, better...clarinets. Firsts. No, no, no. Jack, come on, pull it out. Okay. Ruth? No...there you go. Clever girl. Saxes...sweet mother of God, do you people have ears? If you did, you would suffer...Denise, that B-flat again, if you would...okay, saxes, better now...my snotty remark was said in disappearing ink. Sorry. Horns, now. Oh, that's great, it's wonderful, you aren't just brass, you're precious metal...trombones, baritones, tubas...good... a bit flat, Hughie...there...trumpets..."

A sound like taxi horns gone wild. "Why is this being done to me? I'm not taking this personally, you understand, but why is it being done to me?" The faithful Denise supplied yet another immaculate B-flat. "Firsts...Steve, that slide is out so far your trumpet looks like a stillborn trombone...okay. Now...seconds. Whoa! You two, flat as pancakes...better...thirds...Whoa! Come on, don't suck on those things, blow them!" The predictable reaction came and went and we were ready. We filed onto the stage and I nodded to the master of ceremonies to make the standard music festival-style delivery.

"We welcome now the Misericordia High School Wind Ensemble under the direction of Mr. Kenneth Jackson. They have for us today the premiere performance of a new work by our own Father John Oakley, Supervisor of Instrumental Music." Applause. "The title is *Karegnondi*, the ancient Huron name for Georgian Bay, and it is in three movements, titled respectively 'Hole-in-the-Wall', 'Parry Sound at Sunset', and 'Stormy Weather at Red Rock'. We're really looking forward to this, Mr. Jackson. Please begin."

All life functions ceased except my brain. The score sat in front of me, reassuring as a navigation chart. The players who began the piece raised their instruments as I raised my baton. This was music of places I had known so well since childhood, and my eyes prickled as the mystery of the Hole-in-the-Wall and its little elves in canoes unfolded in murmuring low woodwinds and hushed tympani rolls, very bleak and northern, a bit like the start of Sibelius' Fifth Symphony.

Then the gentle melancholy of Parry Sound at Sunset as I had seen it countless times from the Jackson family yacht *Snarley Yow*. I have no direct recollection, but apparently, at the age of six or so, I had been so overwhelmed by the beauty of a Parry Sound sunset that I had said "This beautiful day will never come again." Father Oakley had appended that wistful remark to the score.

And then, oh, then…Red Rock! Father Oakley at the actual time of composition had yet to be on the Bay, but it did not deter him from writing some of the stormiest, saltiest music I have ever heard. It roared, thundered, and sprayed, the band playing as ones possessed. I still get a liberal sprinkling of goosebumps at the memory and, best of all, the applause started a full two bars before the final cadence.

Father Oakley came to the stage, bowed in his abrupt, bird-like way, for he hated ceremony, and clapped me on the shoulder. "Great job there, kid! Thanks!"

"Thanks for giving us such a great piece."

"I didn't give it to you. I sold it to you."

"So thanks for selling it to us."

"Any time, kid. It was great." He turned to the band, bowed to them, and blew kisses. "Great job, guys. Thanks for everything. Hang in there…"

What a triumph! My colleagues converged on me, even a visibly reluctant Antonio: "It's'a good'a to do'a da new'a works. You should'a make a specialty of it," a nice accolade, but delivered in such a way that suggested "you do'a da new stuff and leave'a da great'a classics to me."

"Thanks, Antonio." But where was Gianetta in my finest hour? I looked frantically, but she had disappeared. So not only had my initial contact been an utter failure, I now had to go home.

"Daddy, let me help you with your jacket," offered six-year-old Katie as I walked in the door of what I had come to call the White House.

"Thanks, love."

"Oh, Dad, you're all wet."

"So I am. Well, I worked hard today. Conducting is hard work. I'll never get fat. Makes you sweat."

"Oh, sure," came Aileen's chain-saw voice from the kitchen. "Just a high school band and you carry on like it was the Berlin Philharmonic."

"A lot of the Berlin Philharmonic guys started out in Just a High School Band."

"You're so pompous."

"If sweating is a sign of pomposity, then I'm guilty as charged."

"It's all a show and you know it. This god-damn job of yours is too much. You go at it as if it were a holy mission or something. You're obsessive-compulsive—"

"Maybe teaching kids about living and working together and finding their own capabilities merits the status of a holy mission. Besides, it reminds them that there is more to life than just subsisting, which is something I'll bet you can identify with."

"I am a Poet."

"Well, you can poem away to your heart's content, but in the meantime, this god-damn job puts bread on the table, and meat when we get lucky—"

"You always throw that at me!"

"You're lucky that's all I throw at you."

"Dad, did they tape the Georgian Bay music?" interrupted Katie, whose mother had refused to have her excused from school to hear it live.

"Don't interrupt!" screeched Aileen.

"I can't take this. It's a zoo," complained Katie, fingertips to temples.

"Don't make fun of your mother!" shrieked Aileen, triggering a scream of fear from Evie. "Kenneth, make her stop!"

"Don't put your fingertips to your temples, Katie," I said tonelessly. "In fact, don't do anything your mother does."

"Damn you!"

"And yes, Katie, they did tape our performance. Let's go and listen to it."

"Anything to avoid relating to me, hey, Kenneth? No adult company ever...you're just a big child anyway...oh, God, I can't cope!" A screaming exit upstairs ensued.

Both girls were in tears now. "Come on, girls, your mother's just a bit tired and edgy these days."

"She's always tired and edgy, Dad," sobbed Katie. "I'm sick of it. You're always working and you're not like that."

"Your mother works at home, Katie, and works hard at what she does. And she looks after you and Evie, your clothes are always clean, dinner is cooked..."

"I'd rather be dirty and have company. She isn't company, Dad!"

"She writes, honey, and it can be awfully difficult. She always has ideas in her head and often they come at really inconvenient times. And other times, ideas get lost when dinner needs getting ready. She gets frustrated."

"Let's hear the tape. I want to hear what Father Oakley wrote. He does all that stuff and he doesn't scream at people."

"He's also not trying to do a job and have a family at the same time." My heart chilled at recalling the story of Father Oakley's family's demise.

"But you are and you don't scream."

"Well, I'm just a nice guy," I said offhandedly. It was a mistake.

"I heard that!" screamed the voice from upstairs. Before I could get further mired, Katie took me by the sleeve and her sister by the hand and steered us into the living room. I closed the French doors and slipped the tape cassette into the stereo. The music began.

"Pretty music," murmured a now-calm Evie.

"Ooh, Dad, that's lovely," said Katie, who'd attended some of the rehearsals.

"They played beautifully," I sighed, enveloped in a sudden oasis of contentment. My skin was now chalky with the dried perspiration of the performance. "Hear those low clarinets...horns, now..." The score slid through my consciousness as if on an imaginary teleprompter. Somehow Father Oakley had enshrined everything that I was into that music, dedicated, as he put it, "to the Misericordia High School Band of Birkenstock, Ontario, and to my good friend K.Y. Jackson. In atonement, John Oakley, S.J."

It was not for the sake of Father Oakley's atonement; the score, in essence, was a memorial to what had once been and that I had given up in an extreme episode of my Neville Chamberlain syndrome. To my regret, I had to turn down the volume for the final movement (the recording machine had lit up like a Christmas tree) to avoid a fresh outburst from Aileen, but I promised the girls we would hear it in full cry sometime when their mother was not in the house.

The music came to its stormy finish. "Oh, Dad, that was just great!" The little girls, oblivious of my swampy state, swarmed all over me. With just these two and no Aileen, life would be very pleasant indeed, and I think in her own way, four-year-old Evie must have been thinking the same thing, for she began to cry again, thin baby hiccups that had a pathos beyond description. She could not articulate her misery, so I just rocked her for a few minutes as

Katie rubbed her back. We were a tight-knit trio in the eye of the hurricane.

"I think your mother is asleep. How about some dinner? What would you like Dad to make?"

"Scrambled eggs," purred a now-calm Evie.

"All right!" approved Katie. There was something about my scrambled eggs that spoke to them.

SNARLEY YOW

O nce our simple repast was done, the girls, fuelled by *Karegnondi*, requested for the time beyond calculation a viewing of the Pictures, the very Pictures that had excited Father Oakley's musical sensibilities. The Pictures for me were a bittersweet union of the pleasure of happy remembrance and the melancholy that it was all gone, dreams sent upon their way by the relentless march of dreary practicality.

The Pictures (any other pictures were merely pictures) dated all the way back to the summer of 1921 and chronicled the summer voyagings of the Jackson family aboard their beloved *Snarley Yow*, a thirty-six foot ketch of indeterminate but assuredly ancient origin. My father and his father before him had also been music teachers ("the bad seed," Aileen was fond of saying) and had been able to spend their summer holidays aboard ship. There was a family joke that both the Jacksons and the Russian imperial family moved aboard their yachts for the summer, the Jacksons having the disadvantage of poverty but the advantage of survival.

Like the traditional summer cottage, *Snarley* was the epicentre of elaborate and unvarying ritual. Starting each Victoria Day weekend, the Jacksons travelled from Birkenstock to Parry Sound (by train in my younger years) each weekend to prepare *Snarley* for the summer's operations. She wintered in a great orange shed at the water's edge and once whatever work Father had decreed was completed, she was rolled out on a cradle on rails and glided like a swan into the water.

Snarley had visited different places each year: Lake Superior, Mackinac Island, Detroit, around Manitoulin Island, and, in Father's last summer, a great odyssey to see his sister in Chicago. Each summer was a *Snarley* summer and when not on a major cruise, she ambled among the magical Thirty Thousand Islands of Georgian Bay, calling at the little coastal communities of Sans

81

Souci, Pointe-au-Baril, Byng Inlet, or Killarney; or anchoring for the night in enchanted bays and coves—Rogers Gut, Collins Inlet, Loon Bay—the yellowish gleam of her oil anchor light reflected in the inky waters against a backdrop of bullfrogs and whip-poor-wills. Cruising was great fun, but Georgian Bay was home to Snarley, and equally, *Snarley* was home to me.

Since I'd spent every summer on *Snarley* for all my life, it never occurred to me to do otherwise. Even after my father's death, when Mother could no longer bear to go near the boat, I carried on with *Snarley* as usual, enlisting friends for crew. It was in that connection that I first met Anna and Hugo Harland. I was taking a break from fitting out *Snarley* in the spring of 1979, strolling about the boatyard, visiting with other sailors, admiring the boats. There was a particularly handsome one for sale, a 1963 Trojan cruiser, which had been on the market for nearly two years. One frets about a homeless wooden boat, and even in 1979 there were a fair number about, so my interest was piqued by the spectacle of a particularly handsome couple (at least, he was handsome while she was simply perfect) examining the boat in company with Donald Shipley, the boatyard proprietor. As I came on the scene, I heard Donald say something vaguely numerical and hands were shaken all around.

"Hi, there, K.Y.," said Donald. "You'll be happy to know our friend the Trojan finally has a new home. Meet Anna and Hugo Harland."

"Oh, my Lord," I said in my worst awe-stricken voice. I was in the midst of reading Hugo's *The Eyesore of Mysore*. The book was aboard *Snarley* at that very moment. As for Anna, her face was all over the place in an advertisement for MudPuppy shoes, as well as on her television program. How I adored those MudPuppy ads; on one of my occasional forays to Toronto, I had missed a subway stop, besotted as I was in my love for the MudPuppy lady. She was right over the subway car door and would not let me go.

Anna and Hugo were used to dealing with dumb-struck admirers and so moments later I was completely at ease with them, discussing what the name of the vessel should be, for none appeared on her, and as all true boat-lovers know, boats have souls and will go to purgatory unless baptized.

Anna leaned toward something from Celtic mythology; Hugo, in contrast, said, "She's a wooden Trojan and therefore has ribs. A Trojan with ribs, according to the package in the drugstore, is called a Screamer…"

"Hugo, don't you dare…"

"Well, look, darling, twin screws, a total of five hundred horsepower, a bow like PT-109, she can't help being a screamer."

"Whatever you call her," I said, "I'd love to do a varnished name-board to go across the transom, you know, a sort of boat-warming present. I'd like to reciprocate some of the enjoyment your books have given me. And, Anna, isn't that you in the MudPuppy ads?"

Anna laughed. The already-brilliant sun strengthened in approval. "I thought only my friends knew."

"Since I know, maybe I can be your friend."

"As long as nothing funny goes on," said Hugo helpfully.

"Darling, don't be silly," purred Anna, rubbing Hugo's tummy. My nerves whined and twanged in agony, the blood roared in my head. Maybe Anna had a sister...but I knew I was doomed to admire from afar, as Brahms did Clara Schumann.

So, although none of us knew at the time, the first chapter in the saga of the Birkenstock Music Camp was already being written, even though the actual event was still a dozen years off, for Anna and Hugo had just purchased Camp Mishipashoo, to be run as an artists' retreat and a headquarters for Hugo's burgeoning collection of wooden boats.

Not much cruising took place that summer. I was informally engaged to help with the renovations at the camp to get it back into operating condition and to help Hugo with work on *Screamer,* for that became her name, above all Anna's protests. In the process, the truth of a lifetime was revealed to me, or I should say confirmed. I had not fully realized this of my own parents until they were gone, but as they had been, Anna and Hugo were friends above everything else and just could not do without each other's company. On the days of being over at the boatyard with Hugo, I was quite entertained at how he could last only until mid-afternoon, to say, "That's all for today, chum. Have to get back to my woman." Sometimes Anna would come too, swearing along with Hugo when things went poorly ("We call it boat language"), fetching tools, becoming mottled with paint and streaked with caulking. Lovely Anna in camouflage. By summer's end, I desperately wanted a relationship like that with a woman like Anna for myself.

They had no children by choice; neither wanted to try to juggle parenthood with a very demanding career and risk, as Hugo put it, screwing the whole works up. Both had the new camp, Anna had her two yoga shows on television as well as the MudPuppy layouts. And Hugo, in addition to producing a steady stream of books, had a new project afoot, the production of the now well-known magazine *Playboat,* to which I have been a charter subscriber and an occasional contributor.

Snarley spent the summer berthed in the creek at the newly-styled Mishipashoo Arts Centre, literally yards away from the spot where the ill-fated Panama Van Lines truck would try to play submarine. Whenever Anna and Hugo wearied of labour, the three of us would take a couple of days off and go sailing around Wasauksing Island or up to Frederic Inlet.

The summer went on its way, as summers do, and all too soon it was Labour Day and *Snarley* was snugged away in the orange shed for her long winter's nap, once again the subject of three generations of flexible payment plans. The Shipleys were kind folk indeed.

AILEEN

For me it was back to teaching and at Thanksgiving, Anna and Hugo closed up at the Mishipashoo Arts Centre, now in readiness for its new function, and returned to their home in Toronto. "We're really depressed," said Anna cheerfully over the phone. "We're throwing a party next weekend...what, Hugo?...yes, I know it's a silly expression...sorry, K.Y., Hugo is on a crusade to purify the language...we're throwing a party...come on, Hugo...next weekend and we'd like you to come. There'll be some interesting people for you to meet, and while I have no sister to give you, I have a good friend..."

Indeed there were interesting people at the party, although I would be flattering myself by saying they were like me or I was like them. The biblically-bearded figure by the fireplace was Robertson Davies, talking to a lady whose back was to me until she turned around, revealing herself to be Margaret Laurence. The bar was in the kitchen, where Farley Mowat had Hugo doubled up with laughter. And in the connecting hallway, Irving Layton was agog at the first woman I had seen who visually, at any rate, could measure up to Anna.

I did not recognize her, but I wanted to. I stood there, furiously trying to think of a suitably piquant self-introduction, one in which I would not be doomed in comparison with Irving Layton. A second-year instrumental music teacher in company with Canada's literary giants—"pardon me," said Timothy Findley as he squeezed past—oh, what was I to do? An opening via Irving Layton was out of the question, for, although I genuinely enjoy poetry, with me it has a shelf life of perhaps thirty seconds on a good day.

Anna rescued me, taking charge with hand of iron, glove of velvet. "Meet Aileen Quail and Irving Layton. This is my good friend, Ken Jackson."

"Miss Quail, Mr. Layton," I mumbled, shaking hands. I think Anna may have arranged something with Mr. Layton, for he excused himself and I did not see him for the rest of the evening. Suddenly I had Miss Quail, The One Who Measured Up, all to myself; she was absolutely magnificent, ash blonde, with eyes of the most startling green, almost like emeralds. It was not long, either, that I determined that she had a backside to kill for.

"Uh, nice to meet you," I fumbled. "You know, you're only the second person I've ever met with the surname Quail. Not too common, is it?"

She looked me up and down in obvious appraisal. Be strong, Kenneth, be strong, or as my mother used to say, be British. Aileen said nothing, so of course I had to say something. It was like getting Siegfried's sword Nothung to do Somethung.

"The only other Quail I've ever met is the principal of my school."

"You teach." Accusingly.

"I do."

"The school wouldn't be Misericordia High in Birkenstock, would it?"

"Why, uh, yes…"

"That's my father."

"What? Really?"

"Yes, really. I don't see much of him, haven't for years, really, since he split up with Mum and married this young popsy almost my age." I had, of course, met the popsy, otherwise known as Suzi, but at the time had no idea of the circumstances.

"Your age? But that's, er…"

"Perverse. But it was his choice. I have no idea how long it'll last."

We left the party a bit early, forsaking the company of Margaret Atwood and Erica Jong, who'd dropped in from New York, and walked for a couple of hours through the dark chill of Toronto's streets in October. To this day I cannot say for certain that it was Love, but it assuredly was the most compelling fascination I have ever known. "A death wish, K.Y.," Father Oakley said to me years later. "I read a book once, Tennessee Williams or one of those southern guys, described a woman as a 'fascinating green-eyed bitch-kitty.' That's her, all right. Oh, she's a caution…"

Well, caution was not part of my vocabulary in those days. Aileen and I were soon "courting", though with one major obstacle, that being in the matter of religion. My family's Roman Catholicism was at best nominal; we went to Mass on an irregular basis, discussed our and other religions freely, never did communion ("symbolic cannibalism", my father called it), and any confession was strictly a family matter. What kept us in the fold were the values we had all learned as children in church (called "separate" in Ontario) schools, the art and music of the Church, and simple tradition, for the Jacksons had been good West Highland Catholics since the beginning of time.

Aileen, on the other hand, was Roman Catholic to the very essence of her being, almost to the point of being reactionary. Even in the liberal and free-wheeling seventies, she was determined to go to her marriage bed a virgin, and the physical designs I had on her were brought to a standstill. Others would have moved onward, but not K.Y. Jackson; oh, not at all, for That Which Was Forbidden, alloyed with my natural Scots pig-headedness, decreed that I should continue to pursue.

So our courtship ground along in its wholesome, physically dull way. Intellectually, though, it was another matter, as one of my great passions is literature, and Aileen's destiny was to be a poet. Such a gloriously difficult and impractical dream, to me, was irresistible, a perversely flammable kindling for my desire. I have always been drawn as a moth to a candle to tales of doomed but valiant endeavour—Scott of the Antarctic and the stories of the Jesuit martyrs in Huronia spring immediately to mind—and Aileen's aspirations elevated her, in my mind, to the same pantheon of the condemned. That I too might be condemned somehow never occurred to me. I was young and invincible, I was the valiant knight that would be at Aileen's side as we rode together into the burning fiery furnace of artistic creativity.

Aileen was working on her master's degree in English at the University of Toronto at the time we met and on weekends I commuted down from Birkenstock in my first car, a terrifying old Toyota I called the Kamikaze. It was a great system; I even had my own room at Anna and Hugo's place, since any form of overnight cohabitation with Aileen was out of the question, and in addition to bed and breakfast, the Harlands were a fountainhead of advice.

Inevitably, the time came to think about the summer, which I did habitually around the end of January, concurrently with the annual Boat Show. Summer meant mothballing my apartment in Birkenstock and moving aboard *Snarley*. I needed a crew for the summer. I needed Aileen.

"You'd go off without me?" she said querulously when the subject was first brought up.

"No, I want you to go with me, you know, as crew."

"You know I can't do that."

"You can't?" Sinking heart.

"I've never sailed and I'm not about to lose my virginity."

87

"I can show you what needs to be done and boats do not necessarily have to equate with the loss of virginity. I do not propose that the scuppers should be awash with the spoor of our love-making…"

"You are revolting! You're an animal, just like the rest of them."

"Well, sorry. Look, the boat is big, there are two separate cabins, and you could have complete privacy."

"How do I know I can trust you?"

"How do you know you can't?"

"The way you look at me."

"You're the most gorgeous and sexy woman I have ever met…"

"Except for Anna. I've seen how you look at her. I think you lust for her and only care for me because she's not available."

"Oh, please! Sure, I'm fond of Anna, but she's more like a, er, big sister. Look, we're getting off topic here. I'm going cruising on my boat this summer, I'd like you to come with me, and it's important enough to me that I'm not about to throw it away by indiscretion."

"I still don't like the idea of being just with you," huffed Aileen.

"Oh, thanks. You said you loved me. You must have lied."

"I do love you, Kenneth, but I want to be proper about this. People will talk."

"This is 1980, not 1880."

"I'm not pandering to the low standards of others. I'll go with you on one condition."

"What's that?"

"That someone go with us. Hugo and Anna, maybe."

"They'll be too busy running the camp."

"Oh, of course. Maybe my dad, if I can get him away from the popsy long enough."

"He's my principal!"

"He's also my dad. Maybe I should try to get to know him better. If there's room, he could even bring the popsy, although I'd rather avoid it."

In the end, the difficulty was solved rather ingeniously. I did have my summer aboard *Snarley*, though in a more static role than I was accustomed to. Aileen spent much of the summer "in retreat" at the Mishipashoo Arts Centre, studying with Irving Layton, doing yoga with Anna, taking a theatre course (where she learned the gesture of fingers to temples), and spending the rest of the time working on her own writing. *Snarley* was berthed in the creek, serving as my accommodation while I made some money as sailing instructor, and also did afternoon cruises on the Sound, crewed by aspiring writers, actors, and artists.

So well-oiled was my progress with Aileen that when she completed her session in August, she allowed as she felt ready for a short cruise Alone With Me. We took a short, gentle voyage down the inside passage to Tadmore and visited the Martyrs' Shrine and the old settlement of Sainte Marie-Among-the-Hurons, obligatory destinations for all Catholics, devout or otherwise, in fact, obligatory destinations for anyone, devout or otherwise. We called at the Naval and Military Establishment at Shenaniga. The weather was beautiful, *Snarley* was magnificent, Aileen wrote a paean to the great ship and her indomitable master. It was all a huge success.

The scope of success can be measured by the fact of our wedding the following June at the end of term. Hugo was best man, Anna the matron of honour, there were no harsh words for Mr. Quail's popsy, the sun shone bright, the future was golden.

On our honeymoon, we were not so lucky, and I am afraid it was completely my fault. Instead of asking Aileen what she wanted to do, I made the bland assumption that a passage on *Snarley Yow* would be fitting, especially in view of the time we had the previous summer. To be truthful, economics did enter into it as well; after squaring finances up with Donald Shipley at the boatyard, little money was left and now we had two people living on one modest salary, for it had been agreed that Aileen should write, untrammelled by the mundane business of having to make money. Between my music and her poetry, enlightenment would come to all mankind generations ahead of schedule.

Snarley's sailing orders, then, were for a circular tour of Georgian Bay. She worked her way north-westwards to Killarney, crossed to remote and lonely Club Island, and then carried onward to South Baymouth on Manitoulin Island. There was a thundering great north-westerly that day and Aileen became miserably seasick as *Snarley* surfed along in eight-and nine-foot seas, her ancient sails and rigging straining to the maximum. Once South Baymouth was reached, Aileen pronounced that she had had enough and was going to jump ship, take the ferry to Tobermory, and get the first bus back to Birkenstock. But the weather became too rich even for the great ferries; the wind backed to the west overnight and blew for two days with gusts up to fifty knots. Along with the usual yachts and cruisers, the ferries doubled up their moorings and snugged down to wait it out.

From fifty knots we went to no wind at all. The ferry *Chi-cheemaun* toiled her ponderous way out of the harbour, other yachts started off under power, and Aileen was persuaded that we would have a calm crossing to Tobermory. She rode sullenly on the foredeck as we motored out and set course south-eastward towards the Bruce Peninsula. *Snarley* was behaving rather oddly, making considerable leeway to the west, and I soon realized that, in the wake of the storm, there was quite a strong westward current flowing out of Georgian Bay. It was like sailing in tidal waters.

I was more than usually perturbed, then, when the engine quit with not even a preliminary splutter. Aileen's head spun around one hundred eighty degrees, like the possessed child in The Exorcist. "Oh, great," she snorted. "God-damned boat's falling apart." It was the first expletive I had ever heard from her and it was like a blow to the face.

But there was no time for discussion, analysis, or negotiation. The current was slowly pushing us toward Lake Huron and we would be in trouble if I could not get the engine to go and there was no wind. To add to the fun, we were at the halfway mark in the ferry route. The two vessels would pass here and I didn't want to be drifting in their way. I disengaged the gear and pressed the starter button. The engine re-started instantly. I put the gear lever ahead and the engine quit as abruptly as it had a moment before.

"God-damn boat's falling apart," repeated Aileen.

"She is not falling apart, sweetheart," I retorted. "Something's fouled the screw. I've got to go in the drink." I stripped down to my undershorts, rigged the boarding ladder, and plunged in. I had forgotten how paralysingly cold the water was on the west side of Georgian Bay and as I fought for air, I could see the problem immediately: some cretin had thrown a green plastic garbage bag in the water and it had wrapped itself around *Snarley's* propeller. I took a breath and dived into the icy depths, my very eyeballs going numb; as I had blessed such a deep propeller in heavy seas, I now cursed it for its inaccessibility. I cut and hacked at the plastic for a moment with my knife (the knife had been condemned as a "pretentious prop") and then surfaced, lungs burning, just as an enormous American cruiser hurtled past, blasting her horn indignantly. The wash hurled me upward under *Snarley's* overhanging stern, my head impacting with a shattering thud against her cypress planking. "Fuck!" I roared impotently.

"Get control of yourself!" came a sharp voice from above.

"Well, then, do something useful and hoist code flag 'M' on the spreader."

"Why?"

Dear God. "To indicate we are drifting out of control." Signal flags were another of my "pretentious props."

"I don't think we need it. It's calm and there aren't any other boats around."

"I am not in a position to debate the matter. Just do it."

"Well, well. Quite the bold captain, aren't we?"

A hoarse "blaat" rumbled somewhere behind me. "Oh, God, what's that?" shrieked Aileen.

"That will be the *Chi-cheemaun* on her way to Tobermory and any moment the *Nindawayma* will be coming the other way. I would like them to have some indication of our situation. Now put the fucking flag up!"

In her agitation, Aileen managed to hoist code flag "B", signifying that we were refuelling, which must have puzzled the good folks on the *Chi-cheemaun's* bridge. The vessel did slow, but more as a courtesy than anything, as nothing could be done about the great wall of water that bore down upon me with the ponderous inevitability of a tsunami. Another roar, like a dozen eighteen-wheel transports sounding off, and in the other direction, bow wave hissing like a waterfall, came the *Nindawayma;* the air shuddered with the grumble of her great diesel engines, another tsunami came at me, and the washes of the two vessels met exactly where *Snarley,* Aileen, and I were. I was shot halfway out of the water, losing my undershorts, and poor *Snarley* was spun around to face almost in the direction from which she had come.

Once the commotion had settled, I dove again, cut the plastic bag loose, and then had to swim around, looking for the boarding ladder, which had gone adrift in the melee. Aileen had vanished from the deck.

Another American cruiser nosed up to offer help, as if to atone for the earlier rudeness of his countryman. A small child pointed over the gunwale and shrieked to another small child, "Look, Barbie, that man has nothing on!"

"Ooh, you can see his bee-hind!" The skipper shrugged, gunned his engines, and made off in the direction of Tobermory. Wearily and with considerable trouble, I re-rigged the boarding ladder by holding it up and wiggling it around until it engaged its fittings. I didn't even bother calling to Aileen for help; she was cowering in the cabin, fingertips to temples, muttering the refrain that was to become so familiar: "I can't cope with this...it's a zoo..."

To the brilliance of memories of summers past, there was now a pewter twilight. Even as a thoroughly disgusted and thoroughly concussed K.Y. Jackson was mooring his beloved ship at Tobermory, Aileen was complaining, "I hate that cabin. It's too dark. I want it painted white."

"Painted!" I screamed. "What the fuck do you want to paint it for? Oh, I beg your pardon," to an elderly couple aboard a cruiser in the next berth.

"What the fuck do you want to paint it for?" I repeated in a low voice.

"Because it's too dark down there, as I said before. I say again..." she mimicked my radio transmission voice.

"That cabin is a goddamn showpiece," I bleated. "All that varnish..."

"Well, if you expect me to go on this thing ever again, you will paint the cabin and I will select new upholstery and curtains. That old green shit has to go."

"It's always been like that," I protested.

"And the Ku Klux Klan has always been evil." The connection between *Snarley* and the Ku Klux Klan was too obscure for me to labour the point. I think it was about that time that Neville Chamberlain returned to earth to inhabit my body.

I consented, although it just about broke my heart, but I kept telling myself that it was unfair to Aileen to expect her to walk into a half-century of family tradition and not have some of herself reflected in it. So, after *Snarley* was out of the water for the season and before the horrified eyes of Donald Shipley, I covered Snarley's gleaming mahogany interior with three coats of white enamel.

"Oh, my God!" screeched Aileen on inspecting my work. "I can't live with that!"

I was stunned. "Why not?"

"It's totally antiseptic, it's so cold, like a hospital."

"You wanted white. You got white."

The fingertips went to the temples. "I didn't ask to be blinded. No, it has to be a softer white, an off-white..."

Two more coats of so-called ermine white satisfied; and then there was the matter of the curtains and upholstery. They were a product of the Depression and of the ingenuity of my mother, who had made them out of cast-off curtains from a C.P.R. sleeping car that was being refurbished. They were dark green, coarse, and getting a bit worn, but still comfortable, and even though over fifty years old still imparted a faint smell that, amalgamated with other faint smells, blended into a true essence of *Snarley*. Of course, the essence was effectively destroyed by the damn paint; and now the coup-de-grace, as it were, was administered by Aileen, who chose some expensive floral patterns, and the end result was unsettlingly reminiscent of J.E.H. MacDonald's painting "The Tangled Garden." *Snarley* was not herself any more, but rather a maritime version of my father-in-law's "popsy". In any event, peace was kept, peace in our time.

Kathryn, or Katie, as she soon came to be called, joined *Snarley's* crew in 1985 at the age of seven months, the third generation of Jacksons to be aboard, bunking in a well-padded fo'c'sle. We did just short, gentle cruises that year (in point of fact, short, gentle cruises were all *Snarley* ever seemed to do any more) and I had an uneasy feeling that the boat was quite out of sorts. It was nothing tangible, no extraordinary amount of bilge water or anything, but she was increasingly sluggish and "hung in stays" when coming about. In a particularly bad moment, I even thought I was starting to forget how to sail.

The reason become clear in the year 1987. Evie had been born in the spring, and so for the second consecutive year, and with a very grudging and piteous send-off, I drove up to Parry Sound to prepare *Snarley* for yet another sailing season. This too would be short, gentle cruises, but one must be practical, one must adapt to current requirements, there must be peace in our time.

I set up a couple of lights in Donald Shipley's orange shed and inspected *Snarley's* bottom. There are, as any wooden boat owners will know, invariably surprises at fitting-out time. I was therefore surprised to see caulking that had been perfectly fine the year before all cracked and split and in a couple of cases actually sagging out of the seams. But the boat hadn't been seriously caulked for four or five years, so I mentally budgeted another thirty dollars for some Sikaflex and went to work. The old caulking had to be removed with a hook-shaped knife in a process called reefing, not to be confused with the reefing, or shortening, of a sail. So I went to work and, to my consternation, I found myself reefing out a lot besides caulking. I was reefing out rotten wood, some of which was still wet, and by the time I was finished, *Snarley* stood on her cradle, her decay scattered about her on the ground. Donald came for a look and after a crawl through the bilge, informed me that seven planks and four frames were in hopeless condition. "Three thousand and a bit of change," was the dreaded verdict.

Heartsick, I suspended further work, loaded my tools back into the car, and drove home to our apartment in Birkenstock. I was heartsick because I did not know when *Snarley* would sail again.

"Back so soon?" said Aileen as I walked in the door. "You look like somebody died."

I sat down with a sigh. "*Snarley* has rot."

"I kept telling you the goddamn thing was falling apart."

"I don't think I need to hear that. It's going to cost about three thousand—"

"Oh, no, it's not."

"What do you mean? You know someone who can do it for less?"

"You're not paying for it."

"What? We can't do it ourselves."

"You're going to sell the goddamn thing. I'm sick of you pouring money into it. With two babies, we need a house. Put three thousand into a house."

"Hey, just a minute, that boat was left to me by my parents. She's a...she's a tradition..."

"Tradition, shmadition!" screeched Aileen in a voice so lacking in humanity that in that moment, she was forever defined for me as "Alien". "I'm so sick of your traditions!" she raved. "You job is tradition, your boat is tradition, it's all tradition, it's all yours, yours, yours, and I'm sick of it!" The fingertips reached for the temples.

Tradition was always a sore point with Alien, and it was not only because of me. Her father and my principal, Commander Philip Horatio Quail, Royal Canadian Navy (Ret.), was also firmly rooted in Tradition, which was why we got on so well, why he entrusted me with organizing any sort of pageantry. It was not for nothing, for example, that Misericordia High School had an annual two-hour Remembrance Day service. For my part, I was (and still am) a devout subscriber to such institutions as the monarchy, as it imparts continuity and stability in an age becoming increasingly addicted to disposability and generally endowed with a genius for chaos. And as the monarchy did for society, so had *Snarley* for me, like a gentle dinosaur, ready to comfort, as she had done at the deaths of my parents, whose ashes had been scattered from her decks upon Parry Sound at sunset.

When my life was disrupted or impaired in some way, *Snarley* was the magnet that pulled the pieces back together. So often I had said, "Every family should have a *Snarley Yow*." Now *Snarley* was in danger, not by the exaltation of wind and sea, but by the degradation of tight money and household politics.

Alien had had no *Snarley*, nor any roots to speak of. Her father, as already noted, had been an officer in the Royal Canadian Navy before his present incarnation as my principal. He had been, of course, periodically at sea, and shoreside residences were changed at irregular intervals: Halifax, Esquimalt, *H.M.C.S. York* at Toronto, Halifax again, Saint John, and so forth. In the process, Alien never had a chance for sustained friendships; to compound the situation, she was an only child to whom the growing alcoholism of her mother and the divorce of her parents was a catastrophe of unusual magnitude. Life had thrown her a curve ball and I, Kenneth Yardley Jackson, was going to do great things for her, extending to her my own family's order and stability, and now it was being figuratively spat on.

I was aware of Alien speaking again, this time in a gently disarming tone. "Kenneth, I know the boat means a lot to you, but I just can't live with throwing away three thousand here and three thousand there."

"Donald said she'd be as good as the day she was built."

"Oh, now, you're not going to buy that. Boats are like cars—"

"No, they are not. They don't depreciate fifty percent the moment they leave the dealer..."

"...boats are like cars, and once you start putting money into them, there is no end to it. And, besides" (now her voice was almost a coo), "it's because of the boat we couldn't have a house, and now with the baby...besides, buying a house will enable us to start something fresh together instead of making do with a hand-me-down... let's make our garden grow, Kenneth."

Peace in our time. Never had I seen Alien in such good spirits as when I went about making the arrangements for *Snarley's* sale, listing her with Donald Shipley.

"What!" exploded Donald. "You really want to do this? I don't mind how long it takes to pay me for the repairs."

"Donald, I have to."

"I feel like an undertaker. You have to? Who said you have to? It wasn't you. I know you too well."

"Well, Aileen—"

"Don't let her try emotional coercion, don't let her scare you into this. The boat is your heritage. Look, try the easy payments thing on her, say, over two years. It comes to just a bit over a hundred a month. And no interest. This isn't very businesslike, but I'm almost as attached to *Snarley* as you are."

Sad to report, I did let Alien scare me. "It's time," she pronounced, "for you to put aside childish things and start seriously relating to me. You relate just fine with the boat because it doesn't have opinions or talk back and you're not married to it. You just own it. It's, well, just a thing, a chattel."

So was a house a chattel, but for peace in our time, I sold *Snarley*, my beautiful *Snarley*, for four thousand dollars as a "handyman's special".

I sighed at the recollection as I closed the picture album. "Bed-time," I said to the little girls. Evie had dozed off. "Aww," said Katie.

Father Oakley, of course, was intimately familiar with the sad saga of *Snarley's* disposal. "Don't let anything like that happen again, K.Y.," he cautioned. "You've been treated like Neville Chamberlain. Now she kicks you around, like poor Richard Nixon. The parallels are alarming. You do, after all, live in the White House."

My White House! The whole teaching staff at the Miserable Accordion, my students, and my musical colleagues knew that part of my history, not from actual telling, but from the changing colours of the paint streaks on my hands from our new home, the home for which the sale of *Snarley* had furnished the most ill-gotten down payment in real estate history.

THE WHITE HOUSE

The White House had a dual symbolism, that of Alien's inability to make a decision, and my dog-like capacity to go to any lengths to please others. It was a pleasant frame bungalow on Broadside Avenue, a shady street in one of the older neighbourhoods in Birkenstock, and was indeed painted white when we moved in. Moreover, the paint was in good shape and I thought it would not have to be touched for two or three years. I was wrong.

Alien pronounced the colour boring, and so, in the summer, when I would and should have been sailing *Snarley*, I was spending all sorts of money on a pale green paint selected by Alien. It was my grimmest summer holiday on record, even a visit to the Mishipashoo Arts Centre providing no relief, as it was too poignant a reminder of the loss of *Snarley Yow*. Most of my time was spent applying the green paint, approximately the colour of cream of pea soup, to the house, and in the middle of this grimmest of summers, it was made even grimmer by an accident with the ladder.

I was all the way up it one sweltering July afternoon and suddenly went all light-headed from the heat. The sensation of starting to fall shocked me into grabbing onto the rain gutter, which of course, not being designed to take the weight of a human body, tore loose, sending me sideways into a freshly-weeded flower bed. Alien had been doing the weeding in safety while I scaled the heights of paintdom; I was severely censured for damaging the flowers and for taking the rest of the afternoon off for X-rays. And when the X-rays revealed two broken ribs, I received, not sympathy, but a blistering attack on my safety procedures, an accusation that soon became darkened with suspicions that I had staged the mishap to delay further painting.

97

Since I hate half-finished projects, the last indictment was born of complete idiocy. After a week of lying about in pain, I could stand it no longer, went aloft, and in a furious burst of activity, I completed the work, cleaned the brushes, put away the left-over paint, and stowed the ladder in the garage.

"Oh, God," said Alien by way of gratification.

"Nice, isn't it?" I lied. I thought it looked horrible.

"Oh, no, it looks horrible. Look, it clashes with the natural greenery. No, that won't do. You'll have to do it over."

Preposterous as it may seem, I consented to do the job over the following summer. Even more preposterous, I was persuaded that I must commence operations forthwith.

"Not now," I protested. "I only have two weeks left of holidays."

"Yes, now, Kenneth. I can't live in it this way." Alien put her fingertips to her temples. "I'd sooner move..."

Since we had only moved to the house in June, I was not disposed to go through that horror again. So, after the selection of Delft blue as the preferred colour, I spent more money at the paint store and attacked my appointed task with less than exemplary zeal. I rolled, I brushed, I wrestled ladders and plastic sheets to protect the flower beds. And catastrophe struck again.

One afternoon, Alien was out shopping with the children. The Delft blue was complete, but I had instructions to do the trim in a darker blue, which I had started. I was out in the garage, shaking up a previously-opened can of dark blue paint when the lid flew off, a globule of paint leapt out of the tin, and hovered in mid-air. It was rather pretty; I had plenty of time to admire the shifting highlights as it hung gelatinously above me, but curiously no time to get out of the way.

It fell upon me in a silent liquid breath of alkyde and other tasty toxins, burning up my nose and cooking my eyes. Blinded and with no-one to guide me, I scrabbled my way into the house, through the kitchen and down the basement stairs, eyes burning, throat and lungs burning, skin burning, everything burning. I felt like a mobile *auto-da-fe*. But no burning could compare with the burning I was to get when Alien got home to behold the dark blue spoor of my misfortune on the sink, on the stove, across the refrigerator, and in a wavering line down the basement stairs.

Nor was all forgiven on successful completion of the work, which, as a bonus, included repainting the basement stairwell. According to Alien, the Delft blue looked cold. "I think the white was best after all, Kenneth. But you can leave the blue trim on..."

The white paint occupied all my autumn weekends, and with the shortening evenings, something akin to panic set in. But my stalwart friends turned out to help and things became so convivial that Alien could not stand the noise and went to stay with her father, the Commander and my principal.

Charlie loved painting and came to assist, bringing his little daughter Jennie, who was mid-way in age between Katie and Evie. "We'll just stick them in the back yard with some raw meat. No man should be required to paint his house thrice. Lock and load! Let's hit it!" Alien particularly disliked Charlie. His use of the English language lacked subtlety and symbolism.

And Father Oakley: "K.Y., just think of this as like painting the Quebec Bridge. You finish at one end and then start over at the other. You must learn to be happy in your work…"

Sweet Marie had grown to hate Alien with the fullest measure of gall ("abusing sweet Mr. Jackson like this") and brought sandwiches and lemonade.

Sister Ingrid: "God is guiding you through this, Ken. I honestly don't know why or how He is doing it this way, but we don't question it. Perhaps He knows where the stir stick is. I certainly don't."

Anna and Hugo both helped, although at different times, as the Mishipashoo Arts Centre functioned until Thanksgiving and someone was required on site at all times. Anna's appearance is, of course, familiar to practitioners of yoga and to viewers of her television programs, both of which were carried by CKUP, our local television station. Yoga I could care less about, but any opportunity to view the heavenly Anna, whether in person or on screen, was not to be missed. She had a perpetually out-of-doors look, well-tanned, sun-bleached hair, and an opulently slender figure, if that makes any sense. And she was nowhere nearly as tall as she appeared on television. I tried to figure out why this was so, of which Hugo remarked, "I used to call her mother the Regal Old Lady. I guess Anna's bound in the same direction."

"Of being old, or being regal?" Anna wanted to know.

"Regal, my dear. I'm the one that's old."

Anna's presence at the whitening of the White House was my anchor to sanity, serving as the Greek chorus of my sorrows as well as my oracle. One Sunday morning, when all other hands, including Alien and the children, were at Mass, Anna and I were on our own.

"Let's not paint for a bit," said Anna. "I think we need to talk."

"We need to paint," I said with more than a hint of desperation. "Herself will give me Hail Britannia if there is not progress, visible progress, of the highest possible standard."

"K.Y., just listen to yourself. The woman has you completely spooked and I hate her for it. The two of you have changed completely. Aileen used to be so bright and fun, but this earnestness and spiritual terrorism has completely smothered our old friendship. We keep in touch only because of you. As for you, you've become a lost soul. She's calling all the shots; just look at this horror you've gone through with the paint, and now you're scared of what she'll say when she gets back. Georgian Bay couldn't scare you, you're in complete control with your concerts, I know about some of the horseshit you go through at work, and yet this one person does this to you."

Anna was dressed in shorts and a long shirt, an ensemble that gave her the appearance of wearing nothing underneath. Blood roared in my ears. It roared louder at her next remark.

"K.Y., we've known each other a few years now. You're sort of the brother I never had, so let me ask you this. What is all this doing to your, ah, love life?"

I laughed bitterly. "Love life? You jest, Big Sister. It's been a virtual write-off for nearly three years. In fact, Alien's behaviour has been so abrasive for so long that Evie was, um, conceived only by the greatest spiritual effort on my part. That's how great my self-estimation has been. And since then, I have been completely unable to, er, do my will upon her."

"Isn't that a great line? I think it was in *A Bungalow in Bangalore.*"

"Great line?" I said. "It's a great scene."

"Hugo's research ethic dictated that we should act it out. He said if it were a movie, I should be in it and he could give in to all his perverse fantasies and watch me. Oh, sorry, K.Y., I'm rambling. I shouldn't inflict this on you anyway. Do go on."

I swallowed, shoving my trembling hands into my pockets. "Yes, right. Well, on account of this, um, situation, she has been calling me variously a loser and, on her especially inventive days..."

"Of which there are many."

"...she has called me a latent homosexual."

A sunburst of laughter from Anna. "No, K.Y., not you! It's ridiculous."

"What makes it really ridiculous, after she had laid that on me a few times, I went to a psychiatrist to make sure, I mean, you hear something enough, you start to believe it. So I made an appointment and went."

"And?"

"Well, what do you think? He said I was so straight he didn't feel right about collecting a consulting fee. He took it anyway, but what the hell."

"What did Aileen say?"

"That the doctor was either lying or incompetent."

"She's hopeless. Have an affair."

"Who with? I'm too busy even to look."

"How about her?"

Climbing out of a car in the driveway was my esteemed mother-in-law, Suzi, known to Alien as the popsy. "That's my mother-in-law."

"Oh, the popsy. She's adorable."

"She really is, but an affair with her would be just too complicated."

"But so exciting!"

"Anna, for God's sake. Hi, Mummy."

"How's my wonderful son today?" Suzi gave me a less than chaste hug, holding me to her just a bit longer than mothers-in-law generally do. Anna's left eyebrow rose slightly. But that was the end of my micro-second dalliance. I introduced the two of them and, since Suzi had come to help, we got back to work.

Aside from myself, Alien's indecision about the colour of the house inconvenienced the lives of seven other people, but if it weren't for them, I would still be painting instead of telling my story.

I wanted to have the whole crew over for an evening to show my appreciation, but Alien would have no part of it. "We can't afford it," she pronounced.

"We can't afford not to," I retorted. "Why can't we afford it?"

"That paint job put us in a cost over-run of a hundred and fifty percent."

"I'm not responsible for that. What I am responsible for is having the best friends in the world who'll come of their own free will and help because they can't stand seeing me doing that all by myself."

"Well, surely you don't think I could help, what with the children and my own work..." The fingers began their probing.

"Of course not. So my friends helped. It's done. I'd like to reciprocate."

"Some other time. Thanks to that boat of yours, we have no money—"

"Excuse me, that boat gave us the down payment for this place."

"And you had spent so much money on the God-damn thing that you were in the poorhouse even before we got married. It'll take years to undo the damage."

"Talk about a price-tag mentality! That boat did more—"

"You're pathetic!" spat Alien. "Without that God-damn boat you have no God-damn definition. Your personality is all from external forces, like an actor who has no personality unless he has a role." The shrew that could not be tamed, oh, here we go again.

The black hole in the middle of Alien's face expanded, a deluge of vitriol in full flood. "What a loser! Practically bankrupt, a latent ho—"

It was enough. The mug of tea I had been drinking flew out of my hand and streaked like a missile at Alien's head. Just wonderful, the spectre of domestic violence invading the House of Jackson. Unfortunately, it missed and shattered against a door frame in a brown shower of tea.

"You're crazy!" screamed Alien, diving for cover in the basement. "Don't come near me! I'm calling the police."

"So call."

I left the house; I had to before my life was ruined further by an eternity in prison for aggravated pre-meditated murder in the first degree. I just wanted to get into the Kamikaze and drive, go anywhere, but the fool keys were in the house and there was no way I was going back in. So I walked, no particular destination in mind, along Broadside Avenue, the great trees arching over the road silhouetted against the last fading light of sunset. It was a beautiful autumn evening, the air soft and with that over-ripe smell of vegetation on the brink of decay. Sounds of normality were all about me: the natter of a television, a phone ringing, guffaws of laughter over a flickering barbecue. All was well with the world, except for me.

I walked for about half an hour, wallowing in self-pity. It was all so wrong; why could Anna not have been mine? The answer was, of course, Hugo, but that aside, Anna would never had treated me the way Alien would.

Gianetta d'Averso. In the wake of Antonio, who knew what she would be like? She might be gentle and accommodating, she might be paranoid. She probably wouldn't want involvement with a man who, at least legally, was married. There was the small matter anyway of properly making her acquaintance.

Suzi. She was my mother-in-law and a working colleague, due to inherit Sweet Marie's duties at the end of the academic year. Somehow Anna's description of her as adorable was working on me and I was having uneasy flickerings of feeling strange and different about her. Oh, no, Jackson, that would be a game with fire to end all games with fire.

Yet, here I was, standing on the pavement right in front of Suzi and Commander Philip Horatio's house. Commander Phil's car was not there; Suzi had said something about him being engaged in what she called Philharmania, his constant improvements on nature, at their cottage at Senekot Lake. All grass, all flowers, all shrubbery stood at attention in the shadows; the White Ensign had been lowered and the halyard wound in graceful swoops about the flagpole, both for appearance and to prevent rattling.

I felt like Freddy in *Pygmalion/My Fair Lady*. I felt like a stalker or a voyeur, watching for a glimpse of Suzi through the front window. There was none; likely she was the recreation room, watching *Dallas* or something of similar spiritual uplift. I even considered ringing the bell, but thought better of it. I was in a curious state of schizophrenia, wanting to be with someone and wanting to be alone at the same time, and since I was alone and hated change, I elected to remain alone and started for home, to spend the night on the living-room couch.

THE SCHISM

As so accurately predicted by the oracle Father Oakley, the sale of *Snarley,* the painting and re-painting of the White House, the numerous concessions of taking Evie to the doctor when I was on music or camp business, none were enough. As Hitler had chosen September, 1939, to unleash his catalogue of horrors on Poland, Alien chose December, 1990, for her own malign move, specifically a couple of hours before my Christmas concert.

By my own estimation, I have presided over more than three hundred concerts so far in my career. By any logic, each time should be easier than the last, but this is not a logical field of endeavour, and the reverse tends to be the reality. On concert day, I cannot eat, I cannot listen to other music, I pace up and down like a caged animal. I spend an inordinate amount of time dressing and observing a tradition (there it is again) of wearing a ring that had been my father's and his father's before him.

This particular pre-concert evening had been fairly typical. It was not the music itself that put me in such a state. It was a steady litany of this sort of thing from my students:

"Oh, is there a concert tonight? But it's my boyfriend's birthday…"

"Sir, I can't find my band folder."

"Mr. Jackson, the bass drum beater is missing."

"I have hockey tonight…"

"But Mr. Jackson, my friend broke up with her boyfriend and she's going to need me tonight…"

Never mind that the concert had been put on the school calendar last June. Never mind that I could do nothing about the missing folder but say, "Was it you or your mother who dressed you this morning?"

Of the bass drum beater: "How long has it been missing?"

104

"Since Thursday."

"And nobody told me."

"Er, I forgot, man."

"You forgot, who?"

"Oh, sorry, sir."

To the distressed friend: "Eighty-six friends need you tonight. You are part of this community. Your presence is not negotiable." Merry Christmas, dear children. And I knew there would be an empty chair on the stage whose erstwhile occupant had said vaguely to another band member after school that he "wouldn't be there tonight."

Two breathless phone calls from young love-goddesses-in-waiting to ascertain the order of the programme and another from a love-goddess-of-the-present to say she would be late because her hair-blower had burned out and the end of the world was nigh.

Thus elated and encouraged, I was shaving and doing my final preening before going over to the school. Alien had long since declined attending any of my performances; after all, they were merely interpretive, performers feeding as they did on the ideas of others, and being high school, well, that was just kid stuff anyway.

She generally stayed away from me altogether on concert evenings, so great was my surprise when she marched into the bathroom and sat down on the (closed) toilet. My, my. Were there to be words of sympathy and encouragement, acknowledgement of all the hard and careful work, assurance that once this was all over I could relax and enjoy the onset of Christmas?

"I'm listening," I said.

"Well, good, because we can't go on."

"What? What do you mean?"

"We have to separate."

"What?"

"You already said that."

"But why?"

"Do I have to spell it out for you? All right, I can't stand this, all the tension, the pacing, the phone calls, the general insecurity. Can't you control these people?"

"There are one hundred and sixty-eight hours in a week. I see them for roughly five. Some responsibility has to be left up to them. Besides, control is not what good teaching is about anyway."

"Well, that's just another rationalization for your general spinelessness."

"Thank you very much. If you think you can 'control' eighty-seven people better than I can, you're welcome to try." These were not the right words to be saying.

"That is not the issue."

"So what is the issue?"

"The issue is that I can't stand it any more, any of it."

"So leave."

"Oh, no, you don't. I have to look after the children and I need a house to do it in. I went through enough to get it in the first place."

"Oh, yes, you suffered deeply. I only sold my boat and painted this place three times."

"And messed up the stairwell."

"I have a concert tonight. Do you mind not messing my head up?"

"That's it, right there! Your work is more important than your home and family, and don't go throwing it up at me that it supports your home and family."

The demands of my work had been a major source of contention right from the beginning. In retrospect, I was absorbed in my work perhaps more then I should have been, although, as I remarked some time back, there was compensation through a very generous array of holidays. However, when your work involves so many people, is essentially in a fish-bowl, and has you name on it, you tend to give it your utmost, on both artistic and general principles. But by now, I was far past trying to explain this rationally, and simply said flatly, "But it sort of does support my home and family."

"Throw up, throw up, THROW UP!" screamed Alien, fingertips to temples.

"This is preposterous."

"I want you out of here by tomorrow night!"

Ding-dong merrily on high. That night, I think, was the birth of the New Me, the Bloodied But Unbowed K.Y. Jackson who Carried On Regardless. K.Y. was mad; K.Y was on the warpath.

The immediate result was one of the best concerts I have ever conducted, one for which I had to save the programme. There was a wonderful thing by Alfred Reed, the *Christmas Intrada*; a grand-sounding edition of the Coronation Scene from *Boris Godunov*, which we did with the choir and the bell choir from Via Dolorosa Elementary; a reprise of Father Oakley's *Karegnondi*; and the usual Christmas favourites, rounding off with the *Huron Carol* (with little electric candles for atmosphere) and *Sleigh Ride*.

The adults adjourned to the Brew-Ha-Ha afterwards. Most of the truly important people in my life were there: Father Oakley,

Charlie Cowell (whose band had the night off), Sister Ingrid (demurely sipping ginger ale), Israel Bond, my principal/father-in-law Commander Philip Horatio Quail, R.C.N. (Ret.), and his wife Suzi, the "popsy".

I must digress momentarily on the matter of Phil. He was the most senior and the most respected principal in our school system, the former commanding officer of the submarine *H.M.C.S. Atsihendo*, and he ran the school in like fashion. Nobody saluted anyone else, of course, but the colours were trooped before all assemblies and students were expected to address their teachers as "sir" or "ma'am". Woe betide anyone who said "Hey, man" or "Look, lady"; they were generally to be found after school doing Deck-cleaning Duty.

The beauty of Phil was that, while he ran a tight school, he trusted my musical judgement absolutely: "K.Y., this is my school, but it's your music program. Do what you feel is musically and educationally right." There were no demands for annual Broadway-style productions, although we did some really good ones from time to time; there were no demands for throw-away "pop" material on our concerts; Phil's only insistence was the permanent retention of The Maple Leaf Forever in our repertoire. When one of those tiresome committees that are the bane of education everywhere ordered that Maple Leaf not be performed because of words considered inflammatory to our francophone cousins, Phil snapped, "Forget the words. K.Y. plays it, he doesn't sing it. It's a hell of a good march. End of story."

Phil and Alien had never been close; after his parting of the ways with her mother, they had very little contact. Alien, it was reported by those who knew, was a virtual carbon copy of her mother, at least in terms of disposition; and Phil spoke of both of them so seldom that there was no sensation of family connection in our relationship, and indeed it was known to but a handful of our colleagues.

The new Mrs. Quail was, of course, Suzi, a well-upholstered beauty nearly thirty years Phil's junior and therefore younger than I. Her recent posting in our music office was a situation that permitted us some "quality time" for comparison of notes, for I was not the only one with household troubles. Matters had been strained for some time between Phil and Suzi, for he ran his entire life the way he did his school, with an almost Germanic preoccupation with order, system, and detail; and as much as I liked and respected Phil, it was easy to understand how oppressive something like that could be to live with.

Not only was their home maintained to the outermost limits, their summertime retreat at Senokot Lake likewise reflected the hand of Phil, especially as it pertained to the landscape. "Renoir said," said Phil, "that it is the duty of the artist to correct nature. That is exactly what I do at the cottage, and as an artist yourself, I expect you fully understand and concur." I failed on both counts; Phil, in contrast, had created a virtual miniature Garden of Versailles in the midst of Ontario's forested and rock-girdled north country. Phil's mania (which we christened Philharmania) drove poor Suzi to desperation, as so little time was left for her; not only that, she had the feeling of being an impediment to Phil's unrelenting quest for visible perfection in an visually imperfect world.

In view of Suzi's opulent charms, I thought it a great pity that she should be neglected so, and in turn she thought Alien's treatment of me was nothing less than reprehensible. So on the afternoons I was working at the office, Suzi and I would sometimes slip down to the coffee shop for what Father Oakley called a "taste", carefully picking a time when he was on the phone, and we would trade stories of the latest calumnies of our respective mates.

Although adversity drove us together and Suzi in her own right was most pleasant company, she had not Anna's Mother Earth/Love Goddess aura nor the womanly mystery of Gianetta d'Averso, whose Definitely Single state had recently been confirmed through my network of spies.

The day after the Christmas Concert that had been such a personal disaster and a professional triumph was, in some ways, fairly typical. The half-dozen or so staff members at school who faithfully supported the music programme congratulated me and my students , and the many others, who never darkened the school after hours whinged, "How did it go? I wanted to come, but I was so tired."

I suspended formal classes while the students heard a recording of the concert and generally unwound while I made some calls to establish new lodgings. After school, I went to the office to catch up on some neglected camp work. That, at least, was my purpose, but nothing could be accomplished without Father Oakley, who had been called away unexpectedly on some school emergency. So it was off to the coffee shop with Suzi and a conversation that began in relation to Christmas preparations in the Jackson household. Suzi was very fond of Katie and Evie, an affection fully reciprocated, the chronologically-cluttered relationship being codified by the appellation "Big Sister Grandma Suzi". Alien, of course, regarded the whole thing with total disdain.

"Well," I said in response to Suzi's question, "our preparations have pretty well gone down the toilet. I'm moving out." I still remember with astonishment how casually I said it. I must have been in shock.

"What!" squawked Suzi, attracting the inevitable solemn clerical stares from the southwest corner of the coffee shop. "What a bitch that woman is, just like her mother. Oh, poor K.Y.! You and Phil sure have not been lucky in love."

"Phil got lucky," I said coyly. My misfortune had not killed my flirtatious ways, but it was not the right thing to say.

"Well, I can't help wondering if I did. He's been too busy and exhausted to touch me for over six months. I'm going out of my mind. Help me. And I can…"

"Whoa, no, not me. Don't forget, he's also my principal, and besides, I'm too messed up to help anybody. My God, trying to explain this to the children…that's what hurts the most. I don't give a shit about the old bag, I'm not even too sorry about leaving the house, but the kids…Evie is too little to really understand, but Katie, it was so sad. She cried in the night and I woke her up and she said to me, 'Dad, I could come and live with you and fix dinner and do the cleaning up and keep you company.'"

Suzi, her spontaneous and ill-advised plea momentarily forgotten, choked on her coffee, eyes glistening.

I continued, "I told her she could come and stay from time to time, weekends and so forth, but with all this work I have to do, there is no way I could be home from school before the girls. Their mother's at home all the time…"

"Delightful for the girls, poor little things. But God have mercy. And at Christmas!"

"That's Alien's style."

"But where are you going to live?" wondered Suzi. "You could stay with us…"

"Oh, no, Suzi, thanks, you're very kind, but I think I have digs already lined up. One of my buddies put me on to it."

"Where?"

"On High Street. Uh, over the Meteor."

"But that's horrible!" Suzi's alarm was well-justified; the Meteor Meatier Eatery was a singularly raucous and unruly barbecue restaurant that stayed open until three a.m. daily except Sunday, when it went into a brief remission for clearance of tobacco smoke and cleaning up of beer slops. Fights and visits from the police were not uncommon.

"Well, it's affordable. I've got to maintain two households now. There's still a big mortgage on the house and Alien has spent a god-damned fortune on decorating, run up a huge bill on the Perma-Debt card, it's ridiculous."

"Oh, sweetie, I'm so sorry. Well, what about Christmas Day?"

"I get one hour with the children."

"One hour! On whose authority? Surely she hasn't got a lawyer yet!"

"Her authority. I'm just too tired, too sad, and too disgusted to fight with her any more for the moment, and the pity of it all is she knows it. The whole thing has been like a perpetual trip to the dentist and I just can't do it any more."

"Then come to our place for dinner."

Alarm bells again, fainter this time, but where I really wanted to be was with Anna and Hugo. They would be my sanctuary, they wouldn't blizzard me with questions, they would let me be a recluse if I needed it, they would let me pour out my sorrows if I needed to; in short, Anna and Hugo would be all that would do.

"Can we leave that on hold? I may be going to see friends in Toronto. I'll probably know tonight." I had some fast phoning to do.

I moved to my new abode the day before Christmas Eve. It was small, it was clean and it was adequate, though slightly fragrant with tobacco smoke from the restaurant below. I could put up with the fire station being next door; equipment would go shrieking off at the oddest hours, but if I ever had a fire, help would be immediate. The view out the back window wasn't much, giving out onto a sort of service laneway along the backs of the stores; had I been inclined to jump out the window, my destination would have been a dumpster filled with rancid meat scraps, bones, and other debris from the coarse diners of the Meteor Meatier Eatery.

Luckily, the place had furniture, at least of sorts, as my exit from the White House had been too hasty and disorderly to move any of my own. It was prohibited anyway by Alien because absences among the furniture would have been "too disruptive for the children". All I took were my books, scores, and recordings, collectively known as my "god-damn shit", and the stereo. That she could spare, since it would cut down on "all that god-damn noise" and give her much-needed quiet in her pursuit of fusion with the sun or whatever her current goal was.

I assembled the stereo and then sat contemplating my music collection. With what to baptize the new Chez Jackson? The *Messiah or Ceremony of Carols* would have been an agony. *La Mer* was out as well; I had been completely unable to listen to it since *Snarley Yow's* departure from my life. After a few moments' deliberation, I settled on Shostakovich's sublimely defiant *Leningrad Symphony* and as I played it against a counterpoint of the most objectionably whining and wheedling country music wafting up from the Meteor Meatier Eatery, I sipped Emu 999 from a peanut butter jar in a determined if pathetic quest for the good life.

One other thing I did manage to retain as a spoil of war was the car (legally as well as morally mine; it was registered in my name), the elderly and dog-eared Toyota that I called the Kamikaze. The relationship between Alien and the Kamikaze, as between Alien and virtually anything or anyone else, was uncertain and unpredictable. For years, she had not taken any interest in driving, leaving all of it up to me. And then, as recently as October, she had decided that she "needed" a driving licence and out of some occult impulse had required of me that I should teach her.

Of that experience, need I say what a horror it was? She refused to spend money on a properly-ordained driving school, perhaps in view of a restricted cash flow balanced against an absurdly bloated Perma-Debt account, but with the baby-sitting money we ended up spending while "on the road", the saving was minimal, if indeed it existed at all.

So I gave Alien her driving lessons and any doubts I may have had of her decision-making abilities were dismally confirmed. She would dither at stop signs while there was a lull in the oncoming traffic, and then when my exhortations to move finally bore fruit, she would drive straight into the path of a bellowing, roaring transport with Godzilla at the helm. And lane changes on the highway were preceded by three or four kilometres of the direction signal blinking impotently at an empty lane, and then when the maneuver finally took place, it was, predictably, right into the path of a bellowing, roaring transport with Godzilla the helm.

Turnings would be missed and U-turns timed to be right in the path of Godzilla and his eighteen-wheeler loaded with untold tons of potatoes from the bountiful fields of Birkenstock County. Alien's nerves were wrecked by the experience, as were mine, and the fact of her actually passing her driving test was the biggest mutual surprise of our short, stormy, and brutal marriage.

Two days after her unexpected triumph, Alien had to go somewhere during the working day and requested use of the car, declaring that she was completely comfortable with it. Fine, I said, and she drove me to school before going on her way. We are talking (or writing) of late November at this point, less than a month before what I came to call The Schism, and it will surprise no-one to learn that as Alien turned into the school driveway, the Kamikaze hit one of those awful patches of virtually invisible ice, lost steerage, scooted up over the curb, and thundered into a hydro pole before an astonished crowd of every music student I had ever taught and would teach for the next twenty years, including the unborn.

To my surprise (and relief, for there was no way of affording a new car), The Kamikaze, disreputable though it was, was judged worthy of repair by the insurance people. That the mishap could just as easily have happened to me is beside the point; it could be certainly understood if Alien were to decline any further driving, at least until the spring. Therefore I was completely unprepared for her demand to use the car, even though I had custody of same, on Christmas Day.

"Well, too bad," I said. "I'm going down to Anna and Hugo's for Christmas dinner."

"Well, thanks for telling me."

"Since I am the legal owner of the car and pay for all maintenance and insurance, and let me remind you that my premiums have now increased thanks to your love affair with that hydro pole, I hardly think I'm accountable to you for its deployment."

"Deployment, shmeployment. You sound just like my father, so Navy, so god-damned pretentious…"

"And this cosmic, incomprehensible poetry of yours isn't pretentious?"

"At least I have original thought."

"And I don't?"

"You just interpret."

"Could you have given birth without Dr. Garth-Alleyne?" Dr. Garth-Alleyne had been Alien's obstetrician.

"What has that got to do with anything?"

"Yes or no?"

"Well, no. Why?"

"As far as music is concerned, the composer is the father, the band is the collective mother, and I am the obstetrician. It doesn't happen without me."

"So who cares?"

"Oh, only the better part of ninety band members, one hundred and eighty parents, a student body of over thirteen hundred, and a significant segment of the community. How many copies of that cosmic cookbook of yours have you sold?"

"Oh, God, I hate you! You're a mean man! Mean, mean, MEAN!"

The children exploded into heartbroken cries. "Merry Christmas!" hissed Alien. "Now see what you've done!"

I was stunned. I could not believe I had said what I had said; it was as though an alternative being had taken over my mouth. The thoughts were mine (and original ones at that), but there was no need to verbalize them. It was like having an attack of diarrhoea. I had to calm down and I did, at least for a fleeting moment.

"Now, about the car. It is registered in my name, bought by me, insured by me, maintained by me. It just came out of the workshop with over six hundred dollars worth of repairs—"

"I knew you'd throw that up at me!"

The girls moaned and whined in the background like a sorrowful little wind.

"I'm not getting sucked into that again. All I want to know is what is so all-important about having the car tomorrow?"

"We're invited to Mildred Willis's for dinner." Mildred Willis was Alien's publisher and lived on a farm away to the west, out beyond New Jamaica. "If we don't have the car," added Alien, "we get no Christmas dinner." She glanced meaningfully towards the children.

"And if I don't have the car, I get no Christmas dinner."

"You don't have the children."

I lost control. "Okay, take the fucking car and enjoy yourself to the fullest. Have a good one, sweetheart!" I flung the car keys on the floor, stamped out the door, and made the lonely trek on foot back to my aerie over the Meteor Meatier Eatery, past windows aglow with seasonal festivity, coloured lights sparkling on the snow, the tang of wood smoke hanging in the starry night. So much for the magic of Christmas Eve, when at midnight the animals could talk, St. Nicholas was expected imminently in his desperate dash to stay at least six time zones ahead of daybreak, when mysterious and indestructible forces of redemption radiated forth once again from Bethlehem, bringing renewed hope to a maddened world as it had done for over twenty centuries. For K.Y. Jackson there was neither hope nor redemption, no children to read the Nativity story to at bedtime, no car, no Anna and Hugo; I felt wretched beyond words as I climbed the stairs next to a mercifully dark and silent Meteor Meatier Eatery.

In my darkened state, I had a flickering temptation to call Suzi; she had complained of late of Phil's idea of Christmas decor, in which Merry Christmas was spelled out along the eaves of their house in International Code flags, a model of *H.M.C.S. Atsihendo* sat on the mantlepiece, her periscope and snorkel sporting sprigs of cedar, and a miniature lead Royal Navy band marched along the top of a bookshelf. Confidentially, I quite enjoyed it, but although Suzi hated it and probably would have loved a wee tryst with "son", I thought discretion the better part of valour.

In the meantime, I had to deal with tomorrow. I would just drink Emu 999, listen to Shostakovich, and sleep. Christmas dinner would be oxtail soup and Animal Crackers, the sum total of my larder. Additionally, I would have to phone my regrets to Anna and Hugo, with whom I had made successful arrangements but days before.

I phoned Anna and got Hugo. "Hugo, I can't make it for dinner tomorrow."

"Dear God, are you sick, or what? And on Christmas?"

Had I lied and said I was, it might have been the end of it. But I did not lie. I told Hugo about the car.

"Has she three sixes in a row in her social insurance number?" was his enigmatic response.

"Hugo, you are about eighty jumps ahead of me. What the fuck kind of question was that, anyway?"

"It is the number of the Beast. Revelations something-or-other, have to look it up…I may as well say it, I think she is a bitch of the first order and so does Anna, although she'd kill me for telling you—"

"Hugo, I'm going to kill you!" came Anna's faint voice over the line.

Continued Hugo: "I'm too young to die. I'm going to escape and drive up to Birkenstock to pick you up… okay, darling, I won't go up tonight…won't kill me?…promise?…my life for Christmas?…what a relief…I'll come up first thing in the morning to get you, pack a bag and stay the night…what, darling?…stay several nights…what, love?…many nights." Even though Hugo was practically a brother to me, the invitation to stay many nights triggered a brief fantasy of wallowing in the perfumed chambers of Anna. "You still there, K.Y.?"

"Oh, uh, yes. Pardon."

"We're not letting that she-wolf screw up your Christmas or, for that matter, your life. Don't worry about a thing. See you in the morning."

I ended up staying the entire week, right through New Year's Day. Anna and Hugo celebrated New Year's in Scots style and their Hogmanay parties were legendary; Hugo always brewed a horrific concoction he called Hognog that was guaranteed to befuddle the intellect and confound the senses. Of course, the usual glittering and eclectic array of friends was present and I had the pleasure of mixing Hognog (the recipe for which has been sworn to secrecy) variously for Robertson Davies (who was as funny in person as in print), Harry Freedman (with whom I had a lengthy and fascinating musical conversation), and Clayton Ruby, who, on hearing that I was from Birkenstock, introduced me to his Birkenstockian colleague (and Hugo's friend) Sheldon Gallstone.

"I'm sorry for your trouble, Ken," said Sheldon. "I hope you don't mind, but Hugo told me. Here's my card; call me if the need arises." Sheldon was a partner in a law firm with the singular title of Pitt, Bull, Gallstone, and Silverstein, Barristers and Solicitors. So began the year 1991, the year of the Osterling Weekend.

THE NEED ARISES

Many needs arose that January. There was primarily the need to be with my little girls, which predictably, Alien made as difficult as possible. There was the need for some personal funds, which were being bled from me more quickly than they could be replenished. In fact, my personal funds became so depleted that I resorted to sweetening my tea with the scrapings from the innards of Oreo cookies. And all the while, the heavenly vapours of the Meteor Meatier Eatery, once again in full cry following the holidays, permeated my abode, driving me to a frenzy of food-lust.

By mid-January, I'd had enough and phoned Sheldon Gallstone to get a formal separation agreement into motion. I had to be able to see my children, I had to be able to eat, I had to be able to live. Nothing was on paper, although for a while I had put off such a thing, as in my mind it would acknowledge that it was all over, it had failed despite my efforts. Oh, well, what the hell, here we go. K.Y. was back and he was ugly.

"Pitt, Bull, how may we help you?" purred the phone reassuringly. I wanted to scream, "Sue the bitch, put her out of business!" But sense prevailed, I asked for Mr. Gallstone, and he was put on the line. We discussed strategy for a few minutes, and then I came to a matter I particularly dreaded. "Mr. Gallstone…"

"Just call me Shelley, like the poet."

"Well, er, Shelley, I don't know how I would pay you. I'm so broke it's ridiculous…"

"It's all thought out. We'll just charge you for disbursements. I'll put my fee into the firm for the sake of billing and you can work it off."

"What doing?"

"I have this beautiful old Taylor cruiser that needs some tender loving care. I keep her up the lake at Genepool and none of the marinas around here know wood any more. Hugo told me a few things…"

Among the needs that might arise, it had never occurred to me that anything marine would be among them. Even though I would be working on someone else's vessel and even though it could not be until spring, I still had been given something of a course to navigate through the dark winter of my soul. For the first time in quite a spell, I had something to look forward to.

In the meantime, there was the present to deal with. Once the initial shock of separation had worn off, I was dealing with a loneliness so all-encompassing that I felt as if my very sanity were being challenged. There was, of course, the factor of the children, the factor that had been in the forefront of my thoughts at the time of the Schism.

But now there was an almost screaming need for a woman. Alien had steadily eroded my self-estimation—I could still hear echoes of her shrewish accusation of latent homosexuality—and with time on my own to find the scraps of K.Y. Jackson that had been scattered about the cosmos, I was coming rapidly to the conclusion that she had had me starting to believe all these awful things about myself. Primarily out of embarrassment, I had never discussed any of this beyond the surface mean-spiritedness with anyone, except with the briefly-consulted psychiatrist: not Hugo or Anna, not Father Oakley, and not even, or I should say especially, with Suzi.

"Suzi's gone all weird," declared Father Oakley one early January afternoon during a "taste" in the office coffee shop.

"What do you mean, 'weird'?"

"She's gone all introspective, which is definitely not Suzi, if you understand my meaning, no disrespect intended, for she is the work of the Lord." Seeing my startled look, Father Oakley laughed. "Don't worry, I manufactured that one for confession. Been a slow week in the sin department."

"I hear you on both counts. Hair styles and fashions seem to be Suzi's thing. Well, we do talk about the ills of our respective marriages, but since mine is down the drain now, it doesn't leave much scope for dialogue. She is, though, without a doubt one of Our Lord's finest creations. Too bad she isn't single, or at least too bad she's my mother-in-law." Father Oakley looked as if he wanted to say something, but thought better of it.

Although the camp had not been much in my thoughts the last while, preparations were still very much under way; the location was determined, a deposit had been made to Anna and Hugo, the teaching faculty had been engaged. Application forms for campers were now coming in at a gratifying rate; arrangements were put

117

into motion for an audition process, not to determine admission to the camp, but to simply determine the most appropriate placement in an ensemble. Support staff were being recruited from our graduates in different universities.

The frequency of meetings, in abeyance since just before Christmas, now picked up, with Suzi in regular attendance as recording secretary. But, as Father Oakley said, she really had become a bit strange and I wondered if things at home were bound in the same direction as my own situation. I took the bull by the horns and asked.

"Oh, it's just the same old crap. Everything is Phil's way. He never wants to go anywhere or do anything except work or putter with navy stuff."

"If you were to go anywhere, where would you like to go?"

"Oh, Las Vegas or Florida or a cruise on one of those big ships where they spoil you rotten and you get thoroughly oinked out on food."

Personally, I blamed Phil not in the least, although I was surprised a cruise didn't interest him. "He says they're not real ships, they're more like floating dude ranches and he thinks they're ugly." Oh, Phil, my man! "So all I get to do is shopping, which I hate doing alone. How about being a good son-in-law and go shopping with me? I'll throw in dinner, how about next Thursday night?"

"Thursday?"

"Your birthday, or had you forgotten?"

"Oh, yeah," I said listlessly. "Am I still legitimately your son-in-law?"

"Until the end of time."

One of Suzi's favourite places was the new Birkenstock Mall, a sprawling temple of commerce by the main highway to Toronto. The Mall had brought a whole new spiritual dimension to her life, naturally unleashing a flood of editorials from Alien, and it was at the Mall that I spent my birthday.

"Does Phil know we're doing this?"

"Oh, yes, and he's sorry he couldn't be here too. Had to go to a joint principals' meeting with the elementary school guys. Says happy birthday and not to worry, it's still all in the family. Now, first, we shop for you. You need some clothes."

I hate clothes shopping, but not to examine the mouth of the gift horse too intently, so I meekly acquiesced. Very quickly I felt like a Kept Man, so much largesse was heaped upon me. "Suzi," I protested, "enough! Don't leave yourself out."

118

"Don't worry, I won't." She didn't. "I need some new underwear. Help me pick some out."

What Suzi had in mind looked more to be of a ceremonial nature than anything to support and stabilize her bounty. "I like this leopard-skin pattern…look how teeny the panties are!…oh, look, there's a garter belt to go with it, oh, this is divine, and look, there's a zebra pattern too, think I'll take it as well…"

Paradoxically, Suzi spent as much on herself as she had on me, but her package was only a tenth the size of mine. We adjourned to a quite pleasant restaurant, had some laughs over the underwear, and took leave with our usual chaste hug.

A week later, my phone rang at 7:30 in the morning.

"Hi, sweetie, it's Suzi."

"Oh, uh, hi. Is anything wrong?"

"No. Have dinner with me tonight. I have a roast lamb and nobody to eat it with."

"Wait a second. Isn't Phil going away to some convention, Montreal or someplace?"

"Yes, he is, so it'll be just you and me. It was his idea. He thought you could use a woman to talk to."

"Well, as long as he's not uncomfortable…"

"He said he wasn't worried about you fooling around." She laughed. "He didn't ask me about me, though."

"It would be like incest anyway. I'll call you 'mummy' when I get there as a reminder. Listen, thanks. You're most kind. What time?"

"Sixish. I'll be a leopard."

"A leopard? What do you mean?"

"The underwear, silly. I'm going to put it on right now, knowing you're coming."

I got to the Quail abode sixish as directed after a day of total non-concentration in which I kept telling myself not to be a bloody fool. Suzi met me at the door, holding out a glass of wine.

"You look more like the pink panther than a leopard," I remarked, alluding to a pink sweater that adhered deliciously to her contours. Her carotid artery was beating visibly in her throat.

"I'm a leopard underneath. A leopard with stockings, yet. I bet I haven't worn a garter belt since I was seventeen. K.Y., you're so adorable when you blush!"

I did not need a doctoral degree to know the situation I was in. I just had to come to terms with the fact of it not being in a novel or happening to someone else. I kept in motion, busying myself looking at Phil's collection of naval artifacts, asking if there were any new acquisitions (Suzi neither knew nor cared) and asking what new projects were envisioned for the cottage (Suzi neither knew nor cared about that either).

Dinner came and went; I helped clear off the dishes, made an errand of mercy to the loo, and when I emerged, Suzi had a fire going and the haunting music from the film *Laura* on the stereo.

"Dance with me, Ken." Ken. She had never called me that.

"Sure. Uh, this is really nice. No man ever had a mother-in-law like this to dance with."

"No woman ever had a son-in-law like this to dance with." I knew it was all crazy and ill-advised, but I was as helpless as a nail near a magnet. We started to dance and within about ten seconds, I started to feel as if my pants were filling up with warm ginger ale. I had not felt such a thing since before Alien's verbal assaults on my manhood.

Suzi burrowed closer, putting both arms around my neck. Her hair and her scent enveloped me. Blood roared in my ears. My biological clock thumped and clanged. *Laura* was coming to her wistful finale. What next? Hobble to the couch, sit down, and try to make conversation? Another dance?

Suzi stepped away and in two smooth motions peeled off her sweater and dropped her skirt. She made a sensual smoothing gesture down her left thigh. "Suzi, for shit's sake!"

"What a vulgar thing to say! I get to see you in your new clothes and I felt I owed it to you to show you me in mine."

"But..."

"Mine just happened to be underwear. Look, I haven't been touched for over six months. I suspect you haven't either. If no-one else is going to appreciate us, maybe we can appreciate each other. Come here and love me."

I went there and I loved her, right there by firelight on the living room floor. I loved her short, dark hair, her full-lipped sensual mouth and big smile, her great big electric-blue eyes, her body that would be a serious challenge to anything seen in Playboy, all that had been forbidden to me for so many years, I loved comprehensively and with an expertise I never knew I had, an expertise that had her slamming her head and her heels on the floor at the moment of eruption.

As our huffing and panting diminished, she locked her legs about me and murmured, "I'm never letting you go, except for work. The rest of the time you will be my love slave."

"But you're married."

"Ever hear of a Meanage-a-Troy?" Suzi's French was a bit lacking, but after the last quarter-hour or so, who cared?

We lay together for no little time, and when I said feebly that I ought to be going, Suzi whispered "Please don't leave me. I want to wake up in your arms."

She did wake up in my arms, somewhere around five in the morning, and promptly slipped away. For a horrified moment, I thought she was going to say it was all wrong (which it was, but my judgement was corrupted beyond redemption) and that I was to leave immediately. But such was not the case. "Catch me," she whispered and pranced off into the pre-dawn darkness. Round and round the house we went, myself blundering into various obstacles, and we re-connected in the most intimate manner in the recreation room downstairs; Suzi mounted the billiards table, put her feet in the corner pockets, and away we went again. The biggest challenge was to not leave any evidence on the felt.

I was a new man, albeit one with no scruples whatever. "What the hell's gotten into you?" said Father Oakley crossly after a camp planning session. "You're not concentrating and everything is funny to you. Did you get laid, or what?"

"Yes."

"I am a Jesuit Father. Confess."

"I just did."

"Anyone I know?"

Though of an earthy disposition, Father Oakley had moral principles beyond challenge. I knew how horrified and disappointed he would be if the name and face were attached to my new inamorata, so I just lied, mumbled no, and sobered up, trying not to think of Suzi at her desk just outside the meeting room in which we were working.

I fancied myself in love with Suzi. Perhaps she had no original thoughts or designs on the universe; perhaps for her the priorities were clothes rather than Copland, eye-liner rather than Ives, shoes rather than Schubert. Art galleries and museums were a bore, concerts a horror, books something to lend tone to one's house, especially if they were those Reader's Digest things in the fake leather bindings. Poetry was something to be ignored.

Suzi was beautiful, she did not judge, and she was fun. After all the heavy, Germanic intellectualism of Alien, not to mention her vituperations, Suzi was the right woman at the right time and I just could not get enough of her.

Of course, discretion on both our parts was taxed to the limit. Thursday afternoons continued to see me at the office for camp work and Father Oakley developed a sudden and unaccountable availability at coffee time; Suzi and I would sit there practically wetting ourselves with suppressed passion while Father Oakley held forth in cheerful oblivion on politics, religion, "good, good painting", or whatever else captured his interest at the time. I tried valiantly to discourse, the nylon sleekness of Suzi's knee moving gently up and down my leg.

She was all I could think of, and as far as Phil was concerned, my sentiment was that he wasn't bothering to make her happy and I was. So amoral had I become that I felt no discomfort whatever in his presence, it was business as usual, and he never appeared to suspect a thing. If I had had time to contemplate my ethical neutrality, I know it would have come to bother me, but the moment there were flickerings, the phone would ring: "Hi, sweetie, it's me and I just have a second. Phil's in the bathroom. I'm lying here with nothing on, thinking about you. Whoops, here he comes. Night-night."

I felt seventeen again. Suzi and I were A Couple. But unlike the average seventeen-year-old couple who feel compelled to parade their status through the corridors of learning, who take elaborate farewells of each other when bound for separate classes, who mew and moan over each other while fondling buttocks in stairwells, public revelation of our relationship would have had the most far-reaching and hideous consequences.

Evening. The phone. "Hi, sweetie," I said cheerfully.

"Sweetie yourself," rumbled Hugo. "There has been a long silence. We were getting a tad twitched. Are you okay? Talk to me."

I talked to Hugo. I talked to Hugo for over an hour. "I can appreciate your dilemma," he said, "but remember you've both been made to feel like a couple of dung beetles. You're both entitled to happiness and if Suzi's situation is anything like yours, you're on pretty solid moral ground, even if it's illegal. That's my judgment, anyway. I bet we never told you that's how Anna and I met."

"What? Really?"

"Yes, well, it's a long one for the phone and we'll save it for a summer evening at the camp on the dock with a glass of Chablis. But suffice to say for the moment that Anna's husband, as was, had the squeeze on her to have babies and she didn't want any, had no craving at all for motherhood and he as good as raped her and she got pregnant and then miscarried…"

"Who needs Chablis? Keep talking."

"Me, I was just treated like shit, as you were. I was struggling to become established as a writer and if I had it to do over I wouldn't. It's horrible. We had no money and I was getting screamed at all the time, stuff about how I was going nowhere and thought the world owed me a living…"

122

"It does."

"Indeed, and now it's paying up like an oil gusher. God, I love being rich. But Sweetheart didn't hang in with me long enough to reap the benefits. Anyway, we'll talk later on in greater detail. Anna and I went through our share of assignations and furtive meetings, so I have some sense of your situation. I like the sound of this Suzi. If she makes you happy, so be it."

Suzi made me so exquisitely happy that, despite my straitened circumstances and the crudities of living perched atop the Meteor Meatier Eatery, life was good and my students wondered at (but enjoyed) my perpetual state of smiles and chuckles, not to mention an unaccountable but gratifying rise in class averages.

On the drab and practical end of things, Shelley Gallstone moved with a speed virtually unheard of in legal circles and by mid-February, a formal separation agreement was in place between Alien and myself. A writing grant to her from old Carlton Lansdowne's newly-founded foundation took the financial heat off me for the time being and I had regular access to Katie and Evie. Finally there was peace in our time.

FORWARD ONCE MORE

We interviewed our so-called Junior Administration team for the camp early in February, all drawn from the ranks of graduates of the various music programs run by the Birkenstock County Roman Catholic School Board. Alice Nestleton, soon to become known as Miss Moneypenny, was to be in command of the office. Scotia, the daughter of Duke McLeod, the Director of Education, and Warren Peace were in charge at the waterfront. Duncan Doenitz (whom Hugo was certain was a great grandson of the great German admiral) and Dow Jones were in charge of boys' camp. Land sports were to be looked after by Eddie Coli, who took perverse delight in signing his name as "e.coli" and was generally addressed as such. Those interviews were handled by Father Oakley, Charlie, and myself.

Sister Ingrid stood in for Father Oakley to deal with interviews for the unit heads for girls' camp. Liesl Schwarzkopf, whose cello-playing notoriety had preceded her, was one of the successful candidates. The other two were a pair of what one might call "dark horses", although in these times of racial sensitivity such a description may not be in good taste. Dark they were; horses they certainly were not. So stunning was their beauty that Charlie and I were totally useless during the interviews; we let Sister Ingrid handle matters, and then grovellingly and shamelessly lobbied her to accept Surrendra Bangalore (late of New Delhi) and Nirvana Saranwraparan (late of Colombo) as unit heads.

"You two are absolutely disgusting," pronounced Ingrid, trying with only marginal success to look stern. "You didn't hear a thing. All you did was goggle like a couple of love-struck teens."

"It wasn't just them alone, Sister," protested Charlie. "It was the combination of them and you that was just too much. Oh, man…"

124

Another Birkenstock Philharmonic Society concert came and went, again under the direction of the odious Antonio d'Averso. When the ego of the man would ever burst, nobody knew. It was an ego so enormous, said Father Oakley, that it required its own postal code. This event was titled "Hidden Treasures" and featured Charlie as trumpet soloist in the seldom-played concerto by Alexander Arutunian; Charlie was developing quite a taste for "legit stuff". The other hidden treasures were Dvorak's *Der Wassermann* ("we tested positive," reported Charlie) and Glazunov's Symphony No. 5. We in the audience were duly amazed, Antonio duly underwent further inflation.

Suzi, in the meantime, was showing some alarming signs of recklessness. The media were full at the time of a salacious new pastime called "lap dancing"; we were both curious as to how it was done and rather than speculate, we thought we would try it out, which we did one evening at her house. Mine would have been safer, but she did not want to be out so much as to arouse Phil's suspicions, so we had our rendezvous in the recreation room (with the famous pool table standing mute sentinel) where a sliding glass door gave out onto the back garden as an emergency exit.

I had parked around the corner in order to conceal the Kamikaze; there was a hydro right-of-way along the back of the Quail property, enabling me to enter (and leave) through a gate at the bottom of the garden unseen by the neighbours.

We spent some time evolving what we thought were the necessary techniques, hampered by the innocence of never having seen lap dancing, and finally had matters established to our mutual and fevered satisfaction. We were in the midst of rocking and swaying our way to the ultimate gratification when, to our horror, we heard Phil let himself in at the front door. I withdrew, grabbed my jacket, and in my swollen and unspent condition fled out the back into a raging snowstorm. At least my tracks would be covered.

I gained the Kamikaze, realized that I was still indecently exposed, tried to restore myself to decency, and found myself frozen solidly to the zipper on my fly. It was a long and uncomfortable ride home, and once parked, I had to idle the engine until I and my zipper were sufficiently thawed to part company.

February in Birkenstock was Music Festival time. There was no premiere for me this year, but we did an arresting combination of Debussy's *La Cathédrale Engloutie* and William Schuman's rabble-rousing *Chester Overture*, earning kudos from the adjudicators for "an exceptionally mature sound". Kudos came too from my colleagues present at the same session, including, to my surprise, Gianetta d'Averso, who, even in the face of my current attachment, looked absolutely stunning.

"Ken, congratulations," she purred, demurely holding out her hand. "*Chester* was wonderful, but what you did with the Debussy was, well, uncanny. Oh, excuse me, here comes my late husband. I have to go."

Seeing the others clustered about me, Antonio had little social option but to add his own best wishes. Naturally, there were reservations: "Good'a reason Debussy never wrote'a for band, but within'a da limits of'a da genre, you did'a verra well, verra well indeed. Mind'a you, it was nothing I would'a have chosen..."

"I would'a not have'a chosen it either," mimicked Father Oakley later. "But it was done so well. Good, good playing. What a dickhead."

"Who, me?"

"No, kid, Antonio. You are one of the great ones. Let's go for a taste."

Despite the volcanically passionate affair with Suzi, Gianetta could still command my attention and meditations on her were revived more than occasionally. Not only was she, in the vernacular, drop-dead gorgeous, but she had the virtue of being single. She was a teacher and a musician and I was certain that it was because of Antonio's arrogance that her marriage had disintegrated. I would not allow any sort of idiot rivalry to interfere with what had potential to be a beautiful partnership...

...but then Suzi would take over my being, usually spontaneously, as she did one Saturday night when Phil was in Toronto for some sort of Naval Reserve function at *H.M.C.S. York,* the local naval facility, and because of the lateness of the hour decided to stay the night in town.

"Come on over, sweetie! I've got a new outfit to show you."

"Suzi, it's eleven o'clock. I'm in bed."

"Alone. Get over here. Then I'll have you in bed in no time."

"But what about the new outfit?"

"I'll show it to you and then I'll take it off. There's not much to it anyway."

I made my way to Chez Quail, parked around the corner, and came in through the back gate of comic memory. I let myself into the recreation room, the pool table standing square and proud, let me tell you, it was a pool table that made a statement.

"Suzi? Suzi, where are you?"

"Upstairs. Don't move. It's modelling session time. Observe."

I observed as Suzi came downstairs in a gloriously tacky outfit of leather miniskirt and a more or less transparent top, transparent enough, at any rate, for me to see that, for tonight, she was a zebra.

Suzi held out a chamois cloth. "You have to earn your pleasure, dear son-in-law. Leather skirts require polishing. It must be done before anything happens."

I had not polished with such precision and commitment since doing the brass on *Snarley Yow*. Round and round I polished, oh, it was all so round, the round cheeks of her Botticellian behind, the round, sleek thighs, just a slight roundness to the abdomen, round and round went K.Y. Jackson, round and round paradise he went.

"Let me check how well you did this. Excuse me," said Suzi, peeling off the skirt and checking the shine. "Very good, son. I am, as you can see, a zebra. Hunt me!" She raced for the stairs, myself in hot pursuit like Cesar Franck's *Chasseur Maudit*, and she led me a great chase until I cornered her in the kitchen by the refrigerator. We panted, warbled, and whinnied like a couple of demented horses as we tore each other's clothes off and slid in a heap down the face of the refrigerator, firmly engaged even before sprawling on the floor…sucked into the fires of passion, searing, hellish flames of exaltation and damnation all at the same time, oh, God, well, no, I didn't think He really wanted to see all this, but wasn't He everywhere, now, what was this I was hearing, "Oh, son…my beautiful son…oh, sonnnnnn!"

"You called me 'son'," I panted, once the capacity for speech returned.

"Only because you called me Mummy."

"I didn't!"

To this day I don't think I called Suzi Mummy under those specific circumstances, but she stoutly maintained that I did and declared that the sin and corruption were the biggest turn-on she had ever known. I was dragged off to bed and it was not until the next morning that it occurred that I had not only slept with my mother-in-law but in my father-in-law's bed at that.

The next morning brought its own surprise anyway. "Oh, God, Ken, wake up!"

"Eh?"

"It's ten-thirty. Phil'll be home any moment!"

I sprang out of (Phil's side of) the bed and dragged my clothes on. Suzi, in the meantime, was near panic.

"You can't go out the back, you'll be seen. Listen, I'll drive you out."

"What?"

"Just do as I say."

127

A carport adjoined the house and Suzi's car, a Dodge Caravan, was parked rear-first, with its sliding door opposite the house door, so I was able to make a boarding almost as smooth, invisible, and efficient as at an airport. I crouched down on the floor and Suzi drove out, only to stop immediately. A chill draft from an opening window poured down upon me.

"Hi, honey," said Suzi brightly. A man's voice, faintly, oh, sweet Jesus, it was Phil! I pressed my face into the carpet on the floor of the Caravan. If I couldn't see Phil, he couldn't see me.

"Just going out to get a paper," said Suzi, who hated newspapers.

"Got one," came Phil's voice faintly.

"The Sun?"

"The Sun! What a junker! No, I got the Globe and Mail."

"Oh, I'm looking for the Sun. Has an article about the Hair Show. I'll just be a minute. I'll make us coffee. Back in a minute." She rolled up the window and drove off.

"You are so smooth," said I from the floor.

"This is too exciting for words. I could take you right there, right now. Just let me get around the corner..."

February became March and winter started to ease its icy grip over Birkenstock County. There were days of foggy drizzle obscuring the hills away towards Georgian Bay. There were days of tepid sunshine, turning the concession roads around East Ganglia and Tantamount into a quagmire. There were a few more days of snow, but it soon turned to slush and disappeared and the sun came out again, the cloud shadows chasing each other over the woodlots north of Annville and High Dudgeon.

The last Thursday before March Break, I went for my usual Thursday afternoon at the office. Neville was out for his Angiogram, Suzi was hunched over her computer trying to look businesslike, but was able to look up and mouth a nearly-obscene kiss in my direction. We had Been Without for nearly a week and it was telling on us.

A serious-looking Father Oakley took me by the elbow and steered me into a vacant conference room, even before I could take my jacket off. My mind screamed. Had he found out about me and Suzi? Should I just own up and get it over with?

Father Oakley closed the door with a sense of moment I had seen him exercise only at concerts. OhGodohGodohGod!

"I've had to make a very tough decision," he said sombrely. OhGodohGodohGod! "Something has come up and I had to think about it, lay awake most of the night..." OhGodohGodohGod! Silence.

"What is it?" I asked in a dry whisper.

"I was offered a promotion." Relief escaped me in a great, stale whoosh. But then curiosity, mixed with apprehension. "To what?"

"Associate Superintendent of Curriculum."

"You? But that's a Suit job. It's at a desk. It's not you."

"I know. I'd feel like a pimp. I may be a priest, but I know what pimps are. I was asked for a very particular reason. Mr. Lansdowne's generosity notwithstanding, there are budget cuts coming and the bean counters will be targeting the arts first. Duke McLeod [the Director of Education] is very pro-arts, is full of praise for our program, wants to protect it, and thinks I'm the guy to do it. I think the Lord called me through Duke and I'm not going to question it. It won't be nearly as much fun, but it is how I can do the most good."

I, on the other hand, could only think of my own personal welfare. "But who am I going to work with?" I all but whined.

"That's why we need to talk. The job of Supervisor of Instrumental Music is not mine to give away and it will have to be posted through the usual channels. But I will have some input into who is taken aboard and if you are interested in it, you would be my recommendation."

"Meeee?" I squealed.

"Yes, youuuuu. You have some prior knowledge of how the place works, who does what to whom—it's Thursday—you're well-organized, you can put things together, you're a good musician, and I could keep an eye on you for when you screw up. Want to think about it?"

"When would this happen?"

"Interviews would be early in April and the appointment would be effective for the fall term."

"Well...I'm honoured, Father. I do want to think about it, but I am very interested, so very interested..."

The school was not itself in the last week before March Break; it was exam time, I had completed hearing all my performance exams ("You got a spare mouthpiece, Mr. Jackson? Mine's in my bag at home"..."We had to do what pieces?"..."What's a melodic minor scale, man? You never told us"...) and the place was like a tomb. I cleared away all the chairs and music stands in the band room for the cleaning crew, tidied up my desk, put my feet up, and thought furiously. There was much I loved about my job; many of my students were bright, motivated, and focused, a real pleasure to work with. We had great music to play and we played it well. Then, of course, there were those who inhabited a different planet, who would die a messy death if left on their own; there was the constant worry over a ninety-thousand dollar inventory of instruments, the niggling nuisances of making sure there were enough clarinet reeds and trying to keep order among those inspired with a gift for disorder. But I would have greater influence, I would have contact with our entire school system, I had sufficient background to be able to help other teachers; if God had called Father Oakley through Duke McLeod, perhaps He was calling me through Father Oakley. The answer had to be "yes"; the talk of the early nineties was of "career paths" and it looked as if mine would be a superhighway. Besides, there would be a modest salary increase, so between that, the professional confidence Father Oakley was showing in me, and the fact of an impending rendezvous with Suzi at my place that night made the world a beautiful place. I turned out the lights and locked the door; I was liberated, I was on vacation for a week. I drove out past a bus loading with students bound for a week of sunshine in Daytona Beach, refuelled the Kamikaze, and drove home to make my preparations. This was one March Break to get off to a rip-roaring start, with a bang, so to speak.

But, as with T.S. Eliot, it was more of a whimper than a bang. A distraught Suzi showed up in her office clothes and not the promised reprise of the highly-polished leather miniskirt. "Oh, sweetie!" she wailed. "I can't stay! He's taking me away!"

"Who? What? What the hell is going on?"

"I was just leaving the office and Phil phones and he says surprise, get home and pack your bag, we're going on a cruise on the something Princess, you know, one of those Love Boat things, and the plane leaves Toronto at 8:50 tonight. I can't believe it, all the times I begged the man to go and now when he wants to, I don't!"

"So tell him you don't want to."

"I can't do that! He sounded so excited and pleased with having arranged it. But I really wanted to be with you. I would have phoned, except Father Oakley was still there and could hear. Damn it to hell anyway!"

Damn it to hell indeed. So there I was, bereft of a week, intermittent to be sure, but nonetheless a week of passion, now wrenched from me. Actually, there would have been a gap in the form of a two-day visit to Anna and Hugo's with the girls in tow, and what was to be a gap turned into the focal point of that year's March Break.

The night of our arrival, after Katie and Evie were tucked safely away, I unburdened fully to Anna and Hugo about Suzi, including the stories in the preceding pages. Hugo listened with apparent sympathy; Anna quite lost control, fell laughing out of her armchair, and rolled about like one possessed.

"I thought you were my friend," I said with mock stiffness.

"I am...I swear it for all eternity...Hugo, are you taking notes on all this?"

"Oh, no, you don't!" said I. "This one's all mine. It won't have one of Hugo's snappy titles, but it's all mine."

A trip to Toronto was not complete for the girls without a trip to the Metro Zoo. Anna had a T.V. ad to do (Club Med, and the end result was out of this world) and Hugo a book signing at Eaton's (*The Nubile Nubians*), so we had a day to ourselves for zoo activity, and we headed eastwards towards Scarborough, across the Bloor Street Viaduct, which to Hugo was the edge of the known world. He had been to Egypt and Senegal, India and Sri Lanka, but never across the Viaduct.

One of the zoo buildings, the Village Edge, was a haven for nocturnal animals, and so was virtually dark, and before my eyes had a chance to adapt, I blundered straight into a woman and had to grab her to keep her from falling down. "Sorry," I blurted. "Are you all right?"

"Ken Jackson, you clumsy oaf!" Oh, no, surely it couldn't be Alien!

"Just kidding. It's Gianetta...Gianetta d'Av..."

"There is only one Gianetta," I said with a sincerity that I think was quite lost on her. My brain fought for something witty and intelligent to say. A slow loris goggled solemnly from behind the glass.

"Er, uh, meet my children. They're around here someplace..."

Gianetta was travelling solo; it turned out that she was, outside of her day job, an artist of exceptional merit and was making a day of sketching some of the animals in the zoo. Katie and Evie oohed and aahed over her drawings over hot chocolate at the McDonald's concession; not only was Gianetta beautiful, but with a compelling diversity of interests in which she took a wonderfully uncomplicated pleasure instead of regarding as the holiest of missions. Although previous exchanges had been of the utmost brevity, we chatted as if old friends, and on parting I pondered on the wisdom of phoning her. It was all very cordial, but there was still some kind of invisible barrier that suggested that talk about art, music, and animals would be as close as I would ever get. Whatever the barrier was, probably a lingering reluctance thanks to the unworthy Antonio, perhaps K.Y. Jackson could dissolve it through judicious caring, attention, perseverance. Anyway, there was still dear Suzi, soon to return from whatever great high-rise hideosity of a Love Boat she was on. If anyone were to be on a Love Boat with Suzi, it should have been me.

The end of March Break came, as always, far too soon. Well-bronzed children, who could afford a trip to Florida and I couldn't, surged into the school hallways, screaming, slamming locker doors, leaping at each other with hugs and kisses and giving souvenirs, although they had been parted for only a week. Working at the office full-time took on a new attraction.

The phone, oh, beautiful, sacred phone, bringer of glad tidings! Here it comes: "Oh, sweetie, oh, God, how I missed you! I almost went crazy! I think I'm in love." Think? I knew I was in love. "I don't know when I'll get to see you…"

"There's always the Shut-Eye Motel…"

"Oh, no, you don't! This is a wholesome, beautiful, spiritual relationship." (Oh, sure!) "I won't sully it and be like, well, you know who."

"Oh, you know about that?"

"Silly. Everybody does. We can do a lot better."

"Billiards tables and such."

"Exactly. I can't play billiards any more without getting wet to the knees. Shocked, sweetie? But it's true. It's happening just being on the phone with you. We'll get together first thing I can manage. Night-night." Waiting would be hard, but, I assured myself, how nice it was to have someone to wait for.

Big things began to happen come April. Auditions were to happen for the camp, which had now acquired the unofficial title of the Osterling Weekend. Father Oakley, smooth operator that he was, had been in New York at a musical trade show and met Eric Osterling, whose music for school ensembles was so much a fact (and a welcome one at that) of our lives. What sort of negotiation went on is to this day known only to Eric and Father Oakley, but it developed that Eric was to be in Toronto late in May to guest conduct the band of the Princess of Wales' Royal Canadian Heavy Artillery. Further, he was very interested to hear of our new camp and found himself commissioned to stay in Canada for an extra week and be with us as Composer-in-Residence. The news of this sent a shock wave of thrill the length and breadth of Birkenstock County, from Foulmouth to Crustacea, from Genepool to New Jamaica, just in time for auditions. Practising and preparation took place with an intensity matched only at exam time.

This was what the public saw. What they did not see was a coming battle of the giants, a titanic duel for supremacy between the two contenders for Father Oakley's position: Kenneth Yardley Jackson and Antonio Superbo Immaculato d'Averso.

"I'm toast!" I wailed to Father Oakley. "He'll walk all over me!"

"Calm down, kid. He's all flashy and flamboyant and so forth, but don't forget that number he pulled with the itinerants last November. I'm on the search committee and I will not hesitate to bring it up. Any right-thinking body would place integrity ahead of flash."

My life was an unbelievable clutter. There was my daily work. There were Katie and Evie. There was camp. There were insidious and persistent meditations on Gianetta. There was Suzi. And now this, well, one needed compound eyes to focus on it all.

Speaking of Suzi, there were two sizzlers in close succession. The requirements of our schools always went through a change each spring, once it was known how many students were to be enrolled in what subjects for the following year. Some schools would have vacancies, others surplus staff members, and the principals' staffing conferences were an annual ritual. The Principals' Staffing Conference of 1991 was also a golden opportunity for Suzi and me to take care of certain vacancies and surpluses.

Both exercises took place in my abode. There is nothing new or innovative to report on the physical end of things, besides which, descriptions of that sort of thing pale after a while. But after the second of these, Suzi became quite introspective as we lay together in the dark.

"You really are a sweetie," she said, "which is why I call you Sweetie. I can't help wondering about a life together for us."

"What? You mean divorce Phil?"

"I kind of hate the idea, especially after that cruise, but you're more my kind of guy. Your way isn't always the only way, you don't judge me because I just like simple, everyday things, and, well, you are absolutely amazing in bed!"

"Not bad for a latent homosexual."

"A what? You're not!"

"That's what Alien said. She had just bitched all the interest out of me and then said I was a latent homosexual."

"Oh, sweetie, she is wrong, wrong, wrong. She may have a giant brain and all, but she doesn't have any idea how to use it. I, on the other hand..."

To this point in *l'Affaire Suzi*, I had been quite content to have her whenever I could, but now the vacancy left by her departed bed-warmth was really starting to bother me; as well, I had genuinely missed her during March Break, and now her suggestion, tentative though it may have been, of a departure from

133

Phil, unleashed a giddy bubble of hope within me. My complete and unfeeling disregard for the possible emotional consequences for Phil bother me deeply in retrospect; I had undergone quite a profound sea-change in the schism from Alien, and it may well be that at the time I subconsciously wanted to punish Phil for having sired something as dreadful as she.

Suzi, out of operational necessity, was primarily a nocturnal occurrence. Daytimes held other considerations, the most prominent of which was what I hoped was my coming elevation to glory, to being what my colleague Dunstan Corrigan called being the Emir of Instrumental Music. The fact of "emir" oozing Islam was not a bother to Dunny; he just loved titles, the more esoteric the better.

My interview took place at 10:00 on a Friday morning, the kind of warm April morning when nature has stopped fooling around and teasing us with shirtsleeve weather one day and snow the next, the sort of morning when the birds are singing an ode to the sun and the rills of winter's run-off gurgle their way along the county road between Ringside and Umbrage. It was an omen. It had to be. The Almighty Himself, despite my multiple and unconfessed sins, was beaming benedictions upon me.

Neville, Father Oakley, and two principals (one each from the secondary and elementary segments of the system) formed the interview committee. I wore a suit Suzi had bought for me, I looked smart, I acted smart, I was smart. I was informed, I was urbane, I was confident, I was all the things I usually was not. I left the interview just knowing the job was mine, my self-assurance not in the least shaken by an incoming Antonio d'Averso as he passed me in the hall, a smirk glued to his face.

That evening, the phone rang. I picked it up. "Hi, sweetie!" I said brightly.

"Excuse me?" said Father Oakley.

"Oh, sorry, Father, I though it was somebody else."

"After what I have to tell you, you'll wish it were somebody else. There's no way to do this gently, but that son of a bitch Antonio got the job. I'm sorry, pal."

I sat speechless, numb with disappointment, with hurt, a much-needed triumph torn from my grasp.

Continued the Father, "I supported you to the hilt. Neville, the weasel, got sucked right in, as did the two principals. They were dazzled by all this international conducting, oh, and the guy is now a doctor of music, for God's sake. I didn't even know he'd been working on it. I don't even know when he'd have the time to work on it. I feel terrible, just awful. If the choice were mine and mine alone…"

"I know, Father. Thanks for calling."

The phone rang again. "Huh?"

"Oh, sweetie, I heard! I wanted to come and be with you, but I can't. Oops, gotta go. Night-night."

The phone rang a third time. I picked it up. "What?" I spat into it.

"Ken?"

"Yeah, that's me." I must have sounded sloppy and I didn't really care.

"It's Gianetta d'Averso."

"What? Who?"

"Gianetta d'Averso. From the zoo."

"Of course! I beg your pardon. Not really from the zoo, of course..."

"No, not born there or anything. Don't live there either. Ken, I heard what happened..."

"News travels fast."

"Israel phoned and told me. He was livid."

"I'll bet."

"So am I. I need to talk to you about this, and soon. Are you busy tomorrow?"

"Tomorrow. Oh, God, I nearly forgot. I have to go and work on a boat for my lawyer. She's up in Genepool."

"The lawyer?"

"No, the boat. The lawyer's a he. This is how I'm paying off a legal bill."

"You too, eh? Who's the lawyer?"

"Shelley Gallstone."

"He's first-rate, he took my divorce case against Himself. Will you be on your own? At the boat, I mean?"

"For the morning. Shelley's coming down in the afternoon."

"I really need to talk to you. I'll bring a thermos of coffee. Where will you be?"

"Box Brothers Marina, down at the end of Lonely Street."

"I'll be there. Tennish?"

"Tennish."

135

THE PLOT

I slept hardly at all. Mixed with the devastation over the new job, the worst I had suffered since the Schism, was raging speculation over Gianetta and the purpose of her call. Why me? Was my reversal a pretext for her to make a call she had wanted to make but was too shy? Why on Earth? And why so urgent?

Shelley's old Taylor cruiser was a beauty. Her name was *Shalom* and in a sense of tradition even more ancient than mine, her name was engrossed on either side of her flying bridge in both English and in Hebrew. For the first time in several years, I donned my paint-and-Sikaflex-smeared work suit, put a dust mask over my nose, on went the safety goggles and a Royal Canadian Navy safety helmet that Phil had given me and that had been condemned by Alien as yet another example of my bloated pretensions.

I put up a ladder to *Shalom,* rigged an extension cord for my lights, heat gun and power sander; I readied my scrapers and other tools, I was alive again, I was the Real Me. A car door slammed outside the storage shed and my whole nervous system went on full alert.

"Ken, are you there?" called the voice I had loved even before I really knew it.

"Over here, Gianetta. I look horrible. This is the Real Me. Hope it doesn't put you off."

"Oh, well, just look at you. There is a certain rustic charm. You are definitely dressed for the job. I'll just sit on this wood thing and talk while you work. Here's some coffee."

"Thanks." I said, trying to keep the flutter out of my voice. "Now, what's up?"

"You got screwed is what's up. I can't stand this any more. I lived Antonio's damned lies for ten years, I've been hurt, now you've been hurt, and I can't stand it any more."

136

Heat gun and scrapers forgotten, I sat down on *Shalom's* foredeck. "I'm listening," I said.

"Tell me what you know of Antonio's background."

"Oh, well, some diploma from the Bologna something, degrees from the University of...what the hell was it, Bari? International conducting engagements, although John Oakley tells me that's really his band trips..."

"Precisely. The University of Bari. It's a postbox number, nothing more. You send money, you get a degree. He's got all three. And the Bologna Collegium Musicum is the same sort of thing. There is a Bologna Conservatory and it's damn good, but this ain't it. Bologna! Baloney is more like it."

"What! You mean he never studied, he never..."

"No!"

"Well, how the hell did he pull off that stuff with the Philharmonic, then? He must have done something right."

"Know who the Chairman or woman of the Philharmonic Board of Directors is?"

"Last I heard, it was Ms. Hook." Ida Hook was a formidable lady lawyer, crusader for women's rights, and a partner in the local law firm of Hook, Lyon, and Sinclair.

"It still is Ms. Hook. And dear Antonio reached his exalted position via the knickers of Ms. Hook, but that's another story. The issue here is that his credentials are, at most, worth the paper they're printed on. They mean nothing. He has a pass degree in General Arts that got him into teaching and all the others are these funny store-bought things. But nobody ever checked. I found the financial statements for them in a desk drawer once when we were doing income tax and he actually threatened bodily harm if I ever told anyone. Then the bastard started crowing about how funny it all was and how he was taking everybody for a ride and he wasn't finished yet."

Gianetta was turning pink with agitation. I think I was too, but not for the same reason.

"So, fundamentally, he's a fraud," I said as evenly as I could. "I have a legitimate Music Specialist certificate and he doesn't."

"You've got it. And there was that stunt he pulled hiring itinerants for the *Symphonie Fantastique*..."

"...which, sorry to report, was tremendous. The bugger must know something about music..."

"You would be surprised how little he really does know," said Gianetta. "First of all, he can read a score only enough to know where he is..."

"What!"

137

"His gift is a phenomenal memory. He can hear something a few times and know it. The thing is, though, that he just regurgitates somebody else's performance. There's nothing at all of him in it. That's why he cleaves to the great masters. You'll never find him doing anything that hasn't been recorded. He'd be sunk."

"This has to be the height of charlatanism!" I snorted. "What an operator! It reminds me of an old movie, *The Great Impostor*, Tony Curtis, let's see..."

"I have both seen and lived that movie. I want you to do something for both of us. I want you to blow the whistle on this creep and I want you to do it, not only because you have been wronged big-time, but because it will carry more weight from you. If I did it, it would be perceived as the bitchy ex-wife seeking revenge."

"You bitchy? Never!"

Gianetta gave me a wicked smile. "You don't know me. In fact, you don't really know who I am."

"What do you mean?"

"My real name is Janet Harwood. And Antonio's real name, believe it or not, is Anthony Adverse, he is from Campbell River, B.C., and he has never set foot in Italy. He went all Italian, which he can't speak, by the way, and tried to force me to do the same. I actually look Italian, but I was damned if I was going to do the phoney accent as well. But he did it round the clock, even when we were making love..."

I nearly fell off *Shalom's* foredeck.

"Are you okay, Ken?"

"Oh, er, fine. All right. I'll talk to John Oakley, who would be deliriously happy to help. He hates Antonio to the marrow."

"I have to go now," said Gianetta abruptly. "Thanks so much for doing this. Call me." She started for the shed door.

"Oh, here, let me walk you to your car."

"That's okay. No need to get down. See you later."

I was left with a swimming head. Suzi was fun, passionate, and quite empty-headed. Gianetta was gorgeous, mysterious, and hugely intelligent. Gianetta, in retrospect, attracted me for the same reasons Alien had, although the thought did not occur to me at the time. But in my confused and jumbled passions, I retreated to the world of teendom, trying to extract meaning out of a peculiar assortment of utterances from Gianetta. Why wouldn't she let me walk her out of the boat shed? It was no big deal just to jump down. But then the way she said "Call me"? There was something more than mere business at work, I was certain of it.

I phoned Father Oakley that evening and told him of my findings. He nearly, as the young people say, went ballistic. "He'll get fired! He'll get sued! He's been paid for having these degrees. Oh, the son of a bitch. You busy Monday afternoon?"

"I have a rehearsal."

"Cancel it. You and I are going to pay a visit to Myles Kenwood in Personnel. He will be very interested in this."

Myles Kenwood was indeed very interested. He was formidable-looking, Nordic and angular, so Nordic, in fact, that a couple of those awful Aryan superiority outfits had been all but grovelling for him to become a member. For Myles, it was a major embarrassment, but would not hesitate to act Nordic whenever he had to, and we knew he would be more than a match for Antonio when the time came.

Myles listened to us with little comment, no expression, and much taking of notes. I began to feel a bit prickly; I prefer being spoken to rather than having notes taken right in my face.

"So that's the story," said Father Oakley. "Now, what are you going to do about it?"

For a challenge like that, Myles would have asked anyone else to leave. But he was dealing with Father Oakley. "First, Mr. d'Averso has disqualified himself for the position here at the office. That much is clear."

Hope resonated in my chest. I felt like a little kid in Grade 1, hand in air, arm stretched to the limit, saying, "Pick me, pick me!"

Myles smiled glacially. "Yes, Ken, you'll get it, but kindly wait until confirmation. Damn, d'Averso's letter of confirmation went out this morning. Oh, well. I'd like to fire him, but the union would be all over me. What I think I can do, though, is restrict him from any promotion or even transfer within this board. And I will certainly require repayment of the extra allowance he has been collecting for these so-called degrees. I do not like being scammed. I just can't understand why nobody checked in the first place, but I wasn't Superintendent when he came aboard. I've just assumed everything was kosher."

Father Oakley took me to dinner that night for what he cautioned should be a "tentative celebration". His elation at cornering Antonio was such that he wore a suit, commanded me to do the same, and said the sky was the limit on the menu. "Eat up, kid, whatever you want," was his instruction. I took him literally and quite made a hog of myself; while he ate sparingly of salad and fruit, I had a steak so enormous that it hung out over the edge of the plate like a rubbery awning, followed by some chocolate thing that had the lining of my stomach creaking in protest.

Other parts of me creaked in protest as well. For once, I could freely and legitimately call Suzi at home. I could also freely and legitimately call Gianetta. The twinge of excitement about the latter hovered about the edges of guilt; given a simple choice between the two, I could not be sure which path I would take. Suzi at least I knew, although with time I was under no illusion that sexual ingenuity was finite and once it had worn itself out, where would we be? Gianetta would be fascinating company, sexually she was uncharted territory, what she would be like on a day-to-day basis I could only guess. Experience had taught me that fascination can mean trouble.

Bloated almost beyond endurance, I let myself in to my premises over the Meteor Meatier Eatery, which was in embarrassingly full cry, to make my phone calls. I elected to make Suzi my first errand.

"Sweetie, what happened?"

I gave a fullish account of that afternoon's meeting. "Oh, sweetie, that's wonderful. Oh, and we can work together every day and have working luncheons, oh, and I'll be your secretary..." Suzi was becoming charmingly breathless. "We'll have to tell Phil..."

"What? About us?"

"No, silly. He'll need a new music director."

"I'll have to talk to him, but I'll do it at school."

"He's out tonight. Want to come over?"

"Better not. I have another call to make..."

"A woman?"

"Ginanetta d'Averso."

"She's single. Watch out."

"You're married. Watch out even more." I was meaning to be funny, but it didn't work. There was a wistful sigh.

"I'm getting a bit confused," said Suzi. "Phil has been so attentive since the cruise. He's been bringing flowers home and we've had wine in bed and candles going and then made love..."

"Suzi, I shouldn't be hearing this."

"But it's amazing. He's turning into a tiger. He bought some rope at a boat store and showed me all these fancy knots and next thing I knew I was all tied up and, oh, my God, there's something so erotic about being absolutely helpless and there's something so erotic about telling you this, oh, oh, he's home now. Night-night."

It took some time to recover from Suzi's inverse verbal voyeurism, and as I did so, I tried to work out some means of phoning Gianetta without her hearing the thumping and banging from the Meteor. I did not wish to be embarrassed by my low surroundings. The phone cord was long enough to reach into a closet. I retreated like an animal into a cave and dialled the call that I had dreamed of making for the last three years. One ringy-dingy, I though absurdly. Ernestine the phone operator. Another ringy-dingy. Good Lord, Ernestine was about twenty-five years ago. A third ringy-dingy. Oh, please answer! *Laugh-In*, the show was called. A fourth ringy-dingy, and then the answering machine: "This is 464-2811. We (we?) can't come to the phone right now. Please leave a message and we'll (we?) phone you right back. Wait for the beep." Oh, she spoke with such class, her t's enunciated perfectly, whoops, there was the beep. I left a message and then retired, feeling both let down and apprehensive. Was this an editorial or a plural "we" that I was dealing with? One never knew these days, and the more I thought of it, the more I knew I wanted to know Gianetta.

Belatedly, I realized the stupidity of phoning Gianetta on a Monday night. She would have been rehearsing with the Ouentaron Symphony and wouldn't be home until late, well, I would just have to wait until Tuesday, what is this, the phone is ringing, although it's well after eleven. I had been asleep already and picked it up, trying to shake the cobwebs out of my head.

"Hello?" I said, trying not to sound querulous.

"Hi, Ken, it's Gianetta. You sound as if I had woken you up."

"Oh, no," I lied. "Wide awake here. I have some neat stuff to tell you. Sit down."

"Don't need to. I'm in bed." My toes curled. What was she wearing, if anything? Was anyone else there? I strained to listen for evidence as I talked.

I reported the interview with Myles Kenwood, the confirmation of the illegitimacy of Antonio's credentials, the limitations to promotion and transfer, the requirement of payback of his allowance for extra degrees. Silence. "Gianetta? You still there?"

"Yes," kind of distantly. And then, "Ken, you're a hero. You've brought our friend Ozymandias crashing to the desert sand, just like in the poem." I could hear a faint rustle of bedclothes over the phone.

"As soon as this is a done deal, let's celebrate and have dinner. That is, if you're in a position to accept social invitations."

"Yes, that would be nice. I have to go now. Call me."

There it was again, almost a brush-off. And yet she had accepted my dinner invitation. But why had she rung off so abruptly? This I did not like.

The life of K.Y. Jackson that spring had an extraordinary number of facets to it, which in tabulated form was like this:

1. The daily routine at school.
2. Meetings and errands relative to the new music camp.
3. Such weekends that I could engineer with Katie and Evie.
4. The destruction of Antonio.
5. The pursuit of Gianetta.
5. Continued activities with Suzi.

Of my daily routine, the less said the better. Although I was very attached to my students, their continual company all day every day was wearing thin and, once my appointment to the office was confirmed, I truly looked forward, although it would not be until the autumn term, to working in an adult environment. And even with Phil Quail in command of a Catholic high school, the hallway atmosphere was degenerating into an industrial clangour of locker doors and screaming girls. They never screamed about anything in particular. They just screamed.

Of the meetings and errands, the errands were by far the more fun. Father Oakley wanted to acquire some new music for the camp and arranged to borrow me from school for a day for a shopping trip in Toronto. One of the major dealers, Gareth V. Thomas, was having a going-out-of-business sale, so, like a couple of vultures, we descended on their store in quest of whatever bargains we could find, and find them we did.

Virtually the only discord in Father Oakley's and my relationship hinged on transcriptions, which is to say music arranged for band from other performing media, particularly orchestra. G.V. Thomas had a whole pile of it, some of which was just being given away, and I thought how happy Israel Bond would be.

While Father Oakley was rounding up "legitimate" band music by Alan Hovhaness, Samuel Barber, Alfred Reed, and Francis MacBeth, I was happily rooting through dusty, yellowed boxes, rhapsodizing, "Look, Father, here's the first movement of the Brahms G Minor Quartet...("You have to be kidding")...*Procession of the Nobles*...("well, that's okay")...oh, look, Grieg's C Minor Symphony..."

"Look, kid, that's taking bastardization a bit far. Grieg expressly forbade performance of the damn thing. Are you about to violate Grieg's wishes?"

"It's for Israel. He got screwed. Antonio's still doing the orchestra at camp..."

"Thanks to that unprincipled son of a bitch Neville."

"...and I want to make it as nice as I can for him. He's our ally."

"You'll be seeing Antonio at the director's meeting next Thursday. Should be interesting."

"Yeah," I said tonelessly. This would be our first meeting since the Fall of Antonio and the Rise of K.Y. Jackson. K.Y. Jackson, though completely in the right, was not looking forward to it. He knew only too well Antonio's powers of bombast and intimidation.

Something funny happened to the Brahms Quartet (for band!) and the Grieg Symphony on the way back to Birkenstock. I never saw them, as well as a few allied works, ever again. I am sure Father Oakley hid them, although he denies it. I can only be sure if he swears on the memory of the Holy Virgin, the only tactic I have not tried on him.

The third Thursday of each month was always a disruption to my office routine. It was also an interruption to Neville's regular and systematic program of Angiograms. The third Thursday was the monthly meeting of secondary-level music directors from all over the Birkenstock County Roman Catholic School Board. The third Thursday of April, 1991, was High Noon for me and Antonio.

I'd hoped to deal with Antonio before the meeting, assuming he would even be there. If he were at all decent, simple shame should have kept him away. But he was not decent, he was there, and I was late. "Buon giorno," he nodded at me, keyboard smile at full power.

The bulk of the meeting had to do with the Osterling Weekend and need not be recounted here. The bonfires of the vanities burned brightly indeed for me as my promotion was announced; in fact, the bonfires still burn brightly enough for me to include that golden moment in my tale. And then adjournment came and my moment of confrontation was at hand. I took Antonio aside. Fighting a wobble in my voice, I said, "Antonio, there's something you should know. I take full responsibility for what happened. Gianetta, in case you were wondering, had nothing to do with it…"

"What'a you did'a was'a reprehensible," pronounced Antonio.

"And what you did wasn't?"

Gianetta appeared magically at my elbow; I think she must have been just outside the meeting room door. In any event, she lit into Antonio, usurping completely my role as avenging angel. "You snake-in-the-grass!" she hissed. "It's time somebody tore the wraps off you."

"This is'a costing'a me a great'a deal of'a money."

"Obtained under false pretences, which you know and I know and Ken knows and everybody knows, so let's not try to kid around. How you can even show your face around here baffles me completely. And talk proper English for a change, for God's sake. Whatever you get, you deserve. Let's go, Ken."

"Hoho, you make'a da girlfriend, heh, K.Y.? She's a wild one, doesn't'a know her place…"

"Neither do you. This sucks the big one. I'm out of here," I snapped.

Charlie Cowell happened to be in the office and as I passed through, he said, "Oh, K.Y., you're such a rebel! You're starting to sound like me. Better you should sound like you. More class."

In being out of there, I had rudely and unintentionally abandoned Gianetta; I had made my point, made a dignified if uncouth withdrawal, but Gianetta had changed her mind about leaving and had a few more things to say, the blistering echoes of which I could hear as I left the office for the cool twilight of an April evening.

The phone was ringing as I entered my divinely-smelling-of-steak abode. "Hello."

'Ken, it's Gianetta. You're stupendous! Are you free for a victory dinner tomorrow night?"

"Well, I do believe I am. I'll pick you up at, what, six?

"Perfect. See you then." Filled with helium happiness, I hung up the phone, which rang even before I had my hand off it.

"Hi, sweetie!"

"Oh, uh, hey, Suzi! How the hell are you?"

"Well, that was a strange greeting, like I'm one of the boys."

"Sorry, just surprised."

"Charlie phoned and said you did a pretty good number on Antonio."

"Nothing compared to the number that got done on Antonio by Gianetta. She was still at it when I left."

"Well, good, whoever did the number," said Suzi. "I never did care for that man. What're you up to tomorrow night?"

Oh, God! "I, er, have a, um, dinner date."

"A dinner date? Sweetie, I, oh, how can I complain, I'm married, oh, this is a nightmare," and she began to weep.

"Suzi, it's nothing. It's just (just?) Gianetta. We're going to nastily and vindictively celebrate the downfall of the great Antonio. That's all. It isn't anything at all." Like hell it wasn't. I loved Suzi, but as of this moment I was in love with Gianetta, and there is a more than subtle difference. But I have a major flaw in that I prefer to say what people want to hear, hence my dismissal of the importance of my date with Gianetta. The weeping stopped.

"Phil's out of town for part of the evening. I wanted to come over."

"Well, uh…"

"I want you so badly, sweetie. I can't go more than twenty-four hours. Tell you what, leave your spare key under your doormat. I'll be there for you when you get home. I'm going to be an animal."

"Leopard or zebra?"

"Neither. Just straight woman. Whoops, gotta go. Toodles."

Two women in one evening. Not bad for a lay-tent ho-mo-sexual. But as with previous dealings with Gianetta, the evening was curiously inconclusive. Gianetta phoned in mid-afternoon to say she would be delayed at school and would meet me at the restaurant. So much for calling for her like a gentleman and escorting her home after dinner, being invited in, perhaps some amorous overtures and laying of plans for the future. But the date was still on and K.Y. was still in business.

We did have a couple of very pleasant hours together, talking about the camp, about music, about art, literature, history, and all the other things that Suzi found such a bore. Being informed was not Suzi's long suit; for Gianetta, it was a way of life. Suzi was an open book; Gianetta was a fascinating enigma, oh, beware of fascination, K.Y.!

Over dessert, Gianetta said, "Ken, I really meant it when I called you a hero. Nobody has ever gone to bat for me like that before."

"That's very kind of you, but I was going to bat for me too."

"But you didn't have to disclaim involvement on my part. I set Antonio straight on that. I didn't think you should have to take all the heat."

"I didn't. I was out of there too quick."

Gianetta laughed.

"What?" I said.

"What you said about it sucking the big one. It stopped him right in his tracks." She looked me with those wonderful black eyes. "What do you suppose the big one is, anyway?"

I dropped my fork, blushing furiously. Gianetta laughed again, but only fleetingly. "Thanks for dinner, Ken. This was really nice. I have to go now, but I'll see you, oh, I guess at camp."

Camp! That was still two months off. Oh, sooner, please, Holy Mary. "Sooner, I hope," I said, prompted by the Mother of All Sorrows, with whom by this time I had a remarkable rapport.

"Call me. Thanks again." An arid handshake in the parking lot, and Gianetta was on her way. I felt stunned. Hero one moment, crumb the next. And it wasn't even eight o'clock; the sun had not set, the birds were chirping, a tractor growled and sputtered in a near-by field. I had a horrid feeling that she might have been on her way to another date; how on Earth to find out? Still in my stupefied state, I set sail for the Meteor Meatier Eatery and home, a bit of a drive since the chosen restaurant was on the outskirts of Panacea, a drive in which the only thing I could think of at all was Gianetta d'Averso.

THE INFERNO

I let myself in and immediately sensed something strange; there was a smell like pine and a sort of vapour through the place, a faint slosh of water, dear Lord, I had clean forgotten about Suzi! The scent, the vapour, and a judiciously-placed trail of intimate garments guided me in a matter of seconds to the bathroom, which had been completely transformed. A black shag rug covered the floor and ran up the outside of the bathtub. The only light was from a gold candlestick at each corner of the bath. And there, in a great mound of suds, was dear Suzi. No enigma, she. "Hi, sweetie," she whispered. "I missed you. Come into the bath with me. I have some champagne here."

Almost numbly, I got rid of my clothes, Gianetta being reluctantly but certainly displaced from my psyche, and slid into the warm, pine-scented water, face-to-face with my erstwhile mother-in-law. She pulled herself up a bit to make more room for me and a bouquet of suds skated down her ample cleavage, guided to a perfect centre by the topography. Her foot found its way underneath me. My foot found its way underneath her. We drank champagne.

"Penny for your thoughts," said Suzi. The heat, the champagne, the angst over Gianetta, the thought of hurting Suzi in any way, all converged on me at once, and I became quite choked up.

"Sweetie, what is it?"

But rather than try to explain it all, I resorted to my formula of saying what I thought was what desired to be heard. "I love you," I blurted. It was not a lie, just a gross simplification. But it was like throwing meat to a dog. Suzi surged forward, trying to envelope me, but we were so slippery that all we did was thrash around, myself shipping water up my nose in the process. I coughed wetly and leapt out of the tub in a great shower of spray, extinguishing three of the four candles. A sleekly gleaming Suzi threshed after

147

me; somehow she ended up perched on the washstand and the games began, her head banging the mirror and cracking it, she wrapped her legs around me and held me to her, I was her prisoner but I wanted no part of escape, she was a heavenly shishkebab impaled upon the skewer of my ardour, the forces were building now, as surely as the rising of the tide, so great was the intensity that we felt as if engulfed in flames. Our bodies spent, we slid in a slippery heap to the floor, how remarkable, there were still flames, oh, shit, the shower curtain had caught fire from the last candle!

I tore the bathroom door open for escape and the burning curtain, under the inward rush of oxygen, erupted into a great, belching fireball, like something from the second circle of Hell. Pursued thus by the flames of carnal sin, we dove for cover and I slammed the door shut, hoping the fire might extinguish itself. But the glow through the crack under the door brightened, the grey haze permeated my quarters. I had no option but to call the Birkenstock Fire Department.

The Fire Department was right next door, guaranteeing a response time of about ninety seconds. In that time, I had to hide Suzi in a closet that had to be almost emptied to accommodate her; there was barely enough time, and then in the mayhem, I could not find my bathrobe (it was in the bathroom and in the process of burning). In fact, the only garment that came to hand was a wispy pair of panties belonging to Suzi. Plainly, they would not do, especially with the fire crew pounding at the door. I grabbed a blanket off my bed, wrapped myself up like someone in a western movie, and answered the door.

In marched the fire brigade with fire extinguishers, brandishing axes, unreeling hoses. The hoses remained at the ready; the bathroom door was chopped down and after a few foggy blasts with the fire extinguisher, it was all over. The firemen gathered their equipment together, the indignant diners from the Meteor Meatier Eatery who had been turned out into the street returned to their tables, and my landlord (and owner of the Meteor), Feodor Gregorovich Ignyshyn, was in full cry, pacing up and down, flailing a gnarled forefinger and crying "Out! Out!"

"Sir, try to calm down," said the young policeman, come to, oh, God, investigate.

"I kennot calm down. Ziss young idiot hass tried to burn the place down…"

"I'm sure nobody tried to burn it down, sir. I'll talk to you in a minute. Now, sir" (to me), "I need your name."

I swallowed. "Kenneth Y. Jackson."

The constable's pencil paused in mid-air. "Mr. Jackson! I had you in Grades Nine and Ten, well, I failed in Ten, played trombone…you probably don't remember me, Connor Clark is my name. My younger sister Kimberley is one of your students."

"Oh, for heaven's sake! Oh, I remember you, Connor. I got you suspended for drinking pina colada out of a trombone mute during the spring concert."

"I had to do it, sir. I was so terrified of being on stage, it was the only way I could get through it."

"In-flight refuelling, as it were."

"Something like that. Now, Mr. Jackson, how did the fire start?"

"In the bathroom. I, uh, had a candle going and it caught the shower curtain."

"Ouch! A candle, Mr. Jackson? Please show me." With Feodor tailgating us, we had a look at the bathroom.

"Oy!" lamented Feodor. "Like Stalingrad. You stoopid, Kennet."

Connor shone a flashlight around the dark and blackened bathroom, looking speculatively at the shag rug, the champagne bottle and glasses, and the heat-wilted candles. His eyebrows rose. "You weren't alone, were you, Mr. Jackson?"

"Um, no."

"A bordello," growled Feodor. "Sinning under my very roof…"

Connor's pencil did little circles over his notepad, like an investigative divining rod. "Who was with you?"

"Connor, if I told you, my career would be over and there would be a messy divorce action with me in the middle."

"You did get me suspended, Mr. Jackson."

Connor, aside from the pina colada, had been something of a nemesis for me, constantly unprepared, inattentive, a prolific skipper of classes. And here he was now, majestic in uniform and with power over a functionally naked K.Y. Jackson.

"Connor, if I could un-suspend you, if I could be an academic bungee cord, I would. But I can't. All I can do is ask your discretion, you know, just between us boys."

"Okay, Mr. Jackson. But you are going to owe me. I don't know how at the moment, but I'll think of something."

"Do you have a boat?"

"Yes, in fact, I do."

"Is she wood?"

"Yes, in fact she is."

"Complete varnish and paint. Totally free."

"Deal. For the record, your bathroom light burned out, you had no spare, and used a candle. It was an accident."

"Bless you, Connor."

"Bordello," snorted Feodor, trying the bathroom light by way of challenge. Luckily, the bulb had exploded from the heat.

There was a knock at the door. To my uncomprehending horror, it was Phil. Suzi's "things" were still arranged for the same purpose as Hansel and Gretel's breadcrumbs, with the obvious drawback in this instance of being far more visible.

"Are you okay, Ken? I was passing by and saw the police cruiser and some of the fire guys out front. What happened?"

I stayed in the doorway, hoping to keep Suzi's clothes out of sight. "Oh, I'm okay. Just a little shaken up. Light burned out in the bathroom and I had no spare bulb, so I used a candle and the damn thing tipped over."

Feodor cleared his throat so comprehensively that he sounded as if to have consumption.

Phil sniffed at the air like an old hound. "Pretty thick in here." Oh, esteemed father-in-law, if you only knew! "Why don't you stay with us until it's all aired out and repaired? Why am I asking? Suzi would never forgive me if you didn't. Therefore, as your principal, I am ordering you to come."

"Oh, now, Phil…"

"Just do it. I'd better get home and mobilize Suzi to get the spare room ready for you. Just take your time, bring anything that needs washing."

Everything needed washing, but that was the least of my concerns. Once Feodor and Connor were on their way, I had to deal with Suzi. She was in a panic. "Oh, sweetie, all my clothes smell of smoke. What am I going to do?"

"Phone Phil and tell him you were here just after he was and you helped me clean up. That'll explain the smell."

"I want you again. That was absolutely the greatest—"

"No time."

"Maybe while you're staying with us, if Phil goes out—"

"Suzi, for God's sake! We came too close for comfort!"

"But didn't we just come!"

I was becoming annoyed. I had come within centimetres of a scandal from which neither of us would have ever recovered, a scandal that would have affected Evie and Katie, and what they would have thought, Daddy and Big Sister Grandma Suzi going at it in a burning bathroom, eclipsed my worst fantasies.

"Just phone Phil and tell him we're on our way."

"You're angry with me." She pouted.

"Don't be silly. I'm just recovering from a slightly bad scare."

Suzi phoned Phil with the story that, well, it was the funniest thing, she had just passed through a few minutes after him, and so forth. She actually did all the cleaning up and organizing of my clothes, most of which were smoked up and in need of laundering, while I got some clothes on and went below to mend fences with Feodor the landlord and start getting things sorted out with respect to insurance. The whole process took sufficiently long for the explanation of Suzi's smoky garments to be logical and reasonable.

Naturally, I had to be punished for my sins. That is part of being a Roman Catholic. If Suzi were Catholic, which she wasn't, she too would have been punished, not only for carnal knowledge of someone not her husband, but carnal knowledge of someone besides her husband. Not only was Suzi not punished, she was the instrument of my own punishment. Lying in bed that night, I had to listen to her ravishing and defiling Commander Philip Horatio Quail, R.C.N.R., Principal of Misericordia High School, and, still on paper, my father-in-law. Absurdly, I felt as if Suzi were cheating on me, especially when Commander Philip, who raised his voice only in the most exceptional circumstances, cried out at the moment of truth, warbling and whinnying.

CALLING IN THE MARKERS

I never did have to do anything on Police Constable Clark's boat. It would have been a pleasure—she was a 1967 Mason—but time was running short, there was so much to do both at school and at camp, and it turned out that I was able to do him a much more significant favour.

On the Tuesday morning after the great Meteor Meatier Eatery fire, I was in the school office and was stranded there for the national anthem and morning announcements. There were the usual things: after-school team practices, a Rugby game at Golgotha High (bus leaving at 2:30 and don't miss it), cancellation of the weekly meeting of the Hieroglyphics Club, tickets on sale for the upcoming video dance sponsored by CKUP-TV, and winner of the Music Camp lottery. Music Camp lottery? I knew nothing of any such lottery.

I looked at the announcement form and noted the signature with more than casual interest. It had been signed by Kimberley Clark, the sister of Constable Connor. Kimberley was in my Period 1 class, following which I asked her into my office.

"About this lottery," I said. Kimberley blushed a crimson so deep as to be on the brink of burgundy. "If anyone should know about this lottery, it should be me. I'm helping to run the camp and I know everything. Except this. Please explain."

Kimberley was a Canadian Everyman's dream. She was petite and pneumatic all at once, with short blonde hair, blue eyes, a great smile, a look of wholesome sensuality. But now she was shaking like an aspen in a high wind. "It's just a, er, little lottery I was running on my own. I didn't have enough money for the final payment for camp and I couldn't ask my mum for more. She's on her own…"

"Oh, I see. Well, why didn't you see me if you had a problem?"

152

"Well, I, uh, well, we know about you and Mrs. Jackson and I figured you had enough to worry about. I didn't want to bother you."

"Regardless of my personal circumstances, and I do appreciate your consideration, I'm still your teacher and I'm still trying to do my job. You didn't need to feel that way. Did you have any authorization from Mr. Quail?"

"No."

"We'll call it a sin of omission. I'll talk to him. I know him rather well."

Kimberley's breath escaped in a great, gum-flavoured whoosh of relief. She started to get up.

"He'll need to know what was offered by way of a prize."

Kimberley returned to her burgundy mode as if I had pressed a button. She shook from head to toe, making little gurgling noises. I thought she was having an attack of epilepsy.

"Kimberley, what is it, dear? Are you all right?"

"Oh, please, Mr. Jackson, I'll be ruined!"

"What was it, then, some sort of scam?" I asked sharply. It was far too soon for another scandal. "Was there a prize?"

"Oh, yes, there certainly was. Is."

"So what's the problem? What's the prize?"

"Me."

"You? What do you mean?"

"You're going to hate me."

"I doubt it. Look, you're a first-rate student and you must really want to go to camp to, uh, whatever you did. We can deal with this if you'll tell me what we're dealing with."

"I sold tickets only to boys and the prize is me."

"The prize is you, as in…"

"Yes. Sex."

"Kimberley, I'm going to get you out of this. I'll tell Mr. Quail that you made a mistake and didn't get clearance and the boys will all get their money back. Well, I won't say boys. We have enough money in the department's account that I can cover you and you can make it back helping me clean up and sort music at the end of the year."

"Oh, thank you so, so muuuch, Mr. Jackson. I owe you for this."

"That's okay. I happen to owe your brother a favour, so this is a way of making it up, at least to your family. That, as far as I am concerned, is the end of it." Unfortunately, it wasn't.

I thought I was handling the whole thing rather smoothly. Officially, it was announced that, through an error of omission, the lottery was cancelled and all ticket-holders could get a refund at the music office. Naturally, most of the would-be-winners had thrown away their tickets when the actual and real winner was announced, and this caused complications, as the prize had been so sought-after that Kimberley did not even know some of the buyers and could not identify them by name. So, in the interests of honour and benefit of the doubt, my petty cash account ended up with a shortfall of fifty-eight dollars.

But the winner, an obstreperous Grade 12 percussionist named Slobodan Djokic, elected to be difficult. We had got off on the wrong foot when I took attendance for his first Grade 9 class and had pronounced his name as "Jock-itch."

"Hey, look, man," said Slobodan, said he. "I won fair and square. I wanna collect my prize."

"Slob," I said patiently, "there is no lottery and there is no prize. Forget about it."

"No, man, I'm not. Do you know what the prize was, Mr. Jackson?"

"No," I lied.

"Well, it was Miss Kimberley Clark herself. I'm gonna collect."

The horror was mounting toward the danger zone, but I remained calm. "Slob, I think you'd rather not. For one thing, Miss Clark's brother is a constable on the Birkenstock Police Force and if anything happened, the finger points straight from him to you. Not a good idea, my friend."

"You can't do that to me!"

"Do what? I haven't done anything to you, except give you some advice. You're on the brink of failing. If you stay away from Kimberley and say nothing to anyone, I think we can arrange a pass for you, provided, of course, that you make an honest effort."

Slobodan shook his head. "Oh, man!" he muttered and shambled out.

THE HOLIEST OF ALL

Slobodan Jokic had the good sense to make the right moves and actually showed up to participate in the Misericordia High School spring concert; he had a lamentable record for "forgetting" or "not knowing" or "having to work, man", but took his final opportunity to make amends, ensure a pass, and not create a scandal over Kimberley Clark, whom I was seeing in quite a new and exciting light.

Even though the spring concert was essentially my farewell to the Miserable Accordion before taking up my new duties, it took something of a back seat to other events. There was, of course, the camp. An enormous amount of work had been going forward: contracts for the junior administration and instructors, records of payments from the campers, endless lists of equipment and supplies, the engagement of Panama Van Lines for transportation, almost daily phone calls to Anna and/or Hugo.

Poor Charlie was just about run ragged. I was now in the office more than just on Thursday afternoons, just to keep up, and one day (not a Thursday, but Neville was out anyway), I walked in to find both Sweet Marie and Suzi just sitting.

"Huh?" I said.

"Listen, Sweet One," said Sweet Marie. Charlie had a desk behind one of the adjacent partitions. Charlie was singing to himself, something that sounded like Waltzing Matilda, but with certain modifications:

"Walking the X-Ray, walking the X-Ray,

Won't you...hell!...come a-walking the X-Ray with meeee...aw, screw this thing..

And he sat on his ass and waited while his pecker boiled,

Won't you...God damn it!...come a-walking the X-Ray with me."

155

"Charlie, what's the matter?" called Suzi. "Do you need a hand?" She winked lewdly at me.

"I'm trying to key in this camp manual and the fool thing won't paginate."

Suzi and I converged to help Charlie, well, in reality, Suzi to help and me to offer moral support. "Now, let's see what the problem is," said Suzi.

"Charlie's having problems with his pagina," I remarked helpfully.

Charlie's chair tipped over as he leapt up, grabbed me, and gave me a whiskery kiss on the lips. "That's it, man, when you talk like that, I just can't handle it. Makes me go all crazy inside." Suzi gaped with astonishment and perhaps a little envy. She did, however, succeed in fixing Charlie's "paginal problem" and peace reigned once more.

An event reared its head in early May, doubtless calculated to steal some of the spotlight from everything else; it was the season's closing of the Birkenstock Philharmonic Society, Antonio Immaculato Superbo d'Averso, Music Director and Sole Conductor, for no guest was to ever darken the rostrum. Visiting artists were to be the All-County Choir (Angela Rumley, Director) and the choir from nearby Annville (the Annville Chorus, Sister Ingrid Harrington, Director). Four soloists had been engaged from the Canadian Opera Co. and the orchestra was to be augmented, thanks to the deep pockets of Ms. Hook, with whom Antonio was now living.

Aside from the physical mass of the performing organization, which only the local arena was capable of accommodating, what set this aside from the usual was that Antonio was to conduct a new work in its world premiere.

This was an ideal pretext to phone Gianetta. "Hello. You have reached 464-2811." How was it possible to bring sensuality to mere numbers? "We (we?) can't come to the phone right now, but at the sound of the beep, please leave a message and we'll (we?) get back to you." Oh, hell, it was a Monday again!

Eleven p.m. The phone rang. "Hello."

"Hello, Ken. It's Gianetta d'Averso."

"There is only one Gianetta."

"I hope it's not too late."

"Well, I'm in bed…"

"So am I."

My head spun. "Not asleep, though."

"Neither am I. What's up?"

"This premiere of Antonio's. How can he do it if he's such a bad reader?"

"Beats me."

"Want to find out?"

"Oh, do you know something?"

"Well, no," I said. "Maybe we should work on it together."

"I'm leaving this one alone. I'm sick of him."

My heart sank. "Oh, that's too bad. I enjoyed our, um, conspiracy."

"So did I, and it did what we wanted it to. But I'm tired of the whole Antonio business. Maybe if you find out anything, you could call me. I have to go now. Good night."

That's it, I thought. I'm not suffering over this woman any more. Unethical though it may be, I'll just carry on with Suzi for the time being, even though I'm starting to feel like a bird in a cage. Why did Gianetta "have to go" when she was tucked safely in bed? To me, it was all but final proof that she had a lover.

I would carry on by myself. Even in the wake of my victory over Antonio, he continued to be so arrogant and so cocksure that my darker instincts were coming to the fore. I wasn't content just to win the battle. I wanted to win the war.

In the same net with Antonio, as it happened, was Neville Park, Charlie's "Walking X-Ray". Neville Park was in the net because he was the composer of the new work Antonio was premiering, a surprise to all of us because we knew him only as a composer of small pieces for Angela Rumley's choir that sounded like Carl Orff being performed backwards. The surprise was all the greater because the piece had been quietly substituted for the Bruckner *Te Deum* in the program, which already featured *Carmina Burana*, only two months before the concert.

Sister Ingrid was not pleased, especially since Mrs. Rumley had known about the program change two weeks before she did. Neville's opus was called *The Holiest of All* and the astonishing fact was revealed that it had been nearly thirty years in the making. When asked what took him so long, Neville steepled his fingers and spoke of how he could only work to the most rigorously high standards in order to serve the Lord through the medium of music.

"Barf," said Father Oakley inelegantly. "The son-of-a-bitch sure picked a great time for all this hoo-ha. Here we have this camp about to happen, biddy Rumley's tied up..."

"Tied up in ways..."

"I shouldn't hear that, K.Y. Sister's all tied up, and she's upset, Charlie's suckered into it, Neville has Sweet Marie working round the clock on some great piece of bio-crap about his divine

157

inspiration. That just leaves you and me and Suzi. Too bad Suzi's married to your boss. I think she likes you…"

The Holiest of All almost was the downfall of the Osterling Weekend even before it started. Despite my teaching schedule and the endless last-minute crises that kept arising relative to the camp, I was put in charge of arranging a speaking tour by Neville to all the Roman Catholic schools in Birkenstock County. Understandably, a high proportion of principals contacted declined because of the short notice and the lateness of the year, whereupon Neville, through me, offered himself at any Sunday Mass for the same purpose, to any priest that would take him. It was like telemarketing and I began to develop a rejection syndrome.

Over a "taste" on a Thursday afternoon, Charlie was looking particularly long of face. Besides teaching, besides the office, he had been playing at the Brew-ha-ha for the past several nights for a special appearance by a black exotic dancer named Afro-desia, and he was exhausted. "She's something else, man. I race home nights and attack the Pipe Cleaner and both ends of me hurt the next morning. Both ends of me hurt right now. Of the two, I think my head is the worst."

"How's Neville's *Holier Than Thou*, or whatever the hell it is, doing?" inquired Father Oakley.

"Neville, he pisses me off, man. There's this chord where I have an F-sharp and the damn thing hangs out like a Skil saw, makes no sense, and fucking Antonio can't figure it out, fact, he couldn't even name the damn note."

"Figures," said Father Oakley.

"So I take it to Neville and he gives me this stuff about how the chord, it's augmented all to hell, represents the epicentre of somebody's conflict. Well, hell, man, I'm just a regular guy, I'm not a philosopher or a profound thinker, I deal with equipment, but even I know that things lead up to conflict, it just doesn't pop out of thin air. I think it's a mistake and Neville won't admit it. And Antonio doesn't know what's going on anyway. If it weren't for *Carmina Burana*, I'd chuck the whole thing."

"You're really getting into the legit stuff big-time, aren't you?" I said.

"*Carmina Burana* is not legit. It's rock and roll."

MISHIPASHOO ARTS CENTRE
SATURDAY, JUNE 7, EVENING

Anna and Hugo gave a reception for the camp staff on the first evening of the Osterling Weekend; their cottage, though reasonably spacious, could not hold everyone at once, so a fair number of us found ourselves being gently regurgitated out into the summer evening. We watched the sun sink behind the trees on the other side of the creek, listening to the chirpings of the little frogs in a near-by marsh. "It's happening, man, I like it," remarked Charlie. "Finally got this thing going. Looks like Rosie was doing okay in the tuck shop."

"Very okay," I approved. "There's a certain *je ne sais quoi* about young love goddesses performing fellatio on raspberry popsicles..."

"Oh, man, I love your mind! When you talk dirty, it just makes me all crazy inside. Think I'll cleave unto the Pipe Cleaner tonight and you can be at our bedside, murmuring words of encouragement."

I thought I should be all managerial and circulate. Dear, beautiful Anna, I saw, had already made a point of acquainting herself with Gianetta; the spectacle of the two of them within one field of vision was as overpowering as Edvard Munch's outsize painting of the sun. Anna knew exactly what to say and do; she slipped an arm around my middle and said to Giannetta, "This is my timeless and eternal friend K.Y. If he and I had ever been single at the same time, I would have shamelessly thrown myself at him. He's a special guy."

"He did a pretty good number on my ex-husband," said Gianetta off-handedly. "I like that."

"I heard," said Anna. "It's like Irish Spring. I like it too. Besides, he's funny and he's cute."

159

Oh, what now? Full and extravagant agreement? "Well, you've known him longer than I have. Nice to meet you, Anna. I have to go now. See you later."

"Well, shit," I grumbled.

"Sorry, love, I tried," said Anna apologetically. "She's like a locked door. You can only go so far and then it's a dead end. That ex-husband is a real piece of work. Give her some time. He may have turned her off of men for the time being."

"If he has, I hope it's only for the time being. But this is awfully hard to handle."

"Try looking for a woman who isn't mysterious. That was the problem with Alien. You need someone, well, like me! I guess we'd better circulate."

Neville was acting as if he owned the whole operation even though Father Oakley, Charlie, Sister Ingrid and I had put it together. He was particularly sluggish of movement this evening, so sat in an armchair holding court, fingers steepled wisely and discussing the art of phrasing. Father Oakley shook his head and went back to a conversation with Hugo about Byzantine art, a conversation punctuated with endearments of "good dog…clever dog" from Hugo to Angus, the Highland terrier.

A rival court was being held by Antonio, emoting something about a radio broadcast in Holland and babbling about his various "colleagues": Seiji in Boston, Christoph in Cleveland, Riccardo at La Scala, Jimmy at the Met. Father Oakley looked pained and went back to a conversation with Hugo, now joined by Israel Bond and Charlie, about Hasidic practice.

Charlie had picked up an intriguing bit of lore in the spring when playing in the band for a Jewish wedding. According to Hasidic or Orthodox practice, the wife, for purposes of intimacy, was covered in a sheet with a strategic hole in it "for access, man," as Charlie put it.

"Ach, so. A bit traditional for my taste, but interesting, no? Yes!" concluded Israel.

"Think I'll try it with the Pipe Cleaner just for the hell of it," whispered Charlie in my ear. "If I can't see her, I sure can hear her. 'Oh, yeaaah!' Outstanding…"

Ms. Rumley, teeth smeared liberally with lipstick, had joined Neville in the holding of court. Even though the Osterling Weekend was only a matter of hours old, they were talking about including an opera elective the following year, and at the mention of opera, the courts of Neville and Antonio coalesced into the worst caricature of an artsy gathering I have ever seen. Father

Oakley, now green of face, was steering Hugo, Israel, Charlie, and me out to the veranda. "There's them," he said, "and there's us."

"I want to talk more about Hasidic stuff," declared Charlie. "I wonder what a clothesline full of Hasidic bedsheets would look like. K.Y., draw it for me. You're good at that kind of thing."

I did a sketch on a serviette. "Cool," said Charlie.

"Good on a vindy day, not blow zo much," approved Israel.

I drew a Hasidic teepee.

"Vot you say? Chewish Indians?"

"Why not? They have as much right to be Jewish as anyone else."

"Beink Chewish iss not a right. You are born into it."

"Not always. There are conversions. Marilyn Monroe converted when she married Arthur Miller. And there was Sammy Davis, Jr. ..."

"Too schmart you are, Kennet. Hey, Hugo tells me you sail. I luff to sail, but I don't know zo much about it. Can you tek me out zometime?"

"I'd love to, Israel, and that steers me to another possibility. Let's try a Hasidic spinnaker." Heads bent forward again while I drew an impression.

Dear Dunny had Eric Osterling cornered for most of the party. It was supposed to be a social gathering, but such was Dunny's obsessive love for music in general and bands in particular that he had brought an armful of scores, mostly Osterling, and was going through them with Eric, alternately brandishing a red pencil and a battery of highlighters. Dunny liked to colour-code all entries: yellow for the flutes, magenta for the oboes, and so forth. Eric was trying to look impressed, trying to control the look of a tremulous mouthful of marbles that comes with a suppressed yawn.

I went to the rescue with a reminder that the morrow was a working day and it was time to wind things up. Dunny looked disappointed, Eric looked relieved, the Neville/Angela/Antonio ghastliness was disbanded, the junior administration cleaned up, and quiet settled over the camp.

I meandered alone back to the cabin I shared with Father Oakley, slapping at bugs, for this was June and June was their season, but I didn't care. I was in one of my favourite places doing my favourite things with my favourite people; it is a perversity that in good times, one looks for things to make them even better, inevitably unattainable things. The evening would have been enchanted had *Snarley* been berthed in the creek and I were aboard, making overtures to Gianetta. But *Snarley* was at the boat works enduring the humiliations of being a handyman's special

161

Steven Duff

and Giannetta, well, *Enigma Variations* could not begin to tell the tale. Never had I seen anyone with such a definite and predictable limit to personal boundaries.

I shrugged and trudged along the road, hearing the chirping clamour of the little frogs around nearby Cole Lake and the gargling sounds of some nocturnal bird. Rather than turning at the footbridge towards the cabin, I treated myself to a walk up to Carling Bay Road, a bit ghastly with the bugs, but I needed a bit of time to settle my mind. The grief over *Snarley*, the horror of the Schism, the elation over the camp and of my new position, the despair over Gianetta, all had come in such close succession. My brain felt like a prune with all it had been subjected to emotionally and I simply had to get control over it or my life at the camp and beyond would be a misery.

One of the problems with being a musician, indeed of being any kind of artist, is the extremes of emotion one experiences. There are the Himalayas and the Andes of exaltation, the Mid-Atlantic Trench of despair, the ying and yang of one's state of well-being. There is no question that it makes life interesting and exciting and there were many times at school, especially around concert time, that I thought my non-musical colleagues led a dull, predictable, plodding existence. There was, no doubt, an element of snobbery involved; I took a wayward pride in how my state might be represented on a graph, taking wild swoops all over the place, and those who in my eyes led an "ordinary" life I called flat-liners because of their relatively even state of existence. But the extremes of my own ying and yang were exacting too heavy a price; for the time being at least, I would have to be a flat-liner, an emotional armadillo, for my own self-preservation.

Pleased with my resolution and with my imagery, I turned back, barely able to discern the road in the extreme darkness of the northern night, headed for the slumbering camp and for a few hours of oblivion.

162

A DAY AT MUSIC CAMP

The first full day of what became known as the Osterling Weekend established a pattern that became fairly typical of what was to follow. Our young musicians were surprisingly subdued at breakfast—Father Oakley wondered if they were shell-shocked by unfamiliar surroundings—but once the morning rehearsals began, it was a whole different story.

Father Oakley and I did a patrol of all rehearsal sites to make sure everyone was accounted for, that there were no shortages of music or accessories, generally that everyone was happy.

"I think everyone is happy," remarked Father Oakley. "I know I am. This is like a dream come true, all these beautiful trees and rocks, the Bay, being around kids and instruments, why, it doesn't get any better."

"No, it doesn't," I agreed, although the current lack of female company for me was troublesome and my dormant longings for Suzi began to be not so dormant. But that was not a matter for the company of a Jesuit, albeit earthy, man of the cloth.

"Hi, Hugo, how are you doing, kid?"

"Better than the last few days. Donald Shipley is coming to pick up my Ackroyd dinghy that your moving van squashed…"

"Not my moving van, it's Panama Van Lines' moving van."

"Be that as it may, I have clearance from the insurance company to get the boat fixed. From now on, no moving vans beyond the footbridge. What a good dog" (to Angus of God). "Now, there's another vehicle that scares me."

The Hog, Charlie's new HumVee, was parked outside the office. Charlie was about to do some errands in Parry Sound and was assembling a list. "Let's see…couple of bras, size A, for the Pipe Cleaner…some rolls of gauze…how the devil did we ever forget?…correction fluid…more bristol board…"

"What, already?"

163

"Yeah, man, Surrendra and Nirvana are real big on signs, like they never had any in India or wherever…what else, now?…car wash, deposit at the sperm bank, and that's it, boys and girls, I'm outta here, lock and load, va-room!"

Moneypenny shook her head and went back to work, mumbling something about there being no dull people at camp. Father Oakley went in search of Eric Osterling, to remove him from the clutches of Dunny if need be, and I took my ease on the little front veranda of the office to rest my feet and enjoy a few quiet minutes. Kitty Sark hopped up into my lap. Pete the caretaker stopped by on the tractor for a moment. "Hey, Ken," said he through compressed lips. "Hot mernin', eh? You got ennathin to drink here?"

"Not officially, but unofficially we have a cooler of pop in here and we'll sneak you one."

"Much obliged, eh?"

"No need to be obliged. You keep this place going. You're what Father Oakley calls one of the great ones. What kind of pop would you like?"

"You got PeeCee ginger ale?"

"We have."

"A PeeCee would be reely nice, it's my favourite, but don't tell Rosie, eh?"

Pete's wife Rosie worked part-time for the A & P.

"Our secret, Pete."

"Much obliged. Thanks for the pop, eh? Have a nice mernin'."
PeeCee in hand, Pete chugged up the road, the tractor's sound swallowed up in the musical fragments mixed so naturally with the sounds of nature. I had not felt such contentment since the days of *Snarley Yow* and felt as though almost fully reborn. Kitty Sark purred in feline accord.

The mid-morning break came and went, the students settling into their sectional rehearsals and master classes. A whole new combination of noises started up. I was just getting up for another happiness patrol when the same little lad who'd mislaid the twenty dollar bill the previous day came down the road, escorted by Duncan Doenitz and again looking very sorry about life.

"Have a little fellow with a big headache here," said Duncan. "There was nobody at the infirmary. What should I do?"

"Nobody? No sign of Mrs. Vomet?" Mrs. Vomet was the camp nurse. Mrs. Vomet was supposed to be on duty. I was not pleased with Mrs. Vomet.

"No sign of Mrs. Vomit. Her car wasn't there."

"Dear God. What is your name?"

"Rick O'Shea, sir. My head hurts so bad I think I'm going to be sick."

Duncan and I walked Rick up to the infirmary. Mrs. Vomet had left the supply cupboards unlocked, another no-no, but a beneficial no-no in that we could find something for young Rick to make him feel better. Duncan and I knew nothing about pharmacology, but Rick was able to help: "See if you can find some 222s. A couple of those should do the trick."

I found the 222s. "How old are you, Rick?"

"Twelve."

"If your headache is so bad as to make you feel sick, let's try three. Here's some fruit juice. Drink lots to chase them down."

Ordinarily, the camp had no infirmary; since Hugo and Anna catered to adults, they were able to rely on Parry Sound's medical facilities, but with young people, it was a different situation and the establishment of an infirmary was one of the conditions of approval by the Birkenstock County Roman Catholic School Board. Mrs. Vomet was the sister-in-law of one of the trustees and chose this moment to make her appearance.

"Sick call is after lunch," she twanged. She was skinny to the point of emaciation, her fingers stained with nicotine.

"My understanding," I said evenly, "is that you are to be available at all times. We are not medically trained. You are."

"So what did you do for this boy?," said Mrs. Vomet as if we were accountable.

"Gave him three 222s."

"Gave him what?"

"Three 222s."

"Where did you get them?"

"From the supply cupboard. Which was not locked."

"You had no right..."

"Mrs. Vomit, you had no right to put me in that position..."

"Mrs. Vomay, if you please."

"Sorry, I didn't realize. I had to do something and this was the only way. I'll take responsibility, even if you weren't around to take yours."

The whole conversation was taking place right in front of Rick and Duncan, not at all a professional way of handling things, but the woman had been confrontational from the start, leaving me little latitude.

"I'll thank you not to tell me how to do my job."

"I'm not telling you how to do it, Mrs. Vomay. I'm just telling you to do it, and if you have any problem with that, you can take it up with Mr. Park. Have a nice day. Rick, I hope you feel better real soon. Come on, Duncan, we have chores to do."

I was all red, hot, and shaky; I am not good at this sort of thing, but Mrs. Vomet had crossed the proverbial line in the sand. The thought that I had crossed her line in the sand did not occur to me.

The Hog was parked at the office. Charlie was back. "Man, picking out bras is not easy, all these colours, numbers, styles, and sizes. I almost walked off with a double D. Damn thing would have fallen off the Pipe Cleaner. I took it out of the package to check it out, just being a skilled and thorough consumer, and it blew me away. It was awesome. Love to be a fly on the wall when that one gets bought."

"Better still, be a fly in the cup," I said.

Charlie had a habit of squinting when impressed beyond endurance. It did not happen often, but it was happening now. "K.Y., you have one of the greatest minds in Christendom. One of these times, I'm gonna forget myself and kiss you full on the lips."

"You already did that time your, er, pagina didn't work."

"Oh, man! That was arguably the greatest moment of my entire life. Triumph in the midst of despair. Don't back away, now. Don't go being like Father Oakley…"

During lunch, I was summoned to the phone to speak to a hysterical Mrs. O'Shea, who was definitely not in a tranquil state. Mrs. Vomet, as a matter of camp procedure and protocol, had just spoken to her about Rick's headache and my treatment thereof.

"Three 222s!" screamed Mrs. O'Shea.

"Yes, Mrs. O'Shea, I gave him three, I thought it was safe, and he is at lunch, looking a lot better."

"Three 222s!" screamed Mrs. O'Shea again. "I'm coming to fetch him home!"

"Mrs. O'Shea, there's no need, he's perfectly all right—"

"No, he isn't! He is possessed."

"What do you mean?"

"Thrice two hundred twenty two is six hundred and sixty six. It is the number of the beast, oh, you wicked, wicked man, you have made my child the Anti-Christ. That camp is a Babylon!"

"Just a moment," I snapped, the antipathy toward Mrs. Vomet being rekindled and redirected. "You had me worried that I had done something wrong."

"You did, you did, you did!" Somehow I imagined Mrs. O'Shea splattering her telephone with foam.

"Mrs. O'Shea, the nurse was not available and I did the best I could with what I had. If you need a witness, I have one. There is no need to remove Rick from camp. If you like, I will have Mr.

Park, the camp director, phone you and get this all straightened out."

"The Book of Revelations does not get straightened out. It is going to happen and you started the process, using my Ricky…"

"Mr. Park will phone you."

"I expect to hear from him within ten minutes."

Neither Neville nor Angela Rumley were around. They had gone "into town for lunch". I told Father Oakley what had happened and he bellowed with laughter, thinking I had made a joke.

"Father, this was no joke. I have to ask you to call this woman. She's nuts."

"I know Mrs. O'Shea," said Moneypenny, looking up her number.

"What's she like?"

"She's nuts. Rick was in a play at his school in February, something about the early Vikings and their pagan practices. He sang a song about Yggdrasil the ash tree and Mrs. O'Shea went ballistic and pulled him out of the show. Said they were making him do devil music. Stupid woman didn't know the difference between paganism and Satanism. Took Rick to an exorcist. Here's her number."

Father Oakley placed the call. "Mrs. O'Shea, this is Father John Oakley, S.J. I understand you have a concern about our treatment of young Rick. In my opinion, Mr. Jackson acted correctly, although granted the quantity of medication may have been somewhat excessive. But if it had been three 292s, Rick would be in hospital having his stomach pumped out. You need not be concerned…" Father Oakley winced, holding the yammering phone a foot from his ear.

"Mrs. O'Shea…excuse me…can I say something? I honestly don't think there is any symbolism to be drawn from the 222s. It's just a trademark and has no religious connotations. The thesis for my degree concerned this very subject and earned me honours, so I have a pretty comprehensive background. In fact, I established a quite solid theory to the examination committee that Hitler was the Anti-Christ and that World War Two was the Book of Revelations happening and it's all behind us. Tell you what, I'll keep a personal watch on Rick and let you know if anything in his behaviour changes. If anything is amiss, it will show up in the next couple of days. I'll phone you each evening, just to reassure you. Would that be all right?"

The telephone murmured assent and Father Oakley hung up.

"She's nuts, isn't she?" said Moneypenny.

Father Oakley shook his head. "I think I have her calmed down, but good Lord. Rick seems like a nice kid. It's a wonder he isn't unglued half the time."

"Nothing bothers him," said Moneypenny. "He's amazing."

"You look unglued, K.Y.," said Father Oakley, steering me outside. "Go get some dessert, we'll do a happiness patrol for each of the afternoon periods, then I want you to take the rest of the afternoon off, get out on the water for a bit, maybe take Israel for a sail. Get him singing 'Anchors Oy Vay' or whatever. I want you both to be happy."

Happy Israel and I were, too. We took off for a couple of hours before dinner in the remaining functional Ackroyd dinghy, sailing to Loon Bay and back, the sail pulling like a plow-horse, the water cackling gleefully along the lapstrake hull, sun and water interacting in a moving glare of fractured light.

"Iss beautiful," rhapsodized Israel. "No attitoods, no artsy airs, noboddy tryink to scroo you. I sink I vant a boat too, do some clean livink, get away from zis silly crap, no? Yes!"

THERE IS A BOMB IN GILEAD

Locally, they were known as the Happy Gang, but happy they definitely were not. Cathy and Mike MacIntosh were overdrawn at the bank, their Perma-Debt card was at its maximum, they had three children all under four, and their one-year-old marriage, an ill-advised venture to begin with and based on Cathy's eligibility for Mothers' Allowance, was *in extremis*.

No blows had been struck, but it was plain to their neighbours in the village of Snug Harbour, just a few kilometres west of the Mishipashoo Arts Centre, that something big was in the offing. Domestic conversations escalated in their vitriol. On a quiet evening, the sound of Cathy calling Mike a fucking loser echoed through the village; in fact, the word "fuck" and all its variations and modifiers formed such a large proportion of Cathy's vocabulary that it had been degraded to the status of punctuation.

Once the warmer weather came, discretion on the part of the burghers of Snug Harbour was thrown to the winds, for there were now no closed windows to erase the sounds of strife from the MacIntosh household, now regarded locally as the "Happy Gang". That which could not be avoided, then, had to be embraced, and there was nobody within a quarter-mile radius of their home who was not privy to their altercations.

Fidelity was an "F" word whose meaning did not have much currency with the Happy Gang. Cathy found a bra in the conjugal bed one day that was not hers and loudly, if inadvertently, announced the event to the community in a scalding phone call to her husband by an open window. It was duly reported in the surrounding houses to any spouses absent for the actual revelation, and from that time, it became a tradition for the men of Snug Harbour to keep bras in their beds. To be sure, they were their

169

wives' bras, but a new age of pleasure and adventure was taking root in the community and has persisted to this day.

Revenge was *de rigueur*. Cathy loudly trumpeted her intention to "spread her legs for someone who cared" and took to vanishing for entire nights, leaving her husband to care for the children, whose optimistic, childlike vision of the world underwent an understandable revision. Almost overnight, the men of Snug Harbour were all assuring their wives and girlfriends how much they cared; with the obvious and noisy exception of the Happy Gang, Snug Harbour was rapidly evolving into the love capital of Georgian Bay.

The stress was taking its toll on the children. Little Caitlin, the eldest, was training her kindergarten confreres to say "fuck." "That's my mum's favourite word," she explained to her befuddled teacher. Alan, the second child, who was three, regressed under the pressure and demanded a bottle for his breakfast. Cathy went into full eruption, got on the phone with Mike at work to rave about what a terrible father, husband, and provider he was being, and had to bear the ultimate responsibility for Alan's deterioration.

The One Who Cared, the one for whom Cathy was now spreading her legs when the opportunity afforded itself, was a science teacher at the local high school, who had once worked in the C.I.L. explosives plant at Nobel. The C.I.L. plant had closed shop some years before, but the One Who Cared, having worked there, fully understood the nuances and subtleties of high explosive and, as a gift to Cathy to show the depth of his feeling, made her a car bomb. Duly expressing her appreciation, Cathy took the bomb home, set the timer for two o'clock in the morning, and put it in Mike's moth-eaten and decrepit Aerostar minivan, intending the detonation to be a warning.

Cathy was therefore both puzzled and disturbed to find the Aerostar intact when returning the next morning from the bed of the One Who Cared. Her vendetta was further complicated by Mike, a construction worker who was not needed on site until noon, pending delivery of some piece of equipment or another. Therefore it was not until about half past eleven that he went out to the van and opened the back door to stow his tool box. Mike was a singularly disorderly individual and kept both his car and premises in a manner more fitting to Tobacco Road than Snug Harbour, and yet he had an uncanny knack for spotting something out of order. In this way, Cathy had underestimated him; some indifferently folded-up plastic tarpaulins were not as he remembered, he shifted them for re-stowage, and saw the bomb.

Mike was not one to get excited, a contributing factor to his present marital problems, for Cathy loved excitement. He regarded the bomb for a moment, phoned the Provincial Police Parry Sound detachment from his cell phone, opened a beer, and shuffled up the road for a walk until such time as the bomb was cleared or exploded, whichever should happen first.

Constable William "Beaver" Lumber of the Ontario Provincial Police happened to be making his rounds up by the nearby village of Dillon and was at the MacIntosh residence within minutes, converging with another police cruiser. Constable Lumber volunteered, against the advice of his colleague, to take the bomb, leaving said colleague to deal with a profanity-spouting Cathy and a frantically bottle-sucking Alan, and headed back to headquarters in Parry Sound. He tried to call in on the radio, but the scurvy thing, which had been a bit temperamental the day before, was refusing to transmit. Well, then, things would just have to wait until he could phone in.

Like all policemen, Constable Lumber enjoyed a break with a coffee and a doughnut. A coffee without a doughnut was like Daphnis without Chloe, Tristan without Isolde, Romeo without Juliet. Generally, there was something about the combination that induced a sense of well-being. Unlike his fellow officers, however, Constable Lumber avoided doughnut shops when in uniform because of the prevailing cliche in the public mind. But he had a system. His house was right on his regular patrol route in Carling Township, he had a six-month supply of doughnuts in a special freezer, and an accommodating wife who would start the coffee-maker at his signal of three short honks as he turned into the driveway. The time was about right for a break, home was just a few minutes away, and he had to make his phone call to the detachment and see what to do about that there bomb.

Like Pete and Rosie, the Lumbers spoke in the low-key and unhurried manner of northern Ontario country folk.

"Hey, Elsie."

"Hey, Beave. What's new?"

"Got a bomb."

"Bomb, eh?"

"Yup."

"Where is it?"

"Car. In the trunk."

"Saints above! What do they want you to do with it?"

"Dunno. Radio's down. I'll phone 'em now." He punched in the number of the dispatcher's desk in Parry Sound. The dispatcher was an excitable young gee-whizzer named Gina Moistrin.

"Hey, Gina. It's Beaver."

The phone murmured. "Yup. Radio's down. Yup...okay...well, I got a bomb." The phone squealed in agitation.

"I don't know when. I don't know what makes it go. Never seen one before...oh...okay, Gina. You'll find me at Mishipashoo, it's right down the road...eh?...okay, I'll tell 'em."

The phone in the music camp office rang. Moneypenny answered. "Birkenstock Music Camp, how may I help you? Oh, hi, Mr. Harland. Mr. Jackson's here. I'll hand you over to him."

No prelude. "K.Y., we have trouble. There's a bomb in a car at a neighbour's house just back of the concert tent. They're sending the bomb squad down from North Bay, but they'll be a couple of hours, and in the meantime they can't move the damn car and we have to keep that area clear."

"We can rehearse the orchestra by the sailing area, oh, shit, music stands, percussion..."

"Forget it. Stay away. Nobody knows how powerful this thing is and we can't take the chance."

We had a fast war council over lunch, a lunch attended by a sheepish Constable and Mrs. Beaver Lumber, in refuge from the bomb area. Antonio, whose afternoon operations were most affected, waived any sympathy on our part by electing to be difficult. "I cannot'a function in an environment with'a bombs'a going off, I cannot'a do my job..."

We concocted all kinds of different rehearsal plans, none of which suited Antonio, and eventually abandoned the orchestra's afternoon schedule and assigned its members to act as mentors to the younger performing groups. There was no point in trying to disguise the situation, so I simply explained it to the campers during post-lunch announcements, met with the orchestra afterwards, and delegated the members more or less arbitrarily to their temporary duties. They were, for the most part, good-natured about the situation, not even the most notorious prima donnas indulging themselves. These young people were acting in a far more mature manner than their conductor.

Rosie phoned from her work at the A. & P. "Rosie here, from the AynPee. Radio says there's a bomb out there, eh? You guys all okay? Pete around?"

"Everything's okay, Rosie," I assured. "Pete's helping Charlie keep kids away from the, er, site. The bomb squad's coming and we should be all cleared up by the time you're off work."

"Glad Pete's with Charlie, eh? Charlie's a real good fella, real conservative, like."

"Oh, yeah," I agreed with a roll of the eyes.

Charlie and Pete were stationed up the road to discourage any sight-seers and on the other side of the Lumber homestead, the police had a roadblock, to the consternation of the driver of a refrigerated truck (and of Anna) trying to make a delivery to the camp kitchen. Hugo thought we might have to send the truck over to the landing at Nobel and ferry the supplies out in *Helen Louise* and *Screamer*.

Except for the orchestra, it looked like a normal music camp afternoon. The usual Ivesian fragments of music arbitrarily combined with the sight and swoosh of wind in trees; Dunny Corrigan's young band thumped and growled up the road in the Theatre Workshop, and Angela Rumley's choir, in the dining hall, was well on the way to mastery of her specialty *There is a Balm in Gilead.*

The bomb squad from North Bay were, by our estimation, somewhere between Dunchurch and McKellar when Cathy's bomb, mistakenly set for two p.m. rather than a.m., detonated in a hail of debris. It blew the police car completely apart, sending Charlie fleeing as the trunk lid swooped down upon him from an azure sky. The Lumbers' family car was also a write-off, as were most of their windows and an aluminum garden shed that was sent cartwheeling into the bush in a hail of rakes, hoes, and shovels. "Outstanding," pronounced Charlie, apparently unshaken by his near-demise.

As it happened, the Lumbers' property was served by an artesian well, whose pipe was ruptured by the explosion, and in a matter of moments, the camp road was washed out in a great sluice of brown, muddy water.

"This is even more outstanding than originally estimated," elaborated Charlie, lighting up a cigarette. "Let's get that food over here."

"I think Hugo was going to send it to where we could get the stuff by boat."

"Nah. Watch this. Come on, K.Y." Summoned thus, I climbed into the Hog. Its great diesel roared to life, and the vehicle lunged off the road, pausing for me to open a gate, and surged through a cow pasture behind the Lumbers' house. It thrashed and lurched like an unbroken horse, terrifying the cows, a crucifix chained to the rear-view mirror whipping and gyrating. I lost track of how many gears the Hog had, but Charlie was working them all, undeterred by the boulders and stumps that did their level best to capsize us.

173

We regained the road, just as the delivery truck was backing up to get turned around. "Stay put, man, and give us a hand," Charlie commanded the surprised driver. A full cargo of dairy products was hurriedly stowed in the Hog and transported, via the cow pasture behind Constable Lumber's house, to the camp kitchen.

"I guess Sea-Lift Command bit the dust," said Hugo mournfully as the whole Junior Administration team was mobilized to unload.

"Yeah, but how many camps have a HumVee at their disposal?" said Charlie. "Lock and load, boys and girls, come on, we don't have all day, all these poor children to be fed..."

After dinner, a muddy, grass-festooned, but proud Hog led a triumphal parade to the faculty concert, decorated with boughs of cedar and, to Charlie's disgust, bunches of wildflowers. "Man," he said to me during the concert, "I figured there'd be wacko stuff, but from within our ranks...this I hadn't bargained for. There really was a bomb in Gilead. I'm looking forward to tomorrow."

"Why?"

"To see what else can be screwed up."

THE RESCUE

As every family of instruments has its own characteristics, so
have the players. String players are the most prone to being
prima donnas and among their younger ranks is an enormous
proportion of self-designated Perlmans, Zukermans, and Yo Yo
Mas. On Day Three of the Osterling Weekend, the start of
Antonio's symphony orchestra rehearsal, now restored to its home
in the concert tent, was delayed by an argument between two
cellists as to tuning.

"Well, I'm gifted," huffed one of them, who happened to be our
old friend Rick O'Shea, just promoted from the Concert Orchestra.

"I'm a genius. Mr. d'Averso said so," snapped his adversary.

"Quiet!" screamed Antonio. "*Disgrazia! Stupidi bambini!* I
will'a tune you, and I'a never called anyone'a here a genius. Only I
am entitled..."

Brass players tend to be animals, purveyors of loud noises.
Instinctively, their dynamic awareness embraces louder and
loudest—blastissimo, as Father Oakley calls it—and they require
unusual finesse in their training to produce truly musical results.
But, carefully taught and directed, there is nothing that can match a
first-rate brass section for sheer gut-churning excitement. I have a
particular affection for low brass, even though I am not a brass
player by background, but the volcanic possibilities are irresistible
and have contributed to some notable performances at
Misericordia High School.

Percussion. Out of every seven or eight, there is a true
percussionist who has the necessary initiative and organizational
skills to navigate the minefield that is percussion, who does not
mislay things, who does not leave a rehearsal without putting all
the toys away, who is musically literate, who does not scorn the
triangle. The rest are simply drummers of little flexibility who are
to be more pitied than laughed at.

175

I leave the woodwinds for the end because I am a past practitioner and have spent much time in that milieu. Sister Ingrid, you may recall, was a choral specialist, and once said playing wind instruments put you into a "milieu that could kill yieu". Within the woodwinds, the sanest artists are the clarinetists, of whom I was one for quite a number of years. Flutists are all right, as long as they do not refer to themselves as "flautists" and act like instant Rampals or Galways. Oboists are high-strung and temperamental, probably because of all the back-pressure from blowing such a tiny reed, and are given to frequent fits of weeping. Bassoonists are cheerfully gross and in temperament are really honorary brass players.

Saxophones deserve a paragraph of their own. What can be said of an instrument made of brass but fingered and blown as a woodwind? The physical schizophrenia of the instrument extends to the personality of the players, many of whom veer in the direction of John Coltrane and specialize in all sorts of instrumental shrieks and hiccups. They are usually frustrated in a symphonic setting, since there is no scope for the byways of saxophone style, and a saxophonist of Daniel Rubinoff's or Paul Brodie's sensitivity, by way of shining example, is a rarity indeed.

The instrument itself, being brass, is relatively impervious to water, although the pads suffer and must be replaced, but that is a fairly simple if time-consuming task. So, if an instrument must take the deep six, from a mechanical if not artistic point of view, the saxophone is one of the better choices.

Kimberley Clark, she of the ill-advised lottery, was a saxophonist and an exceptionally enthusiastic one. She loved practicing to the point of addiction and was the sort of student who would show up in the music room at ten to four on a Friday afternoon, just as I was treating myself to my weekly quick getaway, to sign out her instrument, round up some extra music, and just chat and pass the time of day. It could be exasperating after a rough week, but who could criticize?

It was not cause for particular notice, then, to hear Kimberley having a quick toot just before lunch out on the footbridge over the creek. Moneypenny was making some preparatory rattlings of keys prior to locking up for the noon hour when the saxophone stopped abruptly and a howl of consternation went up.

I stepped out on the office porch and, in less time than it takes to tell this, took in a cluster of agitated girls on the footbridge, gesticulating at a foaming turbulence below them in the creek. I raced down the bank of the creek, dove in, and, among a swirling column of bubbles, there was poor Kimberley, weighted down by the neck with a tenor saxophone, and struggling limply to surface.

I thought my head and lungs were going to burst. I got Kimberley by the leg, but it was so sleek and well-shaven that it slipped out of my hand in a fleeting feeling of silken femininity.

I kicked myself to the surface for air, gulped hugely, and went down again. With all the bubbles and the brownish cast of the water, I became disoriented and for a moment of unparalleled horror, I thought I had lost Kimberley. A weak kick to my face and there she was, hovering limply in a state of neutral buoyancy. I got her under the arms and kicked to the surface; conveniently, the current of the creek had carried us under the bridge to a spot by Hugo's launching ramp, and there my feet found bottom.

A number of campers and staff helped us ashore and there was the mighty Hog, stationing itself for ambulance service. Kimberley, relieved of her saxophone, was laid out in the back and I started the resuscitation process Anna had taught us just before the start of camp. Because I was thoroughly winded, it was a pretty spastic exercise, and, initially, not a pleasant one, as Kimberley managed to gush a litre or two of creek water all over the floor.

"Oh, man!" cried Charlie, starting the engine.

"Shit, Charlie, what are we doing? What about an ambulance and a paramedic crew?"

"The Hog is the ambulance and you are the paramedic crew. We can be at the hospital by the time an ambulance could get here. Lock and load!" Spinning a hail of stones, the Hog lunged forward and tore up the road, just that morning having been restored to service by the Carling Township Roads Department. Bouncing around in the back, I worked on Kimberley, not at all certain if she had even survived, but by now the operation had become totally devoid of emotion. I was into a rhythm now that could not be stopped.

At the junction to the main highway southbound to Parry Sound, a police cruiser, despatched by Gina Moistrin, who had been alerted by Moneypenny, was waiting to escort us.

I could hear the siren starting its chilling glissando, could hear the Hog hitting full stride, could hear Charlie's exultant "Woo-hoo!" as we swept through Nobel and raced down past the old golf course, past the Parry Sound Mall (where Charlie had once gotten lost but would never admit it), and down Joseph and Church Streets to the hospital. At about the time the Dairy Queen was drawing abeam, Kimberley, evidently thinking she was having an erotic dream, clutched me to her and started frantically French kissing me.

I was moaning in protest. She was moaning in delirium. "Oh, baby, baby," said Charlie helpfully.

177

Kimberley's big electric-blue eyes fluttered open. "Oh, God," she wheezed. "Mr. Jackson! Huh…what's happening, where are we? Why am I all wet?"

"Because.." began Charlie, and then abandoned what he was going to say.

"You fell off the bridge into the creek with your saxophone—"

"Is it all right?"

"It is, just has to dry out and we'll replace the pads. How do you feel?"

"My throat is sore, my head hurts. Why were you kissing me like that?"

"C.P.R., you know, mouth-to-mouth."

"I guess I should be embarrassed…" Her voice trailed off and her eyes met mine with a disturbingly penetrating look. Kimberley Clark was eighteen years old. I did not need this.

"Don't worry. Here's the hospital."

While Kimberley was being checked over and warmed up, for the water had been damnably cold, I stood out in the sun to dry of as best I could. After an hour or so, Kimberley was adjudged fit to return to the camp under instructions to rest for the afternoon; we stopped at the Dairy Queen for a hamburger ("I just love these BrazierBurgers," said Charlie with the inevitable mispronunciation) and then headed homeward. The usually-gregarious Kimberley was all but silent, a condition I ascribed to fright, cold, and the usual after-effects of such a shock to the system.

The afternoon rehearsals were in progress by the time Charlie parked the Hog by the office. The duskily beautiful Surrendra Bangalore walked Kimberley to her cabin to change clothes and rest for a while; I rounded up a set of spare tenor saxophone pads from the library, took up station in a rocking chair on the office porch, and set to work to rehabilitate Kimberley's instrument.

Pete came by for his afternoon PeeCee ginger ale. "Hey, Ken."

"Hey, Pete."

"Heard."

"Heard what?"

"'Bout whatcha did."

"Oh?"

"Real good."

"Oh, thanks."

"Welcome." Pause. "Didja get scared?"

"Not really. There was just no time to think."

"Sometimes best not to think, eh? Guess that's how folks get through wars. Saw 'Platoon' with Rosie a bit ago, eh? Damn near ran screamin' right out of the the-ayter..."

Pete poured the rest of his PeeCee down and went off to do his afternoon chores.

Anna came by to offer purring congratulations. "If it weren't for you, I wouldn't have known what to do," I said, tweezering another recalcitrant pad into position.

"I hear young Kimberley thought you were up to something else. Charlie told me. In fact, Charlie phoned me to tell me. He thinks it's wonderful."

"She'll be all over Mr. Jackson," came Moneypenny's voice through the screen door.

"Come on, you guys," I whined with the secret pleasure that lies beneath elementary school denial.

Come half-past two, rehearsals were finished and streams of students with instrument cases and/or music folders began their ant-like migration to the first of three hours of musical or art options or athletics and water-sports. At 2:35, there was a thump as someone sat down in the other rocking chair; when Hugo had bought the camp, he had made it a law that all verandas had to be equipped for "settin' and rockin'".

The someone was Kimberley. "Mr. Jackson, we need to talk. I don't know how to thank you for rescuing me."

"That's very thoughtful, Kimberley, but it wasn't just me. There was Mr. Cowell, there was Moneypenny, I mean Alice, alerting the police—"

"You pulled me out and it was your arms I was in when I woke up."

"You weren't exactly—"

"Maybe I dreamed some of it. But what I have to tell you is that all afternoon, I've been feeling strange and different about you. I've sort of had a little thing for you since Grade 9, but this has put it in a whole new dimension. I know you're almost double my age, I know you're my teacher and I'm your student, but I'm also a woman."

I concentrated on the saxophone, saying nothing. Just feet away, things were going on as usual and here I was in this divine fantasy world, only it wasn't that divine; Suzi was married to my ex-father-in-law, Gianetta was single but for some reason unavailable, and here was this exquisite young woman approaching me very honestly and frankly (as distinct from "coming on" to me) who was half my age and with the power to put me in jail.

"I'm saying this to you in a public place," continued Kimberley, "because I don't want you to associate me with anything underhanded or sleazy." She nervously fingered a crucifix hung about her neck. "You already saved me from a sleazy situation with the, um, lottery, but I was so desperate…"

"I know and I won't judge you for that."

"You don't judge people and that is one of the many things I like about you. I know we can't see each other at camp, but maybe—"

"Phone, Mr. Jackson," came Moneypenny's voice from the darkness of the office.

I went in to take the call. "Sweetie!" warbled the phone.

"Oh, uh, hi, Suzi."

"All this time apart and that's all you can say?"

"This is a busy place."

"Oh, Sweetie, I can't stand this any more. There are some kids who have to write final exams and I'm bringing them up tomorrrow. I'll be there for lunch. Find us a place for the afternoon."

"Suzi, I can't!"

"If you really want to, you can. See you, darling. Toodles."

I hung up, glancing self-consciously at Moneypenny, who said nothing, but wore her usual look of alarming wisdom.

I returned to the veranda. Kimberley was still there and had taken up the task on the saxophone. "Leave it alone," said I gently. "I want to do that for you."

She looked up, eyes glistening. I felt a twinge of panic; had I said something wrong?

"You're the first person who has ever wanted to do something for me. My dad checked out when I was six, my brother is much older and into his career, Mum is alcoholic and given to slapping me around…everyone has left me. Please don't ever leave me, Mr. Jackson."

Now it was my turn to be wet of eye. "I won't leave you. I'll always be your friend."

"I want it to be like it was when I woke up today."

"That was hardly a normal and typical situation."

"I want it to be normal and typical, like every morning."

"I am truly honoured, Kimberley…hi there, Duncan…but I don't see any way…anyway in another couple of years, you'll be quite a different person—"

"If you're trying to tell me I'll outgrow what I feel, it won't happen. You gave me life all over again. That gives us a relationship only a few couples have, and pardon me if that sounds presumptuous, but that's…hi, Nirvana…that's the only word I could think of."

Now it was my turn to feel strange and different. This was not like talking to a student. This was man-and-woman stuff. Despite myself, I began to feel intrigued.

"You may have a point there…hi, Eddie" (to e.coli)…"look, there's too much traffic here for a conversation. I have to stay—"

"That's okay, I know you have a lot of responsibilities. I know pretty well what you have to do and this is one student who doesn't take it for granted. I'm going for a walk to clear my head and even though I can't do it in public, consider yourself kissed. At great length. See you later." No physical contact and yet I was now in a state of total desire. I hoped I wouldn't have to get up for a few minutes.

The other rocking chair, warmed by Kimberley's divine *derrière*, had no time to lose its residual motion (or warmth) before being occupied, no less, by the incomparable Giannetta, of whom I had seen virtually nothing since the inaugural party. "Hello, there."

"Oh, uh, hi, there, um, Gianetta."

"You sound as if you couldn't remember my name."

"Sorry. Been a rough day."

"So I heard. I missed seeing it, but I heard you were spectacular."

Frankly, I too thought I had been spectacular, but didn't want to ruin the ambience of the whole thing. "I just happened to be there and knew what to do."

Giannetta squeezed my forearm, the first time, except for those dry handshakes, that she had ever touched me. I nearly had a coronary. "You certainly did. That's glamorous stuff, rescuing young maidens from a certain death. She's one of your own kids, isn't she?"

"Yes."

"Well, I'll bet she'll be thinking of you very differently from now on. Why are you blushing and gulping like that?"

"Ah, it's just the heat. I think my body thermostat is all screwed up."

"Well, just don't let her mesmerize you. Keep yourself available for us older women. I have to go. See you later."

I was now and truly confounded. Was Giannetta trying to give me a message? Did she walk away because the rest of what she had to say was a private inner thought that didn't lend itself to settin' and rockin'? All this female attention in one afternoon, of varying stages of mystery, was all too much. Kimberley's saxophone was ready and there was an hour left before dinner, so I borrowed a canoe and went for a quiet paddle out through the gap between Goat and Grave Islands and back.

Charlie was hobbling noticeably at dinner time. "Man," he explained to me, "the Pipe-Cleaner got me."

"What do you mean?"

"What do you think I mean, dummy? She thinks we're heroes. She might get you too. Don't bother resisting, you'll get hurt. Isn't this great? An adventure a day. What will the morrow bring?"

THE RETURN OF SUZI, AND OTHER DELIGHTS

The morrow brought, not just one, but two adventures. I lay awake much of the night, my sleep, such as it was, punctuated by vaguely erotic phantasms of Suzi (with extreme justification), of Kimberley (with the freshness of sheer novelty), and with Gianetta (with no justification but much wishful thinking.) The sensually genial spirit of Anna glided in and out of my nocturnal imaginings, acting as a sort of celestial real estate agent, engineering the formation of a heavenly menage a quatre. It was on shaky knees indeed that I made my dewy pre-breakfast rounds to unlock the various rehearsal sites, my footsteps crunching on the roads and pathways in the morning silence, for the Mishipashoo Arts Centre was a place that awoke quietly. Campers straggled past on the way to breakfast, a crow cawed noisily off in the bush, a cow mooed in the pasture back of the concert tent, a modest cataract of the creek tinkled and gurgled where it passed under the road.

Hugo dropped by the office right after breakfast, Herbert the crow perched on his shoulder. "K.Y., can I borrow you for fifteen minutes or so?"

"Okay by you?" I said to Moneypenny.

"You're the boss."

"I guess I am. Sometimes around you I forget. What's up, Hugo?"

"I'm a bit worried about *Helen Louise*. She always takes a bit of water, but it's on the increase. I hope it's not rot or something. Come down for a look."

Helen Louise was Hugo's 1928 Gidley cruiser and the flagship of his fleet. She was berthed just downstream of the now-famous footbridge, along with *Screamer* and the assortment of camp

183

canoes, sailing dinghies, and rowboats. As we boarded her, the whir and gurgle of her electric bilge pump could be heard.

We took up the cockpit floorboards and spotted the trouble immediately. The stuffing box, the fitting where the propeller shaft came up through the bottom, was dribbling a silent little stream, an ailment easily fixed by tightening a couple of nuts.

"This is simple," I said. "You didn't need me."

"Maybe I didn't need you, I just wanted you, no, that didn't sound right. It's just that I haven't been able to catch up with you. How are you doing? I saw you talking to Gianetta yesterday. Tell me what was said. Tell me everything."

"Get me a socket wrench set and I'll talk."

The wrench was duly procured and I talked while Herbert the crow picked bits of debris from the bilge and dropped them overboard ("clever bird").

"It was pretty strange…"

"Conversations with her usually are. You get to a certain point and then you get cut off at the pass."

"You too, huh?"

"I think she's that way with all men. I think Antonio has made her anti-men. If it were my choice, he wouldn't even be permitted on the grounds."

"She was all admiring about my great rescue," I continued. "I was hoping it might open the door. But there was something else. The girl I fished out told me all this stuff about how different she was feeling about me…"

"Anna told me the French-kissing story. I thought it was great. Can I use it in a book?"

"Be my guest. I'm not entirely certain, but I don't think it was just ga-ga schoolgirl prattle. For the first time since she started studying with me, I felt as if I were talking to a contemporary…"

"Kids grow up too quickly. It's mass culture, in which, I'm sorry to say, I'm a major player."

"Why are you sorry?"

"I'm sorry about the effects of it all. There's a sort of universal demographic now in which age counts for nothing. There's no longer any hierarchy of knowledge or experience; the kids have so much more at their fingertips than you and I ever did, but much of the time it's the wrong kind of knowledge. You don't have to be able to read to watch television. What we are getting is knowledge without wisdom, or, to put it more bluntly, street smarts without literacy. But I'm off track. Tell me about the young lady."

The stuffing box continued to drip. Hugo and I were long overdue for a good chin-wag. "Well," I said, "I don't know how valid my judgement is. The teacher-student relationship among musicians is not your ordinary one. Psychologically, we inhabit the same space and so the boundaries get pretty blurred." I laughed uneasily. "Kimberley's a pretty mature gal, has had some adult situations to deal with, and me, I never quite made it as an adult. I'd rather be nine again. Alien used to call me a man-child."

"There are worse things to be. Anna and I have the same sort of impulse. We sometimes walk around the camp together and say, 'My God, this is our job?' Just the other day, Anna said we were like a couple of bunnies playing in the sunshine at the end of a rainbow."

"You should—"

"I already did. You know, we ought to fix this thing so you, er, we, can get back to work."

I hunched down to get at the leaky stuffing box. I gingerly tightened the nuts, careful not to strip the threads. "There are little holes in the nuts. If you have some thin wire, we can hog-tie them to keep them from loosening up."

"Let's see what the ship's stores have to offer," said Hugo, rummaging under the helmsman's seat. "Sometime I must organize this shit. Herbert's pretty clever, yes, Herbert, but his sense of organization needs some refinement. Aha, here we are."

As I worked with the wire, I remarked that Suzi had called the previous day. "She has to bring up exams today for some unfortunates who didn't get exempted. She instructed me to, uh, arrange some, er, mutual space for us."

"I thought you were hoping for that to cool down."

"I was, until she called. Just hearing her again made me lose my judgement, but I know it's all stupid."

"Remember what I said about how she made you happy. That's what counts. You know, I think *Helen Louise* will be wanting a sea trial, you know, to make sure your repairs are okay. Why don't you take Suzi out in her this afternoon, show her the islands and the Hole in the Wall, go for a swim in that bay on Mowat Island."

"However I may be of service to you, Mr. Harland."

"There is some justification for this. I have to do a screenplay of *Chaos in Laos* and I haven't started. I have to get to work pronto and show what in this business they call 'product', or my agent will go bananas. I've been procrastinating like mad, finding all sorts of excuses and diversions. I hate screenplays, it's just like writing the god-damn thing all over again. And I have to make sure *Helen Louise* is okay. Somebody's coming to do a magazine layout aboard her tomorrow."

"However I may be of service to you, Mr. Harland," I repeated.

185

I had a brief encounter with Kimberley just before lunch. "My mind is made up, Mr. Jackson. I'll wait for you if you can wait for me. Please think about it. I'm not trying to rush you into anything. I'd rather go slow and get it right." She withdrew before I could respond. I stood there in the middle of the road, immobilized like a deer in the headlights of a car, and a car slid to a stop right in front of me, engulfed in a boiling cloud of dust. It was Suzi.

"Sweetie!"

"Suzi, ssh! The children…"

"Only the children prevent me from taking you right here and right now. Oh, Sweetie, I've been going out of my mind. I'm a tiger today, got a new outfit, but I didn't do the garter belt."

"Suzi, pipe down, for God's sake. Look, we have the use of Hugo's cruiser this afternoon, so just try to contain yourself."

"You're scolding me," she pouted.

"Don't be silly." My blood pressure had gone into overdrive at the mention of her tiger underwear. Silly and goofy Suzi may have been, but she still had power over me.

She joined me for lunch in the little faculty dining room; to my dismay, I could see Gianetta, who so far had kept her distance, coming towards me and then at the sight of Suzi changing her mind and joining Sister Ingrid, Mrs. Rumley, and Neville Park, who was expounding as usual, fingers wisely steepled. My heart sank; this was not a good combination of personnel. I hoped that we would not be spotted on our afternoon departure.

Father Oakley was most accommodating about my impending absence, apparently still quite innocent of Suzi's and my relationship. "Go ahead, kid, and have fun. Everything's shaken down now and, unless there is another Bomb in Gilead, it should be a quiet afternoon. Tell you what, I could use some down time myself. You can cover for me tomorrow afternoon."

I felt a bit circumspect taking *Helen Louise* out on my own, despite Hugo's confidence in me. I was not accustomed to powered vessels of her size and she only had a single screw to manoeuvre on in the tight quarters around her berth. I need not have worried, however; she handled like a charm, as well-designed boats generally do, and Suzi and I were off in early afternoon, ploughing a furrow of dancing fragments of light over the breeze-ruffled waters that I knew and loved so well. Suzi knew the whole story and just stood quietly beside me as Helen Louise swung west and then south to clear Goat Island. We chugged along past Wigwas and Green Islands, rounded Horse Island, and set course for the narrow and steep-sided Hole-in-the-Wall. The local excursion ship, the *Island Queen*, came surging out of the gap on her afternoon sailing, and *Helen Louise* attracted considerable attention from the tourists, who waved expansively as we sliced through the swells of the larger ship.

We passed through the Hole-in-the-Wall, west to east, and then circumnavigated Wall Island to head back west to Mowat Island. One of my favourite spots from the days of *Snarley Yow* had been a beautiful wooded bay on the north side of Mowat, sheltered from all winds but a stiff north-westerly and with great pine and spruce climbing a lofty shoreline reminiscent of our west coast.

No other boats were in the anchorage; I ran *Helen Louise* astern to kill headway, dropped anchor (a big old Herreschoff), and shut the engine down. There was only the gentlest lapping of water and rustle of flags as *Helen Louise* trimmed herself to the wind.

"This is the most beautiful place I've ever seen," said an awe-struck Suzi. "A beautiful place to make memories, dearest son."

"You're doing the incest thing on me."

"Exciting, isn't it?" Suzi peeled off her clothes down to a bikini bathing suit so scant that from the back it was hard to discern whether she had any bottom on. With a convulsive flex of her luxuriant backside, she launched herself over the stern, to surface with a startled shriek, for, it being only early June, the water was still very cold.

I rigged the boarding ladder and was about to take the plunge when Suzi called, "Here, catch!" Her top, such as it was, came spiralling wetly through the air. She rolled onto her back, her breasts surfacing like twin pale islands with tiny pink navigation beacons. We swam only for a handful of minutes and then, between the cold water and the heat of desire, we went back aboard and adjourned to the cabin. Naked, wet, and pebbled with goosebumps, we fell onto the starboard bunk to work out almost a fortnight of thwarted desire. "This is the first boat I've ever liked," panted Suzi. "This is...really nice...oh, son...oh, God, I think I am in heaven...my darling...oh, baby...faster...oh, God, I'm...going to...to...oh, sweet mother of God...going to...EXPLODE!"

I too exploded; and then we dozed off for perhaps an hour or so. When I awoke, Suzi was on top of me, we were joined once again. "Don't move," she whispered. "Just lie still. I've always wanted to rape you. Now I'm going to do it." Keeping still was a real chore. I clutched the bedding, I wedged my feet under the sides of the mattress. Relentlessly, like a benign dominatrix, Suzi drove both of us to a squealing frenzy that did not go un-noticed by a crew of senior citizens whose thirty-five foot ketch had anchored nearby during our nap. I dressed, got the engine going, raised anchor, and *Helen Louise* crept sheepishly out of the bay.

Charlie had work to do in the office over dinner hour, doing some repairs, he said, to the p.a. system, and would I bring him over some food, which I did. I dined again with Suzi and again Gianetta gave me a tentative look and then retreated to another table.

For an hour or so after dinner each evening, there was an informal concert by members of the faculty on a voluntary basis; Charlie, Sister Ingrid, and I took turns as stage managers and announcers, and tonight Ingrid was stage-managing and I was doing what we called disc-jockey duty. Charlie was still in the office puttering with the p.a., although it seemed to be working just fine.

One of tonight's performers was to be Gianetta on the oboe, and just before the concert, she handed me a note:

Doing *Tunis* from Ports of Call. By Jacques Ibert, which you probably know. Please Sit down in front when I play.
G. d'A (ha)

I shrugged in acceptance; there was no time to analyse the "ha". The concert began, and Gianetta was first on. As per her request or demand or whatever it was, I took up station at the front of the house. Gianetta checked her A with our official accompanist, the massive and odoriferous Fat Pat, whom I fervently hoped was not up-draft of Gianetta...although if Gianetta passed out, I would have to revive her... but then the music began. Almost as if on the wind came the piano opening, a mysterious, syncopated seven-to-the-bar figuration. And then the mournful wail of the oboe, sounding is if it were coming up out of a grotto, spiralling into the evening sunlight. The audience was mesmerized.

Onward Gianetta played, her eyelids at half-mast, the perfumed harmonic-minor music working magic the like of which I have seldom encountered. The middle section of Tunis is fiendishly difficult, all manner of runs and grace notes; I was familiar with it, knew what was coming, prayed for Gianetta to be okay with it.

She was more, far more, than okay. In my silent encouragement, in willing that all should be well, I was staring at her and at the point in question, realized that she was staring back, straight at me, with an expression as hooded as the mood of the music, was she playing it just for me, oh, yes, there was no mistaking, a barrier had been demolished, a spiritual Berlin Wall taken down. The music reverted to the opening style and Gianetta drew back into herself.

188

The applause verged on the hysterical. I announced the next performer and then went backstage to congratulate Gianetta, but to my dismay, she had disappeared.

"Just ran out the back as if it were the worst thing she'd ever done," said Dunny Corrigan. "Funny. She's a wonderful player, really excellent. You don't hear stuff that good too often. As I said, she's really excellent. Wonder why she took off like that. She just won't have any idea how she touched us. She's really excellent."

For my part, I was flat-out troubled. The whole thing was just too strange, but there was no chance for investigation with Suzi present. She was to stay the night with Sister Ingrid in her cabin, thus obliterating any chance of a third coupling, but two had been sufficient for me; in any case I was monopolized for the evening, staying in out of the bugs with Suzi up at Anna and Hugo's house for what Hugo called a "happy hour". Happy it was for Suzi, but sorely shadowed for me.

Hugo and Anna's house was hard by the mouth of the creek on the east side; directly opposite, on a rocky promontory, was the Arthur Ransome Memorial Outpost, a firepit and general meeting area, where our students adjourned for a campfire and snack after their evening activity. Just before ten o'clock, they gathered as usual, tonight in a bright silvery moonlight. Their campfire flickered in yellow reflection in the black water, snatches of song and shouts of laughter dissipated out over the bay. Our conversation veered naturally to camp experiences, to regrets that camping was now so much less a part of Canadian childhood, of how summer jobs and cheap European holidays had taken their toll.

"It's just another example," said Hugo, "of what K.Y. and I were talking about earlier today, about how childhood is just being traversed too quickly or being skipped altogether...hello, what's that?"

"What's what?"

"That. Listen."

We listened. "That" sounded like something breathing heavily just behind the house. Hugo and I went to the back door and shone a light into the bush, fully expecting a moose or some such. There was a loud rustling sound and a thump that acoustically did not match the surroundings. "Uh," said a voice. Suddenly, the sounds over by the campfire had ceased. The campers were listening too.

"Oh, baby," sighed the voice thickly. "I love everything about you...so smooth, so young and beautiful..."

"Sweetheart," purred a directionless response. "Oh...kiss me there, right there...nibble me...now the other one..."

"What the dickens," whispered Hugo.

The female voice again: "Shall I put it on you? Oh, good, I wanted to...oh, you're magnificent...stupid foil...there...let me unroll it..."

There was a groan of pleasure as it was unrolled, followed by a rubbery snap. Hugo had stopped breathing. Anna and Suzi had joined us. They were not breathing either.

"Unh," said the original voice. "Oh, baby, you're the best..."

"Oh, no. You're the best." Sundry whimperings and bleatings. Moneypenny was to report gleefully the next day that some of the little girl campers crossed themselves at this point. At the time, our collective mentality was in gridlock, able neither to comprehend nor function.

"You can be on top...no, I love your weight, I want you to crush me...oh, you're in, you're in, oh, so divine, oh, baby, wonderfulwonderfulwonderfulwonderful..."

"Shit!" I snapped. "It's bloody Charlie. He's been puttering with the p.a. all evening. He's rigged something up."

I ran for the office, only a hundred or so metres distant. "Fuck me, fuck me," rasped a voice.

"I am, I am..."

"Harder, faster...harder, faster...oh, Holy Virgin Mother."

"Outstanding," said a voice in the dark.

I scrabbled to a halt. "Charlie, what the fuck is going on?"

"What you said."

"What do you mean, what I said?"

"Fuck, is what you said. That's what's happening, man. Listen. Isn't that just great? Reminds me of the *Poem of Ecstasy.*"

"Who in hell is it?"

"They're not in hell, which you could tell if you took the trouble to listen."

"I'm coming," murmured the forest.

"So am I," replied the rocks and the woodland creatures.

"Summer marches in, just like in that Mahler thing," said Charlie. "Cool."

"Who is it?"

"It's Warren and Scotia. They've been banjoing each other nightly ever since camp began. They use that little room where the p.a. is and I caught them at it the other night. Told them to knock it off or else. Now it's or else. I rigged the thing up so it was on without looking to be on. And now my artistry is reaching its climax. Hold me, K.Y."

"Fuck off, you perverted buzzard."

Twin cries of primal rapture tore the darkness and then silence descended. I tiptoed down to the office and took up station on one of the rocking chairs while legions of subdued campers surged past on their way to bed. Charlie quietly joined me as camper noises diminished and the growing quietude was broken only by the occasional slap of a screen door.

"Is the coast clear?" whispered a voice behind the office door.

"No, it isn't," I said loudly. "Get out here."

Thick, terrible silence.

"Let's go in, man, and take them alive," said Charlie. The door was locked, but I had a key. And, as Charlie had described, there were a terrified Scotia McLeod and Warren Peace.

"How did you know we were in here?" blurted Warren.

"Whole camp knows, man," said Charlie mercilessly. "It was broadcast on the p.a."

"The p.a. was on?"

"Yes, dummy, the p.a. was on. I doctored it so the lights and the V.U. meter wouldn't show. You're toast, buddy."

Scotia burst into sobs. "What'll my dad say? Oh, God, I'll be ruined. There'll be a scandal." Scotia's father was Duke McLeod, Director of the Birkenstock County Roman Catholic Board of Education and one of our primary supporters.

"Should have thought of that the first time you got caught," said Charlie relentlessly. "Go to your cabins and pack your bags. You'll be going home with Mrs. Quail in the morning."

In obvious shock, Warren and Scotia shuffled off into the darkness.

"I kind of jumped the gun there, man," said Charlie. "It wasn't really my place to do that, but I figured you would anyway."

"I don't know. Why in hell did it have to be Scotia McLeod, of all people?"

"It's the law. This is the Osterling Weekend. And there are four days left. Woo-hoo!"

And this day wasn't over with yet. I thought I should tell Neville and went to his quarters, which were dark, but not vacant. Perhaps inspired by Warren and Scotia's public demonstration of mature love, Neville was in the throes of an Angioplasty and likely would brook no disturbance. I set course, then, to Anna and Hugo's for the dual purpose of telling them what had happened and of escorting Suzi back to where she was staying.

I never made it. Silhouetted against the moon-splashed water at the end of the dock was the solitary figure of Gianetta, sitting on the bow of a dinghy with her back to me. Cautiously, I walked out to her, afraid to intrude and yet having to know why she was there.

"Hi, Gianetta."

"Hi."

"Are you, uh, all right?"

"Functioning."

"You did a hell of a lot more than just function at the concert. It was absolutely brilliant."

"It was okay. I think I could have played it better. I wanted to. It was for you."

"For me?"

"It said everything I want to say in words but I can't. There's this damnable invisible barrier around me and I can't break it down and I don't think anyone can do it for me. Antonio came close, but he is such a pig, he's like…"

"Like who?"

"Sit down and I'll try to tell you. I've never told anyone else any of this before."

"Don't tell anything you're not comfortable with."

"I don't know how far I'll get with it, but I have to try. If I have to stop, well, I'll need you to understand. The bottom line—how I hate that expression—is that I really don't like being on my own, but it's the only way I feel safe. In fact, it's a miracle I ended up doing music. I had some pretty peculiar early associations with it."

"Oh, oh," I said in a small voice.

"Oh, oh is right, though with an odd variation. I started out on clarinet when I was in Grade 9 and I really loved it, to the point of addiction, actually, and my teacher, his name was Mr. Goebbels—"

"What?"

"Yes, really. Mr. Goebbels offered me free private lessons—"

"Oh, shit."

"It wasn't quite what you think, in fact, I didn't really know what was happening at the time until one of my friends explained it to me. But what Mr. Goebbels did at the end of each lesson was to stick the bell of the instrument in his crotch and say to me, 'Now, blow!' So I…"

"…huffed and puffed…"

"…and after a minute or so, he'd start to sweat and his eyes rolled about and he'd make all these spluttering and gulping sounds. Then he'd tell me abruptly to go home. Dummy me. I thought I was being trained in breath control or something."

"Well, Mr. Goebbels kind of disappeared part way through the year. Not only did he have this odd specialty, but it was not exactly gender-specific.

"Then in Grade 10 there was Mr. Purvis. Purvis the pervert."

"Sounds like Rupert the Bear or something."

"Come to think of it, he did look a bit like Rupert the Bear. How do you know about Rupert the Bear?"

"Used to watch it with my kids."

"At least you had some justification. I used to watch it on my own. Still do when I get the chance."

I was liking Gianetta more and more. There was a child in there somewhere. But what she had to tell me was not childlike.

"Mr. Purvis had the ultimate system. In each theory class, he'd pick the prettiest girl and seat her at the back of the room."

"And you were the prettiest."

"Well, he thought so. So there I was. It started one day during seat-work; I was writing away and he came to see how I was getting on. He put his hand on my back in the friendliest way and next thing I knew, he had, with consummate mastery, undone my bra."

I stopped breathing. The glory of Gianetta unfettered and free.

"So there I was, not exactly deprived in that particular area, with no support, hugging my books to me as I left class. It was completely bizarre."

"So you never got to tell anyone."

"Well, no. Nobody would have believed it. A few years ago, I ran into one of my old friends and we got to reminiscing about our teachers. I told her about it and it turned out the same thing had happened to her. We checked around and found two more girls, just from our year, who had been, er, undone by Mr. Purvis. Even though it was years after the fact, we thought we'd try to bring action, but he had vanished to Inuvik or someplace and it was just too much bother."

A fish splashed out in the water. I could hear footsteps and voices on the near-by road and realized with horror that it was Anna and Suzi, but I could hardly abandon ship under the current conditions.

"These events," continued Gianetta, "just turned me off men and the way my friends were all carrying on about boys, I felt like an outcast. I never lacked for dates, but I sure disrupted the usual timetable of Man the Hunter."

"Which is?"

"First date kiss, second date French kiss, third date feel her up, fourth date bare tit, fifth date digital exploration of the erogenous zone, sixth date the Big One, and I am being conservative. With me, step three was it. I won't say I didn't enjoy being felt up, but it lost its charm when Purvis's expert little fingers would weasel

193

themselves into my imagination and then it was all over. I may have gotten lots of dates, but I was also the most-dumped girl in my class. Until Rupert."

"Rupert?"

"There really was a Rupert, and not a bear, either. He came into my class from England in Grade 11. Rupert was everything I wanted. I don't care for jocks and other rugged types and Rupert was no jock. He was a gentleman, he was sensitive, loved music, especially opera...he cried all the way through *Madame Butterfly* and wasn't embarrassed... was a wonderful painter, loved literature and theatre. He was very funny, too. We had some great laughs together. Rupert and I were an item for almost two years."

I tried not to speculate on Rupert's adherence to the timetable of Man the Hunter. "It took Rupert a full year to get all the way through the timetable of Man the Hunter, if you understand my meaning."

"I do," I gulped.

"But the awful part is that he wasn't interested in me at all."

"What?"

"I have a twin brother."

"Oh, no."

"Oh, yes. Rupert was, as they say, a practitioner of the alternate lifestyle. I was simply a pipeline to my brother Fred."

"So what happened to Fred? What did he do?"

"He and Rupert had gotten to be very good friends, and then Rupert started being Man the Hunter to Fred and Fred beat the living shit out of him. Rupert was heartbroken and moved to Sarawak."

"Jesus," I murmured.

"So I was a basket case all through university. I trusted nobody, but, God, it was lonely. Then, in third year, I got a gig and who was the conductor but..."

"Antonio!" we chorused together.

"Well, didn't wee Janet...don't forget that was my name...didn't wee Janet just wake up and read the tea-leaves. All the women had the G.T.s for him..."

"The G.T.s?"

"Genital tension." I gulped with a sound like a breeching whale. "But I was the Chosen One. He was bright, he was, I thought, educated. He was, I thought, wealthy. Turned out he did some funny things with money too, but that really isn't within the scope of this conversation.

"Antonio also took his time with the timetable of Man the Hunter, in fact, he was so leisurely that I came within an inch of screaming 'Fuck me, fuck me!', it was that intense. I startled you, didn't I? He had these beautiful, manicured hands, so smooth and skilled...oh, I'm sorry, Ken...but I just wanted his hands all over me, and when it happened, I thought I had died and gone to heaven."

Ruefully, I thought how rough and unkempt my own hands were from a week of fighting tractors and moving equipment.

"So," continued Gianetta, "it was like a fairy tale. We got engaged and the day after I got my degree, we had this great Italian wedding, for which all his relatives were hired. May I remind you that his real family lives in B.C. and are totally Anglo. Oh, you should have seen all the *zias* and *zios*..."

"The which?"

"That's Italian for aunties and uncles. And cousins galore, all of whom disappeared after the wedding, never to be seen again. Turned out Antonio ran a modelling agency on the side as a scam and that was what paid the bill.

"You know about how I was required to change my name to Gianetta."

"It suits you. You look Italian."

"Actually, I'm of Irish background with a known dollop of Spanish from the Armada thrown in. Anyway, the rest of the whole sorry tale of Janet Adversity you pretty well know, except that after we were married, Antonio took to wearing women's underwear when we made love. Said it made him feel closer to me when he wore my kind of clothes."

The moon by now was well into the west and the camp was silent. To the east, a train could be heard blowing for the road crossing north of Nobel. "I love that sound," sighed Gianetta. "'Yet there isn't a train I wouldn't take, no matter where it's going.'"

"Edna St. Vincent Millay," I said.

"I like men who know their poetry."

"It's the only one I know."

"Doesn't matter. I've told all. Now you have to tell all."

There is no need to recount this part of the conversation as the sorry details of life with Alien have already been covered. But when I finished my narrative, by which time the moon was hanging low over Carling Bay, Gianetta asked, "Who was that woman you were with at lunch and dinner?"

I though this was going to be easy. "That's my ex-mother-in-law who happens to be married to my principal."

"She's crazy about you. It was written all over her. And you looked far more attentive that the usual son-in-law. I know something's going on and it's good."

"Good?"

"It's good because it made me a bit jealous, the first normal feeling I've had for years. It's the old thing, you know, when something isn't available or you have to struggle for it, it becomes so desirable. That's why I went so weird with *Tunis* tonight. I was thinking far more of you than I was the music."

"I loved it."

"I'm glad. I have to go now" (oh, no!) "but I'd like it if you could walk me to my cabin. The moon's gone now and I can't see without it."

We trudged up to Gianetta's cabin, our new intimacy almost tangible, and yet the barrier was still there; something told me I shouldn't even try to hold her hand, and I didn't. Nor was there so much as a friendly hug, just a business-like "Good night, Ken. Thanks for listening." What could have been my personal Transfigured Night was just another ambiguous encounter, another return flight on a spiritual boomerang.

LET'S GET THIS WORKING!

Predictably, Suzi was petulant at breakfast. "You didn't come back to me last night. Who was that woman on the dock?"

"It was one of our faculty members with some personal problems."

"And counselling them is part of your job? Especially when they are drop-dead gorgeous?"

"My job is anything that needs to be done. And this needed to be done." Gianetta, at another table, was acting as if I were not even in the room. "Besides, you're married."

"Meaning?"

"Well, among other things, you don't own me." I knew it was the wrong thing to say, but before I could make amends, the young walrus figuration of Dunny plunked itself down at our table.

"Hi, folks, mind if I join you? Good…great morning, wasn't that a great moon last night? Reminded me of Schoenberg's *Transfigured Night,* love that thing even if it's just for strings…great having Osterling here, the man's a giant, wonder if Oakley can get him back next year, you know, all my university buddies are just green that I'm here when he's here, this is the best fun, it's really excellent…"

Amends were further inhibited by a summons for me and Charlie to meet with Neville Park right after breakfast at Hugo's cottage. A tear-stained Scotia McLeod and a disconsolate Warren Peace were present. Remnants of breakfast clung to Neville's shirt-front. He steepled his fingers and began.

"As Roman Catholics and musicians, we are committed to the highest ethical and artistic standards. It is part of what we are. Miss McLeod and Mr. Peace, you have violated those standards. And so, I am sorry to say" (oh, God, he knows about me and Suzi!) "have you" (ohGodohGod), "Mr. Cowell."

"Meeeee?" screeched Charlie.

197

"Yes, you, for your shabby little escapade with the public address system. What should have been a private matter among us is now known to the entire camp. What I do not think is known, however, is the identity of those who were...um..."(Warren and Scotia looked at the floor) "engaged in vile, shameful, and illicit sexual intercourse on camp property, although since neither of you have responsibilities after dinner, anyone can put two and two together.

"However, what has happened has happened. Now we have to do damage control. Legitimately, the two of you should be let go. And, Mr. Cowell, what you did was so tasteless, disruptive, and ill-advised that your presence as well is now less than desirable.

"We have the dilemma, of course, that Miss McLeod's father is the Director of Education for the Birkenstock County Roman Catholic School Board." Neville summoned every drop of awful majesty that he could for his pronouncement. "We have the dilemma that, even though we said anyone guilty of inappropriate behaviour would be let go, replacing you at this stage would be difficult indeed."

"A couple of Anna's waterfront staff could fill in," said Charlie. He was out for blood.

Neville's steeple wavered, as if in a high wind. "Replacing you at this stage would also be difficult. Now, Mr. McLeod is one of our leading supporters. The fallout from all this could be devastating to the camp and will, of course, mean the *most acute*, most acute, embarrassment, humiliation, discomfiture, and perplex to the McLeod family."

Scotia was so wracked with sobs as to sound about to be sick. "Want a bowl?" asked Charlie chivalrously. She shook her head and wiped some drool from her mouth.

"Under these considerations, if Scotia is retained, so, out of fairness, is Warren."

"But..." said Charlie.

"Ah, ah, ah," said Neville imperiously, raising his hand, leaving the other frozen in its steeple position. "I have weighed all these considerations and have decided to proceed with the status quo. However, Miss McLeod and Mr. Peace, you will be under staff supervision at all times from now on to prevent further fornication and other lascivious, inappropriate, and sinful behaviour. Miss McLeod, you will be permanently attached to Sister Ingrid and will be with her at all times when not on duty. Mr. Peace, you will be attached to" (Charlie and I looked at each other) "Mr. Jackson under the same conditions."

Oh, shit, I thought indignantly. What about my own fornication and other lascivious, inappropriate, and sinful behaviour? An understanding with Warren would have to be forged.

"Further," decreed Neville, fingers steepled once more, "while on duty at the waterfront, the two of you will be required to shroud yourselves from each other's view to discourage lustful and pornographic thought."

"But, sir, if we have to do a rescue..."

"Ah, ah, this is not a matter for discussion. I would have to say, young lady, that you have gotten off very easily, very easily indeed."

"Yes, sir. Thank you, sir."

A thump of footsteps sounded on the veranda. It was Father Oakley. "Father Oakley," announced Neville, "has kindly taken the time to hear a full and detailed confession. Mr. Jackson and Mr. Cowell, you are excused."

"Gutless fucker," grumbled Charlie on our way up the road. "He's scared skinny of Duke McLeod. Now those kids get off scot free, although I don't think I'd care to be confessing something like that to Father Oakley." He grabbed my arm. "I gotta confess something to you, though."

"What?"

"The Pipe Cleaner was in bed reading a Danielle Steele book last night when the, uh, broadcast took place. When I got in, man, she came at me, she tore my Bare Naked Ladies T-shirt to shreds..."

"Oh, no, not the one Eddie Robertson signed."

"Yeah, man, it was my Shroud of Turin, torn right through the middle of Eddie's signature. I got totally trashed, gouges all over my back, Jenny thought Mummy and Daddy were having a fight. In point of fact, Mummy and Daddy were having the time of their lives, and unprotected at that. I know it's not very Catholic, but we don't want to spawn like some people. If a kid results from last night, it'll be called Scotia if it's a girl or Warren if it's a boy. What is going on over there?"

It was slightly past ten o'clock, the time for a fifteen-minute break before sectional rehearsals. Even though the camp had been in session for only four days, instant traditions had popped up like toadstools, one of which was to see how many could stand on the footbridge during break without it collapsing. So far it had resisted. But this morning, nobody was on the bridge. Rather, a pod of students was oscillating slowly around a Mercedes by the office. And then the pod began to move slowly in the direction of *Helen Louise's* berth.

"Oh," I said, "Hugo said something yesterday about a magazine layout being done aboard his boat."

"This is going to be some layout, then. Look who just got out of the car."

"Holy shit, it's Vesuvia Siliconti!" The discerning reader will recall Vesuvia Siliconti as the star of a mindless T.V. soap-opera/thriller called *Sea-Watch*; the discerning reader will further recall that her role required Vesuvia Siliconti to be clad in the most economical of swim-wear, and, although she was fully-attired this morning, her mere presence had acted as a magnet to our young of both genders, for the boys worshipped Ms. Siliconti and the girls wanted to be like her.

Hugo, elegantly dressed in whites and with an electric blue ascot (he had borrowed it from Antonio), escorted Ms. Siliconti along the dock, followed by a coterie of photographers, managers, and bodyguards, the pod of students slowly following. Since the dock was a floating one, it began to submerge under the weight of ardent young humanity. Crew on board, *Helen Louise* let go her lines and set out into the first breeze of the day on her designated mission.

Ruefully, I discovered that Suzi had left, and despite my jumble of feelings about Gianetta, despite Kimberley Clark's evident designs on me, despite my irritation at (I thought) being accountable to Suzi, I was still too fond of her for ill-feeling; at least, she was a known quantity in all aspects of the feelings department.

At this point, she would have been on the highway around Mactier or Foot's Bay or someplace and therefore beyond communication, so I phoned the office in Birkenstock.

"Music Department, Mrs. Cadbury speaking."

"Sweet Marie!"

"Sweet Mr. Jackson! How is my golden boy this morning? How I've missed you. Why do I have to be retiring just when you're coming here full time? What should be deliriously happy has been tainted…how's everything?"

"Oh, fine. Look, can I leave a message for Suzi? She left before I could tell her something."

"I know," whispered the phone cavernously.

"Know what?"

"About you and Suzi. She told me. She's going out of her mind. Hello? Are you still there, Sweet One?"

"Uh, yes."

"Here I stayed away from you only because you were married, and then the second you were available, she beat me to it. Now I'm

200

all jealous. But, yes, my lovely, I'll leave a message. What shall it be?"

"Just that I called and I'd like, no, I'd love it if she called me."

"Certainly, dearest Mr. Jackson. My lips are sealed."

Anna was out on the dock in a state of dudgeon so high as to be stratospheric. "Anna, you look to be in a state of the highest dudgeon."

"I swear I'll skin Hugo alive. I knew he was doing some sort of photographic thing, but he never told me it was Vesuvia Siliconti."

"How could he do anything with all those other people? And why would he want to when he's married to the supreme love goddess of the century?" Anna had no inkling of my sincerity.

"You're such a dear. But the way he dressed up for her and fawned over her, well, it was disgusting. And with all those campers around…"

"Hey," said Pete, wandering up. "How about that Eye-talian girl, eh? Sure got everyone greatly excited, havin' someone from the television and all. Can't wait to tell Rosie. Tried to call, but she's havin' a real busy mernin' there at the AynPee."

"Are you greatly excited, Pete?"

"Nah, not me. Got my Rosie. But even if you're on a diet, nothin' says you can't look at the menu, eh? Hey, Ken, I'm dried right out. Got a PeeCee for me in the office?"

A message came for me in mid-afternoon that Suzi would call at six, a time that we could talk in private. I told Moneypenny I would lock up the office , she went ahead to dinner, and Suzi called as arranged. She was convinced that I had something going with Gianetta; if I had, it was still too cloaked in mystery and ambiguity for me to be able to say yes, so I was able truthfully to say no. I got her calmed down, rang off, and closed the office, just as Vesuvia Siliconti's Mercedes purred past; a solitary Hugo stood at the end of the dock, silhouetted against the shimmering waters of Georgian Bay. I walked out to him to ask how things had gone, but I needed to say nothing. I had never seen Hugo terror-stricken, but he was now, cuddling Kitty Sark for security and comfort. "Oh, shit, Anna's going to skin me alive."

"She said she was going to," I reported reassuringly.

"Nobody told me there was going to be porn stuff. I thought it would just be bathing suits, Sports Illustrated or something."

"Porn stuff?"

"Of the most blatant kind."

"And you saw?" I asked almost reverently.

"Don't sound so reverent. Yes, I saw. I had no choice. What a nightmare. I'm just too much of a prude for this kind of thing."

"Embarrassing?"

"It was appalling." Hugo deposited Kitty onto the dock and climbed aboard *Helen Louise*. "There's a nice, high point off the end of Muriel Island, well, you know the place. I got the boat positioned there and then Vesuvia takes it all off, and, let me tell you, she is stacked in the grand tradition, like Monroe and Russell and Novak. So she got on the stern seat, like this" (Hugo sat as sensually as he could, chest out, hand suggestively on thigh), "and then she did this" (Hugo cupped an imaginary pair of breasts and fixed his face in an obscene kiss that made him look like a carp), "and then she rolled over and stuck her ass right up in the air, like this."

In a losing battle not to laugh, I made a noise like a fire extinguisher going off. Kitty fled in fright.

"This isn't funny," reproved Hugo. "Then she stood up, bent her knees, and started flapping them in and out, in and out, like this." Hugo demonstrated, looking like an eagle flapping its wings while standing on its head.

"What the hell is that supposed to mean?"

"The wind had, er, dried her out. She said 'Let's get this working', flapping away to get all moistened up again. Then she flopped down on the stern seat again and spread her legs as if on an examining table. And there's this photographer fellow clicking away and the other guys standing around as if it were all normal. And this shit was going on by the hour. Now it's going to be in *Hustler* magazine or some damn thing. They paid me a fortune and my name's going to be in the magazine and everything. I signed before I realized it."

"Oh, shit, you mean 'Vesuvia Siliconti was guest aboard distinguished author Hugo Harland's antique boat' or something?"

"Oh, yes, and Anna's going to kill me. Listen, could you come up to the house while I tell her? Maybe having you there will keep her calm."

Hugo repeated his illustrations for Anna and I don't know which of the two of them was funnier. Anna could never be mad if she laughed, and laugh she did, ending up in a whimpering heap under the dining room table. Hugo's confession completed and after a suitable rest period, the three of us staggered up to the dining hall for a belated dinner, Anna holding hands with both of us for a few fleeting moments of paradise.

I persuaded Hugo to do a third performance for Charlie and, after some reflection, for Father Oakley during evening activities. Father Oakley guffawed (remarking that he would be unable to get through confession without losing it) and Charlie, not generally susceptible to that sort of thing, laughed until he cried. "A new star is born in the lexicon of the Osterling Weekend," he declared.

"What's that?"

" 'Let's get this working!' "

AN ORDINARY DAY

The sixth day of the Osterling Weekend, a Thursday, was as ordinary a day as we ever had during that remarkable time.

For Neville Park, our Maximum Leader, it was his last day, and it was fitting that it should be a Thursday, of being on his own with Ms. Rumley, for the attractive but formidable Mrs. Park was expected that night, to stay with Neville until the end of camp. There was also a sense of impending finale; the last faculty concert had been the night before and the remaining two evening performances were to be presented by the students.

I had not had any contact with Kimberley for the last couple of days, beyond the occasional greeting in passing. It looked as if her ardour was born of the euphoria of rescue and was perhaps going on its way of its own accord. For me, there was a vague sense of disappointment, of unfulfilled curiosity, alloyed with relief. A third party in my theatre of affection would be just too difficult to deal with. I was not prepared, then, for the contents of an envelope in my mailbox, marked 'Mr. K.Y. Jackson—Personal and Confidential.' Moneypenny smirked knowingly as I took it outside to open it, for it had been hand-delivered.

In the envelope was a sheet of birchbark, beautifully decorated with little plants and animals indigenous to the camp and with these words of Henry Wadsworth Longfellow:

As unto the bow the cord is,
So unto the man is woman;
Though she bends him, she obeys him,
Though she draws him, yet she follows,
Useless each without the other!

Also in the envelope was a slip of paper and on it was written,

204

Dear Mr. Jackson,

I can't stop thinking of you. I made this for you and I'm sorry it took so long, but, as I said the other day, better to go slow and get it right.

Love always,
K.C.

"Sir, can I talk to you for a moment?" I looked up. It was Scotia McLeod, looking as if she wished the world would end.

"Hi, Scotia. Cheer up."

"I can't, all the things I said, and broadcast all over the place. I never hated anyone until now, but I sure hate Mr. Cowell."

"He did warn you."

"I know, but, well, Warren and I are so totally like in love and can't, like, get enough of each other. I know you've been through it too and you understand."

I wondered what she knew what I had in fact been through, but never had a chance to find out. "I hope this isn't an imposition," she said, "but there are some people wanting to go sailing this afternoon and we can't do any real instruction. I hear you know quite a bit about it. Would you be willing to take a boat out with someone at five o'clock?"

"Would I be willing? Twist my arm."

"You're a sweetie, Mr. Jackson. Thanks so much."

I reported to the waterfront shortly after four thirty. "Mr. Harland said to take *Olivia*," said Scotia. She was shrouded as per Neville's instructions, in ludicrous contrast to her freckled, sunburnt face, but curiously the shroud merely emphasized her desirability. I swallowed. "Your crew will be here at five."

"Thanks, Scotia." I boarded *Olivia* and set about my preparations, taking off the sail cover, hanking on the jib, shipping the rudder, making sure all lines were running freely. *Olivia* was a little beauty, a sixteen-foot Grew dinghy that Hugo had named (to Anna's intense but temporary irritation) for the singer Olivia Newton-John. When Ms. Newton-John had been awarded the Order of the British Empire some years before, Hugo had added the letters O.B.E. to the ship's name on the transom.

Footsteps on the dock. "Hi. I'm here."

I looked up. It was Kimberley. "Oh… hi. Who and where is the rest of the crew?"

"Just me."

"Oh, uh, okay." I gave Kimberley a short orientation and then we paddled *Olivia* out to where the breeze was and hoisted sail. Within two minutes, I could tell that Kimberley not only knew how to sail, but knew how to sail very well. I let her take over the helm.

"You don't need me here. You're very good."

"I missed you and got Scotia to fix it up for me."

"I got your birchbark. It's beautiful."

"I'm glad. When do you think you can get divorced?"

I wanted to cry "whoa!", but something held me back. "I probably could any time, but you attend to your education first. Savour what's left of your youth. Don't get into adult situations any sooner than you have to."

"Can you promise that I won't lose you?"

"Kimberley, honey, you have university ahead of you—"

"Without you. I'm going to die—"

"No, you're not."

"But then I won't be your student, and that'll be easier. We can spend time together and I won't die after all."

"Kimberley, I think we should just confine ourselves to being good friends."

"I want more. I want it all. My mind is made up, I told you that. Ready about...helm's alee."

I retrimmed the jib and we flew off on the other tack.

"Ready about...helm's alee."

"What, already?"

"Yes, already. You do as I say, Mr. Jackson. If I have to be a dominatrix, well, so be it. Ready about, helm's alee."

Frantically we tacked up to Carling Bay, south and then east around Goat and Grave Islands, and back to the camp. Kimberley was a gutsy sailor and was not perturbed as an ugly parfait of several different shades of blue, grey, and yellow developed toweringly to the west and moved in quickly on a freshening wind. "Like me to take her?" I offered.

"I can handle her, kind sir. Gybe-oh!"

The sails slammed across and a silver streak of water sluiced over the gunwale. "Shit!" I said involuntarily.

"Shit!" said Kimberley triumphantly, laughing for the first time since the Rescue. "Tell me we wouldn't make a great couple! Oh, look at that sky. I do believe we're in for an adventure."

"We're going back in."

"But of course. Good sailors don't take stupid chances."

Gusts of wind tore at *Olivia,* sending her stout, clinker-built hull slicing madly through the rising seas.

"Know what my big dream is?" shouted Kimberley above the racket.

"What?"

"That we should have our own yacht and whenever it stormed, we'd just bull our way through it and when we found our harbour at the end of the day, one of us would say 'We must get out of these wet clothes!'" She laughed again. "You should see the look on your face!"

"I'll bet. Want me to take her in?"

"No way, I mean, no, thank you."

Kimberley brought us in at full tilt; I was certain we were going to ram the end of the dock, but at the last moment, Kimberley spun *Olivia* into the wind, doing a landing so gentle that a kitchen sponge would have sufficed as a fender. We berthed the boat in her slip, secured her lines, got the jib stowed and the sail cover on, as Kimberley chanted, "Come on, rain, come on, rain!"

"What?"

"So that we'll have wet clothes to get out of."

"At this point, it would be a pretty academic exercise." Jackson, you idiot, what are you saying?

"No, even in separation, it could be pretty exciting. I'd just think of you as I undid—"

"Kimberley, this is sexual harassment. I want you to stop right now."

"I'm not stopping, now or ever. Remember the bond between us. I said it couldn't be broken."

"What would your mother think?"

"My mother is too wasted on alcohol to think. That's why we have no money and I had to try my, er, lottery to get to camp. Effectively, I'm on my own and I hate it. I want you to care for me." She leapt out of the boat and all but ran up the road, now devoid of campers as they made their way to dinner. I finished bailing and, mind churning almost painfully, followed as gusts of wind sent dust devils before me and flailed the trees, exposing the pale underside of their leaves. As I got to dinner, the storm broke.

STOP, DROP, AND ROLL

Friday was the final full day of the Osterling Weekend and the last day of the timetable that had been established over the course of so many meetings. On that account, there was a whiff of melancholy in the air, reinforced by the overcast left over by last night's storm and the long faces worn by Mr. Park and Mrs. Rumley, their lengthy idyll now terminated by the presence of Mrs. Park.

As the working day started, Father Oakley and I did a joint happiness check, more out of a sense of ceremony than anything. The Concert Choir were putting the final touches on what may have been the most authoritative rendition of *There is a Balm in Gilead* of all time. "They should know it anyway," grumbled Father Oakley. "Bet Biddy Rumley has done the damn thing a hundred times."

Mrs. Cowell, Charlie's beloved Pipe Cleaner, had the Concert Orchestra hard at work on something by Purcell. As she conducted, her extreme length undulated like a snake standing on its end. In fascination, we watched as, without pause, she steered the piece, some Chaconne or another, to its end; it really was beautiful and as the last note was released, there was a chorus of "Yes!" and "All right!", all but drowned out by the war-cry of "Oh, yeahhhh!"

"Great job, guys," applauded Father Oakley. "Just no 'oh, yeahhhh!' when you finish it at tomorrow's concert, okay?"

"Oh, yeahhhh!" chorused the orchestra.

Our next call was to the Symphonic Band, of which Giannetta was conductor. We stood watching and listening for a few minutes, during which there was no acknowledgement of our presence. Concentration was one thing, but this felt more like being simply ignored. "I think we're being ignored," said Father Oakley. "She's a strange one. She'll talk to you, very friendly, and

208

then suddenly it's as if somebody threw a light switch. I don't know what her problem is, but it's not our place to fix it. She does do the job, which is the most important thing. Let's carry on."

Dunny Corrigan came scuttling down the road. "Dunny, what the hell is wrong?" Dunny should have been with his band. "It's okay, Osterling's got it for the moment. He did this new piece for us, finished it yesterday…"

"Dunny, for God's sake, we didn't actually commission him to write something for us. We don't have a budget for it…"

"It's okay, Father, he did it as a present for the camp…"

"And it just so happens your band is to do it. Who's to conduct?"

"Me, so I'd better get back there. Come on up and hear it, it's really excellent. What a wizard the man is, this is really exciting, everything I ever dreamed of, my university buddies are going to be green over this one, just listen to that, will you? He was up most of the night working on the score, this is just like with Mozart, you know, the ink hardly dry, and these kids, they're wonderful, they read so well, it's like working with a Hollywood studio orchestra…"

"Dunny."

"Yes, Father?"

"Take a breath before you pass out. Pull yourself together…"

"But this is so exciting. A first performance…"

"You're doing it tomorrow?"

"Yes. They'll have it ready. Everything else is set to go, so we can spend all day on it."

"It" was called the *Mishipashoo Overture*. "Hey," said Father Oakley, "Dunny's a hustler. If he thinks they can do it, I'll just stay out of the way."

We lingered for a few minutes outside the Theatre Workshop to hear the new work. Eric had spent some time making adjustments and corrections and now Dunny took over on the podium to do a complete take against a counterpoint of barn swallows as they flew in and out an open window, oblivious to the sound about them, until a piccolo solo based on their song. Puzzled, they paused to listen; for that moment, we could not look each other in the eye, moved as we were by this fleeting union of life forms.

"Nice piece," said Father Oakley as we trudged over to the Wind Ensemble. "That Dunny, though, he's a caution…now, there's dear Israel, doing Bruckner with a band."

"Israel did the arrangement. So much for you trying to hide that music from G.V. Thomas…"

"I did not hide it."

209

"Could you swear on the Holy Virgin?"

"I don't have to."

"Oh, sure, Father."

Israel finished his Bruckner, the scherzo from the Seventh Symphony, as we strolled into his headquarters in the old barn. "Bravo, guys," said Father Oakley. "Just remember that's orchestra stuff."

"So?" said Israel, hands on hips. Looks of anticipation bloomed in the ranks of the Wind Ensemble; they loved it when Israel and Father Oakley went head-to-head. So, for that matter, did Israel and Father Oakley. For my own part, I usually did, but while they debated, I could not evade the dewy stare of Kimberley Clark from the saxophone section, a distillation of youthful womanly perfection, of maturity and lingering girlhood, of the capacity to sail the hell out of a boat and say "shit", of the caring and affection to send me lines by Longfellow on birchbark.

"K.Y? Hey, are you awake? Come on, kid, we still have things to do."

On our way up the trail to the Symphony Orchestra, our last port of call, Father Oakley said to me, "It's young Kimberley, isn't it?"

I sighed. "Is there no escape?"

"You haven't, er, done anything, have you?"

"Oh, no, she's just been kind of…strange since I fished her out of the creek."

"What girl wouldn't be? Snatched from the jaws of death by a good-looking, intelligent, single man who is not a stranger, now seen in a different light…"

"Father, I had no idea you felt that way!"

Father Oakley spun away in horror. "It's bad enough with Charlie, don't you go all queer on me too."

"Neither of us is queer."

"I know, but it scares me when the two of you act like it. Now just listen. She's beautiful and she's bright and she's attractive. Just remember this will pass. She's just a kid. She's dazzled by what you did, but then we'll all get back to Birkenstock and get on with our lives."

"She has a job helping me close up the music room for the summer."

"Then leave the music room door open, kid. Don't go screwing up your life. And don't forget, you're still a sitting duck after what Alien put you through. Be nice to Kimberley, but not too nice."

"Yeah," I said disconsolately.

Father Oakley, sensing my confusion, patted me on the shoulder. "Let's hear that said with spirit."

"Oh, yeahhhh!"

Antonio, in flat-out rivalry with Israel, was also embroiled in Bruckner, the first movement of the Fourth Symphony. It was the one work by the orchestra on tomorrow's programme; as Antonio had put it at an organizational meeting the previous afternoon (before the wild voyage with Kimberley), "I choose'a da first move'ament of'a da Fourth Symphony by'a Anton Bruckner because of its title *Romantic*, which'a so'a vividly portrays Bruckner's reverence for'a da nature of which'a we are so much of a part here at'a Mishipashoo..."

Father Oakley shook his head at the memory. "Dickhead," he muttered. "Well, Neville decreed the son-of-a-bitch should be here, so it's on his head if the damn concert goes on all night. Charlie'll be pissed, though, if he's still here at midnight cleaning up."

Neville Park was not to be present to bear any responsibility for Antonio. By the time the concert was to begin on the Saturday afternoon, Neville was in the burn unit at Sunnybrook Medical Centre in Toronto, via the Parry Sound General Hospital. This is how it happened.

After the afternoon rehearsal of this last day, there were no electives, athletics or waterfront activities. The campers were left to their own devices under limited supervision while student staff rounded up all chairs, music stands, and percussion equipment for marshalling in the concert tent and the barn, where two concerts were to be run concurrently the next day to save time. Charlie, Sister Ingrid, and I, in consultation with Pete, had organized who was responsible for what, and after lunch, the three of us were taking a stroll along the road in front of Neville's quarters in an oasis of calm before the games should begin.

For us, the games began a bit sooner than anticipated. As we ambled along, we encountered Rick O'Shea, whom Antonio had despatched with a message for Neville; as Rick stopped to exchange pleasantries with us, the front door of Neville's quarters flew open and the usually-sluggish Neville came running, running for the first time in living memory.

"My God, he's running," I said in surprise.

"Look, Mr. Park's running," said Rick.

"Praise be to God, Neville's running," said Sister Ingrid as if witnessing a miracle.

"I do believe that the Walking X-Ray is running," said Charlie.

It took us a moment to realize that Neville was on fire. Flaming garments peeled from him as he raced towards the water like a pregnant giraffe in a stampede.

"Jesus, Mary, and Joseph!" exclaimed Sister Ingrid, crossing herself.

I gaped in astonishment.

"Sir," called Rick to Neville, "Ronald McDonald says if you're burning, stop, drop, and roll."

"Outstanding," said Charlie, squinting with amazement.

Neville, wheezing mightily and making a whooshing sound like a giant burning marshmallow, charged past us and launched himself into the creek, sending up a swell that rocked the nearby sailing dinghies. Steam spiralled from the subsiding wavelets.

"Take that, you miserable hog!" shouted Mrs. Park from her doorway.

"He and the Hog cannot be mentioned in the same breath," said Charlie. "Speaking of which, the Hog to the rescue once again. K.Y., Neville is floating face down. He will drown unless saved. You're the master at C.P.R. I recommend you do something."

Charlie raced up to the office, where the Hog was berthed in its usual spot. Rick, Ingrid, and I slid down the bank into the water, where Neville lay, as Charlie said, face-down; we turned him over, dragged him into the shallows, and I contemplated the face framed in nicotine-stained wattles, the jaw hanging slackly open, the yellow, camel-like teeth. Why, oh, why couldn't this be Gianetta? Almost retching, I applied myself to ministering to the charred, half-nude Neville.

The Hog slid to a gravelly halt; out spilled Scotia and Warren as well as Charlie and it took the three of them, plus Ingrid, Rick, and myself, to get Neville up the slope and into the back of the Hog. Mrs. Park continued to stare malevolently from her veranda.

Rick started to quote a line from *Hamlet* about lugging the guts.

"Rick, show some respect," reproved Charlie. "Scotia, you take over C.P.R. You and Warren will ride with me into town, all three of us in the same vehicle, babe. Ain't life grand? We're outta here; let's get this working!"

Once again it was the ever-alert Moneypenny who summoned the Ontario Provincial Police; and it was Constable Lumber who had the honour of providing police escort to Parry Sound General Hospital.

"We had better look after Mrs. Park," said Sister Ingrid.

"It looks as if Mrs. Park was looking after Mrs. Park and doesn't need us," I said.

"Well, we should see what's going on." Anna, attracted by the hullabaloo, was on her way as well, so she and Ingrid went to deal with Mrs. Park ("just us girls") while I single-handedly dealt with supervising the movement of chairs and equipment. We had, after vigorous negotiation with Charlie, come to count on the Hog for rolling stock, so with just the villainous old Cockshutt tractor (driven, this time successfully, by me) and its spavined trailer, the process took twice as long as envisioned.

Mindful of the McIntosh saga of a few days before, I was speculating that Mrs. Park had found some intimate artifact of Mrs. Rumley's in the cottage and was therefore completely taken aback by Sister Ingrid's report. "She knows he's diddling around, but she can't really get anything on him," said Ingrid. "What set this one off is that he ate a chocolate Easter rabbit she had been saving."

"What?"

"She's addicted to chocolate and had bought a whole bunch of those chocolate Easter bunnies on sale. She had one for camp and Neville ate it. So he got burned, not over a woman, but over a chocolate Easter rabbit. It would not be Christian to laugh, would it?"

"No," I said solemnly.

"Thank you, K.Y." said Ingrid, squeezing my arm in a most un-nun-like gesture. "I need your strength."

Mrs. Park was shortly in custody in Parry Sound on charges of aggravated assault and attempted arson. By the time Mrs. Rumley had rushed to Mr. Park's bedside at Parry Sound General, the bed was vacant, the scorched Mr. Park on his way to Sunnybrook by air ambulance.

"Wish I could have gone too," said Charlie wistfully. "I've always wanted a ride in a chopper. Well, one more day. God, this is fun. I thought we had run out of stupid things to happen, but I guess I was wrong."

CONCERT DAY

While the best company anyone could ask for, Father Oakley was not the easiest room-mate for one who has always regarded himself as constitutionally lazy. During the Osterling Weekend, indeed when the Mishipashoo Arts Centre was in session, breakfast was at 7:30 and to allow myself time to get up and do my morning rounds, 6:30 to me was a respectable, indeed virtuous, time to rise.

Virtuous I could forget. Father Oakley was up with the sun, in early June at about 5:00, to go for a run followed by as cold a shower as he could summon. On the last morning of the Osterling Weekend, Father was off right on schedule at 5:20 for his run and I turned over for the forty minutes I thought were left to me and to which I was entitled. Half an hour later, he was back. "K.Y., we have trouble."

"Come on, Father," I whined. "This is too early for jokes."

"This is not a joke. Get your ass out of bed and come with me."

The trouble was the concert tent. After the student concert the night before, it had been left shipshape, chairs in neat rows, music stands and percussion equipment at the ready, other equipment not needed for the concert but ready for shipment back to Birkenstock stacked neatly to the side. Now, at 5:50 in the morning, a good half of it lay in a dew-sodden heap, poles tilted at various angles. In the middle were two humps, one large, one small, like a cat and kitten under a blanket. Several befuddled cattle stood nearby, staring at the tent and chewing their cuds.

"Come on, cow, over here," invited the smaller hump under the canvas. "Pretty please...come on, asshole."

The larger hump whiffled indignantly and there was a sound of chairs being knocked over.

"Shit," said the smaller hump, inching its way under the soggy canvas. "Go that way, over there…no…no…atta girl…what a good cow…clever cow."

"Mooooo!" came a muffled exclamation.

"Hold still, Bossy, your horn's snagged…ow, shit, you stupid bitch. If I had a prod it'd be a different story…there we go…good cow…"

The larger hump emerged with a look of consummate desperation on its face and galumphed off to join its sisters. An equally-desperate Charlie clawed his way out into the open, saw the two of us, and said peremptorily "What're you looking at?"

Father Oakley answered with a question of his own. "What the hell happened?"

"Oh, man. I couldn't sleep, so I went out for a spin in the Hog, went over to the highway for a coffee and donut. Came back, saw this neat road, guess it was an old logging road, thought I'd try it out. Damn road dead-ends out back of this field and I didn't realize it until I was through the fence. There's a place a truck can drive through, but with a thing the cattle can't walk on. I came right out into the field, scared the shit out of the cows, and they took off in a real live stampede. I tried to head them off, made a royal mess of the field, but they went straight for the damn tent, right through the fence on the other side of the field, as if they'd been programmed. Mercy me," lisped Charlie, "what are we going to do?"

Father Oakley took charge. "K.Y., get Pete. We'll need him to fix those fences before we're sued. Charlie, go get all the junior admin. kids and Ingrid. Let's get this working!" All three of us flapped our knees in what was now accepted as the Osterling Weekend Salute.

Pete, who lived just across the road, was apparently not surprised to have me knocking on his door so early. "Beautiful mernin', eh, Ken?" said he through lips stretched to the maximum by sheer *joie de vivre*. "Like a cuppa java?"

"Need you to fix a fence. Some cattle broke through, got into the concert tent…"

"Oh, my. Thought I heard a bit of a ruckus, eh? Thought I was dreamin'. Be with you in two shakes of a lamb's tail."

An astonished repair crew converged on the sorry heap of the once-proud concert tent that had taken nearly three hours to erect at the start of camp. The temporarily shell-shocked Charlie was back in charge. "Warren and Duncan on that corner…Dow and e.coli and Moneypenny on the other corner…Father and K.Y. here…Rita and Scotia over there…Sister and Surrendra and Nirvana right there…ready now? What do we all say?"

215

"Let's get this working!" We all saluted, but for a hapless and innocent Sister Ingrid, who merely looked puzzled, then shrugged.

"Lock and load!" commanded Charlie in a voice that flushed some startled starlings out of the nearby woods. "Now, heave!"

We heaved or hove or whatever, feet scrabbling for traction on the slippery grass. Sister Ingrid skidded in a cow pie, fell, and exclaimed "Oh, scissors!"

"Sister, I love it when you talk dirty. It just makes me all crazy inside. Come on, come on!" urged Charlie.

"You could pull too, Charlie," panted Father Oakley.

"Heavens to Murgatroyd, so I could." Charlie was all we needed and the key tent poles lurched into a more-or-less upright position.

"Hold her right there...I need a hammer...If I had a ham-mer..."

Pete had three hammers. He, Charlie, and I hammered the tent pegs in, we straightened up the chairs, got rid of the byproducts of the trapped cow's desperation, and made it in time for breakfast.

The morning was given over to dress rehearsals that were little more than a run-through for the "on-somms" to get used to their new venues, for only the Symphony Orchestra would be performing in the same place where it rehearsed. Charlie, Ingrid, Father Oakley, and I were all over the place, ensuring that all personnel were where they were supposed to be at the designated times. I made a point of being at the concert tent when Gianetta was rehearsing the Symphonic Band. Further, I made a point of asking if she had everything she needed, was there anything I could do?

"No, thank you," she said brusquely and left the moment her rehearsal was over. I was in a state of stunned misery; Kimberley was a sweetheart, but too young; Suzi was beautiful and intensely erotic, but with little to offer in the spiritual, aside from the complications of her being a married woman. I could sense everything I wanted in Gianetta, she had taken me into her life for a few fleeting minutes on that magical moonlit Transfigured Night; and now she had withdrawn and would be off to Germany in another week. Maybe she would accept a dinner invitation before she left. But I knew in my heart that she would not.

"Mr. Jackson," said a frazzled-sounding Moneypenny on the p.a. "Please come to the office a.s.a.p." Oh, God, what now? Mrs. Schwarzkopf with another complaint? Mrs. O'Shea and her demons?

It was a blissful, grinning, and swaying Scotia McLeod awaiting me, propped up in the back of the office. "I think she's been drinking," whispered Moneypenny, "and the parents will start showing up in less than an hour. That includes her dad."

I sat down beside Scotia. "Mr. Jackson!" she exclaimed, trying to put her arm around me. Her timing could not have been worse. Kimberley Clark came into the office for something, saw me being clutched to the bosom of Scotia McLeod, and stamped angrily out, her mission incomplete. One of the wise eyebrows of Moneypenny rose ever so slightly.

"Scotia!" I said sharply, "what's going on?"

"I feel wonderful, just lovely. I never realized just how adorable you really are. If Warren and I ever break up, I'm yours."

"Scotia, this is really stupid."

A similarly inebriated Liesl Schwarzkopf came lurching in at the door. "Whoo!" she cried, and, finding no seat available, plunked herself down in my lap.

"Get out of here, Liesl," said Scotia indignantly, and started to laugh hysterically. "Isn't Mr. Jackson the cutest thing?"

"The best. I love the movies he picks."

"Will you two smarten up!" flamed Moneypenny. "There are parents arriving now. This is a great time to pick to get stoned! Mr. Jackson, we'll have to hide them."

"Hide Mr. Jackson with us!" Screams of idiot laughter. And who should walk in but Mrs. Schwarzkopf.

"Aha! I should haff known! Mr. Checkson und his den of iniquity. Ach, *mein liebchen*, drugged to ze gills. Mr. Checkson, your days are numbered, you haff ruined yourself, but you vill not ruin mein Liesl, such a good girl, a good, wholesome Catholic girl. Und *kleine* Scotia too! Mr. Checkson, vot dretful substance you giff these poor girls?"

My brain had locked completely. And to add to the horror, there was Duke McLeod, Scotia's father and Director of Education for the Birkenstock County Roman Catholic School Board. Even dressed casually, Duke carried a great air of majesty and authority, and here I sat, Liesl in my lap and Scotia with a gentle hammerlock about my neck. I wanted a sword upon which to fall.

"Daddy!" gurgled Scotia. "Isn't Mr. Jackson the most delicious thing you have even seen in your life?"

Warren Peace walked in, took a look, shook his head, and left.

"That honour falls to your mother," said Duke demurely. "Have you been using felt markers?"

"Yes, she was," said Moneypenny.

"Were they Marks-a-Million markers?"

"Yes, sir, they were."

"I know what to do, then. Scotia gets high on them if there isn't enough fresh air. Scotia, honey, come on. Walk with Daddy. What about this other young woman?"

"Her too," explained Moneypenny.

"I can only manage one at a time. Can somebody help her to walk it off? It only takes about five minutes. And tell whoever bought those things, they're not Board-approved."

"Help, please, Mr. Checkson."

In a growing crowd of parents, we navigated our now-subdued inebriates across the footbridge to quieter pastures. Absurdly, I realized that behind the Germanic bombast, Mrs. Schwarzkopf was a mature and extremely attractive version of her daughter.

"I sink I owe apology, Mr. Checkson."

"You almost gave me a heart attack."

"Vell, I apologeiss. Should not jump to concloosions. I haff brought nize Chairman picnic lunch, all manner of wursts und ozzer goodies, too much for chust me und Liesl. Vould you choin us? I vould like to make peace offerink." Her voice dropped to a whisper. "I haff bottle of Moselle in bottom of bazkit."

Liesl and Scotia were back to being themselves, though rather sheepish and hung over, within a quarter of an hour. We did a final check that all signs and directions were in place, the ones writ large with the fateful Marks-a-Million, and they were, except for one that Liesl, in her delirium, had posted upside down. Curiously, Nirvana and Surrendra, our other prime sign-makers, were unaffected by the markers. Surrendra ascribed it to racial superiority.

"Ve eat now," commanded Mrs. Schwarzkopf. "Und no Moselle for you, my darlink, not after zot dretful substance you sniffed. Mr. Checkson und I vill haff to trink it all."

"Mum, I didn't sniff it, I breathed it accidentally."

"Voteffer. You haff Yinyer Ale. Mr. Checkson und I haff the Moselle."

I found myself regretting the limited time I had for our picnic. Not only was there something terrifyingly alluring about Mrs. Schwarzkopf, almost Black Widowish, she was a very interesting woman with an absolute devotion to music, art, literature, and philosophy. Additionally, there was no evidence or mention of a Mr. Schwarzkopf, although she wore a wedding ring, so I assumed that he simply wasn't able to come up for the day from Birkenstock.

I excused myself to attend to some last chores; with Neville hors de combat, Father Oakley had said to me, "Would you be M.C. in his place? I really should, but you're good at that stuff and

I hate it." So I took a short walk to think of what I would say and, after months of planning, the moment of truth arrived. It was 1:30. It was concert time, the swan song for the Osterling Weekend.

I presided at the concert tent, the location for the Symphonic Band, the Wind Ensemble, and the Symphony Orchestra. For Gianetta and Antonio to share the same concert location had not been intentional, but simply a function of the relative seniority of the camp "on-somms". Somehow they just had to live with it.

The family support for our venture that we knew we had could now be seen. It was little wonder that our students were so good and so well-adjusted; they had their families behind them one hundred percent, supporting them, believing in them, and, most important, loving them.

It was, as in *Wind in the Willows*, a golden afternoon. The sun shone, a westerly breeze sighed through the adjacent trees, there was a sense of summer's beginning.

Duke McLeod, still and forever unknowing of Scotia's broadcast amours, welcomed the audience and spoke for a few moments of the great value of musical study to a child's development, of the consequent development of teamwork, commitment, and decision-making; of intellectual and emotional development and simple sensitivity and response to beauty.

"Music and its sister arts," said Duke, "form a sort of membrane that keeps humanity in check and reminds us of what we can really do. Anyone can destroy, as we can see in the daily papers and television. But it takes someone very special, like our students and their teachers, to create."

Hugo and Anna were introduced and Hugo said some very kind words about how the camp was in good part a product of his and Anna's friendship with me.

And then the concert began. As Gianetta made her way to the podium, I tried to catch her eye, but she stared straight ahead. Oh, well, I thought, she's focused on the performance. And it was a good one, very good indeed.

Then came the Wind Ensemble under the direction of the unwilling but valiant Israel Bond, with his strictly great symphonic classic programme. Not only was the music great, but so was the playing; a Bach Prelude, one of Dvorak's Slavonic Dances, and then the scherzo from the Bruckner Seventh.

And then was Antonio d'Averso and the Symphony Orchestra with the first movement of Bruckner's *Romantic* Symphony. Having two works by the same composer on the same programme went against my own principles, but both Antonio and Israel had been adamant to the point of pig-headedness. All I could do was say that it was a great afternoon for Bruckner and while the stage

219

was being re-set for the orchestra, I remarked on how music teachers had an unusual affinity for Bruckner, since he himself had been a teacher and therefore One of Us. Mrs. Schwarzkopf beamed from the front row; Bruckner was one of her favourites.

As usual, the semi-literate and unscrupulous Antonio managed to impress everyone, including, to my disgust, me. His inamorata, Ms. Hook, was also beaming from the front row, seated next to Mrs. Schwarzkopf. And for a final touch, I had to add a caution at the end of the programme: "The orchestra's performance of this wonderfully rural music has attained an unusual dimension of realism. Please remain seated for a moment...there are some loose cattle in back of the tent and for everybody's safety, we have to figure out a way to get them out of here. Just sit tight for a moment. Junior Administration and counsellors, come with me."

We made a semicircle around the cows, who had found a gap in the fence that Pete had overlooked, and herded them back to where they belonged, the audience looking on approvingly. Someone summoned Pete to finish fixing the fence and the audience migrated along to the barn, where the Concert Band was to do a second performance of Eric Osterling's *Mishipashoo Overture*, a musical recounting of the original Mishipashoo, a spirit of Ojibway folklore who appears as a black panther dwelling in the deep and presiding over the waterways.

Refreshments in the dining hall, cars and busses being loaded, handshakes, hugs, kisses... and then a hush as quiet settled over the camp. It was all over and we were a subdued group who went to help load the van that had made it from Birkenstock, with the message that the other van had lost a wheel and another had been sent in its place. Pianos and the contents of the barn were loaded and to our collective relief, the second van showed up soon after. Charlie was the mastermind of the operation; he loved every facet of transportation and shared Hugo's regret that we couldn't have shipped everything by sea.

We formed a human chain at the concert tent and ferried everything out and stowed it in the van. We struck the tent, folded and stowed it, and in the cool of the evening, the sun just grazing the trees to the west, we were done.

There was only one thing left and that was the long-anticipated Last Supper at the Serviette Union in Parry Sound. We dispersed to take showers and finish loading our cars; and then, in convoy, we traversed the familiar route out Carling Bay Road to the Killbear Road and then over to the southbound highway towards Birkenstock and Toronto. Eric Osterling, who could have left right after the concert, had elected to stay for the last rites, as had, interestingly enough, Mrs. Schwarzkopf. Her forbidding mein in abeyance, she laughed, not uproariously, but laughed at the stories we had to tell. And we told them all, though omitting the sad tale of Warren and Scotia and heavily editing the saga of the scorched Neville Park. The man's life was enough of a mess already.

Dinner was finished, the harbour lights were on, the Hog was about to go to the car wash. "I want the last word," said Charlie. "There are others more entitled, in fact, most of you are more entitled, but there is something that absolutely must be said and I must say it, lest we forget. Please stand."

We stood.

"Let's get this working!"

CODA

The Osterling Weekend had a long gestation and, like the may-fly, a brief but radiant lifespan. And because of certain events that surfaced like jetsam in its wake, it had a lengthy coda such as might be found in a Mahler symphony. Proportionally, it was like a thin paperback supported by two outsize bookends.

This is only in the physical sense. Spiritually and intellectually, the Osterling Weekend would loom enormously in the lives of our students fortunate enough to be there. Because of so few distractions, they had a clearer idea of their musical and social capabilities; and they would return to their schools in September with something extra to contribute to their respective school programs.

My heart and head were full as I drove homeward along the dark and empty highway. We had battled all manner of the unforeseen and we had won. Musical miracles had happened. But what of Giannetta? She had left right after her performance and hadn't even stopped to say good-bye. Classes were over at the Miserable Accordion and Kimberley Clark would be there to help me close up for the summer; and of that prospect, I felt some desire, much curiosity, and a bit of fear. Having such a sweet young thing so overtly enamoured of me was a responsibility whose implications grew daily. My power to demolish her life if I were not careful was almost more than I could accept. I even thought of cancelling our arrangement, but she had tried something foolish, I had covered her financially, and, to put it bluntly, she owed me and it was my social duty to collect.

Then there was Suzi. I had no idea of what sort of scope there might be left. Likely she and Commander Philip Horatio would be at their cottage for much of the summer, they might invite me up

222

with Evie and Katie, but obviously the activities that pleased us the most were out of the question.

At the one and same time, I endured and savoured the time with Kimberley. Her acceptance into the Faculty of Music at the University of Toronto was waiting in the mail for her when she got home from the Osterling Weekend and she took me to lunch by way of celebration.

"I should be taking you to lunch," I protested.

"I'm a grad now and you have no power over me, dear Mr. Jackson, so don't argue. And since you gave me life, I think I can give you lunch."

Although I speculate to this day what might have happened that week, it was too hot and our work was too grotty (to use a favourite word of Hugo's) to be conducive to any sort of physical overtures, save hugs of greeting and farewell at either end of the day. Kimberley was off to do fire-fighting for the Ontario Ministry of Natural Resources at Sioux Lookout for the summer, a matter for me of relief mingled with regret.

"I love you, Mr. Jackson, I truly do," said Kimberley at the end of her last day of clean-up duty. "I asked you to wait for me, but I know now it would be unfair. If you're still single when I get my degree, well, maybe I could be the second Mrs. Jackson, and how the first could have dumped a cute thing like you I'll never understand. But whatever happens, you'll always be very special to me."

From Suzi: "Oh, Sweetie, I don't know what to do! Phil's taking me for another cruise."

"Another cruise?"

"Another cruise, this time a European cruise, all over the place, and we'll be gone from mid-July until the last week of August. Oh, what are we going to do?"

"It really doesn't sound as if you need me any more."

"Oh, Sweetie, don't say that...but...Phil is loving me half to death now...it just can't go any further with you and me. It's not really fair to anyone." She started to cry. I went numb. For comprehensive female companionship, even if illicit and immoral, Suzi was all I had.

"Er..." I fumbled.

"I think we'll have to break it off. I have a marriage again and I can't throw it away. And I can't keep you on a string. But I will always love you." The line went dead and then there was the drone of the dial tone.

I tried Gianetta's number. "Hello. You have reached 464-2811. We" (we?) "aren't home right now, but at the sound of the beep, please leave a message and we" (we?) "will get right back to you." Disgustedly, I hung up. Gianetta was probably at the airport anyway, boarding the Lufthansa or whatever would take her to Germany. That day had been the end of term, usually a day to be relished to the fullest, the opening of the portals to glorious summer, at the end of which would be my new position. But what a disaster! No woman, no boat, no anything, and Hugo and Anna now full tilt into their summer season and with limited time for heart-to-heart conversations.

The hour was late, but it being Friday, the Meteor Meatier Eatery was going full blast and my floor shook with the pulsations of Kenny Rogers. Two tomcats fought out in the laneway. Delinquent tires screeched on High Street.

I took a long bath and was just out of the tub when the phone rang. Gianetta wanting to be mine? Kimberley saying please wait after all? Suzi recanting? Or, God forbid, something had happened to Evie and/or Katie? I picked up the phone. "Hello."

"Mr. Checkson," clucked the phone. Had I performed some other corruption to the innocent? What was this?

"Oh, hi, Mrs. Schwarzkopf. Um, nice to hear from you." I closed my eyes. What had I done or said since our entente cordiale picnic to arouse her ire, especially at 10:30 at night?

"Mr. Checkson, I vill come to ze point immediately. First, I apologeiss for calling zo late at night. Plees forgif me."

"Of course, Mrs. Schwarzkopf."

"Second, ze purpose of my call." Oh, here we go! "Chust got call zot I haff two tickets to *Das Rheingold* Sunday night at ze ArtPark in ze Niagara Gorge. I know it's schordt notice, but I vould like to inwite you to go vis me und be my date for ze evenink." Surely she meant guest, but who was to debate the point?

"Well, yes, I'd love to. Thanks, Mrs. Schwarzkopf, that's very thoughtful of you."

"If ve haff date, you must call me Edeltraut. I inzist. I look forvard to Sunday, Mr. Checkson. Vell, if you call me Edeltraut, I call you Kennet, okay?"

"Okay." Better that than K.Y., at least on a first date, oh, come on, she called it a date, but surely it was an eccentricity of her English. I dozed off in a stupour of exhaustion, sorrow, renewed interest, and not a little bit of terror. Edeltraut Schwarzkopf; it was a name to strike fear into the stoutest of hearts.

Come Sunday afternoon, when I went to pick her up, Edeltraut looked absolutely magnificent, a great cumulus of creamy blonde hair piled on her head, cheeks naturally rosy and healthily Aryan, wearing a sort of sheath thing—I am completely ignorant of fashion terminology—that left no curvature to the realm of mystery. Liesl let me in the door and tried not to smirk when I beheld the stupendous glory of her mother. And there was no Mr. Schwarzkopf to tell us to drive carefully and enjoy ourselves.

On the long drive to and from ArtPark, I learned much about Edeltraut Schwarzkopf. What she had to tell me, in abridged form, went like this:

"Ven I met you in person ze ozzer day, I sot to meinzelf, very nice, pleasant young mann. I sink I vos too hard on you ven you vore at kemp, all zat business about zot movie mit der glowing condoms. Pleasant young mann, und very intelligent und attractive too. You are divorced? Zeparated?"

"Separated. Probably divorced sometime in the fall."

"You haff lady friend?"

"Well, no."

"Nize young man like you should haff lady friend." Was she acting as someone's agent? Was she maybe marrying off Liesl? What was going on?

Continued Mrs. Schwarzkopf: "I am vidow. Mein husband, Sigismund, vos drowned."

"I'm so sorry. What happened?"

"Heppened in Chairmany ven Liesl vos six. Sigi vos sailor, how you say, yachtsman. Fell oaferboard in big race in Baltic Sea. I vos devastated, no uzzer mann after mein Sigi. Ve had boat of our own, vich I zold. No more boats, said I."

My heart began to sink.

"But fourteen years of mournink iss enough, no? I chust existed for meine kleine Liesl und now she's at uniwersity und I am all alone. Must schtardt to liff again."

Das Rheingold was almost as stupendous as Mrs. Schwarzkopf. Aside from the Rhine itself, no setting could have been more perfect, and the performance would have, had he been alive, brought Wagner himself to his feet. But a concert review this is not. We must proceed.

On the return trip: "I sot of takink motel for night, but Liesl vould haff been uncomfortable. Zis iss ze first time she hass effer seen her mama go out on ein date. Besides vich, you might haff been uncomfortable alzo. Ve kennot be too *schnell* mit zese sings, ken ve?"

"Being too *schnell* is not good," I agreed earnestly.

"I like you, Kennet. You heff schtyle und integrity. I sink I am a bit older zen you, but could be eggziting, yes?"

I thought of Anna, my beautiful yardstick of womanhood; she was older by five or six years and exciting beyond compare. She was also my oracle. I would have to consult her.

"She's certainly great-looking," said Anna of Edeltraut. "I think Hugo and I have to meet her, though. We have to make amends for introducing you to Alien. We feel a responsibility. Bring her up to the camp for a weekend...she will have to ask us for your hand in marriage..."

It was a highly proper (and highly successful) visit. Edeltraut and I were chastely lodged in separate quarters, matters moved at an appropriately un-*schnell* pace. I gave Mrs. Schwarzkopf, or I should say Edeltraut, a gentle re-introduction to sailing in the dinghy *Olivia*, sailing out to the Pancake Islands for a picnic, and she was absolutely agog at the open Georgian Bay.

As we tacked out beyond Killbear Point, Edeltraut kept her back to me every time we came about; she spoke little and I thought she might be reminded of her departed Sigi and be grieving for him. I felt a pang of jealousy, but told myself not to be an idiot; divorce you recover from, but widowhood was another matter and I would just have to live with it.

Finally I could no longer stand it. "You're thinking of Sigi, aren't you?"

The majestic and indomitable Edeltraut had tears in her eyes. "I sink of Sigi effery day. Vos kind of you to sink of zat. Yes, I am sinking of Sigi, but how he vould like you und vant you to take care of me."

I was so touched at what she said that it was my turn to look away. "Kennet, I vant you to look at me."

"Er..."

"Kennet, zere is somsink else."

Oh, no! An old lover come back into her life?

"Um, what?"

"You are showink me magic today; ze vind, ze sea, zis pretty boat, und zen, out zere, vell...ze beauty und desolation of nature, ze feeling of being face-to-face mit creation itself...now I fully unterschtant vy you call Georgian Bay your home." Edeltraut knew what I had been through relative to *Snarley Yow* and to Alien.

"Vun day, Kennet," she added, "I vant it to be mein home too."

Anna and Hugo's report: "She's beautiful, she's mature, she's very bright, she's understanding and compassionate, and if initially a bit formidable, well, she's a real treasure. We don't say this casually, but, believe us, she's the one for you. Keep us informed of progress."

"In detail," said Hugo.

"Hugo!"

A fortnight later, my phone rang.

"*Mein liebchen!*"

"What's this 'liebchen' stuff, pal? Ohhh, you thought it was Mrs. Schwarzkopf, didn't you?"

"No, Father, I was calling you '*liebchen*'."

"Horseshit," said Father Oakley inelegantly. "I have something for you that is just so hot it sizzles. You remember that Holy Whatever that Neville wrote? Antonio's one and only premiere?"

"I thought it was pretty good, except for that F-sharp or whatever that pissed Charlie off."

"It was pretty good. And it wasn't by Neville."

"What?"

"Like I said, this one is hot, but it's awful too. It's kind of like the Mozart Requiem. Neville commissioned the thing from a guy named, hell, Mahooo or something…"

"Roger Mayhew. He died just a bit ago, I think…"

"Had leukemia, the poor bastard, and it must have been his last work. Neville got him to write it and paid the commission out of Board funds. I don't think our Neville's going to be around for a while. I was sorting out some of his papers, and what a rat's nest that was, at the office, and I found the commissioning agreement and an invoice, made some phone calls to Mrs. Mahooo, and that was that."

"Good God."

"Well might you say, kid. That F-sharp that had Charlie bent out of shape was a simple mistake that anyone who knew about music could have fixed."

"That's one part of the mystery. But what about Antonio?"

"Before he died, Roger Mahooo recorded the piano version of the score and Antonio memorized it. Roger had accidentally hit the F-sharp that was also mistakenly in the score. Neville paid Antonio for the project."

"Out of Board funds?"

"You've got it, pal. We have corruption here on a scale known only in certain third-world dictatorships. You'll have a lot on your plate in the fall. Oh, and those Orff-in-reverse-sounding ditties Neville wrote for dear Angie."

"Oh, yeahhh!"

"Oh, no, not you too. They were indeed some of those *Schulwerk* things done backwards with new words. Charlatanism has reached new heights. On a happier note, how are things with Mrs. S.?"

Things with Mrs. S. were very fine indeed. Katie and Evie had met her and, though over-awed at first, had become very fond of her and told her that they liked the way she had made Daddy happy. They also got on well with Liesl and thought she'd make a wonderful honorary big sister.

I had found a true friend in Edeltraut and could sense something strong and enduring taking shape; our daily, as they were now, doings together were reminiscent of my parents and, for that, matter, Anna and Hugo, the two bunnies playing in the sunshine at the end of the rainbow. *Schnellness* was still being avoided, but that was fine; the angst ("ein gut Chairman vord") over Gianetta and the sexual convulsions over Suzi were pretty well a thing of the past, although I did have a number of vivid dreams of Suzi's womanly architecture, her unbridled passion, and the feeling of magnificent inevitability as she advanced upon me. In that respect, it was well that Edeltraut and I were not being *schnell*; calling Suzi's name in the wrong circumstances would have been a disaster.

Since I was at the office full time come autumn, I had to go back to work a week earlier than if I were still teaching. Sweet Marie had retired and Suzi had transferred to another office, just as well under the circumstances. So there we were with two new secretaries, indeed a virtually new staff. With Neville out of the picture, Father Oakley was, by his request, relieved of his "Suit" job and was the new Director of Music. I was in charge of instrumental music; and, since Angela Rumley had unexpectedly "gone on sabbatical", Sister Ingrid had taken her place in an acting capacity. Charlie was to continue overseeing operations by the itinerant teachers. It was as if there had been a total *coup d'état* without a shot being fired.

But the defining moment above all others was on the Wednesday night of that week. The phone rang. "Mr. Checkson."

"What? Edeltraut?" I had not been called Mr. Checkson since our first date.

"Yess. I haff serious matter to discuss mit you."

I reached for an invisible panic button. "What is it?"

"I haff done much sinking. Ve haff to talk."

Oh, God!

"What is it, is something wrong?"

"Zot iss for you to chudge, Mr. Checkson. I haff done much sinking. About mein past. Sigi luffed to sail und after he died, I lost interest und sold ze boat. Now I vant to sail again—haha, gotcha! —und I haff bought anuzzer boat."

"You did?" I was now officially in love.

"Yess, but oldt von. Needs much vork. I need help."

"Where is the boat?"

"Parry Zound."

"Was there a name on the boat? It might be one I know."

"Vos a name, yess, but ein really strange von. Made no sense."

My scalp prickled. "What was it?"

"Like I say, fonny name. *Snarley Yow.*"

POSTLUDE

For medical reasons, Neville Park took early retirement from his position as Director of Music for the Birkenstock County Roman Catholic School Board. He made a good recovery from his burns, but the strain on his heart from his desperate dash to the creek, in concert with hypertension, borderline cirrhosis, and high cholestorol, made it inadvisable that he should continue his work. He has retired on a disability pension.

Mrs. Park was sentenced to five years of community service in the form of care for her husband. Her only respite from caring for him is on Thursday afternoons, when, as part of his medical care, he must go for an angiogram.

Gianetta d'Averso left the teaching profession at the end of the 1991-92 academic year, sold all her possessions, and took orders as a Carmelite Sister.

Antonio d'Averso has been remanded for trial on a case of sexual molestation. He is alleged to have had intercourse with a minor member of the Annville Chorus on the floor of a church following a dress rehearsal for the Berlioz Requiem. Spiritual ecstasy was claimed as a motivating factor. In the meantime, his teaching certificate has been suspended and he has been relieved as music director of the Birkenstock Philharmonic.

Israel Bond returned to the Birkenstock Philharmonic, augmented it with the stronger elements of the Ouentaron Symphony, and celebrated his return with a performance of Mahler's *Resurrection* Symphony that was broadcast on TVOntario. He continues as music director at Golgotha High School.

Dunstan Corrigan took over from Antonio d'Averso at Stigmata High School and in commemoration he commissioned *The Wounded Hands* from Eric Osterling.

Mr. and Mrs. Charles Cowell had a son in March, 1992. He was christened Warren and it is generally conceded that he was conceived during the Osterling Weekend.

Eric Osterling is semi-retired and has moved to Florida. He returned to the MishipashooArts Centre for the 1992-93, and -94 Birkenstock County Roman Catholic School Board music camps.

Anna and Hugo Harland continue from strength to strength in their various endeavours. Hugo has just completed *The Secret Passions of Miss Manners* and *A Pillow of Strength* was recently made into a T.V. movie with Anna in a leading role. She was nominated for a Gemini award.

Warren Peace and Scotia McLeod were married in June, 1994 and in December of that year, Scotia gave birth to a daughter, who was named Heavenly.

Angela Rumley took a sabbatical from the Music Office for 1991-92 and then decided, on the basis of an unexpected inheritance, to take early retirement. She is currently on a round of medical treatment for reasons unknown; her appointments are for each Thursday afternoon.

Sister Ingrid Harrington assumed the duties of Angela Rumley at the Music Office. She is now officially designated Supervisor of Choral Music.

With the retirement of Neville Park, Father John Oakley was designated Director of Music for the Birkenstock County Roman Catholic School Board. He also composed the soundtrack for Hugo Harland's TV movie *A Pillow of Strength* and was nominated for a Gemini Award. This title has become immensely popular in an edition for band.

Commander Philip Horatio and Suzanne Quail had a son just before Christmas, 1991. He was christened Kenneth.

Kenneth Yardley Jackson took Father John Oakley's place as Supervisor of Instrumental Music for the Birkenstock Country Roman Catholic School Board. He and Edeltraut Schwarzkopf were married in June, 1992, at the Centennial Church in Carling Township. Father Oakley performed the ceremony, Hugo Harland was Best Man, Liesl Schwarzkopf the Maid of Honour, and Charles Cowell was chauffeur. Their honeymoon was a summer aboard a newly-refurbished *Snarley Yow.*

By her request, Kimberley Clark, whose mother passed away from alcohol poisoning in April, 1992, was formally adopted by Kenneth Yardley Jackson and Edeltraut Schwarzkopf Jackson. All subsequent conversation between her and Jackson has remained confidential.

231

Aileen Quail Jackson was re-married in December, 1993, to Emerson Dewey, senior partner in the accounting firm of Dewey, Cheetham, and Howe. She was short-listed for the Canadian Broadcasting Corp. Poetry Contest the following year. Aileen lives with her new husband, Katie, and Evie in Caledon, Ontario, the children spending holidays and summers with K.Y. and Edeltraut Jackson.

K.Y. Jackson's 1979 Toyota, nicknamed the Kamikaze, was retired from active service in the spring of 1992. Its headlights tended to diffuse their light at speed, returning to normal when the vehicle slowed down. Inspection revealed the fenders so corroded and lacking support that they spread apart in any sort of headwind. The end came on a routine errand when the transmission fell out on to the pavement of a parking lot.

FINE

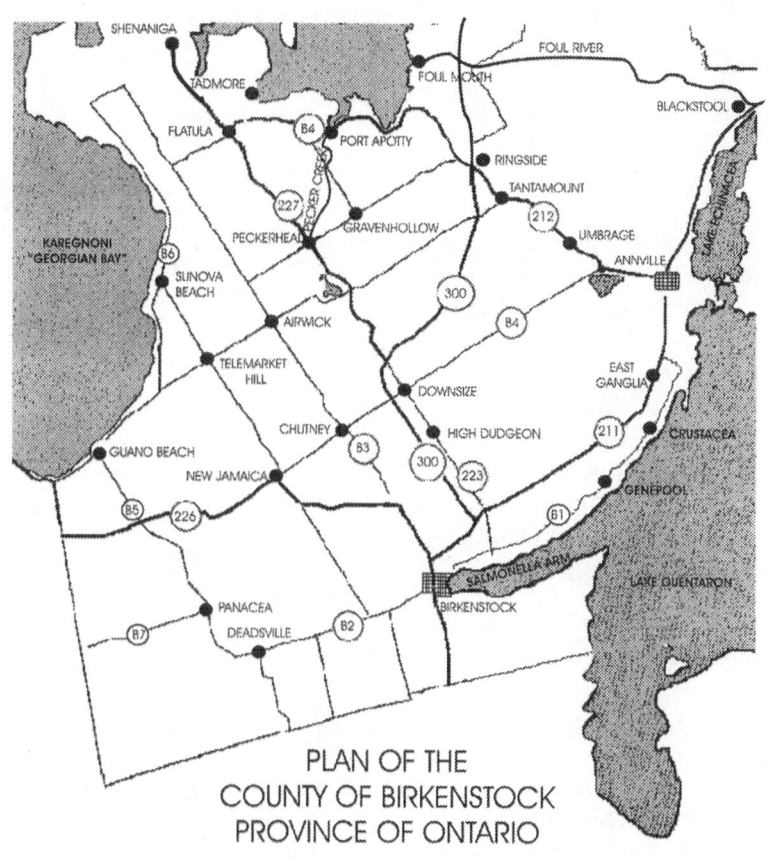

PLAN OF THE
COUNTY OF BIRKENSTOCK
PROVINCE OF ONTARIO

A HUGO HARLAND BIBLIOGRAPHY

Published exclusively by
Gold, Frankenstein, and Muir, Toronto

Fiction:

I Shot the Pillsbury Dough Man
So Long, Ceylon
A Bungalow in Bangalore
A Scirocco in Morocco
Chaos in Laos
A Widow of Opportunity
The Nubile Nubians
A Pillow of Strength
The Pathological Pathan
A Garage in Gorazde
A Synagogue in Senegal
The Secret Passions of Miss Manners

Non-Fiction:

A Rubble of Rubles: The Collapse of the Soviet Economy
Sikh and Ye Shall Find: A Study of Immigration Patterns from Southern Asia
Make Mine Manhasset: The Evolution of the Modern Music Stand
Roman Catholicism and the Art of Wooden Boat Restoration
From All Woks of Life: A Study of Canadian Immigration from the Orient
Emission Impossible: A Study of Male Impotence in the Post-Trudeau Years
The Shiftless Paradigm: My Crusade Against Change
A Vortex in My Cortex: A Study of Strenn in the 1990s
Those Lazy, Hazy, Crazy Days of Sumer: An Adventure in Archaeology
A Dominion of Minions: A Short History of Canada's Civil Service
A Rapture of Raptors: Basketball Comes to Toronto
The Oracle of the Coracle: Traditional Boat-building in Wales

MUSICAL WORKS OF Father John Oakley, S.J.

Karegnondi – Suite in Three Movements for Wind Ensemble

Chaconne a Son Gout – for String orchestra

A Pillow of Strength – available for both symphony orchestra and wind ensemble (advanced)

Lapp Dances – An Arctic Journey, for wind ensemble

Exorcisms – for wind ensemble

Suite for Triangle Unaccompanied

Pas de Onze, from the ballet Ocean's Eleven

MUSICAL WORKS OF ERIC OSTERLING

Mr. Osterling's musical catalogue is handled by the Hal Leonard Corp. Inquiries may be directed to halinfo@halleonard.com

ACKNOWLEDGEMENTS

While writing is necessarily a solitary venture, a finished product does not happen without the help of others. In that connection, I want to say a special thanks to my colleagues and friends, James Ferris and Paul Rayment, for reading the manuscript; James A. Brown, another staunch friend, for his alchemy with a computer to create the map of Birkenstock County; and to my eagle-eyed wife Debra, who has gone through the manuscript and hunted down the gremlins within.

Special thanks as well to Eric Osterling, whose music has been embraced by many generations of music students and their teachers, for lending his *persona* to this story.

ABOUT THE AUTHOR

Steven Duff retired in 1996 from a 32-year career as a music educator in Scarborough, Ontario. During his tenure in Scarborough, he was active as a teacher, conductor, music festival adjudicator, and administrator. Following his retirement, Mr. Duff moved to Parry Sound, Ontario, to begin a new career as a writer and artist; as well as freelance writing on such varied topics as history, transportation, and the arts, he has had four published novels to his credit prior to *The Osterling Weekend.*

When not writing or painting, Mr. Duff enjoys sailing and maintaining an outsize collection of classic boats, as well as reading, engagement in community affairs, and listening to music without preoccupation with upcoming rehearsals and concerts. He is a grandfather of two and lives with his wife Debra and their toy poodle Bruno.